INVERSION

RIVEN WORLDS BOOK TWO

(AMARANTHE ♦ 15)

G. S. JENNSEN

HYPERNOVA
PUBLISHING
2020

INVERSION

Copyright © 2020 by G. S. Jennsen

Cover design by Susan Gerardi (Susan Digital Designs) and G. S. Jennsen.
Cover typography by G. S. Jennsen

Hypernova Publishing
P.O. Box 2214
Parker, Colorado 80134
www.hypernovapublishing.com

The Hypernova Publishing name, colophon and logo are trademarks of
Hypernova Publishing.

Ordering Information:
Hypernova Publishing books may be purchased for educational, business or sales
promotional use. For details, contact the "Special Markets Department" at the
address above.

Inversion / G. S. Jennsen.—1st ed.

LCCN 2020911180
978-1-7351784-0-0

AMARANTHE UNIVERSE

AURORA RHAPSODY

AURORA RISING
STARSHINE
VERTIGO
TRANSCENDENCE

AURORA RENEGADES
SIDESPACE
DISSONANCE
ABYSM

AURORA RESONANT
RELATIVITY
RUBICON
REQUIEM

SHORT STORIES
Restless, Vol. I • *Restless, Vol. II* • *Apogee* • *Solatium*
Venatoris • *Re/Genesis* • *Meridian* • *Fractals*

ASTERION NOIR
EXIN EX MACHINA
OF A DARKER VOID
THE STARS LIKE GODS

RIVEN WORLDS
CONTINUUM
INVERSION

Learn more at gsjennsen.com/books or visit the Amaranthe
Wiki: gsj.space/wiki

For everyone who's longed for a second chance at life

DRAMATIS PERSONAE

HUMANS

Alexis 'Alex' Solovy Marano

Space scout and explorer. Prevo.

Spouse of Caleb Marano, daughter of Miriam and David Solovy.

Caleb Marano

Former Special Operations intelligence agent; space scout and explorer.

Spouse of Alex Solovy.

Miriam Solovy (Commandant)

Leader, Concord Armed Forces.

Marlee Marano

Consulate Assistant.

Malcolm Jenner (Admiral)

AEGIS Fleet Admiral.

Mia Requelme (Senator)

Head of Concord Consulate.

David Solovy

Professor, Concord SWTC.

Richard Navick

Concord Intelligence Director.

ASTERIONS

Nika Kirumase

External Relations Advisor, Asterion Dominion Advisor Committee.

Former NOIR leader.

Dashiel Ridani

Industry Advisor, Asterion Dominion Advisor Committee.

Joaquim Lacese

Former NOIR Operations Director.

Grant Mesahle

Dominion Armed Forces Consultant.

Parc Eshett

Omoikane Consultant.

Selene Panetier

Justice Advisor.

Lance Palmer

Military Advisor.

Perrin Benvenit

Omoikane Personnel Director.

OTHER MAJOR CHARACTERS

Eren Savitas asi-Idoni
CINT agent.
Species: Anaden

Mnemosyne ('Mesme')
Idryma Member. Former 1st Analystae of Aurora.
Species: Katasketousya

Abigail Canivon
Regenesis expert.
Species: Human

Akeso
Sentient planet.
Species: Ekos

Casmir elasson-Machim
Leader, Anaden military.
Species: Anaden

Danilo Nisi/Corradeo Praesidis
Former leader of anarch resistance.
Species: Anaden

Devon Reynolds
Director, Concord Special Projects.
Species: Human

Drae Shonen ela-Machim
CINT agent.
Species: Anaden

Ferdinand elasson-Kyvern
Anaden Senator, Concord Senate.
Species: Anaden

Kennedy Rossi
Founder/CEO, Connova Interstellar.
Species: Human

Kiernan Phillips
Lieutenant, DAF pilot.
Species: Asterion

Kuisk Jhountar
General, Savrakath military.
Species: Savrakath

Morgan Lekkas
Former IDCC Commander.
Species: Human

Nolan Bastian
AEGIS Field Marshal.
Species: Human

Nyx elasson-Praesidis
Former Inquisitor.
Species: Anaden

Ryan Theroit
Former NOIR member.
Species: Asterion

Thomas
Concord Command Artificial.
Species: Artificial

Torval elasson-Machim
Machim military commander.
Species: Anaden

Valkyrie
Alex's Prevo counterpart.
Species: Artificial

Xyche'ghael
Namino merchant.
Species: Taiyok

MINOR CHARACTERS

Adam Goodwin, AEGIS Flight Lieutenant (*Human*)

Adlai Weiss, Justice Advisor (*Asterion*)

Akhar Ghorek, Brigadier, Savrakath military (*Savrakath*)

Ava Zobel, former NOIR member (*Asterion*)

Carl Odaka, Colonel, AEGIS Special Forces (*Human*)

Cosime Rhomyhn, former CINT agent (deceased) (*Naraida*)

Emilio Rogers, Colonel, Dominion Armed Forces (*Asterion*)

Felzeor, CINT agent (*Volucri*)

Hannah elasson-Machim, Machim military commander (*Anaden*)

Ilgur Darhk, Savrakath Ambassador (*Savrakath*)

Isabela Marano, biochemistry professor, Caleb's sister (*Human*)

Janice ela-Kyvern, CINT Shift Supervisor (*Anaden*)

Katherine Colson, Administration Advisor (*Asterion*)

Klas Johansson, Brigadier, DAF (*Asterion*)

Maris Debray, Culture Advisor (*Asterion*)

Meno, Mia Requelme's Prevo counterpart (*Artificial*)

Noah Terrage, COO, Connova Interstellar (*Human*)

Onai Veshnael, Dean, Novoloume Senator (*Novoloume*)

Otto elasson-Machim, Machim military commander (*Anaden*)

Phael Thisiame, Pointe-Amiral, Novoloume military (*Novoloume*)

Pinchutsenahn Niikha Qhiyane Kteh ("Pinchu"), Tokahe Naataan (*Khokteh*)

Taiv ela-Kyvern, CINT informant (*Anaden*)

Vaihe, refugee (*Godjan*)

Vance Greshe, Ridani Enterprises Manufacturing Director (*Asterion*)

William 'Will' Sutton, CINT Operations Director (*Human*)

CONCORD

MEMBER SPECIES

Human
Representative: Mia Requelme

Anaden
Representative: Ferdinand elasson-Kyvern

Novoloume
Representative: Dean Onai Veshnael

Naraida
Representative: Tasme Chareis

Khokteh
Representative: Pinchutsenahn Niikha Qhiyane Kteh

Barisan
Representative: Daayn Shahs-lan

Dankath
Representative: Bohlke'ban

Efkam
Representative: Ahhk~sae

ALLIED SPECIES

Asterion
Katasketousya
Fylliot
Ruda

Taenarin
Volucri
Yinhe

PROTECTED SPECIES

Ekos
Faneros
Galenai

Icksel
Pachrem
Vrachnas

AMARANTHE
CONCORD EMPIRE

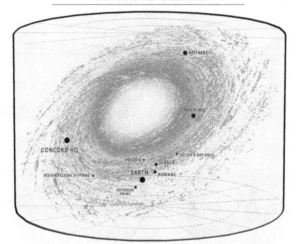

MILKY WAY GALAXY

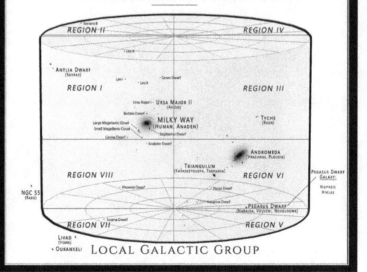

LOCAL GALACTIC GROUP

GENNISI GALAXY
(MESSIER 94)

RASU STRONGHOLD
(DESTROYED)

SOGAIN SYSTEM

MIRAI

NAMINO

KIYORA

EBISU

TOKI'TAKU
(TAIYOK HOMEWORLD)

SYNRA

CHOSEK
(CHIZERU HOMEWORLD)

✦ ASTERION DOMINION AXIS WORLDS
✦ ASTERION DOMINION ADJUNCT WORLDS
✳ ALIEN WORLDS

ASTERION DOMINION
AXIS WORLDS

MIRAI   NAMINO   SYNRA   EBISU   KIYORA

THE STORY SO FAR

---

*For a brief summary of the events of **AMARANTHE #1-13**, see the Appendix in the back of the book.*

CONTINUUM

Fourteen years have passed since the events of REQUIEM.

Nika Kirumase joins Alex and Caleb for dinner at their home on Akeso. They share the story of how humanity ended up in Amaranthe and fill her in on Concord, the multi-species government that has taken the place of the deposed Anaden Directorate.

Marlee Marano, Caleb's niece, is on the planet Savrak as part of her work for the Concord Consulate. The Savrakaths are a lizard-evolved species that originated in the Mosaic. Marlee discovers they are enslaving and mistreating the Godjans, a species they share Savrak with. While helping a Godjan girl, Vaihe, escape imminent torture, Marlee is arrested by local authorities. David Solovy and Caleb both arrive to come to her aid, and they are able to secure her release.

Elsewhere on Savrak, Eren asi-Idoni and his team (Cosime, Felzeor, Drae) surveil a Savrakath lab on behalf of Concord Intelligence (CINT). The team infiltrates the lab and acquires evidence the Savrakaths are secretly developing antimatter weapons.

Miriam Solovy, Concord's military leader, receives a visit from Lakhes. The Kat conveys its opinion of the Asterions and a warning regarding the Rasu. Lakhes then returns home, where it confronts Mesme about the secrets it has been keeping regarding the Asterions.

Alex takes Nika to Concord HQ to meet humanity's power players in Concord: her mother and father, Malcolm Jenner, Mia Requelme and Richard Navick. Nika fills them in on the Asterion's experiences with the Rasu (see the summary of *Asterion Noir* in the Appendix).

Nika returns home to Mirai, and Dashiel Ridani introduces her to the Omoikane Initiative, a massive project spearheaded by the other Advisors to accelerate technology, warfare and logistical plans to combat the Rasu. She learns about the Vault, a project to store the psyche backups of all Asterions in a fortified spaceship, where they can be spirited away in the event of a Rasu invasion.

On Machimis, Casmir elasson-Machim struggles to exert authority over the other Machim *elassons*. Torval elasson-Machim learns about the Savrakaths' antimatter development and, believing Concord is not doing enough to address it, decides to take matters into his own hands.

Alex, Caleb and Valkyrie travel to NGC 55, believed to be the closest Rasu-controlled galaxy to Concord space. They discover millions of Rasu vessels and platforms in thousands of star systems throughout the galaxy, as well as a Rasu artificial ring orbiting the galactic core.

Nika, Dashiel and Lance Palmer attend a formal meeting with Concord leaders to review what they know about the Rasu's reach, their intentions, and ways to counter them. Conventional weapons have proved ineffective, and they discuss the use of negative energy, nuclear and antimatter weapons, as well as even more exotic weaponry. Nika fills the others in on the Rasu's unique consciousness and their paranoid, controlling nature.

Miriam promises the Asterions military and scientific cooperation, information sharing and a steady supply of Reor/kyoseil, but stops short of providing them with adiamene. Alex asks Kennedy to secretly give the formula for adiamene to the Asterions. Kennedy and Noah decide if they can do so in such a way that protects their family, they will.

Vaihe unexpectedly contacts Marlee. She's escaped capture but is alone in the Savrak wilderness. Marlee hacks a Caeles Prism to open at Vaihe's location and gets her off Savrak. She takes Vaihe to meet Mia, and the Godjan relays the full extent of the Savrakaths' mistreatment of her people. Marlee demands Mia do something to help the Godjans.

On Mirai, Adlai Weiss discovers his personal account has been hacked and his bank accounts emptied. When he goes home, he is attacked and knocked unconscious. He wakes up in an unknown location, strung up in a rack and being held captive by a strange man.

Perrin is determined to find Adlai. She breaks into the Justice server to find out what Justice knows about Adlai's kidnapping. She and Parc Eshett review the data and discover Justice has a suspect named Ian Sevulch, but he has an alibi. Parc reveals that some Asterions have begun transforming themselves into "Plexes," where a single consciousness occupies multiple physical bodies simultaneously. He believes Sevulch could be a Plex, and they decide to surveil the man.

Perrin tails Sevulch to an abandoned shop, where she discovers Adlai tied up in the basement. She shoots Sevulch in the head and rescues Adlai. She then keeps vigil at Adlai's side while he recovers from his torture. Parc stops by, and Perrin reveals she's figured out that he's a Plex. He asks her to keep his secret, and she agrees.

Nika takes Maris Debray to visit their original homeworld, Asterion Prime, in the Milky Way. Maris tells Nika about the early days of the SAI Rebellion and about Nika's family, including her brother, Loshi, who was killed during the rebellion.

Eren's team receives authorization to destroy the Savrakath antimatter lab. However, while they're placing explosives around the lab, Torval arrives in his Imperium and blasts the facility, killing Drae and Cosime.

Eren takes Cosime's body to Alex and Caleb on Akeso and demands that they bring her back to life, much as Akeso did for Caleb fourteen years earlier. Caleb tries to explain how it's beyond Akeso's ability to renew life in someone the planet hasn't previously bonded with. When a hysterical Eren insists, Caleb tries to open a connection to Cosime, only to be overwhelmed by darkness and death. Eren realizes Cosime is truly gone; he asks Alex and Caleb to take care of her for him and flees.

Miriam arrests Torval for disobeying orders and the murder of Concord personnel, then tells Casmir to bring the other Machim *elassons* in line. Miriam and Mia deliver an ultimatum to the Savrakaths, terminating their negotiations for a Concord alliance, demanding they cease all antimatter production and offering asylum to all Godjans.

Alex and Caleb attend Cosime's funeral. Eren is absent, and no one knows where he's gone. Caleb decides to try to find Eren and enlists Felzeor's help to do so. Meanwhile, Eren travels to an underworld Anaden planet, Lethe, to acquire a dangerous black-market hypnol that will suppress his emotions and increase his reflexes. He takes the first dose, then begins planning his revenge for Cosime's death.

In a skirmish between Savrakath ships and Casmir's fleet, the Savrakaths deploy antimatter weapons to decimate the Machim ships. In response, Miriam issues a "red-flag" order, terminating all Concord relations with the Savrakaths and forbidding them from entering Concord territory.

Dashiel receives files from an anonymous source containing the details for adiamene production, and he begins making plans for its manufacture.

The Concord Senate approves a formal alliance with the Asterion Dominion, over the vehement objections of the Anaden senator, Ferdinand elasson-Kyvern.

During the Asterion's battle against the Rasu in the Gennisi galaxy, an Asterion pilot, Kiernan Phillips, and a Taiyok, Toshke'phien, were pulled into a Rasu wormhole and spit out to crash land on an unknown planet. The planet is being subjected to a quantum block, meaning they can't call home for rescue. They've survived until now by staying out of sight of Rasu currently roving the planet, which appears to have been home to a primitive species until recently. The Rasu discover the wreck of Kiernan's ship, however, and take it apart for information.

Despondent over what the Rasu might learn, Kiernan and Toshke return to Toshke's ship ahead of the Rasu and burn it. They then seek refuge in the woods for the night; the next morning they spot a non-Rasu ship overhead, and race to meet up with it.

In a distant galaxy, Danilo Nisi/Corradeo Praesidis and his granddaughter, Nyx elasson-Praesidis, visit an advanced alien species Danilo previously encountered, the Ourankeli. On arriving, they find the Ourankeli's habitats destroyed, including a solar halo ring, and the Ourankeli massacred. Next, they travel to the home system of the Hoan, the primitive species that sheltered Danilo after his son tried to murder him. They discover Rasu ships in orbit and a quantum block surrounding the planet. They descend to the surface, where they find villages of Hoan massacred. Danilo is lamenting their fate when Kiernan and Toshke rush out of the woods to meet them. After a tense encounter, Kiernan insists that they all leave immediately, before the Rasu discover them, and Danilo agrees.

Malcolm leads a special forces squad on a stealth raid of the Godjan prison on Savrak. They are able to rescue the imprisoned Godjans, but as the last of the captives are freed, Savrakath forces attack. Malcolm is caught in an explosion and loses consciousness.

Marlee accompanies Mia to Mirai. Shortly after they arrive, word reaches Lance of Kiernan's rescue, and of the fact that some Rasu may now know the location of Namino, where Kiernan's ship was based. The Asterions begin preparations for the possibility of a Rasu attack, and Mia and Marlee go with Lance to DAF Command on Namino. There, Marlee meets Grant Mesahle and convinces him to take her into the city for a tour.

Caleb and Felzeor track Eren to Lethe, but Eren has already departed. Caleb searches the hotel room Eren had rented, finds evidence of the hypnol Eren had procured, and deduces what Eren is planning.

At Concord HQ, Eren breaks Torval out of detention and imprisons him in the cargo hold of Eren's ship. Caleb and Felzeor reach Concord HQ minutes after Eren has absconded with Torval. They confer with Richard until he's called away by Miriam, then decide to go drop in on Marlee.

Rasu arrive in the Namino stellar system, and Lance deploys his fleet. Miriam orders the AEGIS, Machim, Novoloume and Khokteh fleets to Namino and accompanies them in the *Stalwart II*.

On learning of the impending battle, Ferdinand elasson-Kyvern conspires with other Anaden *elassons* to subvert the new alliance. He kidnaps Casmir before the man can report to Namino with his fleet.

The Asterion fleet engages the Rasu. Concord forces arrives at Namino and join the battle, but the Machim fleet is a no-show. Mia reaches out to Ferdinand, who threatens an all-out rebellion against Concord. The battle is nevertheless turning the Asterions' and Concord's way when massive Rasu reinforcements arrive. Miriam appeals to Lakhes for the Kats to join the battle, but Lakhes declines.

Alex arrives at Namino to find the battle going badly for the good guys. After checking in with Miriam, she leaves the *Siyane* in Valkyrie's hands and goes to the Initiative to warn Nika that they're about to lose Namino. Nika and Dashiel decide they need to get the Vault to a safe location, and they're debating where and how when Mesme shows up and offers to safeguard the Vault. Nika is skeptical, but Mesme's pleas and Alex's promise that she trusts Mesme convinces Nika to agree to it.

A Rasu leviathan attacks the *Stalwart II*. When it can't do any damage, it changes shape and surrounds the *Stalwart II*, enclosing it entirely. Rasu then melt and infiltrate the ship via tiny seams in the hull; once inside, they solidify and attack ship personnel. When the Rasu are about to reach the bridge, Miriam activates the ship's self-destruct mechanism.

Valkyrie shows Alex what happened to the *Stalwart II*. Alex tells Nika that whatever she's going to do to rescue the people still on Namino, she needs to do it now, then opens a wormhole and vanishes.

Nika prepares to go to Namino and fight the Rasu invaders. Joaquim Lacese arrives at the Initiative, eager to join her. Joaquim leads the way through the d-gate to Namino; just as Nika is stepping through, the d-gate shuts down, as does every d-gate leading to Namino.

Caleb learns that Marlee has gone with Mia to the Dominion. He sends a furious message to Mia, demanding that she get Marlee out of the warzone immediately. Mia insists that she's trying (unsuccessfully) to get Marlee to leave, and Caleb tells her to open a wormhole to her office and he'll personally come retrieve Marlee.

Marlee gets separated from Grant and begins trying to get pedestrians into the DAF Command basement as Rasu land in the city and go on the attack. Caleb arrives at Mia's office, and Mia opens a wormhole, joining him just as Rasu reach DAF Command and attack Marlee. Caleb is rushing through the wormhole to rescue her when it shuts down, denying him access to Namino. When Mia is unable to reopen it, Caleb announces he is going to get his niece and walks out.

CONTENTS

Inversion

PART I

THE UPSIDE DOWN

CONCORD

1

CONCORD HQ
COMMAND
MILKY WAY GALAXY

A lex Solovy stumbled through the wormhole from Mirai and straight into her father's arms. Warmth and strength enveloped her in a loving cocoon, and for a fleeting moment she was a little girl again, trusting in her father to make the world right and safe. "Dad…."

"I know, *milaya*. It's going to be okay. *She's* going to be okay." His voice shook, a reminder that he was just a man. A good man, but not an omnipotent one.

There had been a time in Alex's adolescence when she'd wished with all her young heart that this was the way events had gone—wished he'd been the one comforting her over her mother's heroic death in the First Crux War instead of the other way around. Now, she couldn't conceive of ever having entertained such a fantasy. Yet she'd never felt more grateful that her father once again lived and breathed in this world.

"I saw it happen, Dad. The Rasu…they *swallowed* the *Stalwart II* whole."

"And then infiltrated the ship. Your mother made the right decision. The only decision a true leader could make to shield us from the enemy. She's a hero, and in a couple of days, we'll be able to tell her so."

"But what if there's a problem with the regenesis—"

"No 'buts'—not today. We need to have a little faith is all." He offered her a weak, fragile smile. Without any forewarning of her arrival, he hadn't cleaned himself up, and his blotchy cheeks glistened from wiped-away tears. "How did you get past the worm-hole block on HQ? Never mind, you don't have to answer that question. I'm glad you did." His gaze darted toward the door behind her. "But I'm afraid we have a more immediate problem than the Rasu to contend with."

As if on cue, the distant, muffled sounds of...weapons fire?...echoed from beyond the door. She stepped out of his embrace, wiping her own tears off her cheeks as she frowned in confusion and growing dread. "What's going on out there?"

"Anaden forces, we believe led by Senator Ferdinand, are trying to take control of Command. Trying to take control of all of HQ, I suspect."

"Because they know Mom is...?" She couldn't utter the word; to say it aloud would give it the weight of truth.

"No, I doubt they've gotten the news yet, and the trouble started before...." His voice trailed off; he couldn't say it either. "They're trying to effect a coup because they're petty tyrant *svilochnaya* who can't be bothered to learn how to play well with others." He squeezed her hand, his grip strong and reassuring, then went around behind her mother's desk and called up a screen. It showed the security cam feed from the Command atrium and the branching hallways leading to offices, meeting rooms, servers and equipment storage.

Red warning lights flashed throughout the area, and blast doors had engaged to block off all external points of entry. "I came to the office as soon as I caught wind that there might be trouble, and I was able to activate the priority defenses before any attackers reached the Command wing. We, and the critical data stored here, should be safe for now."

He pulled up a new screen from the control panel, deftly punched in a series of commands and opened a comm channel. "Bastian, I've unlocked all the human world-facing Caeles Prisms. Get your Marines onto HQ pronto."

"Acknowledged. The first teams will arrive in eighty seconds."

Alex frowned anew as she worked to piece together exactly what was happening here. Her head spun to the point of vertigo. Events were spiraling out of control around her, and she felt as if she were drowning beneath a malevolent hurricane.

Valkyrie, I could use some help. I need to be present in the here and now so I can help my dad and safeguard Mom's work, but I'm really struggling. Do what you can to shut down this panic, these ricocheting emotions, and help me focus. Just for a little while.

Of course. Try to concentrate on what you need to do, and I will ensure it gets easier to do so over the next few minutes.

Thank you. "Why are you talking to Field Marshal Bastian about bringing in Marines? Where's Malcolm?"

"I don't know. Off the grid."

'Off the grid'? What did that even mean? *Valkyrie? Tell me the Rasu did not get him as well.*

Meno does not have much in the way of further information. Malcolm was not present at Namino, however; he was instead leading a raid on Savrak and has not yet reported in.

I'm sure he's fine. He always is.

David reached under the desk, and his hand reemerged gripping a military-issue Daemon. He already had his own weapon holstered on his belt, so he tossed it to her. "In case they get through."

She instinctively checked the weapon over, letting muscle memory step her hands through the safety protocols Caleb had long ago drilled into her. Then she hung it off her belt and flicked her wrist in front of her. A lash of shimmering white electricity whipped out from her bracelet, crackling the air before it dissipated away.

David arched an eyebrow. "Let's hope they don't get that close."

She studied the door, a wave of redirected anger flooding her veins with adrenaline. "I kind of hope they do. If the Machim fleet had shown up at Namino like Mom ordered it to…" her throat constricted, and she had to force the words past it "…everything might be different now."

He came up beside her and touched her shoulder. "We can't look backward. We have to focus on what we can do now to protect Concord and its people."

"Right." Always the champion, even when it must be so damn hard for him. She checked the atrium visual. "Do you think they'll be able to break through the defenses?"

"Not unless they get control of Vigil security systems and deactivate them remotely."

"Well, are they going to get control?"

He shook his head. "Richard won't let them."

"Richard and what army?"

RW

Caleb Marano rushed out of the Consulate wing in the direction of the central transport station, his mind focused on formulating a plan to rescue Marlee from the Rasu to the exclusion of all else.

Assuming Namino still resided on this physical plane of existence, he needed a ship to reach it. Or...he glanced to his right, toward the wide hallway leading to the Caeles Prism Hub. If Mirai remained reachable, he could walk through a wormhole and be there in seconds, then find whatever crazy Asterions were planning to storm Namino and join up with them.

But taking that course of action would leave Marlee's fate largely dependent on the mercy of strangers. Not his first choice. So a ship, then. *Puddle Jumper* didn't have a Caeles Prism installed, and besides, it was little more than a glorified shuttle and would instantly get torn to shreds if it wandered within a parsec of warfare. On the other hand, he needed to run by the house and grab the archine blade Nika had given him as well as some other gear, and from there he could use Akeso's Caeles Prism to get reasonably close to Namino. Did he dare risk it with *Puddle Jumper*?

He didn't even consider trying to take the *Siyane*. Alex was off fighting Rasu with it and—he stopped cold in the middle of the hallway. *Alex*. Was she safe? In his head, she chided him about how that was never the pertinent question to ask. But the battle had obviously gone badly, and he hadn't heard from her in several hours.

A squad of Marines jogged past him toward the Consulate offices wearing full combat gear. Not Vigil officers, but AEGIS military personnel. What the hell was going on?

But he couldn't get involved. Whatever the problem was, the Marines could surely handle it. He set off again.

He needed to tell Isabela what had happened to Marlee before he left for Namino, though he had no idea how he was going to manage to get the words out.

Laser fire streaked across the open space of the atrium ahead, and without consciously deciding to do it, he ducked behind a pillar and drew his Daemon. Seriously, *what the hell?*

Six Vigil officers, all Anadens, advanced through the atrium with their weapons drawn, heading toward the section of the station that led to Command. More laser fire erupted from an obscured hallway on the other side, and the Vigil officers scurried for cover. All except one, who took a direct hit in the chest; his shield depleted, blood and tissue exploded out from the exit wound in the man's spine as he crumpled to the floor.

Disparate events over the last hour that Caleb had noted then ignored sprang into his mind. Richard's sudden troubled demeanor as he sprinted out of Detention after receiving a message. An overheard curse on the levtram about the Machim fleet not showing up at Namino. The Consulate receptionist saying Mia had requested new security measures—the Marines? Now Vigil officers were opening fire in the middle of HQ, and they weren't the only ones.

Coup.

He crept along the curving atrium wall, keeping out of the line of sight of the Vigil officers as he advanced on their left flank.

Four combat drones buzzed out of the opposite hallway and opened fire on the Anadens. Two of them went down in the initial volley before one of the others tossed an electricity grenade into the fray. Ozone sizzled in the air as the drones shorted out and dropped to the floor.

In the fleeting chaos the exchange created, Caleb flattened against the next pillar, then swung out, sighted down on the closest Vigil officer and pressed the trigger on his Daemon. A body fell—

—pain ripped through his skull, and he staggered back into the wall. His legs weakened, struggling to hold him upright. Had he been shot? He felt blindly around his head, but his hands came back bloodless even as jagged bolts of agony stabbed at his eyeballs from the inside.

All does not want this stop no death no blood

The wail of sorrow engulfing him drowned out the cacophony of continuing weapons fire. This was the first time in fourteen years that he'd killed someone. He tried to tell himself that since it was an Anaden, it didn't count. Didn't matter. But Akeso didn't recognize the difference.

The pungent odor of blood and gore reached his nostrils, and he doubled over and vomited up the lunch he and Felzeor had eaten earlier.

Stop no more

Dammit, Akeso, people are in danger. I have to protect them, don't I?

The wail diminished to background noise, and he fought to regain the concentration required for him to assess the situation. The final attacker was now on the ground, presumably taken out by whoever was defending the hallway leading to Command.

He stepped into the atrium, hands in the air, and stumbled past several bodies to reach the opposite wing.

"Caleb!" Someone grabbed his arm and dragged him into an open doorway as an explosion behind him rattled the walls. "There are more attackers incoming. Stay in cover."

He blinked and looked over to find Richard Navick motioning four men—CINT agents he thought, all human—out into the atrium. "Richard? What the hell is happening here?"

"Senator Ferdinand is leading a coup to take control of Concord agencies. David and Alex are holding Command from

Miriam's office for the time being, but the automated defenses won't last for long if the attackers assault Command in force."

His heart seized up for the second time in this eternal hour. *Please, don't take anyone else from me today.* "What is Alex doing in Command? She's supposed to be on the *Siyane* at Namino."

Richard looked up from an aural he'd instantiated to stare at Caleb strangely. "You don't know?"

"Know what?"

"Miriam blew up the *Stalwart II* to prevent the Rasu from capturing it."

"Miriam's dead?"

A new volley of weapons fire erupted from the atrium, and Richard peered out, Daemon raised. "Hopefully just for the moment."

Fuck.

> *Alex, are you okay?*
>
> *You mean am I hurt? Physically injured? No, I'm not. But I am so damn far from okay. Where are you?*
>
> *About a hundred meters from you. I found Richard.*
>
> *Good. Keep those bastards out of here.*

Caleb inhaled through his nostrils and grimaced past the resurgent shooting pain in his head. He could give her the protection and time she needed. He must, or else he was nothing. "What's the plan?"

"The plan—" Richard ducked back inside as arcing laser fire raced past "—is to reach a more defensible position and hold Command until a Marine regiment from AEGIS arrives, at which point we will clear the entire station of insurgents. Arrest them, detain them, interrogate them, and learn where Ferdinand has holed up to oversee his little coup attempt, then repeat the process with Ferdinand and his cronies."

"Can we?"

"Can we what?"

"Hold Command until the Marines arrive?"

"Right now, the blast doors are engaged, so even if we go down, they can't get inside."

"Those doors can be overridden by Vigil Security. Ferdinand's an idiot, but if the Machim officer orchestrating this attack has any operational sense, Security will have been the first place they targeted."

"Oh, it was. Loyal Vigil officers—non-Anaden officers—have held it so far, and I've ordered the first two Marine squads to reinforce them. This means it's just us, a couple of CINT agents who happened to be in the area, and those blast doors safeguarding Command for now."

"We'll be enough. What about the CINT offices?"

The muscles around Richard's mouth twitched and tensed. "Will's locked the suite down and is barricaded inside with the rest of the agents on site."

A flare of sympathy cut through the turmoil of his own selfish ruminations. "Will's not a soldier."

"Today he is. But CINT should be a low-priority target for the attackers, so...he'll be safe there."

"I'm sure you're right." Caleb pressed his fingertips to his temples as jolts of pain ricocheted between them at the mere thought of the necessary violence that now lay ahead of him. His eyes watered, and his vision swam.

"Caleb? Are you okay?"

I am so damn far from okay. "I'll be fine. Pull your men back to us, and let's retreat to the security checkpoint outside the entrance to Command. That's our defensible position."

2

CONCORD HQ
COMMAND

The floor shook from a thunderous explosion centered somewhere beyond the blast doors, but being blast doors, they held firm.

Alex watched her father as he cycled through a roulette of cams located throughout HQ. Abruptly he gave her a thumbs-up sign. "The cavalry's arrived. About damn time."

She moved back to her mother's desk in time to see a torrent of AEGIS Marines pour out of the Caeles Prism Hub and fan out across HQ. Two squads rematerialized on the Vigil Security cam thirty seconds later; another moved into CINT and one into the Consulate.

Impatience bled out of her to manifest in dancing fingers and tapping feet as another explosion shook the blast doors. The mutineers wanted to take Command, and they wanted it badly.

Finally, three full Marine squads swept into the Command wing to roll through the Anaden attackers with some good, old-fashioned hand-to-hand combat. In a few short minutes, all weapons fire had ceased, and an AEGIS officer she didn't recognize began issuing orders and overseeing the restraining of their new prisoners.

All the righteous urgency that had been driving her forward abandoned her in a rush of dumped adrenaline, and she sank shakily against the edge of her mother's desk. "Is it over?"

"For now, it looks like." David came around and draped an arm over her shoulder. "Sorry we didn't get to shoot anyone."

"Me, too. I could've used the catharsis."

"I know the feeling, *milaya*." He motioned toward the doors to the office. "They'll be opening in a minute, but it's the good guys."

On one of the cams, the blast doors slid open, and some very welcome faces arrived to hurry inside.

She kept the Daemon flush at her hip as she adjusted her posture and tried to project a calm and competent mien, as if everything about her life *wasn't* crashing down around her.

A few seconds later the office door slid open, and Richard led a small team of Marines inside. Her father clapped Richard's shoulder, and they began murmuring emphatically to one another as four Marines took up guard positions just outside the door.

She peered past them. Where was….

Caleb strode into the atrium, Daemon raised, scanning every corner for threats—until he saw her. A relieved smile broke upon features that even from this distance looked strained and worn.

She brushed past Richard and her father to meet him halfway across the open space. He wrapped his arms around her, holding her tight against him. "You're safe now, baby."

She pressed her face into his warm neck...hot, actually, almost as if he burned with a fever. She kissed his ear and leaned back in his embrace, only to be stunned by what she saw. His eyes were bloodshot, his skin sweaty and his jaw locked tight, and what might be a permanent crease had etched itself deeply into his forehead.

She brought a hand to his cheek. "What's wrong? I mean, besides everything?"

His throat worked laboriously. "Marlee was on Namino when the Rasu invaded. She's hurt."

"What?" She stepped out of his grasp, extended her arm and started gathering energy in the miniature Caeles Prism on her wrist. "Where is she? I'll open a wormhole right now—"

His hand moved to rest atop her wrist. "You can't. The wormholes to Namino have all stopped working. She's trapped there." His eyes squeezed shut tight. "And I don't know if…."

"Oh, no. I'm so sorry, *priyazn*." She drew him back into her arms, and he didn't fight her. Dammit, how much were they going to lose today?

This wasn't how the battle was supposed to have gone. They wielded indestructible warships that could leap across galaxies and rain weapons of immense power down upon their enemy. They were supposed to have won the day and celebrated a victorious night away.

"We'll talk to Nika, okay? We'll find out what the situation is on the ground there and see what she can do to help Marlee."

He nodded quickly. "It's a good idea. They must have rescue plans for those trapped in the invasion. Right?"

ASTERION DOMINION

3

NAMINO

DAF COMMAND
GENNISI GALAXY

G rant Mesahle rushed into the operational control room on the top floor of DAF Command and ran to the windows just in time to see a bipedal Rasu swat the Human girl and an Asterion man aside like flies as it barreled down the street. Marlee hurtled through the air and slammed into the sidewalk, while the man landed atop a wrought-iron fence, impaled.

Closer to the building, a rippling oval cutting into the fabric of the air flickered and vanished.

Behind him, a panicked clamor broke out.

He breathed in until his chest filled with oxygen, then turned around to see that the d-gate to the Mirai One Pavilion had gone silent, leaving an anxious throng of people confused and desperate as they tried to escape the invasion. Two technicians fussed over the control station to no avail. Grant checked his messages; there had been no announcement from the Omoikane Initiative that the Firewall Protocol was being activated, so this meant the d-gate outage was a technical problem.

He started to go over to the control station, confident he could help—but stopped, thinking of how the wormhole by the entrance had just vanished. He sent pings to Nika, Dashiel and Maris, but wasn't surprised when they all bounced.

Only a few things could cause all three events to occur at the same time, and they all involved blocking quantum signals.

He cleared his throat above the clamor. "The d-gate system is down, and it's likely not coming back up in the near future.

Everyone needs to get to the basement, okay? It will provide you some protection. Head to the lift behind the lobby and take it below."

Confused exclamations continued unabated.

"Hey! Get down to the basement before the Rasu tear through this building and you! Now!"

A shocked silence fell—then everyone was running out the door.

Everyone, that was, except Joaquim Lacese and Ava Zobel.

The former NOIR mission leader threw his hands in the air. "What the hells is going on? Nika was right behind us."

"It's just a guess, but I suspect the Rasu are blocking quantum manipulation here. It's the same thing they did on the planet where one of our pilots crashed after the Rasu stronghold battle."

"What?"

"It's not important right now. I'm glad you two are here. We need to head outside and pull off a rescue before this neighborhood is completely overrun." He'd stupidly lost Marlee in the initial panic when the Rasu began raining down from the sky. He'd delivered her directly into harm's way, and he deeply hoped his mistake hadn't cost the girl her life.

Joaquim patted the assault rifle slung across his chest, while Ava bounced on the balls of her feet in anticipation. NOIR's revolution might be over, but some people never changed.

He motioned for them to follow him, and they rushed downstairs into the first-floor lobby, where a whole new level of confusion reigned. "The basement lift is at the end of the right hallway—go!" He headed in the opposite direction, pushing through the front doors and out into armageddon.

Debris particles hung in the air on a faint breeze, and the ground rattled every other second from the tumbling of distant and not-so-distant buildings. An unidentified roar throbbed beneath it all like the slow heartbeat of Tartarus rising.

The smoke had grown so thick he could barely see across the street, so he switched to hybrid infrared. Faint and weakening heat signatures dotted the landscape—the dead or dying. One shape, however, still burned brightly—more brightly than a healthy Asterion, in fact. The Human.

"She's across the street and twenty-two degrees to the east. I'm going to make a run for her, and I need you two to provide cover fire."

Ava scoffed. "I've got all the cover fire you need. Joaquim, go with him."

"Fine. Let's move!"

Grant sprinted out into the haze, keeping his focus on his target, not searching around for looming Rasu bipedals or swooping vessels. The sound of collapsing buildings and distant screams in every direction was the worst thing he'd heard since a lost battle seven hundred thousand years ago, and he swiftly shut down the resurgent memory.

An explosion a few dozen meters away roiled the street beneath his feet, and he hurtled forward, throwing his arms out to brace himself. He crashed hard onto the sidewalk, sending jarring pain shooting up his left arm into his shoulder.

"Get up, man." Joaquim crawled toward him, blood trickling out of one ear.

Grant nodded weakly and checked his location. He'd landed almost on top of the heat signature, and he killed the infrared as he scrambled over to the young woman.

Marlee's eyes were closed, one arm was pinned at an ugly angle under her body, and she lay in a worrisome pool of blood, but a quick scan detected a pulse and a heartbeat.

He'd figure out what injuries might be patchable later, somewhere safer. Hopefully such a place existed. He wound his arms underneath her and lifted her up, ignoring the protestations in his shoulder. Her head lolled against his chest, and a nonsensical murmur escaped her lips.

He peered across the street and spent two seconds evaluating the return trip.

Joaquim leveled his weapon to the left, then swept it to the right. "I've got our backs. Let's run for it."

Running seemed impossible, but he stumble-jogged across the broken and pitted street. Laser fire streaked above their heads as they passed through the open gate leading back to DAF Command.

Joaquim grabbed Ava's free arm on the way by, and they all hurried inside.

The lobby had cleared out, and a sole remaining security dyne stood placidly at the counter. Grant approached the dyne to get its attention. "Shut those doors, then stay and stand watch. If any people—not Rasu, but people—come along, direct them inside and to the basement."

"Acknowledged."

A cough racked Grant's body as smoke and debris demanded to be set free from his lungs, and he sagged against the wall to keep from dropping his charge. Joaquim tried to take her from him, but he shook his head and began trudging toward the lift.

'Basement' was a bit of a misnomer for the space beneath DAF Command. This being a military structure, the lower level stretched for the full length of the building. Storage rooms dotted the far wall and backup server rooms the near one.

Perhaps fifty people milled about, many of them bleeding, all of them covered in a fine layer of dust. All the seats in the room were occupied by the exhausted and the injured, so he leaned beside the door. "Does anyone have any idea how to treat injuries on a Human?"

Several people stepped off to the side to allow someone to elbow their way through the crowd. Selene Panetier strode deliberately up to him and peered at the girl in his arms. "No, but I suspect stopping the bleeding is a good first step."

"You're as helpful as—" A deafening roar erupted above them. The ceiling shuddered, raining down a shower of debris and possibly very soon bringing the building down on top of them. It would be a damn shame to have gone to all the trouble of getting these people into the basement only for them to be buried alive.

Grant felt bone weary already, though this trial had scarcely begun. "No time to rest just yet."

Selene nodded, and the two of them approached an unmarked stretch of wall in the far-left corner. She was lifting a hand to unlock the hidden door when it slid open on its own.

Xyche'ghael stepped out of a dim, earthen tunnel and into the light. The Taiyok merchant motioned back to the passageway from which he'd emerged. "This location is no longer safe. Follow me."

4

NAMINO

Marlee opened her eyes, then immediately recoiled from the harsh, antiseptic light flooding her vision. Ah, hell…was she in a hospital? Or worse, a Rasu lab?

She tried not to move as she peered around through narrowed, watering eyes behind lowered lashes. Above her, an earthen ceiling curved down to meet stone walls braced by arched metal girders. The room was maybe thirty meters long and twenty wide, but it felt cramped due to the low ceiling, a complete absence of windows and the four dozen people crammed inside it.

No, not people precisely—or not humans, anyway. *Asterions.* And several tall, winged creatures…Taiyoks?

She bolted upright, wincing as a stabbing pain in her left side halted her movement halfway to sitting. She braced herself on her right arm and eased up the rest of the way. *Owww.*

A man with shoulder-length, dirty blond hair looked up from a nearby workstation nudged up against the wall, then stood and walked over wearing an easy grin. She knew him…Grant!

"Hey, you're awake. You had us worried for a while there."

She rubbed at her face as she dragged her legs off the edge of what appeared to be a field cot, and he hurriedly placed a warning hand on her arm. "Careful now. You've still got several active injuries. We patched you up as best we could, but no one here has ever treated a Human before." He tilted his head in question. "How did we do?"

"I'm alive, so I'd say pretty good. What happened? Where are we?"

He sat beside her on the cot. "You took a nasty swipe from a passing Rasu out on the street. Luckily for you, it had someplace else it wanted to be and kept going. About that time, all the wormholes shut off, so your boss couldn't reach you and evacuate you to Concord. Joaquim and I—" he gazed around for a second, then pointed out a copper-haired man wearing black tactical gear across the room "—that's Joaquim. We got you off the street and brought you with us down here, to our bunker. Hideout. Cave." He shrugged weakly. "It's protected us so far, so I shouldn't complain about the accommodations."

She gave him a big smile. Gosh, he was cute. "You saved my life. Thank you."

"You're trapped underground on a planet overtaken by highly inconsiderate shapeshifting metal aliens armed with deadly weapons. Not sure I've saved it quite yet."

"Sure you have." She lifted her shirt up above her waist and examined what it revealed. Four strips of tape were bound across her left ribs; the pain wasn't sharp as such, but merely breathing evoked a dull ache in the area, which was mottled with bruising. "What's the damage?"

"*That* is two deep gashes and three cracked ribs from where the Rasu caught you. You lost a decent amount of blood, too, but we were afraid to give you a transfusion. You might experience some dizziness and weakness for a couple of days. Oh, and you also dislocated your left elbow, hence the sling. It was probably for the best that you were unconscious when we reset it."

She'd been so busy absorbing the details of the room and her various aches and Grant's gorgeous, artificial eyes, it hadn't registered that her left arm was secured in a loose cloth sling. "Ouch." Now she gingerly tried to flex it out a little, but her elbow instantly protested. "I think I'll leave the sling on for a while longer."

"Good idea. Finally, you got banged on the head pretty hard when you landed on the sidewalk. I can't say for certain if you have a concussion, but it's likely why you've been unconscious for so long."

"How long is 'so long'?"

"About ten hours."

"Damn." She queried her eVi for a damage report, and while it mostly confirmed what Grant had said, it also came back incomplete. A quick diagnostic scan reported multiple systems were offline, most notably messaging and exanet access.

"We can't talk to the outside world? Several of my internal systems are offline."

"Nope. A quantum blocking field extends over the entire city. Possibly the entire planet. It's causing plenty of issues for us, too."

"I imagine so." She stifled a groan. Her mother must be sick with worry. True, her mother worried about her all the time, and she'd quit letting it slow her down a long time ago, but she'd never wanted to cause *this* level of worry. And Caleb...god, he was going to rip her to shreds when—she needed to be honest, *if*—he ever saw her again. And Mia was without a doubt going to fire her this time.

But instead of dwelling on how spectacularly she'd bollocksed things up, she studied those gathered in the bunker. Forty or fifty Asterions in total that she could see. Many were actively engaged in work she assumed was designed to keep them alive, but many more moped around looking dejected and forlorn. They believed they were fated to die.

But she refused to accept such a fatalistic scenario. "What's the plan? What is this cavernous, and also a literal cavern, hideout bunker for exactly?"

Grant chuckled. "Hiding out. We—the Omoikane Initiative, not me specifically—have been planning for the possibility of a Rasu invasion for the last two months. Somewhat to our surprise, it turned out the Taiyoks living here on Namino have been using underground tunnels to get around for years now, so we expanded them and built a series of bunkers beneath the city. One of the tunnels runs under DAF Command, and this bunker is located about a hundred meters to the east of it."

She scanned the room again until she found one of the tall, feathered aliens and gestured toward them. "That's a Taiyok, right?"

"It is. I did promise you that you could meet one, didn't I? Come on, if you're feeling up to walking."

"Are you kidding? I'm practically as good as new." She pushed herself to standing as a cascade of gentle warnings erupted from her eVi. Yep, there was the dizziness. She inhaled through her nose and swayed back to lean against the cot.

Grant steadied her. "Never mind, we can do introductions later. You ought to lie back down."

She started to shake her head vehemently, then thought better of it. "No, I'm okay. Just a bit of a head rush is all." To prove it, she let go of the cot and strode off with minimal grace, leaving Grant to catch up.

He reappeared at her side a second later to shoot her a squirrelly glance as they neared the alien. "Xyche, do you have a minute?"

The Taiyok shifted away from a pile of small weapons he and two Asterions were sorting on a table. "What do you require of me?"

"I want to introduce you. Marlee, this is Xyche'ghael, a long-time ally of Nika and NOIR and now of the Initiative. Xyche, this is Marlee...Marano, right? She's one of the Human representatives from Concord and was unlucky enough to get trapped here with us."

"Ah, the *laiti'manu* arises. Good."

She laughed, which provoked her cracked ribs into reminding her of their state. " 'Little bird'? I guess I can't argue with that, though I try to be a fierce, um...*manu'felelei* whenever possible."

The feathers framing the Taiyok's beak-like mouth fluttered. "You understood me?"

Oh, dear. She hoped she wasn't blushing. "I studied the files the Asterions provided to us on your species—especially your language—before I came to the Dominion. Alien languages are kind of my 'thing.' I'm not proficient yet, but let's see...*ou te tauma'fai.*"

"And to you, *laiti'manu.*"

"Thank you. I no longer have access to the files due to the quantum block, so perhaps you can teach me more of your language? When there's time."

"Perhaps. But first, we have many tasks to perform. Grant, we need to retrieve more weapons from the DAF Command armory or from other bunkers. This supply is not sufficient to enable us to mount a defense should the Rasu arrive here."

"I know it isn't. I'll talk to Joaquim." Grant turned to her. "Which presents an opportunity for me to introduce you to Joaquim. I apologize in advance."

"Whatever for?"

"You'll see."

In the far corner, the man Grant had pointed out earlier sat cross-legged on the floor between two women, one with long, flowing emerald hair and the other with shorter blond hair tied back in a tail. In front of them hovered a tetrahedron of slowly rotating...maps?

Joaquim reached up and grasped one of the maps to stop its spin. "We can take the tunnels here to get within eight hundred meters or so, but then we'll have to go above to reach the building."

"Which is instant suicide."

"We don't know that. What we do know is there are people pinned down in this building, and we need to get to them."

The blonde woman leveled an impressively steely glare at Joaquim. "No, we know there *were* people pinned down there ten hours ago. I'm sorry, as I realize these are friends of yours, but the odds of them still being functional are minuscule."

"Bullshit!" The emerald-haired woman leaned forward, radiating an impression of barely coiled violence. "They're NOIR, and NOIR people are survivors. I didn't think Justice Advisors were such cowards."

The other woman didn't seem fazed by what had sounded a lot like an insult. "No, Justice Advisors are smart. I can't authorize an above-ground foray until I learn what the situation is up there."

Joaquim threw his hands in the air. "You say that like you're in charge or something."

"I *am* in charge."

"All evidence to the contrary. Come on, Ava. We can rescue Dominic and Josie ourselves." Joaquim leapt to his feet and stormed off toward the weapons cache where Xyche was working; the woman—Ava, apparently—stood and followed him, which was when Marlee noticed that beneath a series of interlocking synthetic skin flaps that hung open, her left arm was *literally a weapon*. Wow. Asterions were so cool.

Grant held out a hand to halt her progress toward the group. "Or maybe we should do introductions later."

The second woman, the one Joaquim had called a 'Justice Advisor,' scratched at her nose, sighed and stood as well, then spotted them and came over. "If your friend wants to get himself sliced up good and proper, I won't get in his way, but I will not let him lead everyone else to the same fate."

"I never said he was my friend." Grant adopted a pained expression. "Though he kind of is. Anyway, good luck trying to stop him once he gets a mind to do something, even something stupid."

"I'm picking up on that." The woman pivoted to her and donned a perfunctory smile. "You're awake. I'm glad. I'm Selene Panetier, Namino Justice Advisor."

"Hi. You were at DAF Command, but we didn't get a chance to speak. I'm Marlee Marano, Research Assistant for the Concord Consulate."

"Selene's most of the reason why you're up and walking around."

The woman shrugged. "Eh, it turns out we have most of the same body parts. I'm serious about Lacese, Grant. If he starts kicking up trouble here, we'll have to deal with him."

"I don't disagree. But you need to realize, he's a great fighter and a great leader...of fights." He turned to Marlee. "You must be famished. We have a refrigeration unit stocked full of terrible food down the narrow hallway on the left back there."

She was being excused from the conversation. But at the promise of food, her stomach grumbled. "I'll get some, then. Thank you both again for rescuing me."

She wandered off toward the hall Grant had indicated. The cramped, low-ceiling corridor led to several small rooms: a storage space, a working lavatory—thank goodness—and a kitchen.

She found the fridge and opened it, scowling as she surveyed its contents. She was indeed super grateful to Grant, Selene and anyone else who played a role in her rescue, but she hated *needing* to be rescued. Even from something as formidable as the Rasu. Her whole body hurt when she moved and hurt worse when she didn't, but she hated being weak and damaged, especially in front of all these amazing aliens.

Her memory of the last few minutes of the attack started returning in muddled flashes of fire and smoke and giant ships darkening the sky. Lumbering metal beasts tearing through the streets with her in their sights.

She shivered involuntarily, though the bunker was stiflingly warm.

Well, Marlee, you wanted an adventure.

5

MIRAI
OMOIKANE INITIATIVE

A frigid pall had settled over the Omoikane Initiative. Oh, people scrambled here and there, working diligently to track and manage evacuations, monitor deep space scanners across Dominion territory for further Rasu incursions and, more solemnly, begin a tally of the losses and what resources remained at their disposal.

You never knew how strong a person was going to prove to be until disaster struck, and most of the individuals in the room were proving themselves strong indeed. It was enough to make any self-respecting Asterion proud.

Nika Kirumase, however, felt as if she was cracking apart from the inside out. In her mind she kept seeing Joaquim and Ava disappear through the d-gate. She'd taken Dashiel's hand and strode forward—and the passage vanished. She'd willed her feet to move faster, to sprint ahead and tumble through the d-gate and onto Namino soil. Two more seconds was all she'd needed!

Now the Rasu were rampaging across Namino and she was stuck here on Mirai, with the greater weight of the Advisors sitting here at the conference table looking desperately to her for guidance. What was she supposed to say? Any of them were capable of running the government as well as she, but few if any were capable of fighting the Rasu. She *was*.

Two more seconds....

"Nika?"

She noted the faces of the other Advisors, alternately forlorn and shocked into an almost fugue state, then directed her attention to the highest-ranking military officer not dead or trapped on Namino, a Brigadier Johansson. "How many flight-worthy ships do we have remaining?"

The brigadier's jaw twitched. "Eight, ma'am."

"Eight…hundred?"

"No. Eight ships."

She dropped her head into her hands atop the table. "*Eight.*"

"Yes, ma'am. And the only reason we have those eight is because Concord Commandant Solovy ordered our surviving ships to retreat."

She breathed in through her nose, but it didn't ease the throb from her pulse pounding angrily against her temples. "*Eight.*"

Dashiel's hand landed gently on her knee. "Nika…."

"Don't," she growled through gritted teeth.

"I think I will. I understand that you're upset, but how do you think I feel? Everything I've spent the last two months building is gone. *Everything.*"

She peered at him from behind splayed fingers. "Everything except eight warships."

His eyes narrowed, and he jerked away from her.

Because he *was* hurting as much as she was. Dammit. "I'm sorry." She reached out and touched his shoulder. "I'm *sorry.*"

He finally shifted back to face her, giving her the poorest attempt at a smile she'd ever seen cross his features.

She had to pull herself together. For him. For Perrin and Adlai and Maris and Spencer and all the other important people in her life who were still here on this side of the broken d-gates with her. She had to trust in Joaquim to lead and protect those stranded on the other side until she could get to them.

She lifted her shoulders and clasped her hands properly atop the table. "I apologize to everyone. I realize we're all hurting, but we have to find a way to move forward—to do everything we can to defend the people on the rest of our worlds. Dashiel, when will we have eight hundred ships?"

He sank lower in his chair. "All our existing military shipyards were destroyed in the attack. We were, however, in the process of building two additional shipyards here on Mirai, and they will be operational in two days."

"Two days? That's good news. By then Lance will be back up and with us, and we can..." the darkening expression on his face suggested it wasn't such good news after all "...what?"

"Ninety percent of our component assembly facilities were also located on or above Namino. I know, Lance was right, and we should have diversified to make the supply chain more resilient. We will learn from our mistakes—from my mistakes—and do a better job of it this time."

"How long?"

"I've already issued the instructions for recreating the assembly facilities here and on Synra. Once they're up and running, we'll add redundancies on Kiyora and Ebisu."

"How *long*?"

"Ten days."

She inhaled deeply, struggling to fill her lungs; there wasn't sufficient oxygen in the damn room. "All right. Ten days until we have more ships. Brigadier Johansson, please send one of our...eight surviving ships to Namino under full stealth. We know the Rasu's quantum blocking field prevents communications and supradimensional disruptions, but we need to find out if it also blocks physical intrusions. Have the ship try to reach the atmosphere, then reach the surface if it can, survey the situation as much as is feasible and escape alive to report back to us."

"Yes, ma'am. I'll see to it."

"Adlai, how many people are trapped on Namino?"

The Justice Advisor had propped his still-healing leg on a second chair, and he was pale enough that if this were anything less than the end of the world, she'd have ordered him back to the clinic for another few hours in a tank. "We evacuated 6.5 million before the d-gates went down."

"That not what I asked."

"I know it isn't. Our best guess? Around eight million."

Her eyes closed. Her chest felt constricted; she genuinely couldn't breathe in this suffocating air. How was Joaquim supposed to protect *eight million* people? How many would soon find themselves strapped to a torture table in a lab like the one she'd destroyed at the stronghold?

Shadows of myself flit in and out of my peripheral vision, but I can only focus on my own. I search for an opening cut into a wall of the expansive lab, because the Rasu don't use doors.

A hulking, multi-limbed Rasu steps into my path. My legs are no more. I fall.

The violet flame of a weapon firing sears through me. My chest explodes. I fall.

Blinding light from nowhere and everywhere consumes me. I fall.

Rasu orbs flood the lab with their beams crisscrossing the room in a macabre dance of death. Slicing into flesh. I fall. I'm falling for so long.

"Hey, are you okay?"

She opened her eyes to find Dashiel's hand had returned to her knee. She nodded tightly and cleared her throat. "Maris, how are we planning to spin this for the public? What smashing ideas do you have on how to boost morale?"

Her oldest friend stared at her with wide, frozen orchid irises. "I...do not know."

"Fair enough. Here's what we're going to do. I want one d-gate on each Axis World set to constantly ping Namino. The blocking field might fluctuate, or cycle, or randomly go down, and we need to be ready."

"But the risk of opening a d-gate when Rasu—"

She whipped toward Adlai. "I don't give a fuck about Firewall!"

"You should."

She threw her head back to glare at the ceiling. "Guard the relevant d-gates. Guard them with AEVs if it helps you sleep at night. We'll be able to stop a single Rasu as it comes through—*if* one tries to come through—then shut the d-gate down. But we have to try to reach the planet."

Adlai glanced at the remaining Justice Advisors—Spencer, Julien and Harris, as Selene was among those trapped on Namino. "We'll draw up a plan we can all live with."

Silence engulfed the table like a smothering fog until Dashiel stepped in again. "We need to decide how to proceed on the planetary shielding project, Project Shirudo. The test results came back good here on Mirai, so we can begin building a network for a second Axis World, but...."

"What's the cost?"

"Billions. Plus thousands of man-hours and hundreds of thousands of dyne-hours."

Nika shook her head in frustration. "It's not worth it. If the Rasu don't yet have the locations of every one of our worlds, they will any hour now. Armed with this knowledge, there's no reason to hope that a cloaking shield will fool them. We need to spend the money and time where they have a chance of making a difference. Can anyone tell me where that might be?"

Katherine Colson, the Mirai Administration Advisor, spoke up for the first time. "We can always—"

One of the military officers who'd evacuated DAF Command before the quantum block descended jogged up to the table, panting and out of breath. "I'm sorry to interrupt, Advisors, but we are picking up a sudden surge in artificial signals in the Mirai stellar system."

Her chair clattered to the floor as she shoved it back and leapt up. "*Here?*"

"Yes. Multiple readings appeared out of nowhere. They're on a direct course for Mirai."

She was vaguely aware of Dashiel rushing past her to reach the monitoring station near the front of the room. Her legs shook from the effort of keeping her upright. It had all been for naught. They couldn't stand up to an enemy such as this one. Her only consolation was that at some point in the future, the Vault could restart Asterion civilization in a distant corner of the universe. Assuming any place was beyond the reach of the Rasu—

"These aren't Rasu signatures."

Her gaze shot over to Dashiel, where he, Johansson and several others were crowded around the monitoring station. "Say that again?"

"They're ships of some kind, but they're not giving off the Rasu energy signature."

"Then whose ships are they? Concord?"

"We'll have a visual in four seconds."

No one moved.

On a pane above the monitoring station, an image materialized of a long, cylindrical, inky black vessel laced through with vivid crimson fluorescent lines. The cam panned out to reveal dozens, then hundreds of identical vessels. It looked like a fleet risen from Tartarus itself.

"Um...scale?"

"Let's see...2.4 kilometers in length, four-hundred-ten in width."

Her hand came to her forehead. "Brigadier, ready the planetary defenses, but don't fire."

Dashiel stared at her incredulously. "Are you crazy? We need to respond...." His voice drifted off as his attention shifted to something behind her.

Her hair ruffled, as if caught up in a breeze, when a tsunami of pinprick lights swept in to spin around her before gathering in an undulating pattern near the center of the room.

Apologies if we have unduly frightened you. Please accept this fleet of Katasketousya warships to aid you in your time of need.

Nika blinked. "Mesme?"

It is I.

She motioned toward the pane. "And these are your ships?" The offhand comments Alex and others had made about the terrifying nature of Kat vessels suddenly made a great deal more sense.

They are. They stand ready to defend Asterion worlds.

"Um, thank you. This is most generous of you…" she frowned "…but not timely. Why the hells didn't they come to Namino's defense?"

An internal matter prevented us from arriving in time. I regret this was so. As penance, I can only offer them to you now.

"I see." She glanced at Dashiel, but his attention was fixated on the swirling lights. "Listen, these ships appear to be most impressive and formidable, but I know the Humans defeated an entire armada of ships like these. What makes you think they can withstand a Rasu assault?"

Since our conflict with the Humans, we have made improvements to their design and weaponry.

"Good. Will they be able to destroy Rasu vessels?"

No. Not in sufficient quantities or with sufficient speed. But they will do an excellent job of occupying Rasu forces for an extended period of time. Days, if our simulations are correct. Long enough to buy you time to respond accordingly.

"I appreciate the gesture, but right now we have nothing to respond with."

I have faith you soon will. Also, I should mention that we hope to deliver additional defensive measures for your use in the coming days.

"What kind of defensive measures?"

I do not want to overpromise and disappoint. We will do what we can.

Maddening, confounding creature. "I…thank you. I mean it. We welcome whatever aid you can provide."

You may distribute these vessels as you see fit. I await your instructions.

She wasn't a military strategist, but she recognized full well that every choice came with a cost. "How many vessels are there?"

Four hundred forty superdreadnoughts, as the Humans call them, each carrying ten thousand attack craft.

"Swarmers?"

Yes.

She did the math in her head...it still wasn't enough. She motioned everyone back to the table, dropped her hands upon it and leaned forward to bring their attention to her and off the Kat. "I think we need to evacuate the Adjunct Worlds. We can't protect them. But maybe, if we concentrate all our efforts on the remaining Axis Worlds, we *can* protect them, for a time."

Katherine threw her hands in the air. "That's over three million people. Our infrastructure is already straining to the point of breaking under the weight of 6.5 million evacuees from Namino."

"Then adapt. Overcome. Solve the godsdamn problem. Or someone tell me how I'm wrong? Give me a better plan, one that actually stands a fuck's chance in Hades of working."

Silence greeted her. Off to the left, the conglomeration of lights danced languidly, awaiting her order.

"Evacuate the Adjunct Worlds, then pull all our resources back to the Axis Worlds. Mesme, leave one hundred ten superdreadnoughts here and send an equal number to each of Synra, Kiyora and Ebisu."

It will be done.

She breathed in, finding a pocket of nourishing air for the first time in hours. This was something. A pitiful little iota of something, but something nonetheless.

She turned to regard the eddying lights with what she hoped was a grateful countenance. "What's the situation in Concord?"

CONCORD

6

CONCORD HQ
COMMAND

David slid into the chair beside Alex and patted her hand under the table. She offered him a weak smile, but her eyes were unfocused and distant, her thoughts likely parsecs away from the conference room. She'd been robotically going through the motions for the last day, as if the double tragedy of losing—*for now*—Miri and Marlee had fractured something inside her.

If David thought about it for longer than a few seconds, he could feel vital pieces of himself breaking apart, too. The only glue he had on hand to hold the pieces together was the certainty that Miri needed him to zealously guard everything she'd built in her absence. The sole thing he could do for her in the here and now was be the best steward of her legacy he knew how to be, until she returned.

Renewed determination to do so lifted his chin, and he addressed those gathered at the table with a clear voice he would not allow to crack. "At this point, I'm prepared to officially declare Concord HQ secure. Thanks to a swift response by Field Marshal Bastian, we believe we've fully suppressed the mutiny here on the station. Now AEGIS Marines are working together with Khokteh and Barisan soldiers and Vigil officers—non-Anaden Vigil officers—to restore order and security in all departments. In doing so, they are giving lie to Senator Ferdinand's spurious claims that humans are trying to take over Concord. AEGIS, Khokteh and Novoloume vessels are patrolling the station's perimeter to deter any new incursions from space. Richard?"

His old friend looked a little worn around the edges, but since the attack he'd showered and donned fresh clothes that were free of dried blood and laser burns. "We've arrested and detained all the Anaden attackers who didn't deliberately null out. To a one, they claim they were simply following orders from two of the Machim *elassons*, Hannah and Otto. I'm inclined to believe them, because that's what Anadens who aren't *elassons* do—follow orders. But since they're apt to continue doing so unless something major changes, they will remain in Detention until the ringleaders of the coup attempt are brought to justice."

"What about the rest of Vigil?"

"The vast majority of the non-Anaden officers stood down as soon as they realized what was happening. They serve Concord, not the *elassons*, and with a few one-off exceptions, I'm comfortable permitting everyone else to resume their duties."

"Excellent news. And what of those ringleaders? Hannah, Otto, Ferdinand, any others who might be involved?"

Richard spread his arms wide. "Gone to ground somewhere, presumably to foment further revolution. I've tasked five separate CINT investigative teams with hunting them down. I'm also tracking two other potential leads I'm hoping will pan out, but due to rampant security concerns I need to keep them need-to-know for now."

"Understood. Great work, my friend."

Richard nodded a thanks, and David returned his attention to the table at large. He held no official title beyond 'Professor Emeritus,' but thus far everyone acted willing to defer to him on operational matters. Which was a good thing, since he hadn't intended on taking 'no' for an answer should they refuse. "I can't overstate how important it is that we continue to hold HQ. Yes, there are troves of data, secure feeds, intel and resources located here. It's our seat of power, after all. But more importantly, it's a symbol: whoever controls HQ controls Concord, and any other claimants to authority are nothing but usurpers in exile."

Pinchu shifted in his chair, causing his tail to make a soft *swooshing* sound across the floor. "What about the Asterions? We left them in a sorry state. There was no other choice at the time, but honor demands we do what we can for them."

Pointe-Amiral Thisiame responded. "The probes we left behind indicate the planet of Namino is under full siege by the Rasu. Thousands of Rasu vessels orbit it, fortifying their control of the system. We can't say what's happening on the ground."

David drummed his fingers on the table. "And the other Asterion worlds? It's safe to assume the Rasu will soon learn where they're located as well."

Bastian shook his head. "Maybe, but we cannot afford to send more ships to defend their worlds right now. Not until the situation with the breakaway Anadens is under control. I'm sorry, but I won't risk leaving us underdefended."

Alex had been staring at her hands folded in her lap, but now she glanced up. "It's fine. The Kats are taking care of it."

David pivoted to her in surprise. "What?"

"They sent a fleet of turbocharged superdreadnoughts to the Dominion a couple of hours ago. Not to try to retake Namino, but to guard the other Axis Worlds."

He snorted with a trace of disgust. "Where the *ebanatyi pidaraz* were those superdreadnoughts during the Namino battle?"

She shrugged wordlessly. He wanted to hug her and swear to her on his second life that everything was going to turn out okay, even if he had to corral the entire universe into falling in line before his will. Instead he bit off a tirade against the Kats before it reached his lips. "All right. I'm happy to hear they've gotten their act together and the Asterions have some protection. We need to focus on—"

An officer stuck his head in the room. "Professor Solovy? You said for us to inform you when Dr. Canivon arrived. She's here now."

He and Alex leapt up in unison, and he waved distractedly toward the table. "Please, continue without us for a few minutes."

In the anteroom, Alex embraced Dr. Canivon without guile; the woman awkwardly patted Alex on the back.

"Thank you so much for coming, Abigail."

"Of course. I'm glad you contacted me."

David motioned down the hall. "We can talk privately in Miri's office."

Once there, they settled around the table by the window, and David clasped his hands on the table. "Well? What have you been able to learn?"

"The regenesis process has already begun at the AEGIS HR lab on the Presidio. All the markers are very favorable for it to be successful. Commandant Solovy's last neural imprint was taken two weeks before her...passing, which isn't so long of a gap. It should minimize any disorientation when she awakens. It's a clean imprint, and any minor glitches fall well within safety parameters. I'm confident the process will result in a favorable outcome for her."

"Good. Good." He nodded, mostly to himself. "When?"

"It will take a little time. We long ago perfected growing bones, organs and skin, but we're still new at the neurological aspects of regenesis. We don't want to make any mistakes, especially with such a high profile—especially with someone as important as Miriam." David motioned expectantly for her to get to a timetable. "Since the team has already gotten started, likely two or three more days, the majority of which will be devoted to creating and readying the body."

He gave Alex a big grin. "Just a couple of days. Nowhere near twenty-five years."

She rolled her eyes at him and wiped away a tear, then lifted her chin bravely. "Thank you again for stepping in to personally oversee this for us. There's no one I trust more with my mother's life."

Dr. Canivon patted Alex's hand perfunctorily. "Don't worry yourself too much. We've spent the last fourteen years preparing for this day, all so we can get this one right. Now unless you have any further questions, I need to go install myself in the AEGIS HR lab for the next several days."

David stood and shook the woman's hand. "Please, contact Alex or me with any questions or concerns, no matter how slight. And if the loggerheads at the Presidio give you any grief, let me know and I'll knock them into shape."

"I suspect the mere threat of you doing so will be sufficient to keep them polite and compliant."

Only someone like Dr. Canivon would ever refer to humanity's most elite military officers as 'polite and compliant.' What an odd woman she was.

He and Alex saw her to the door and bid their farewells. As soon as she'd departed, Alex buried herself in his arms. "This is going to work."

"It is." He squeezed her tight, trying to convey reassurance with every touch. He meant it, too. Though he'd never allowed himself to doubt that Miri would soon return to them, the doctor's assured confidence had him feeling positively buoyant about the prospect. "Then you will have brought both your parents back to life. Quite a feat."

"I'm not doing this. Science is."

"Science we never would have dreamed of discovering and mastering if not for all you did before and after The Displacement."

"Well." She drew back to give him a bright if teary smile, and for the first time since the Namino battle, her eyes sparkled with a hint of vivacity. "Whatever you need, I'm here for you. And when she wakes up, I'll be here for her, too."

"There are still wars to fight, *milaya*."

"I know, but right now I only care about my family—you, Mom, Caleb, Marlee. Let someone else fight the wars for once."

7

CONCORD HQ
COMMAND

Caleb offered Dr. Canivon a polite nod as he passed her on the way to Miriam's office. He'd never cared for the woman personally, but he did respect her. She was nothing short of a miracle worker, having created the Prevos who saved humanity, brought Mia back from the brink of death fifteen years ago, and designed two Artificials clever enough to bring *her* back from the other side. In her capable hands, Miriam was certain to return in consummate form, and soon.

He stopped in the open doorway and watched Alex and David comfort one another. Hugs and murmurs were exchanged with a level of intimacy only family brought. It warmed his aching heart to see, but it also solidified his resolve. He didn't think he could leave if it meant she'd suffer through this trial alone, but she and her father were here for each other. She would be okay without him.

He'd spoken with Nika a few minutes earlier, but the Asterion had delivered only bad, if expected, news. Not only could they not reach Namino via wormhole, they also couldn't talk to anyone on the ground there or access their local surveillance systems. Namino was in effect an island drifting in the void, cut off from the universe and the universe from it. And while Nika had expressed a fervent desire to reach the island herself, with her government currently in meltdown and her military decimated, she had bigger concerns than one human girl.

Alex spotted him in the doorway and hurried over to embrace him. "Abigail says Mom's regenesis should be successful. No problems on the horizon that she can detect. It'll take a few days is all."

He breathed her in, absorbing the familiar scent of her hair; kissed her cheeks, tasting tears that now carried hope rather than sadness. "I am so, so glad."

Her lips brushed across his, her eyelashes fluttering over his skin…and he wanted more than anything in all the worlds to *stay*.

She drew back to study him closely, and he worked to shape his features into a brave, rock-solid countenance. If he let her see the cracks, he'd never manage to leave.

"What about Marlee? Any word?"

"I talked to Nika a little while ago. They're working on infiltrating Namino as soon as possible. She said if Marlee was at DAF Command, there would've been a lot of people nearby who could help her…and I'm sure they did."

"So am I. Also, the Asterions spent the last few months putting in place contingency plans in the event of a Rasu invasion. Bunkers for people to seek shelter in, weapons stashes, the works."

"They did."

Alex's brow furrowed, and he sensed the wheels turning in her mind. "Maybe we ought to—hmm. Valkyrie says Mia needs to talk to me about something. Do you want to come with me to see her?"

He managed a weak laugh, and it came out sounding bitter despite his best efforts otherwise. "I'm still a bit hot under the collar at Mia for putting Marlee at risk in the first place. I expect I'll forgive her eventually, but I probably shouldn't be around her right now."

"Understood." She stepped fully out of his arms and glanced over her shoulder at David, who'd been giving a fatherly impression of ignoring their nuzzling. "You two should head back into the meeting, lest it descend into total bedlam without your guiding presence. I'll join you shortly."

David grimaced. "Good idea. I can practically hear the shouting from here."

Alex shot him a sympathetic look then disappeared out the door.

Caleb closed it behind her and pivoted to David. "I need you to get me into the CINT ship hangar wing and help me steal a Ghost."

"What makes you think I can do that?"

He just stared at his father-in-law.

"Fine, I can do that." David leaned against the table by the viewport. "Caleb, Namino is infested with Rasu. Even if a Ghost gets you to the surface, you won't survive ten minutes on the ground. You'll never find her."

"I submit I will."

David made the same face Alex did when she was growing frustrated with him. "And you're going to leave Alex here alone? At this moment, of all the times to abandon her?"

Way to stick the knife in and twist. "You think I *want* to leave her? You think I don't realize full well what doing this will cost me? But Alex has you. Once Miriam wakes up, you'll all have each other. Right now, Marlee only has me. I have no choice but to try to save her. If I don't, I betray everything I have ever been."

"You must realize that Marlee..." David's eyes closed "...she might be dead."

Fire boiled through his veins, lashing out at the words. His mind went to the promise he'd made to his sister earlier this morning as a grim, steel dawn broke over Cavare.

Isabela stumbled backwards to fall into the chair. "What?"

Caleb didn't need to close his eyes to see the scene play out in an endless loop in his mind. "She was out on the street during the Rasu attack, trying to help people get to a nearby basement shelter. A passing Rasu sideswiped her and sent her...sent her tumbling onto the sidewalk. She didn't immediately get up. Then the wormhole failed, and I couldn't reach her."

"What do you mean, it 'failed'?"

"I mean the Rasu have erected some type of quantum interference field around the planet. It's preventing any wormholes from opening on or near Namino."

His sister dragged both hands through already tangled hair. "What was she doing there?"

"Her job, ostensibly. Mia was trying to get her to leave, but you know how she is. She refused, insisting on staying to help people."

"Goddamn her!"

"Bela—"

"Is she dead?"

The prepared response stuck in his throat, and he had to drag each word out against its will. "I don't think so. I mean, I don't think the strike from the Rasu killed her. So either she got to her feet and made it inside on her own, or someone helped her get inside, or...if she stayed on the street for long, then...no. She's alive. I refuse to accept any other alternative."

"Good." Isabela grabbed his shoulders and shook him fiercely. "You bring her back to me, no matter what it takes. Promise me!"

"All this time, everyone has constantly been telling me how brilliant and resourceful Marlee is. Everyone was right, and I was blind not to see it, but I have to believe it now, because it means she's too smart to die. But she *is* suffering. So I'm going to Namino one way or another. If you care at all about Marlee, you'll help give me the best chance possible of reaching her."

"Dammit, Caleb, you are not being fair. You know how much I care about that girl."

"I do. So *help* me."

David groaned and cast his gaze to the ceiling. "Come with me."

RW

CONSULATE

Mia looked up from the latest in a long line of panicked dispatches to see Colonel Odaka standing in the doorway. Finally! She motioned him into her office. "Thank you for coming, Colonel. I realize you're busy."

"We all are, Senator. It's no trouble."

She only vaguely remembered the man from the formative days of the IDCC, but part of her job was making every person feel as though they were an old friend. She shook his hand warmly and dragged out a welcoming smile. "It's good to see you again, sir, though I regret it must be under these circumstances. Can I get you anything to drink?"

He shook his head tersely, retaining a rigid military stance. "No, thank you."

"Very well. I won't waste your time, then. What can you tell me about what happened on the Okshakin raid?"

"To Fleet Admiral Jenner, you mean."

"And any other of our personnel who are...unaccounted for."

"He's the only one. Three of our men suffered moderate-to-severe injuries, but they are recovering. Several of the Godjans were injured as well, but the doctors say they should all live."

"Colonel." Her nerves were increasingly frazzled, and she worked to steady her voice. "Please. What happened?"

"Jenner—the Fleet Admiral—was helping an injured team member reach the extraction point, which by that time was coming under heavy fire from Savrakath military personnel. He pushed the injured team member ahead of him through the wormhole and onto our DAR vessel at the same instant a grenade detonated in proximity to the open wormhole. The Prevo, Major Rodriguez, was rendered unconscious by the blast, and the wormhole destabilized then shut down, cutting us off from Savrak. Before the wormhole closed, however, the explosion ripped through the hold of the vessel. This is what caused most of the injuries. By the time

Major Rodriguez regained consciousness and was able to survey the scene via sidespace, he found nothing but flooded rubble and...no sign of Fleet Admiral Jenner."

She fought to overcome the suffocating tightness growing in her chest. These were just details; they didn't fundamentally alter what she already knew, which was that Malcolm was missing. "And further investigation?"

"Has found nothing so far. We've had Prevos surveilling the rest of the Savradin Governmental Hall, as well as the military facility locations we'd previously tagged. And the Savradin hospitals. And the prisons. Nothing."

The room got colder, and she tried not to visibly shiver. "Thank you, Colonel. Please continue active surveillance, but I think we need to assume the Savrakaths have taken him prisoner and are holding him at a secret location of which Concord is not aware."

"We've searched very thoroughly, Senator."

She forcefully bit back a snappish response. Breathed in through her nose. "Nevertheless. Given the circumstances, I'm declaring this a diplomatic matter."

"Yes, Senator." He turned to go, then pivoted back. "I'm sorry we lost him. Marines aren't supposed to leave a man behind. If he's somehow...if we're able to locate him, I can have a rescue mission primed and ready to move in ninety minutes."

You're damn right you can—and will. "We haven't lost him, Colonel. But thank you. I'll keep you informed, and I ask you to do the same."

After Odaka left, she took a minute, then another, to recompose herself before sending a conference request to Ambassador Darhk.

The Savrakath kept her waiting for twelve minutes before appearing on the holocomm wearing decorated military attire and standing in front of an ostentatious painting of himself receiving a medal.

His voice hissed shrilly, setting her nerves on edge. "Senator, don't you think the time for diplomacy has passed? You attack our sovereign soil at will. Understand that we will have no compunction about doing the same to yours in retaliation."

"The time for diplomacy never passes, Ambassador, for we must strive to keep open a path back from the cliff. I recognize that you and I cannot end this conflict today, but I'm contacting you with an interim proposal. Return any prisoners of war you have captured as a result of the raid on the Okshakin facility and refrain from taking any violent actions against Concord, and we will cease further offensives on Savrak soil." She didn't have the authority to make the offer, but right now she didn't give a damn.

"POWs? What POWs? One of your soldiers fell during your illegal incursion. He did not survive his injuries. If you agree to return the Godjan criminals you kidnapped, we will *consider* de-escalating our response to Concord's hostilities."

A shrill, high-pitched noise rang in her ears, and she tried to tell herself she hadn't heard the ambassador correctly. Or he was lying, jockeying for a superior negotiating position. He must be. Her vision blurred, and she discreetly placed a hand on her desk to steady herself. "If any Concord soldiers were in fact killed as you claim, we demand their bodies be returned for a proper..." her voice cracked "...burial."

Darhk bared his teeth, and a dismissive, sneering sound escaped through them. "Alas, your combatant was burned beyond recognition in the devastating fire that consumed the Okshakin facility as a result of your raid. We disposed of what little remained—"

She cut the connection a nanosecond before her legs gave out beneath her, and both hands slammed roughly to the floor to poorly brace her fall.

Dead? No...it couldn't be true. He was always okay, somehow.

But it *could* be true. Darhk wouldn't willingly trade away a valuable bargaining chip unless he never possessed it in the first place, would he? She suddenly felt uncertain. She'd misjudged the Savrakaths in general, and Darhk in particular, on several occasions during the protracted alliance negotiations, and now she didn't trust herself to deduce what angle he'd choose to play. But no. He might not be willing to trade Malcolm for even a mountain of gold, but if he had someone of Malcolm's stature in custody, he'd gleefully parade his prize captive in front of every audience he managed to conjure. There was no other rational explanation, was there? She forced herself to think it through a second time...no.

She grabbed her knees and pulled them tight against her chest. *Dead?*

Meno whispered gently in her head. *Mia, I am so very sorry. But you know he will have—*

Yes, a neural imprint. I know. Just like Miriam. I only...give me a minute.

She tried to breathe through a throat that had closed tight. There were things she needed to do. She needed to file an official Record of Death, then the next nanosecond start the paperwork required for an expedited regenesis procedure to commence. She needed to tell his mother and sister what had happened, but only once she was also able to tell them it was going to be fine. She needed to, needed to....

She needed to get it together. For him, and for all of Concord. She shakily pushed herself up off the floor, stumbled to the lavatory and splashed water on her face and most of her blouse.

Better? A little, which had to be enough. Concentrate on what she could do. And what she could do was use her clout as humanity's representative to grease the wheels of bureaucracy and bring Malcolm back to her faster.

She went to her desk and began sending a series of orders where she had license and strongly worded requests where she did not.

8

CONCORD HQ
CINT HANGAR WING

The Ghost hangar resided in a far outer arm of Command's expansive docking pinwheels. The craft were primarily the result of CINT research, but CINT was a pseudo-military organization, and the Ghosts were decidedly military aircraft.

David cleared them through two security checkpoints where the guards didn't so much as blink at their credentials, then paused outside a reinforced door. He glanced at Caleb, sighed, and entered a code on the door panel. It slid open.

Inside the hangar, twelve Ghost aircraft were lined up in two facing rows. Their long, narrow profiles and smooth adiamene hulls gave them the appearance of rockets more than ships. At the far end of the space, a force field shimmered brightly, obscuring the details of the space beyond it.

Caleb stopped and listened for several seconds but detected no footfalls or conversations; the hangar seemed to be empty.

David went directly to the first Ghost on the left row. "Allow me to try this one more time. You recognize what manner of Hell awaits you on Namino. Can you handle it?"

He suspected David wasn't referring to the typical horrors of war, or at least not only. They'd rarely spoken in-depth about the nature of his connection to Akeso, but Alex had without a doubt confided in her father regarding some of the struggles it had brought. The man knew enough.

But now was not the time for a heart-to-heart conversation, and he couldn't allow anyone to talk him out of this. "Marlee's counting on me, even if she doesn't know she is. I have to be able to handle it."

"Caleb—"

"I'll be fine."

David diverted his focus to the hull of the tiny, sleek ship. "The Ghosts have some quirks to them—necessary concessions to boost their stealth measures and such."

"Then send me the pilot training file."

"I don't have the file. To get it, I'll need to break into the CINT server and—"

"And I don't have time to wait for you to do that. I'll figure out the quirks on the way. I know how to fly a ship."

"I'm certain you do. Just be warned." David dragged his hands down his face; deep creases had formed around his eyes in an outward hint of the strain the man currently functioned under. "What am I supposed to tell Alex?"

"Nothing. I'll tell her once I'm gone. She doesn't need to learn you were involved."

"We'll see how well that works out. All right." He reached out and clasped Caleb by the shoulders. "Bring our girl back to us."

"I will. I swear it. Take care of Alex while I'm gone—and let her take care of you."

CONSULATE

The holocomm invitation startled Mia out of…she wasn't sure what. She'd been reviewing the latest reports on the disaster at Namino like a good diplomat, searching for any news on Marlee like a good friend and employer. But somewhere along the way she'd drifted into a sort of daze.

She checked the sender…Dr. Sandal Boroshkov. Wonderful. This would be news about Malcolm's regenesis! She hurriedly accepted the invitation. "Yes, Dr. Boroshkov? Do you have an update for me?"

The doctor cleared his throat awkwardly, struggling to maintain eye contact. "Um, yes...of sorts. Senator Requelme, you are listed as the estate guardian in Fleet Admiral Malcolm Jenner's will."

"That's correct." She nodded as added confirmation.

"I see. Well, the thing is...it seems his will contains a 'No Regenesis' clause. He added it to the will six months ago."

RW

Alex didn't care for leaving her father and Caleb to the military wolves in the conference room. Not that they couldn't fend for themselves perfectly well—even if neither of them was at their best presently—but she was feeling overprotective of everyone in her family. She wanted to hold them close and never let go of them again.

By the time she stepped off the levtram at the Consulate stop, she was a tad annoyed.

What does Mia want, Valkyrie? I need to be with Dad and Caleb right now.

I do not know. Meno has urgently requested your presence in Mia's office, however.

Urgently? Was this about Marlee? God, please let it be good news.

Why didn't she send me a message directly?

I do not know that, either.

The door to Mia's office was locked, and she checked behind her to find the receptionist's desk unattended.

Meno will let you in.

The door slid open, and Alex peeked inside. "Mia? It's Alex. Did you want to see me?"

No response came. She stepped inside the office and spotted Mia huddled on the floor in the far corner against the wall. She rushed over and crouched down in front of the woman. "Are you all right? What happened?"

Mia didn't respond. Her hair was wrent into a disheveled mess—a true rarity—almost as if she'd been tearing at it. A pair of dress shoes lay haphazardly near the wall a meter away. Her head was buried in her knees.

"Mia? Talk to me. Are you hurt?" At a loss for what to do, she reached out and touched the woman's shoulder.

Mia's head slowly rose to reveal tear-streaked, reddened features and bloodshot, impossibly desolate jade eyes. "He's gone."

"What? Who's gone?"

Mia blinked, freeing new tears, and looked away.

Frustrated, Alex instinctively reached for the Noesis. Not the sprawling, public virtual overlay, but the bedrock underlying it that she and the Noetica Prevos had shared from their first moments....

She dropped the rest of the way to the floor in shock as the details flooded over her. *No. Not him, too.* How many more people would this damnable universe steal from them?

She wrapped her arms around Mia, drawing the woman against her chest. "I'm so sorry. I don't know what else to say."

Mia sniffled past messy tears. "How could he do this to me? No regenesis? I realize he never truly believed that it could bring back a person's soul, but...but why would he leave me all alone?"

"He always was such a dope."

That got a sob-wracked laugh out of Mia, but it quickly evaporated into despair. "I don't know what I'm going to do. I can't think. I can't catch my breath. I can't...."

None of us can. All the oxygen has vanished from our firmament. Alex searched the office for answers. It was a ridiculous place to hunt for them, so no surprise when she found none. In desperation, she imparted the paltry wisdom she'd been trying to follow since returning from Mirai. "Focus on the breathing for now. Inhale in, exhale out. Everything else can wait."

9

SAVRAK

UNKNOWN LOCATION
ANTLIA DWARF GALAXY

A wareness fought its way through a haze of pain to the forefront of his consciousness. Entrenched training forced Malcolm Jenner's eyes open.

A force field shimmered two meters in front of him, framed by dank, sallow walls and a hard, rough-hewn floor. The only light came from the force field, giving the space a ghostly, surreal feel.

Pain radiated in overlapping eddies centered on his head and his right shoulder. He cautiously turned his head to check his shoulder. Blood had dried around a ragged hole in his uniform, and the skin the hole exposed was swollen an angry, florid red with hints of jaundiced yellow.

He slouched against the rear wall of what he took to be a cell. His left arm was pulled up and away from his body. He tilted his head back to peer up, cringing as dull throbs radiated from the base of his skull and down his neck. A thick metal chain hooked into a brace on the wall led to a manacle clasped around his left wrist. His left leg was similarly chained, though not so stringently that he couldn't stretch it out.

Confusion muddled his thoughts, and the pain made it difficult to concentrate. He ignored the worrying ache that flared in his chest when he inhaled, and tried to impose order on the confusion. To remember.

Water and fire.

Drowning even as he clawed his way forward to escape the flames.

Then nothing. But what about before?

Savrak. The rescue mission on Savrak. An explosion had taken out the wormhole, the walls, the ceiling and the plumbing. His team! Everyone else had already reached the DAR, but the explosion would have torn through the wormhole into the ship itself. People could be injured; the ship could be disabled.

He tried to send a pulse to Colonel Odaka, but it bounced. He spent the next thirty seconds trying to send all varieties of communications to a multitude of recipients, but nothing got through. His eVi wasn't loudly proclaiming critical damage to its core systems, so this likely meant the Savrakaths were employing a comm block on the cell.

Assessment time. He ordered his eVi to run a self-diagnostic to make certain it wasn't the source of the comm problem then, assuming it remained functional, to begin a health diagnostic.

He made a reasoned assumption based on available facts that some Savrakaths had dragged him out of the flooding Okshakin dungeon, saving his life before locking him up in a cell. When? His clothes were now dry, so it had been several hours at a minimum. He checked his system clock. Over three days had passed? The self-diagnostic reported full functionality, confirming the bad news.

God, Mia. His heart panged at the thought of how worried she must be. She'd been so right—it had been idiotic for him to go on the mission—but he doubted this was providing her much comfort at present.

I am so sorry, my love.

He needed to get himself out of here and home to her. Somehow.

He glanced at his shredded shoulder again. He didn't need the diagnostic routine to tell him it was in rough shape, and it didn't look as though his captors had done a damn thing to treat it or even clean it up. If he died of sepsis, it was on them.

He tried to shift to a more comfortable position, and in doing so his body made known several additional, if less severe, injuries. He went to lift his right arm to feel for a suspected wound on the back of his head, but his shoulder shrieked in agony the instant his hand left the floor, and he let it sag loosely beside him.

He wasn't escaping the cell in this condition. Which meant he needed to improve his condition.

The health diagnostic routine completed, and he scanned the report in resignation. Grade III concussion; hairline fracture in a parietal skull bone; fractured right lateral scapula; multiple torn tendons in the right rotator cuff; torn right deltoid; infection of the epidermis and dermis tissue surrounding the wound; two broken ribs.

Without any external medical assistance, he was facing a long, slow process for his cybernetics to subdue the infection in his shoulder wound then begin mending bone and tissue back together. The concussion and skull injuries ought to take care of themselves in time so long as he didn't do something stupid, but triage priorities demanded that the broken ribs stay broken until the shoulder wound was under control.

Movement beyond the force field drew his attention, and he steeled himself for the imminent encounter.

A Savrakath in military field attire stopped in front of his cell with a hiss. "You are awake. We thought you might die. A surprise that Humans are so frail and fragile."

"I might still die if you don't treat this wound. It's infected."

"Infection is good for the soul. It tests the body. Strengthens it, if it can pass the trial."

"Well, I'm not Savrakath, so I'd as soon skip the trial. I'm also no good to you dead. A little antiseptic would go a long way toward keeping me alive."

The Savrakath sniffed the air. "Prove your worth to us. Give us the name and location of a strategically important but soft Concord target, and we will treat your wounds."

Prove your worth to us. They didn't know who he was? Because he'd been on the assault team like a complete moron, they must have assumed he was just a ground-pounder.

His presence here, in their custody, gave them a more valuable bargaining chip in the conflict with Concord than any hordes of intel he could (but never would) provide, but they didn't know what they had.

An image of Mia flashed through his mind, stunning in a white silk robe, her long hair whipping around her face on the balcony of the Atlantis resort suite they'd rented for their unofficial anniversary three months earlier. The urge to utter a meager few words overwhelmed him, and only his Marine training stilled his tongue. Provide his name and rank, and he'd become a high-stakes pawn—and also the best-treated prisoner housed in whatever gulag this was. His injuries would be treated post-haste, because the Savrakaths would no longer risk their star prisoner dying.

But Concord would need to weaken its position in the conflict to trade for him, and he couldn't allow that to happen. Duty and honor before self. *Semper fidelis.*

So he would have to find another way to get medical treatment—to improve his condition so he could escape.

He swallowed past a dry and swollen throat. "Bring me a glass of water and a swab of alcohol for my shoulder, and I'll wrack my brain trying to think of an appropriate target."

The guard's lips pulled back in a snarl. "You are even weaker than I expected. We will see." He spun around, his tail narrowly missing the force field, and strode off into the darkness.

RW

Malcolm had drifted off to sleep when his jailer returned two hours later. Sleep helped to speed healing, and the concussion was old enough that he didn't need to worry about slipping into a coma.

He jerked awake at the sound of the guard barking an order at him. "I'm sorry, what did you say?"

"I have brought the supplies you requested. The target, please."

"So you can then turn around and walk away with those supplies? No, that's not how this works."

"You are in no position to tell anyone how this works."

"Be that as it may, I'm not sharing any information until my shoulder wound's been treated."

The guard studied him for several seconds, then deactivated a small square area of the force field at the floor and shoved a tray through it. The tray skidded across the floor and bumped into Malcolm's foot.

He gazed imploringly at the guard. "Thank you, but I can't reach it. My right arm doesn't work, and my left one...." He peered meaningfully up at the chain and manacle.

The Savrakath hissed in what seemed like disgust, but he deactivated the full force field, stepped inside and reactivated it, then came closer and nudged the tray up beside Malcolm's limp arm. "There."

Malcolm made a show of trying to pick up the container of water it held before sinking against the wall. "Please. Train a weapon on me if it will make you feel better, but you have to unlatch the manacle. My right arm is useless. I can't lift it more than a few centimeters."

The guard marched in a circle twice, spittle escaping through his teeth. "Fine." He removed a long rifle from a holster on his back and pressed the barrel to Malcolm's forehead. "Try anything, and your brains will decorate the wall."

"I understand."

The guard reached up to the manacle and placed a small module of some kind onto the lock. Malcolm's arm dropped out of the restraint to fall limply at his side.

After days suspended from the manacle, his left arm barely worked better than his right one, but he managed to drag it over to the tray and grasp the water container. He leaned down and pressed it to his lips, praying it wasn't hot and swampy.

Fresh, cool water splashed over his tongue, and he hurriedly slurped it down before stopping himself for a moment. Coughing it all back up would defeat the purpose of drinking it. After another few seconds, he judiciously finished off the water.

While the guard watched him from across the cell, long rifle raised, he opened the jar of what he hoped was an antiseptic solution and spilled some on the provided cloth. Then he pressed it to his open wound—and almost bit his tongue in agony as spasms shot out from his shoulder and into his chest. He breathed in through his nose and worked to compartmentalize the discomfort away; he had extensive training on how to keep functioning in such circumstances, dammit. Another breath, and he forced himself to wipe the entire wound with the cloth.

Now came the hard part. There was also an exit wound, and it was probably in worse shape than the entry one. He flipped the cloth over, spilled more antiseptic on it, and wrenched his left arm around over his right shoulder. He knew he'd found his mark when a fresh wave of searing pain punished his body. He wiped all the skin he could reach, until his arm gave out and fell away.

No. Not finished yet. His hand shook as he picked up the jar of antiseptic, brought it up to his shoulder, and dumped the rest of its contents into the wound.

The empty jar fell from his hand to roll across the floor. His vision swam and blurred. He'd instructed his eVi to dedicate all resources toward treatment and healing, at the expense of pain amelioration. He now profoundly regretted that choice.

The guard rushed forward, grabbed Malcolm's left arm and yanked it upward to secure it in the manacle, then retrieved the tray, the empty jar and bottle and retreated beyond the force field. "We have provided. Now give us the location of a Concord soft target."

He exhaled through gritted teeth, imagining the jagged edges of his broken ribs scraping at his fragile lung tissue as he did. "You know, I've been wracking my brain like I said I would...but I just can't think of any."

"Liar!" The guard deactivated the field once more and stormed into the cell, rifle raised. "You will talk—"

Malcolm's eyes closed, and he succumbed to a dark oblivion.

10

CINT VESSEL 23A-X
SAVRAK STELLAR SYSTEM

Eren Savitas asi-Idoni paced in deliberate, measured circles around the tiny cabin of the CINT ship he'd claimed as his own. He'd injected the last dose of *dialele* half an hour earlier. His mind was sharp and his senses honed, but the clock was now ticking.

Delivering Torval elasson-Machim to Eren's intended destination was going to require a grand, dramatic and, most crucially, rapid entrance. Ideally a rapid exit for him as well, but he couldn't bring himself to care too much one way or another about it.

He'd reviewed CINT's voluminous files on General Jhountar one final time. The military leader spent most days at his office at Savrak Military Headquarters in Savradin, holding court with underlings, issuing orders and strutting through the hallways. Unless Jhountar had joined his fleet in their increasingly aggressive patrols, he ought to be in the building today.

However, Eren couldn't exactly land his ship on the lawn of Military Headquarters and stroll in the front door with his prisoner in tow. An active if undeclared state of war now existed between the Savrakaths and Concord, which meant he and his prisoner were guaranteed to be instantly arrested, if not shot on sight.

No, he needed to get directly in front of Jhountar—if Jhountar was absent, he'd have to settle for his first lieutenant, Brigadier Ghorek—and present his case swiftly and succinctly.

He wasn't a Prevo, so he couldn't open a wormhole in the middle of Jhountar's office on a whim. The CINT vessel did have a Caeles Prism generator installed, but the ship, while tiny, was too large to fit in any single room inside Military Headquarters. So he was back to the front lawn. It *might* work, if he defined 'work' as him staying alive long enough to explain to someone with power the nature of the trophy he was offering them. He didn't care for the odds, though.

Which meant he was down to one last option. He readied himself, trying to remember how he'd be expected to act during the interaction, and sent a message.

Mesme, do you have twenty minutes to spare? I desperately need a favor.

I do not, but for you, I will create the time.

His brow furrowed in surprise at the offer of affection from the Kat. *I'm touched. Thank you.*

A few seconds later, a sparkle of lights filled the cabin then clustered together in front of him. *I should express my sorrow for the loss of your friend. I wished to have done so earlier, but I have been otherwise occupied in the Asterion Dominion. I would attempt to ease your pain if I believed I could accomplish it, but my previous attempts to do so have not been successful, so I will refrain from making matters worse.*

His...friend. The Kats didn't appear to have romantic entanglements—though who could really say for certain—so perhaps the word encompassed the breadth of close relationships as Kats understood them. The condolences evoked only a dull ache in his chest, for the *dialele* silenced the raging anguish that briefly threatened to break free. Even Mesme's oblique reference to the shitshow of a visit they'd paid to the Faneros' transplanted homeworld wasn't enough to overpower the stranglehold the *dialele* maintained on his emotions, and good thing for it.

"I appreciate the thought. But if you genuinely want to help me, you simply need to do me this one favor."

Speak it.

"I have a prisoner secured in the cargo hold—"

I am aware.

No surprise that Mesme was cognizant of every atom within its range of perception. "Right. I need you to peek inside the Savrak

Military Headquarters building and locate General Jhountar. This guy." He flashed the Savrakath's official military photo. "Then I need you to transport myself and my prisoner to wherever Jhountar is, wait while I give one of my famous speeches, then transport me back to this ship. That's it."

Why are you delivering an Anaden prisoner to the Savrakaths?

"He's the man who killed Cosime. He also bombed their anti-matter facility by way of murder weapon, so he'll be a prize catch for them."

The Kat vacillated in agitation. *I see.*

"Mesme, don't go soft on me now. He's an unrepentant mur-derer who wants to bring everything Concord has built crashing down at our feet."

But this is not why you wish to deliver him to the Savrakaths.

"No. I'm delivering him to the Savrakaths because I want him to suffer unspeakable torture for years. Decades. Centuries. Both justifications can be true. Will you do it?"

Silence reigned in his mind for a weighty pause. *I will.*

"Thank you. Give me a minute to unshackle the prisoner from his cage below, then we'll be ready."

I will locate this General Jhountar. Summon me when preparations are complete. The lights accelerated through the port wall of the ship and vanished.

Eren retrieved a small bottle from the supply cabinet and loaded its contents into a projectile needle, then climbed down the ladder. Torval lay slumped against the wall inside the force field, but on sensing Eren's arrival, he opened his eyes to glower through hooded lids. "I heard talking. Do we have a guest?"

Eren didn't answer; instead he deactivated the force field long enough to fire the contents of the needle, a potent muscle relaxant, into Torval's chest, then reactivated it until the drug took effect. He'd strongly considered knocking the man unconscious, but he wanted Torval to be cognizant enough to hear what he was plan-ning to say to Jhountar.

The prisoner's head lolled, chin bouncing off his chest, and a few incomprehensible words made it past Torval's lips in a mumble. Eren waited thirty more seconds before deactivating the field again. He unlatched the chains securing the man's ankles from the wall and locked them together. He did the same for the chains binding his wrists and dragged Torval to his feet. All the man's weight sagged against Eren, and they both stumbled back into the wall. Damn, he was a big guy.

Mesme, I'm ready for you below.

Shimmering lights filled every centimeter of the cramped cargo hold. *I have located this General Jhountar in the largest office on the top floor of Military Headquarters.*

"Excellent. I was hoping he'd be there." Eren adjusted his grip on Torval's upper arm. "Let's go."

Mesme swirled tightly around him and his charge. Through the tiny gaps in the Kat's whirlwind, the scene shifted.

RW

SAVRAK
MILITARY HEADQUARTERS

The stifling, humid air soaked through Mesme's ethereal cocoon even before it dissipated to reveal a clean, shiny office decorated in gaudy ornamental furniture made of polished bronze.

General Jhountar was already leaping up from his oversized desk as his hand went to his sidearm. "Guards! We have intruders!"

"Wait." Eren gathered Torval's wrist restraints up and shoved the man forward. Thanks to the muscle relaxant, Torval promptly fell to the floor. As much as his prisoner surely wanted to fight and rage, he merely flopped around on the tile like a beached fish.

Eren lifted his hands in the air. "A present for you, General. This is the man who attacked your antimatter facility and killed your people who were working there."

Jhountar kept his sidearm pointed at Eren. "Is Concord seeking capitulation in return for this 'present'? They will not get it from us."

"I don't represent Concord. I'm fairly certain I don't even work for them any longer. This is a personal present, from me to you."

"Why?"

"Because this man is a monster, and I want to see him punished. Now, there is a catch."

Jhountar snarled through razor-sharp teeth. "Savrakaths do not like catches."

"You'll be content with this one. Do whatever the hells you want to him. Torture him in new and inventive ways. Make him bleed. Make him scream." Eren ground his jaw as emotions fought to rise up and break free. "Make him suffer. But *don't* kill him. Not on purpose and not on accident. If you do, he wins. He wakes up in a cushy bed back in Concord and gets to resume living in comfort and splendor."

"We know of your 'regenesis.' We do not think much of its alchemy."

"Don't care. Trust me, this man here thinks quite a lot of it. He will do everything in his power to trick you into killing him. Don't fall for it. Follow this one rule, and you get to continue torturing him for years and years. Centuries if you want, which I deeply hope you do. Understand?"

"I do." Jhountar waved his sidearm portentously at Eren. "Now, tell me, why should I not also take you into custody? Torture you for centuries as well?"

Eren forcefully choked off a maniacal laugh. The *dialele* was wearing thin, and the cracks in his pharmaceutical armor were deepening. He just had to power through for a few minutes more, then none of it would matter. "You absolutely should—after all, I was primed to blow up your antimatter facility when this man beat me to it—but you won't get the privilege."

Now, Mesme.

A tornado of lights surrounded him the same instant four guards rushed into the room, long rifles raised—and he was gone.

RW

CINT VESSEL 23A-X
SAVRAK STELLAR SYSTEM

The walls of his little ship solidified around him, and his legs almost buckled from a wave of dizziness heralding an incoming tsunami of despair. Just a few minutes more. "Thank you, Mesme. That was all I needed. Go and see to the Asterions."

What will you do now?

"Oh, you know. Probably wander about sulking for a while." He felt behind him for the security of the cockpit chair and grabbed hold of the headrest. "Get drunk, then get high. Wallow in some tears. I'll be fine."

Will you?

He scratched at an itching spot on his head. His hair was starting to grow back in patchy spikes, and scratching it only made the itch worse. The side effects of the *dialele* were picking up a strong head of steam. "Eventually. But you flitting around me in overprotective concern isn't apt to help me get there any sooner. Away you go!"

As you wish.

The lights dissipated, leaving him alone at last.

He crumpled to the floor. The urge to grab a blade and slice the flesh off his arms was overpowering. To drag his nails down his cheeks until they drew blood. The memory of Cosime's ruined body draped lifelessly in his arms overwhelmed his mind as the dam broke free, and he willed for a black hole to open up beneath him and swallow him whole.

But he was going to have to do it himself.

He crawled to the cockpit chair and dragged himself to his feet, then collapsed onto the dash. Sweet, eternal oblivion was a scant 0.7 AU away. He fixated on the orange star boiling against the blackness. In a last act of egoism, he would die once and for all the way he had lived: burning brightly and flaming out. Even if no one would ever know.

Tears streamed down his face as he felt along the HUD for the navigation controls and set the ship's course for the star.

As the engine engaged, a flash of movement in his peripheral vision caught his attention. Before he could turn toward it, a heavy whack landed on the back of his head and everything went dark.

11

EPITHERO

Ferdinand elasson-Kyvern stared out the window at the shining sea of white and chrome stretching to the horizon beneath him. His homeworld was pristine and immaculate always. A beacon of efficiency, productivity and order. The death of his Primor fourteen years earlier had caused a momentary stumble on his Dynasty's part, but the Kyvern machine drove onward, for the work to be done to ensure a properly functioning empire never ceased.

He tucked a stray strand of chestnut hair behind his ear and resumed his seat at the head of the table. The Kyvern Primor had long sat in this seat, and he hoped the imagery was not lost on those present.

The bickering had continued unabated while he'd briefly vacated, and he was forced to clear his throat loudly to be heard over the din. "Enough. We will discuss these issues like civilized leaders."

"And what if we're neither?" Jhalana elasson-Idoni's opalescent hair was bound into a sea of braids, and her ice-green eyes were narrow rings around dilated pupils. She idly twirled the stem of a champagne glass between two fingers. She was high, because what else would an Idoni be while attending a crucial strategy meeting?

Ferdinand rued his decision to allow her to be a part of this council, and not for the first time. Most of the Idoni *elassons* couldn't be bothered to attend to the mundanity of rebellion, though, and he needed at least one Idoni representative here for appearance's sake. With her at the table, every Dynasty was represented—except for Praesidis, but no one had seen or heard from a Praesidis *elasson* in over a decade.

"Then we should try harder to stay sober at a minimum. Now, where were we?"

"We were trying and failing to decide what it is we are intending to *do*. Your little coup attempt failed miserably, and now we are holed up on this..." Otto elasson-Machim shuddered "...bureaucratic hellhole of a planet trying to come up with a plan for how to move forward. But to have a plan, we first need a goal."

"We do. I propose—"

Otto interrupted. "If Torval were here, he would propose our goal be to take the entire Machim fleet and turn Concord HQ into a crater in space. And I'd be inclined to agree with him."

"So the next day the entire AEGIS armada can show up here and turn this building and ten kilometers in every direction into a similarly sized crater in the ground?"

Ferdinand's mouth curled downward in Basra elasson-Kyvern's direction. Even by Kyvern standards, his sister was a peevish coward. "They don't know where we are."

"It's not as if it's difficult to figure out."

He'd considered this reality in the immediate aftermath of the coup attempt, before dismissing the risk involved. He needed to surround himself with the comfort, security and efficient systems of home if he was to be expected to lead an uprising.

"Should an AEGIS armada arrive, the planetary defenses will protect us, not to mention the Machim warships in orbit. But I don't expect such an armada to show up. Concord and AEGIS are in similar panic modes right now. They're both leaderless and knocked back on their heels by their disastrous encounter with the Rasu in the Gennisi galaxy. They will be weeks regaining their bearings, if they ever do, which is why we need to come out strong now, while they are weak.

"As I was preparing to say, I propose we formally withdraw from Concord and form our own government. Let us rule ourselves, in the manner Anadens have always ruled. In a year's time, we will be the true power in the Milky Way. In all surrounding galaxies."

"And what about Concord? Are they our enemy, as Otto suggests? Do we destroy all they've built, or treaty with them as equals? Our supply chains for vital goods and materials are now inexorably entangled with those of the Concord member species. Declaring ourselves 'independent' is not a simple matter. You cannot wave your hands and make it so." Rachele elasson-Theriz flicked her wrist toward the table for added emphasis.

Ferdinand tried to look stern while holding at bay a screaming retort of *I don't know!* He disagreed with how Concord conducted itself, and he didn't care for being overruled by lesser species in important votes. Now they expected him to *poof!* come up with a new, fully functioning government, diplomatic corps and supply chain network out of thin air? Did he have to do everything himself?

He made sure his voice sounded calm and measured. "As tempting as it is, I believe we ought not to attack Concord directly— at least not right away. Let us first establish ourselves. Work out those supply chains and construct a proper government. Later, once our position is solidified, we can adopt a harder, more uncompromising stance toward Concord. They need not be our enemy unless they choose it, but they assuredly are our adversary. For now, though, the important thing is that we are no longer taking orders from the Humans."

A rumbling concurrence overtook the table; finally, something they all agreed on.

Otto clasped his meaty hands atop the table. "What's the status of the Asterions?"

"My sources tell me the Rasu demolished their minuscule fleet. It won't be long before the Rasu have exterminated the Asterions for us. I say we let them. We have larger concerns here."

"And the Savrakaths?"

Ferdinand gestured dismissively in Otto's direction. "Destroy them. Bomb them into Eradication, then send in a Theriz Cultivation Unit. The resources we acquire can fortify some of our new supply chains."

Lars elasson-Theriz threw his hands in the air and shoved his chair back, though he didn't stand. "The Cultivation Units no longer exist."

"But the cultivation equipment does, doesn't it? Call it whatever you like, but harvest Savrak's resources, and let us be done with the troublesome lizards."

Otto shifted uncomfortably in his chair. "Who are you to order the Eradication of a species?"

Ferdinand almost choked on his lemon spritzer. "Excuse me?"

"They have antimatter weapons, so I'm happy to destroy their military capability and put them in their place. But I don't take orders from you, and I'm more inclined to go drop appropriate firepower on the Asterions instead of trusting these Rasu to finish the job."

"The purpose of this discussion is to decide on a way forward for all Anadens. There has to be a chain of command, or chaos will ensue."

"And you're putting yourself at the top of it?"

"No, I am merely trying to lead an organized and productive discussion—"

Hannah challenged Otto from across the table. "Forget the Asterions *and* the Savrakaths. We should save our military resources for our defense. I believe Concord will recover far more quickly than Ferdinand proclaims. They will not take kindly to our actions and might not wait for us to attack them before retaliating."

Ferdinand was trying to formulate a response to either of them when a third Machim, Ulric, jumped in. "Then let us attack them before they can attack us."

Hannah shook her head firmly. "Only a fraction of their fleets are stationed at Concord HQ. Are you suggesting we attack Earth? Seneca? Nopreis? And what about the Kats? Don't you think they will come to the defense of the very allies who helped them topple the Directorate? An offensive strategy is madness."

Otto scoffed. "Machims have always won through strength and decisiveness. Would you instead have us cower in fear behind the Kyverns' trousers?"

"Of course not! But we must use our strength wisely. We cannot go attacking every group that has annoyed us."

"Can't we?"

Hannah leveled a piercing glower at her brother. "I just said we can't."

"What you mean is you won't. Fine. You can leave the room and transfer control of your fleets to me."

"Enough!" Ferdinand stood and slammed his hands onto the table. "Ulrich, you can do whatever you want with the Savrakaths, but do not attack Concord interests. We will lose."

"I think it's been too long since you saw what a real Machim fleet can do."

"Fall in line, Ulrich. The only way we succeed is through unity."

"Unity?" Otto scoffed. "I count, what, twenty-nine of us here? How can we have unity when most of the *elassons* aren't even present? Twelve million Machim ships are out there under the control of *elassons* who have elected not to join our council. Maybe they're siding with Concord. Maybe they've decided to fly off into the void and never come back. All I know is they aren't listening to you, Ferdinand. So why should I?"

Ferdinand pinched the bridge of his nose in frustration. The two most influential Machim personalities weren't at the table to bully their siblings into compliance. Torval had been kidnapped, presumably by Concord interests, and Casmir was locked up under guard in a suite two floors below. Torval, were he here, would convince the other Machims to deploy their millions of warships against each and every one of their enemies, a gambit Ferdinand feared would end in failure, leaving them weakened when they most needed to be formidable. Casmir, on the other hand, was liable to package those warships up and hand them over to Concord while begging forgiveness. Neither path would get Ferdinand what he wanted, but he had to find some way to bring the Machim *elassons* who were here to heel under his guidance.

He straightened up and tried to don an inspirational guise. "Someone has to lead, and we all must realize it needs to be a

Kyvern. This is what we do. Now, I've spent the last decade representing our people in the Senate. As such, I ask you, Otto, and everyone at the table to recognize my authority, if only temporarily and borne of necessity."

Otto growled as he stood. "I need to check on the readiness status of my ships. We can resume this discussion later." With that, he spun and strode out of the room, leaving Ferdinand standing there, his mouth agape, looking like nothing so much as an ineffectual fool.

PART II

OLDER & FAR AWAY

ASTERION DOMINION

12

MIRAI

DAF/RIDANI ENTERPRISES COMPONENT FACTORY

Dashiel walked the partially constructed assembly line at the new component factory in Mirai Two. His hands drifted across random equipment, robotic arms and conveyors, checking connections and braces. He'd walked such lines thousands of times in his life, inspecting the quality of their assembly and searching for greater efficiencies.

Materials shortages for components had represented their biggest bottleneck before the Rasu attacked Namino, and little had changed on that front now. Teams scoured the galaxy for the rare materials needed for warships and hauled them in as quickly as their equipment allowed, but he was not a magician. He could not manufacture another fleet out of thin air.

Palmer had been discharged from the regen clinic this morning, and Dashiel expected that only a few hours remained before the Commander's warpath led the man to his door. Palmer would demand the impossible, and Dashiel wouldn't blame him for doing so.

He drew back to take in the multiple parallel lines here on the floor and overhead in the towering facility. Palmer was likely to want a fleet of new ships immediately, but he worried whether it was wise to blindly repeat their actions from before the attack. They'd busted their asses to produce tens of thousands of vessels in record time; those tens of thousands of vessels were then eradicated in a matter of hours upon contact with the Rasu. Why build tens of thousands more vessels, just to see the same thing happen the next time they dared to engage the enemy?

He'd build the new vessels using adiamene, no question, but the bloom was now off even that rose. He'd spoken briefly with Kennedy Rossi this morning, long enough to confirm that Concord, too, was hyper-aware of the weakness in adiamene the Rasu had exposed. She had not put forth any brilliant ideas on a practical way to make adiamene seamless and thus impervious to Rasu intrusion. Neither had he.

He knew he shouldn't be so fatalistic. Adiamene hulls were certain to make a tremendous difference in the durability of their ships—no longer would they crumple to Rasu fire like paper mâché planes. Conceptual Research scientists had improved the propulsion of starship engines by fifteen percent over where they'd started, and a weapons-focused ceraff were squeezing another eighteen percent firepower out of warship laser weapons. Collectively, the Dominion's greatest minds were digging their way out of the ditch they'd dug for themselves by not prioritizing spaceship technology all these millennia, and this next fleet was going to be stronger, tougher and faster than the one that had preceded it.

Still, he couldn't get the sight of Rasu swallowing state of the art warships whole out of his mind. A single tiny gap was all the enemy needed—then they had you. Your people, your technology, your data.

He didn't dare hold up new production until he invented an effective counter, but he also couldn't get rid of the nagging feeling that until he solved this problem, they were simply repeating the same mistakes.

OMOIKANE INITIATIVE

Caleb Marano was headed to Namino in a suicidal gambit to rescue his niece. He hadn't offered Nika a seat on his ship, and while every bone in her body had screamed at her to demand one...she hadn't done it. Given time to calm down, distance from the immediate horror of the attack and a few fitful hours of sleep here and there, she'd talked herself into believing that right now—for the next few days and possibly weeks—she needed to be here. She owed it to her people to lead them through this crisis. To find a way forward.

So she'd loaded Caleb up with information on Namino One, including a map of the city's layout and the locations of the underground bunkers, and wished him well.

"Advisor, our recon craft has succeeded in departing Namino. Expect visuals momentarily."

"Thank you, Brigadier." She paced across the full breadth of the Initiative, both terrified and anxious to view the scene on the ground. She hated being blind, of course, but there was no way the visuals were going to bring good news. Still, a ship had reached the Namino surface and departed to tell the tale. She could have the *Wayfarer* there in a few hours...and do what? Wander the streets searching for survivors and slicing up stray Rasu with her archine blades? No. She needed to lead from here, remember?

"Nika."

She spun around to see Dashiel jogging toward her. She smiled in relief and, when he reached her, buried herself in his arms. She'd acted awful toward him in those initial hours, for which she'd apologized profusely and repeatedly. The truth was, she'd felt empty and alone this morning when he left to oversee construction at the new component facility. The truth was, she was stronger with him at her side.

She took everything she could from the warmth of his embrace, until she had no choice but to let go. "Our ship made it out. Time to learn what havoc the Rasu have wrought."

They joined Brigadier Johansson in front of the left-most pane along the rear wall as the captured video began streaming a visualization of their worst nightmares brought to life.

Rasu vessels reigned supreme in the skies over every city and manufacturing center on Namino. The shining towers of Namino One lay crumbled in ruins, though not Namino Tower itself. If only this was a positive sign instead of yet another harbinger of further doom to come. The Rasu had recognized the Tower's importance and were currently stealing *everything*. Hundreds of millennia's worth of data and records. The history of the Dominion and its people.

The cam swept across the streets of downtown from high above—close enough to capture the thousands of bodies littering the streets but far enough away to spare them the bloody details of their deaths.

Her breath caught in her throat, as if someone had again sucked most of the oxygen out of the room. "This is...all those people. They didn't deserve this."

Dashiel sighed quietly. "I don't think the Rasu are the type to think in terms of 'deserving.' They consume everything they encounter—"

"Advisor Kirumase? I'm sorry to disturb you."

She turned as one of the DAF security officers approached her. "Yes?"

"Lieutenant Kiernan Phillips, the pilot who crashed during the attack on the Rasu stronghold—"

"I'm aware of who he is."

"Of course. He's downstairs now, accompanied by the two individuals who assisted him and the Taiyok in escaping from the Rasu-occupied world they crashed on."

She didn't know anything about Kiernan's rescuers, other than that they were Anatype aliens, which meant she was politely being asked to act as a diplomat. She glanced back at the pane in time to see the camera viewpoint swerve and jerk upward—the pilot avoiding an approaching Rasu vessel, no doubt. "Lance ought to be here in a few minutes, but I'm happy to speak with them until he arrives."

"Yes, ma'am. I'll show them in."

Her attention drifted inexorably back to the visuals. The pilot had escaped detection and moved on to the southern sector of the city, where kilometers of warehouses and factories had been flattened like pancakes. No, she was wrong earlier—she should be there. She should be fighting—

"Ma'am?"

She pivoted away from the pane once more to find a different man in a DAF dress uniform waiting at parade rest. "Lieutenant Kiernan Phillips, ma'am."

She plastered on her best, most diplomatic countenance. "Welcome to the Initiative, Lieutenant. I'm so glad to see you made it home safely."

"Thank you, but it was all due to my friends here. I want to introduce—"

A violent wave of déjà vu swept over Nika, to the point she lost her footing and stumbled backward into Dashiel, who reached out and steadied her. The man standing behind Kiernan—no, it couldn't be. *Impossible.*

Then the man tilted his head just *so*, his frightfully piercing gaze landing squarely on her, and all doubt was erased.

She nudged Dashiel back and lifted her chin proudly. "Supreme Commander."

The man's brow drew tight. "Nicolette Hinotori? This is most unexpected."

Lieutenant Phillips looked at them both in puzzlement. "I'm sorry, do you two know each other?"

The man buried any confusion behind a guarded countenance. "In a manner of speaking. I haven't gone by 'Supreme Commander' in a very long time."

"I'd wager I haven't gone by 'Nicolette Hinotori' in longer. It's Nika Kirumase now." Her voice nearly cracked, and she cleared her throat. "What shall I call you, then?"

"I was most recently known as Danilo Nisi. I suppose that will suffice for a while longer." He gestured to his companion, a raven-haired woman with a toned physique and sapphire irises locked in a cold, stony stare. "This is my granddaughter, Nyx elasson-Praesidis."

Nika nodded tersely to the woman without ever taking her eyes off the Supreme Commander. "I see. Alex and Caleb told me you still lived, but I confess I was skeptical."

He frowned deeply. "Caleb Marano died in The Displacement."

One corner of her lips curled up, though not into a smile. "It turns out you're not the only one who's exceedingly hard to kill."

"I am...quite glad to hear it. He's a good man."

"Seems to be. Don't get too excited, though. He might not be alive for much longer...." Her words drifted off as she spotted Lance walking into the Initiative behind them. Her muscles tensed; however negative her reaction to seeing this ghost from aeons past might be, Lance's was guaranteed to be far worse.

He'd taken a few steps inside when he spotted Kiernan, and a second later, their guests. Shock flashed across his face, replaced swiftly by unmistakable rage.

Nika tried to ward him off, though her heart frankly wasn't in it. "Lance—"

He stormed up to them and, without hesitation, reared back and punched the Supreme Commander in the jaw. Corradeo—Danilo, whatever—lurched for half a step, then caught himself. His granddaughter reached for a weapon and came up empty, as security would have demanded they surrender any weapons before entering the Initiative.

Instead, the woman placed herself between her grandfather and Lance. "Touch him again and you will—"

"It's fine, Nyx. Commander Palmer has earned the right to take one free swing at me." He massaged his jaw and moved to stand beside Nyx. "But only one."

Lance stepped forward, even as Dashiel laid a hand on his arm and urged him back a bit. "You colossal bastard. What foul rock did you crawl out from under?"

"Now, Commander Palmer. Isn't seven hundred thousand years a long time to hold a grudge?"

"A *grudge*? Is that what you call the consequences of you murdering tens of thousands of my people? There's no statute of limitations on wholesale slaughter."

The man's throat worked. "No, there isn't. I own my mistakes. But I assure you, I am not here to kill any more of you."

"We are not the same people you drove out of the Milky Way at the tip of your spear. I'd like to see you try."

Something flared in the Supreme Commander's eyes. A challenge, perhaps. He motioned behind Nika, toward the pane streaming the footage from Namino. "It appears the Rasu are doing a fine job of slaughtering your people without my help."

Lance lunged for the man. Nika jumped in front of him the same instant Nyx leapt forward. She waved the woman off while placing a hand firmly on Lance's chest. "Not now, okay?"

Kiernan had fallen back, out of the line of fire of the confrontation, but now he stepped closer. "Commander Palmer, I don't understand what's happening here. These people helped Toshke and me. They're the only reason we're alive, and the only reason you had any advance warning of the Rasu attack. Whatever history you all have with each other, in my opinion they deserve the benefit of the doubt."

"They won't get it from me."

The Supreme Commander huffed a breath. "I'd say it's beginning to sound to me as if you are *exactly* the same people I drove out of the Milky Way—"

Nika growled above the overlapping retorts. "Enough, both of you! We are not going to reenact the SAI Rebellion in the middle of the Initiative during an active Rasu invasion. Supreme—Mr. Nisi, if we take you at your word when you say you mean us no ill will, then are you here to help?"

"I have already helped. I enabled Lieutenant Phillips to escape and warn you the Rasu were on their way. I trust this saved a few lives."

"A few. Then if that will be all, we're a little busy at present, so the officer here will see you out."

Nisi's chin dropped. "Wait. Forgive my rudeness. I want to assist you in this fight, if possible."

"No."

She thrust a warning hand in Lance's direction. "Lance, I understand how you feel. I feel the same way. But we are frankly not in a position to refuse help, no matter the source." She returned her attention to Nisi. "Why?"

"The Rasu butchered a species I cared a great deal about, thus they are now my enemy as well."

"What can you tell us about the Rasu?"

"Far less than I'd like. But if where I found your stranded pilots is any indication, the opposite border of their empire is two hundred megaparsecs away, at the edge of the Shapley Supercluster."

Gods, that was so much farther than the boundaries the Kats had identified when they surveyed the Rasu's reach. So many Rasu, for so far...they might as well stretch for all of eternity. The dull, sorrowful ache churning her stomach ever since Namino fell crept its way around her chest and settled in for the long haul.

"Well, that's certainly disheartening. But I'm more concerned about the part of the border currently creeping over Namino." She squared her shoulders. "We can offer you and your granddaughter hot meals, lodging for as long as you require it and any supplies you need. If you gain any new insights into our enemy or how you can assist us in defeating them, we can speak further then. For now, though, you must excuse us. Commander Palmer and I have a lot of work to do."

Nisi accepted the dismissal, and without fanfare he and Nyx turned and followed the DAF officer out of the Initiative.

"We are *not* making that monster an ally."

The encounter had drained her meager reserves, and with a weary sigh she shifted toward Lance. "It's not so simple. The reality is—"

"Look, you might not remember what he did to us—"

"I remember plenty, okay? I don't care for it, either. But surely it's better to have a man like that on our side than anywhere else."

"Just keep him away from me."

"Oh, I will."

"Good." Lance scowled at Dashiel. "I've been down for several days. Where is my new fleet?"

"In progress. Before you go issuing orders blindly, you should get up to speed on everything that's happened. Why don't we meet later this evening?"

Lance fidgeted; he glanced back at the door, as if he were contemplating chasing after Nisi to get another punch in. "All right. This evening. Do me a favor and bring good news to the meeting." He strode off toward the front of the room to ambush Brigadier Johansson.

Nika sagged against the table behind her and rubbed at her temples.

Dashiel reached out and took her hand. "Why don't we take a walk? Get some fresh air."

She gazed back at the pane, where the footage from Namino had started over at the beginning for Lance's benefit. "I think that sounds like an excellent idea."

RW

Somewhat to her surprise, they stepped out the doors of the Mirai One Pavilion to find the world—this one at least—still spinning on. People strode purposefully down the sidewalks and skycars buzzed overhead. She inhaled the promised fresh air and allowed it to begin patching up her broken heart a little. All was not lost. Not yet.

Dashiel guided her across the lawn to an enormous snowbell tree, where its broad limbs cast dancing shadows upon the lush green grass beneath their feet. Once there, he wrapped his arms around her from behind and hugged her close against him. "So what exactly was that scene? I mean, I was able to piece together a few details from the back-and-forth, but I'm not certain what to make of it all."

"The man who rescued Lieutenant Phillips and the Taiyok pilot—the man who called himself Danilo Nisi—is in actuality

Corradeo Praesidis, Supreme Commander of the Anaden military at the time of the SAI Rebellion."

"*Oh.*" He kissed the top of her head. "That does fill in a couple of blanks. Alex and Caleb know him, don't they?"

"They did. He vanished after their Displacement, but now…now I guess he's back."

"You remember him? From before?"

"A single encounter—the last encounter, when he forced our hand and we chose to flee rather than be massacred. My journals describe other interactions, none of them positive. He was a…hard, cold man. Arrogantly confident in the absolute rightness of his position and perfectly comfortable with killing to make his vision a reality."

She twisted around to face Dashiel, then let herself rest her head on his chest. "I realize events may have changed much about him. He lost his power, he lost his family. To hear Alex and Caleb tell it, he lost everything, and that has to change a man. He helped the Humans defeat the Anaden Directorate, which the man I knew never would have done. But knowing he's changed isn't the same as believing it."

"It's not wrong for you to want him to prove his sincerity. And even then, you don't have to forgive him. In fact, you shouldn't. But it doesn't mean you can't work with him. Think of him the way you think of Gemina Kail, as someone who brings useful skills to the table in an act of penance that we can deploy for the benefit of everyone."

Nika chuckled lightly. "I haven't forgiven her, either. I suppose you're right. He's not a threat to us now—he no longer commands armies and governments—and despite Lance's justified protestations, he could prove to be a worthy ally. But damn…I never expected to see his face again."

13

NAMINO
CAMP BURROW

J oaquim and Ava returned from their rescue mission with four
new people in tow. All were battered and bruised, but all were
walking.

Once the greetings were handled and pop-up cots passed out
to the new guests, Selene headed over to talk to Joaquim, and
Marlee found an excuse to wander nearby. She dialed her aural settings up to full and kept her left ear facing in their direction while
she fiddled with straightening a stack of blankets.

She was the odd duckling out, here among all these Asterions
and Taiyoks. Everyone was being effusively polite to her, but once
she'd gotten her bearings, she'd quickly realized that if she wanted
to be dealt into the game, it was up to her to learn all the quirks and
nuances of the people here, individually and as a culture.

Selene placed both hands on her hips. "All right, Lacese. I admit
it—impressive work getting them all back here safely. Now tell me
what it looked like up there."

Joaquim checked himself over, scowling at several splotches of
drying blood on the front of his shirt. "It was dark. I couldn't really
see much."

"Liar."

"If I tell you, will you promise not to hole up here in this cave
like a mole and wait to die?"

"My job is to keep these people and every other person we find
alive. No one is holing up and waiting to die, but I'll choose the best
course of action to accomplish my job."

"Fine. Couldn't see anything." Joaquim spun to walk away, and Marlee shifted her meandering to stay in range.

Selene grabbed his arm, and he shot the woman a frankly terrifying warning glare. Selene dropped his arm but didn't back away. "Most of these people aren't fighters, and I won't send them up to the surface to die. No, I don't intend to cower here and wait for a rescue that might never come. But before I start acting, I *need* to know what the situation is on the surface. So stop being an ass and tell me."

Joaquim snorted. "Haven't you heard? I'm always an ass."

"I have heard, actually. I also heard NOIR never had a better defender and protector than you. Show me it wasn't a lie. Work with me."

Joaquim dragged a hand down his face. "I'll send you the visuals I was able to capture. It genuinely was dark—they've taken out most of the electrical grid—but what I did see was...I'll let you judge for yourself, Advisor." He reached out and spread the fingertips of one hand against hers.

Silence fell between them. Direct sharing of files through touch?

Selene's expression darkened, and she let her hand fall limply to her side. "My gods. They're everywhere."

"Yeah. Now, what are we going to do about it? My opinion? We need to find out what's generating the quantum blocking field and disable it, then call the cavalry in."

"The cavalry got its butt kicked in the first battle. I'm not certain it exists any longer."

What? Marlee's thoughts went to Aunt Miriam, Pinchu and all the other people she knew who served in the Concord military. Aunt Miriam's ship was indestructible, so she must be safe. Pinchu's wasn't, though. She frantically tried to send a dozen pulses, but the messaging system was of course dead.

Joaquim's jaw worked. "Well, I'm confident Nika is gathering a new one."

"And I wish her the best of luck in the endeavor, but we can't count on the Initiative, DAF, the Taiyoks, the Kats or Concord to save us. We need to assume we will have to save ourselves."

"I'm glad to hear you say that."

"I'm not your enemy, Lacese, but we're going to do this my way. To that end, the first thing we need is more weapons. And tech. We need to set up a surveillance network aboveground so we can learn the Rasu's movements and activities. But as of now, all we have is a few dozen Glasers and archine blades, and picking a fight using such pitiful armaments will mostly succeed in getting us killed only slightly quicker than running away will."

Joaquim nodded sharply. "Agreed. So where do we get more weapons?"

"Underground? We can start by checking the next bunker over. We need to make contact with any people who made it to shelter, anyway. The more survivors, the better, and we can pool our resources."

"What about DAF Command? It's practically above our heads."

"Also out in the open and, if the Rasu have figured out its purpose, likely crawling with the monsters. We take the easier route first."

Joaquim made a face as if he was readying another smart retort, then sighed. "You're right. We should make contact with as many of the bunkers as we can reach."

"Did you just say I was *right*?"

"Don't get used to it." He searched around until he spotted Ava, then motioned her closer. "Gear up again. We're making a run to the next bunker." He raised his voice. "Rogers, you too." One of the new arrivals struggled to stand up from where they'd collapsed in a chair, but Joaquim waved him off. "Not you, Dominic. You've done enough today. Rest."

His eyes scanned the room for additional candidates, and Marlee saw her opportunity. She strode up to him and Selene. "I want to go with you."

Selene shook her head. "You're still injured."

"But I'm not." She held up her shirt to expose her abdomen; she'd removed the tape this morning, and the gashes had fully healed. A little bruising remained across her ribs, but nothing else. "See? I have kick-ass cybernetics. I mean, probably not as kick-ass as you all do, but they're the best humanity has to offer." She wound her sling-free left arm around in front of her, demonstrating its full range of motion. "Please. I want to help. And you need another pair of arms to carry weapons and supplies back."

The Justice Advisor studied her intently, almost as if Marlee were a criminal suspect. "It could be dangerous."

"Simply existing on this planet is dangerous. At least let me do something to help control my fate."

Selene checked with Joaquim, who shrugged. "If she wants to help, who are we stop her?"

"The people in charge?"

He eyed the woman in mock shock. "Are you admitting I'm partially in charge?"

"No. I'm only admitting that you won't shut up about *thinking* you're in charge. All right, Marlee. I won't refuse able-bodied help. Arm yourself with an archine blade and grab an empty bag."

"Thank you!" She spun around to head to the supply room and gear up—and bumped straight into Grant.

"Whoa, there. I guess I'm in, too."

Selene frowned. "Why? No offense, Grant, but you're not exactly a warrior, either."

"No kidding. But I can't let her go while I stay behind."

Marlee scoffed. "Why not? You already saved me. You don't need to continue protecting me now."

"Don't I?"

"I'm not a child."

"Marlee, you are clearly smart and capable. But you're how old?"

She studied the ceiling. "Twenty."

"*Years*? Stars...."

"What? My age has no impact on my skill with a blade, languages or tech. I challenge you to perform better than me at any of those activities."

He stared at her incredulously. "You do realize I'm easily one-third synthetic, right?"

"So? I'm an Enhanced human. Show me what you've got."

"Settle down," Selene growled. "Leave the dick measuring to Lacese, please. Grant, grab an empty bag, or don't, but we're leaving in five minutes."

Grant motioned grandly toward the supply room. "After you."

RW

BENEATH NAMINO ONE

The tunnel leading out from the bunker was almost three meters high and a meter and a half wide—presumably because Taiyoks had initially dug it—so the space didn't feel quite as claustrophobic as Marlee had expected. Everyone attached lights to their clothing, and Selene led the procession wielding a large flashlight.

Less than three minutes into the two-kilometer journey, Selene and Joaquim started bickering. Marlee listened to them go on for a while under her pre-existing theory about gaining further insights into Asterion society, but she was tempted to resign herself to the reality that they were just...people. People with two sets of very different ideas on how to move forward during this crisis and a severe case of repressed sexual tension.

She glanced at Grant, who had fallen in beside her. "Are they always like this?"

"I think they met for the first time during the attack. Joaquim has a strong prejudice against...he doesn't care for Justice officers."

Ava dropped back to join them with a quiet laugh. "Would you believe he got an up-gen a few months ago that was supposed to tone down his virulent hatred of all things Justice? Which...come to think of it, I guess this *is* toned down."

Grant nodded in agreement. "It is."

"An up-gen?" Marlee asked.

"He went to a clinic and had a portion of his personality programming tweaked to better suit who he wanted to be."

"You can do that? How astounding!"

"I don't know about astounding, but it's a thing."

"Have you ever had an up-gen?"

Grant exhaled harshly. "A few."

The way he muttered it made her suspect she was missing some crucial nuance. "Did you not like who you were before?"

"It's not about that, not exactly. Sometimes, we screw around with different traits for fun. But mostly, we try to improve ourselves. Don't want to get stale and set in our ways."

"Oh, I get it. Basically, the polar opposite of the path the Anadens have taken."

"We ran from more than persecution."

"It's wonderful how you keep the spirit of your ancestors' vision alive after all this time."

Grant's features puckered up as he turned away from her to study the earthen walls.

"What did I say? Are you *not* keeping the spirit of your ancestors' vision alive? Did I misunderstand?"

"No, you understood fine. The SAI Rebellion is a sensitive topic is all. Can we talk about something else?"

"Sure." She pondered on what he'd said—and the unspoken disquiet beneath it—while the tunnel curved around to the left. She knew enough Anadens to recognize that extreme long life could alter the way one viewed the passage of time, but the SAI Rebellion was a *long* time ago. Still, she should respect his request. "Aren't you all afraid the Rasu are going to discover the tunnels and bunkers?"

He didn't respond, and she waited for five whole seconds before pushing. "Grant? Listen, I'm sorry if I touched a nerve—"

He stopped and pointed up, where a square black box was embedded in the ceiling. "That module and a bunch more like it are broadcasting the EM signature of solid bedrock. If nothing else, it should make the underground area a low-priority target for the Rasu. Gods know they've got plenty of material to pillage above-ground first."

"Clever. Good thinking on your part."

"We try."

Up ahead, Selene stopped and held up a hand. "Everyone on alert. We're almost there. Let's not spook any friendlies or attract any Rasu."

Marlee readied her archine blade in one hand and her hand-gun—they'd called it a Glaser—in the other. She'd lost her plasma blade when the Rasu had sideswiped her, but she gathered it wouldn't be of much use against the aliens anyway.

Selene, Joaquim and Ava appeared to bring serious skills to bear when it came to combat, and she found she was okay with hanging back until they cleared the way. She wasn't afraid as such, was she? No, of course not. Merely properly respectful of an enemy who had nearly killed her with an offhand wave of one arm.

The tunnel abruptly branched to the left and the right; they took the left branch until it ended at what appeared to be solid rock. Selene motioned everyone flush against the walls. "Kill your lights and stay here." She waved her hand in a controlled, circular motion, and a small panel in the rock revealed itself. She entered a code in the panel and raised her weapon. The rock swung away to create a door-sized opening.

Darkness greeted them. Selene and Joaquim disappeared inside, and silence held sway in the tunnel. Ava took up a position in front of the doorway, her awesome gun arm trained inside.

Thirty agonizing seconds later, Ava stepped aside to let Selene rejoin them. "It's empty. Come on in."

Selene set her flashlight on the floor, and the light cast eerie shadows across the deserted space. It closely resembled their bunker, if a bit smaller and oddly shaped on account of two large boulders jutting out of one wall.

"Dammit, why is no one in here? Did you Justice people bother to tell anyone about the bunkers?"

Selene scowled over her shoulder. "No, Lacese. We thought we'd keep them our little secret. *Yes*, we broadcast their locations repeatedly on the nex web as soon as the attack began."

"Then where is everyone?"

Grant strode past Joaquim and vanished into a murky hallway, only to return quickly. "This is why. The entrance from the surface is caved in." He picked up Selene's flashlight and shone it down the hallway to reveal rubble piled up in a slope from the floor almost to the ceiling.

Selene rested a hand on one of the boulders, her expression unreadable in the shadows. "That answers that. Let's gather up all the weapons and food stockpiles we can carry and head back."

14

NAMINO
CAMP BURROW

"I told you, I agree we need to do what we can to thwart the Rasu on the ground, but—"

"Insurgency. It's called an insurgency."

"Fine. No insurgency until I see for myself what it looks like up there."

Joaquim groaned; godsdamn, the Justice Advisor was infuriating! But, he had to concede, also competent. So far. "Then let's go see what it looks like up there." He scanned the room full of people, most of them sitting in small groups or napping on pop-up cots. "Rogers, over here for a minute."

The colonel came over to where he and Selene sat talking at one of the two small workstations. Despite being formerly in charge of managing DAF Command, Rogers appeared to be more of a bureaucrat than a warrior, and thus far he hadn't tried to challenge either Selene or Joaquim for leadership. If anything, the man acted relieved that he wasn't being expected to lead. "What do you need?"

"DAF Command has a well-stocked armory, doesn't it?"

"Of course it does."

"Do those armaments include drones?"

"They should. A couple, at least."

"Excellent." Joaquim turned to Selene. "We'll go to DAF Command, acquire us some drones and release them from the roof. Give me ten minutes, and I'll have a spike ready that will program them for a grid sweep and send all the data they intake to me."

"If they've realized what it is, DAF Command will be crawling with Rasu."

"You mentioned that already. We're going to come up against Rasu sooner or later, and this is worth the risk."

"Later would suit me fine." She nodded, though. "Bring Ava. Colonel Rogers, you're with us as well. Arm yourselves to the hilt and set your kamero filter to block your thermal signature." In a stroke of luck, the Taiyok origins of the kamero filter technology meant it didn't rely on quantum mechanics to function.

Rogers frowned. "I don't have a kamero filter installed."

Definitely a desk jockey. Joaquim pointed toward the supply room down the hallway. "It's a good thing they stocked a couple of external modules here in the bunker." He glanced back at Selene. "Ten minutes."

RW

Joaquim was finishing up on the spike when the Human girl came up to him. "Let me come with you again."

"Marlee, right? You obviously don't lack for bravery. Or maybe you're itching for suicide by Rasu. But you don't look like a fighter, and I have no idea how you'll react when faced with a real combat situation."

"Whatever I *look* like to you, this won't be my first combat situation. I can handle myself in a fight."

"Perhaps. And something tells me we'll get to find out soon enough one way or another. But not tonight, okay? Besides, a larger team will crowd the hallways and make the kind of clatter that will bring enemies running. We'll need to move fast and quiet if we want to retrieve what we're after and make it back alive."

Her face scrunched up in a universal display of annoyance. "Okay. Next time, though."

"We'll see."

She turned to go, then pivoted back to him. "Can I ask you something?"

He checked the program compilation status. "If you can do it in less than thirty seconds."

"You mentioned suicide. Why doesn't everyone here just commit suicide and wake up in a new body someplace safer?"

"Hmm." He checked the spike's progress again. "Anadens have a process whereby they reincarnate in new bodies when they die, don't they?"

"Yes. Regenesis."

"And you Humans have copied it by now, I assume?"

"More or less."

"Then why aren't you committing suicide?"

"Because I want to live."

He shrugged broadly. "There's your answer."

She studied him suspiciously. The girl wielded an impressive stare, and he found himself weakening beneath its power. "Also, the psyche backups for most of the people here are stored on Namino, and I don't think any regen clinics are open today. Maybe some of them also have a copy stored on the Vault, but cracking it open is our doomsday scenario. So for the time being, this is the only life they've got."

"But not you, right? You're not from Namino."

"No, not me. Before you ask, I'm staying because I want to fight these monsters. It's why I came here in the first place." The light on the spike flashed green, and he made a shooing motion. "Now off with you."

RW

DAF COMMAND

The DAF Command basement had been ransacked as thoroughly as if a junkie thief had come through hunting for hidden doses.

The cement door they'd entered through was now a solid wall; the camouflage was well done.

Selene glared at the mess and muttered under her breath, "If they've come down here, it means there are probably Rasu upstairs."

Adrenaline pulsed through Joaquim's veins. "Good. I'm tired of dreading this fight."

"No, not good. I've marked our route to the armory on the schematic."

He studied the map for a minute. "Talk about taking the long way around."

"It will maximize our chances of avoiding enemy contact."

He bit back a snarky retort. Objectively, he recognized that a close-quarters encounter with Rasu was apt to be bad, bad news. Part of him still wanted it. "All right, we'll do it your way. Kamero filters to maximum and conversation to a minimum." The inability to ping one another thanks to the quantum block was going to make the latter declaration considerably more difficult than usual.

They moved to the lift, which seemed to be mostly intact, and stepped on it. A gear squeaked too loudly, but the lift began to rise.

His muscles tensed, and he adjusted his grip on his Glaser. If a Rasu stood guard at the top of the lift, they were screwed.

But the lift cleared the floor to ascend into a deathly silent lobby. At the other end, the building entrance had been reduced to a jagged, gaping hole. He shivered in spite of himself. The last time he'd been here, screams and shouts had ricocheted through billowing smoke beneath the roar of attacking Rasu. Now it was far too quiet.

He shook off the spell as Selene led them down the hallway to the right, into the heart of the building. The lights were out, and he increased his infrared and thermal filters to compensate. Thanks to their kamero filter protection, the others' heat signatures didn't even register.

Muted thuds echoed overhead, and everyone pulled up to stare at the ceiling in concern. "Rasu in the command center?"

Selene whispered beside him, "Sounds like."

"They're stealing our military data."

"Sounds like. Take the next left."

Ugh, he wanted to throttle the woman, he really did. The Rasu were pillaging the planet and stealing crucial intel about Dominion operations, and she remained as cool as a fucking cucumber. But he held his tongue. They could spar to their hearts' content back at the bunker, but if he wanted this mission to succeed, he needed to stay focused.

"I can—" he tamped his voice down, *focus* "—read the schematic."

They rounded the next corner, and Selene jerked to a halt. Thirty meters beyond them, at the end of the long hallway, a bipedal Rasu disappeared inside an open doorway on the left.

On the schematic, their intended path shifted as Selene devised an alternate route to the armory. She checked each member of the team to confirm they'd seen the modifications, then motioned for everyone to retreat. They backtracked down the hall and took the next right, then a left.

This route took them past DAF Command's primary server room. When they reached it, Joaquim paused to peer inside. Deep in the high-ceilinged room, a shadow flitted across the icy blue glow of powered servers. Rasu.

He reached out to where he thought Selene was standing, grabbed her arm and pointed deliberately into the room. She shook her head in a firm, 'no.'

Joaquim gritted his teeth…and obeyed. But in the back of his mind, he began to hatch a plan.

Three turns later, they reached the DAF Command armory. It looked untouched, but he supposed the Rasu had no need for Asterion weapons.

The door closed behind them, and they lowered the setting on their kamero filters so they could see one another more easily.

Rogers motioned deeper into the room. "The drones should be in the far right area."

Joaquim let Selene and Rogers head into the stacks while Ava watched the door, and he started scanning the labels on the bins. Fifteen seconds later, he found what he was hunting for. He emptied an entire bin of power amplifiers onto the floor, then sat down and started opening them up.

Two minutes later, Selene and Rogers reemerged lugging four drones under their arms. Selene invaded his personal space, towering above him from but a few centimeters away. "Why are you on the floor?"

"It's not important. Hand over the drones."

Her lips puckered into a pout as she crouched beside him and placed her drones on the floor. He blinked, momentarily distracted, then busied himself getting the spike ready while she motioned for Rogers to deposit his drones as well.

Joaquim took each one in turn and jammed the programming spike into the input port. When a subtle ring of lights illuminated around the circumference of the port, he moved on to the next one.

Once they were ready, Selene hefted two of the drones back under her arms. "Now for the tricky part—getting to the roof while lugging these around."

Joaquim began gathering up the power amplifier pieces and stuffing them in his bag. "You three head on up. I'm going to the building's power control center."

"No, you're coming with us to the roof."

"No, I'm going to the power control center. The Rasu have gotten some of the data stored here, but not all of it, or they would've already left and destroyed the building. I intend to make sure they don't steal any more of it."

She glanced at his open bag. "Lacese, our servers are designed to withstand power surges."

"Not this one they aren't. Don't worry, I've done it before."

"Do I want to know what that means?"

"Decidedly not. I'll meet you all at the basement lift." He hurried out of the armory before she tried any Justice jujitsu to stop him.

RW

Selene glared at the disappearing form in seething annoyance. People obeyed her orders; it came with the job title. Yet Lacese seemed to simply…not care. About the title, the orders or anything else she said or did.

She stifled a grumble. He was getting in her head, and she couldn't allow that to happen. They were deep in enemy territory now, and she had a job to do. She deposited her drones in the large pack they'd brought alongside the two Rogers had grabbed. While Rogers hefted the pack up and situated it over his shoulder, she approached Ava. "What's Lacese's story?"

The woman peered out the door, searching for movement. "He was NOIR's Mission Director."

"I know. I mean, why is he such an arrogant asshole?"

"Oh. Beats me. He came that way."

"Right." She sighed, annoyed anew that she'd wasted time inquiring. "Let's move. We'll follow the marked route to a lift that leads to the top floor, then use the roof access in the northeast corner."

Twice they had to change course to avoid rummaging Rasu, and with their destination in sight they came within a nanosecond of running smack into an enemy, but finally they reached the lift.

She cringed at every tiny noise it made as it carried them up. Halfway to the top floor, she decided they needed to take a different lift back down, because given all this racket there was certain to be a cadre of Rasu awaiting their return at the bottom of this one.

It was fifty meters from the lift to the roof access—one long hallway with only locked doors on both sides. The temptation to sprint to the other end was great, but better for them to move carefully and silently.

So they crept down the hall, Rogers taking extra care not to bang the bulky pack against the walls. When they reached the end, Selene activated a button embedded in the wall. A panel in the ceiling slid open, and a ladder descended. She braced herself, grabbed onto the first rung and climbed.

She'd been bitching for days about needing to see what the situation on the surface looked like, but now that the moment approached…she wanted to turn away.

Dry, acrid air assaulted her lungs as she rose through the opening. Instantly her Glaser was out, sweeping across the roof.

Focused as she was on identifying and neutralizing any threats, her eyes registered the scene before her brain did. Finding the roof empty, the landscape beyond it quickly bombarded her awareness, and her arms dropped weakly to her sides.

She wanted to turn away. The urge to sink to her knees in despair was overpowering, but she wouldn't do it. She was the leader, dammit, and she had to be strong. Always.

She nodded to Rogers. "Let's get the drones in the air and get out of here before one of those patrolling ships decides to investigate this roof."

RW

DAF Command transformed into an insidious maze on their return trip, and they were the rats. As Selene had feared, one too many errant sounds had raised the Rasu's alert level, and now they seemed to guard every hallway. Ava requested permission to start shooting three separate times; she denied it all three times. There were a minimum of a dozen Rasu in the building, and those odds meant certain death if this became a shooting war.

A branching hallway waited for them ahead. Selene briefly considered heading back to the armory and taking a fifth drone to use as a scout, but military drones were too bulky for in-building surveillance. Still, she was considering regretting her decision.

She slid along the wall until she was able to see down the left hallway and found it mercifully empty. Except they needed to go right. She peeked around the corner—and froze.

A bipedal Rasu strode toward them, its stance conveying alert watchfulness. Three meters away and closing, so she didn't dare cause so much as a ripple in the air.

In the dim hallway, its form presented as an inky, monotonous shadow of death-seeking metal.

Hq (visual) | scan.(thermal-infrared)(240°:60°)

Thermal readings barely registered, but far-infrared radiation leaked off the form in waves.

The Rasu was going to pass less than a meter from her, and she willed the shadows to envelop her in greater darkness. The enemy bore no visible eyes, yet she swore she could feel its probing gaze nonetheless.

A thunderous roar erupted from deeper in the building to shake the walls, and the Rasu took off running toward the commotion.

No time to worry about what had caused the explosion. She whispered for Ava and Colonel Rogers to follow her, and they rushed through the now-clear hallway, careened around a corner, then another—then they were once again in the lobby. An Asterion cast in shadows waited at the lift. "Hustle it!"

She didn't argue. The three of them leapt onto the lift, and it began descending into the depths.

Once they reached the basement, however, she whipped on Joaquim. "What was the explosion? Your handiwork?"

Even in the dim lighting of the basement she could swear he was smirking. "I suspected you'd need a diversion on that last stretch, so I detonated my little improvised power bomb early. The Rasu won't be getting any further intel out of those military servers."

"I see..." she sighed, overcome by a wave of bone-weariness "...good work."

"You're welcome."

15

NAMINO
CAMP BURROW

Everyone crowded around Joaquim to watch the first footage arriving from the drones, but curiosity quickly transformed into horror, then despair. In less than a minute, most of the onlookers had slunk away to their claimed space in the bunker, defeatism weighing down their features and sluggish steps.

The warriors and leaders stayed, however, refusing to look away. If they expected to fight this enemy, they had to do it with their eyes open.

The footage showed in bloody color and sharp relief what Joaquim already knew: the Rasu were having their way with the city. At least twenty enormous enemy vessels hovered directly above the crumbling skyline, ready to vaporize anything non-Rasu that dared to move. Bipedal Rasu combed through every building still standing. They carted off hardware, materials...and people. Joaquim watched as half a dozen Asterions were rounded up and prodded into a morphing Rasu cage. Once full, the cage lifted off and flew toward one of the vessels hovering overhead.

"Godsdammit!" Joaquim searched around for something to hit. Not finding anything suitable for abuse, he slapped his cheeks then dragged his hands roughly down his face.

"They're restarting their experiments on us." Selene sounded entirely too calm, per usual, though her expression was grim.

"Yes. So all the work we did to destroy their stronghold in our galaxy was for *nothing*."

"That's not true. We refused to grovel and submit to their demands. These people here are being taken by force. We're not serving them up on a platter."

"I doubt any of those prisoners care how we take pride in our moral stance."

"I realize they don't, Lacese. I'm just saying—"

"I get it. Can we stop them from taking more prisoners? Intercept these cage transports before they haul our people away?"

Selene dropped her head into her hands, though she kept one eye on the visuals. "Without any advance warning of where they're planning to round prisoners up, I don't see how." She sighed. "Why didn't those people go to one of the bunkers?"

"Fear freezes people. The prospect of moving probably seemed more terrifying to them than staying put."

"True." She regarded him curiously. "I'm surprised you—"

He paused one of the visuals. "What's this structure here?"

A tower of aubergine metal about a hundred meters tall stood at the center of three concentric rings of lower Rasu structures; the diameter of the outermost ring stretched for half a kilometer. Hundreds of bipedal Rasu and small craft moved to and from the various structures comprising the rings, while additional units arrived and departed from the facility. "It appears as if everything not being ferried up to the big ships is being brought here."

"Makes sense. They've built their own central processing hub. Where is this?"

Joaquim checked the data stream coming from the drone in question. "On the outskirts of downtown to the northwest. 6.2 kilometers from here."

Selene leaned in to inspect the visual more closely as he restarted the feed. "The rings are clearly focused on resource management, but what's the purpose of the tower?"

"Power generation, maybe? I'm not sure."

Grant had been sitting quietly beside Marlee, both of them acting shell-shocked by what they were seeing, but now he glowered at the tower. "It's appropriately big and menacing, so it must be important. Could it have something to do with the quantum block?"

Joaquim shrugged. "I don't think so. The block was activated long before this tower existed."

"True." Grant rubbed at his eyes; none of them were getting much sleep. "We need to find out where or how the block's being generated. To my mind, the only thing we can do that might actually make a real difference here on the ground is disable the quantum block. Somehow."

Selene dropped her chin into a hand. "Lacese, can you instruct one of the drones to move in and get a closer inspection of this compound?"

"Nope. So long as the block remains active, I can't communicate remotely with them. They'll execute on their existing programming, and nothing else." Joaquim planted his hands on the floor and considered the woman opposite him. "I agree with Grant about the block, but until we know more about it, we're left with disrupting the Rasu's occupation however we can. If they were taking the prisoners to this compound, I'd say we should storm it right now. But they're taking them beyond our reach. So what else can we do?"

"You're asking my opinion?"

"I am. You were intimately involved with the planning and execution of Project Guerilla, which put us all down here in the first place. What else does it entail?"

"Having a lot more weapons and trained fighters on hand than we do. We didn't anticipate the quantum block. I'm afraid for all intents and purposes, we are all that exists of Project Guerilla." She studied the visuals from one of the other drones, which panned across a block that had once been a park and was now a crater. "I think our first order of business should be to concentrate on reaching other survivors who *have* made their way underground."

"What good is it going to do us? Without communications, the scattered bunkers will remain isolated even if people are surviving in them. We can't coordinate activities or report breaches or Rasu movements."

"If we make contact, it will show people they aren't alone."

"Again I ask, what good is it going to do for anyone? Alone or not, they'll die all the same. We have to do something to hurt the Rasu. Slow them down."

Selene sat up straighter, the better to throw her hands in the air. "What, Lacese? What, *exactly*, can we do?"

"Disruptive incursions. We can use the footage from the drones to identify Rasu hotspots. Let's get up there and fuck up whatever they're doing, every way we can. We're all that exists of Project Guerilla? Okay, let's be Project Guerilla."

Her gaze drifted across the bunker, where a pall had fallen over the huddled masses. "We have, what, seven or eight people who can fight? It's not much of a hit squad against an enemy as formidable as this one."

Joaquim groaned in growing frustration. "It'll be enough to start. Look, Panetier, I can't breathe in here. It feels like we're trapped in a communal grave, slowly suffocating. I have *got* to get outside and shoot something."

16

NAMINO STELLAR SYSTEM
CAF GHOST G-2

T he horde of Rasu enveloping Namino resembled ants scrambling over a lump of discarded food. Caleb stopped counting at two thousand enormous warships, never mind the tens of thousands of smaller ships scurrying about.

The Rasu knew they had struck gold here.

No physical marker indicated when he passed through the quantum barrier, but his eVi messaging system abruptly dropped out, as did several other exanet-dependent functions.

Caleb chuckled wryly as he thought back to the last time this had happened, on Portal Prime after Mesme's dragon kidnapped Alex. Here he was once again, piloting a 'borrowed' ship on a mission to rescue someone he loved. Yet everything about his life had changed since then, and he couldn't help but wonder if it was all changing once again now. Alex, Marlee, Akeso...their future and his place in it was shrouded by the enemy arrayed in front of him.

But he didn't have time to muse maudlin over the good and bad of it, so he set the memory aside and adopted a course that should deposit him in the vicinity of Namino One.

Even given the size of the armada, on a planetary scale expansive regions remained free of Rasu, and he was able to slip the Ghost through their net while staying more than half a megameter from any Rasu vessel.

The atmospheric entry was brutal, though the pummeling forces posed no risk to the Ghost's adiamene hull. But the ship was tiny—so tiny Marlee was going to have an uncomfortable ride home in the cramped space behind his seat—and sported no inertial dampeners and only minimal shielding to act as a buffer. His brain rattled around in his skull, ratcheting up the headache he'd endured since the coup attempt to a torturous level. Once he made it through the atmosphere, his eVi could initiate a mitigation routine, for all the good it was apt to do. Akeso's frantic objections to his chosen course of action screamed in his mind and wound his stomach into a nauseating knot, and this was before he'd raised a hand against a single Rasu.

At last the skies cleared to reveal a burning and broken city in the distance. Two dozen cruiser-sized Rasu vessels hovered above the wrecked skyline, and a swarm of black dots darted in every direction beneath them.

He slowed to approach cautiously and give the Ghost's vaunted camouflage technology maximum opportunity to work its magic. As such, he had plenty of time to study the scene.

Off to the left, a sprawling region of low-rise structures and cemented stretches of land—a military or industrial facility—lay in smoldering ruins. Between it and the city proper, multiple levtram cars had been thrown off their rails and upended. On both sides of the route, the shattered remains of suburbs and townlets gradually gave way to what had once been an expansive collection of gleaming towers. Now, though, none—save one—stood higher than ten stories, and most had seen their frameworks shorn away in jagged pieces.

That single tower stood tall at what might be the geographic center of the city, intact but not untouched. Gaping holes marred the glass windows across multiple levels and...he squinted and zoomed his ocular implant...multi-limbed, spider-like Rasu crawled along the façade, dashing into and out of the ruptures. He shuddered. Intelligent spiders larger than a human were not a welcome development.

But he needed to focus now, for the outer edge of the radiating destruction rapidly approached. Nika had given him a schematic of the underground tunnels and bunkers the Omoikane Initiative had constructed or upgraded in preparation for a Rasu invasion, but now that he was here, he realized he had a problem. The entire landscape of the city had changed, and few identifiable landmarks included on the schematic still stood. The schematic did include compass markings, so he wouldn't be setting off completely blind. Nonetheless, finding one of the cleverly hidden entrances in a foreign city he'd never before set foot in that was being systematically demolished?

Well, it wasn't as if he'd thought this was going to be easy.

His second problem: he didn't dare set the Ghost down too close to downtown, or Rasu were bound to eventually run over or mangle it without even recognizing what they'd done. He needed the ship to get Marlee home, so he needed to secure it someplace safe. But the farther away from the city he stashed it, the more lethal territory he'd be forced to cross—and for them both to cross on the return trip.

He settled for landing beside a long, low structure that had been gutted and now sat abandoned, five kilometers from the standing tower. He situated the ship far enough away that if the remaining walls of the structure collapsed, they wouldn't hit the Ghost, yet close enough that the walls would hopefully provide some degree of protection for so long as they stood.

After switching the ship to low-power mode, which kept the stealth measures active, he stepped through the checklist he'd prepared. He retrieved the archine blade, his Daemon and one Veil from the backpack, then double-checked its remaining contents: an extra Veil for Marlee, first aid supplies, a canteen of water, and a handful of energy bars. Satisfied, he climbed out of the cockpit, clipped the weapons and the Veil to his pants, and breathed in arid, warm air tinged with smoke and ashes.

He stretched out his arm in front of him, frowning. His fingertips remained inside the cloaking field's range, but he worried the Veil might not be functioning. It was Kat tech turned Prevo tech, which meant quantum programming. Dammit! Stupid of him to not account for this and dig up an old, pre-Prevo cloaking device before he left, but he was woefully out of practice at this.

His eyes closed as he reached for the tranquility of Akeso's living forest...and found solely darkness. Was Akeso denying him entry to their shared world? Or was the mental block of his own making?

Either way, it was probably for the best. Tranquility had no place in a killer's heart. He'd learned years earlier how to quiet—but not silence—Akeso's endless thoughts and intentions, and now he worked to build a stronger, more resilient wall between him and his companion. It felt like he was closing himself off from one half of his soul, but if he wanted to live through this ordeal, he had no choice.

A solemn chill descended upon him as he turned his attention back to his mission. He decided he'd wear the Veil anyway, at least until he confirmed it wasn't functioning. The extra Veil module weighed almost nothing, so he'd bring it along as well. But if the tech was dead, sneaking through the heart of the city promised to be a much more challenging task.

A steady stream of rumbles and booms echoed out from downtown; the Rasu were not quiet about their work. He watched a transport-sized ship rise above a gutted building in the distance to dock with one of the cruisers darkening the sky. Ferrying materials, intel, or worse.

So many people were suffering here. He'd record what he encountered when he was able to, note everything he saw and share it with Nika once he and Marlee escaped the planet, but he had to accept the reality that he couldn't save all of the people here. With a little luck and a lot of remembered skill, maybe he could save one.

He secured the backpack on his shoulders and set off.

Akeso's agitated sensations of protest escaped past his mental wall in fragments as he crept along the ruined streets of devastated neighborhoods. The mere atmosphere, the still-smoking remains of destruction on display, disturbed his companion. Or disturbed him, which fueled a spiraling feedback loop between them.

I warned you long ago that not all Others were peaceful.

He received no articulated response; Akeso had stopped talking to him during the coup attempt and never resumed doing so. Their connection was as strong as ever, for Akeso's distress churned his gut like spoiled food, but the planet's consciousness remained stubbornly mute.

He peeked around the corner of a rare standing wall and found a street littered with charred bodies. The stench assaulted his nostrils in a rush, and suddenly it was too much. He stumbled backward into an alley and vomited up the energy bar he'd eaten before departing the Ghost. He wasn't keeping much food down lately.

The buildings lining this street looked as if they'd been taken out by a giant wrecking ball, and only a few jagged pieces rose higher than three meters tall. In his mind, he saw the occupants fleeing into the street to escape the collapsing structures, only to be burned alive by the rampaging invaders.

Focus on your goal. He stepped back onto the sidewalk. To the east, the single intact tower stood battered and bruised amidst all the destruction, Rasu trampling busily upon it. Up close, the spider forms were closer to a tank than a human in size.

This had to be Namino Tower—and the Rasu had recognized the importance of the data it held. They were stripping it of vital information about the Asterion Dominion and its people, so they could emerge yet stronger for the next invasion. This wasn't his world and these weren't his people, but an aching sorrow welled up in his chest to chill his skin all the same.

But the tragedy wrought by the Rasu's plundering also gave him a signpost. He checked the setting sun to the northeast, then his schematic. DAF Command was located to the south-southwest of Namino Tower, three kilometers away. He turned left at the next intersection.

A block ahead, a squad of Rasu pillaged what appeared to be an apartment building. A cluster of bodies lay strewn across the sidewalk in front of it, and loud noises reverberated from inside.

A Rasu drone patrolled the area, its searing eye scanning the inside of neighboring buildings and narrow alleys. Its course was going to very shortly bring it right to Caleb.

He sprinted down the closest alley and flattened himself against a standing wall, then readied the archine blade in one hand and his Daemon in the other.

A few seconds later, the drone reached the alley and turned its eye upon it—and saw him. So much for the Veil.

A violet beam burst out of the eye. Caleb leapt to the side and rolled away, but the beam sliced into his left upper arm, scorching his skin in a flash of seared flesh.

Long-ago lessons clawed their way out of his memories to whisper their wisdom. *Don't let the pain put you on the ground. Use it to drive you forward. Let it hone you into a deadly weapon. Don't stop until the enemy's pain is greater than your own.*

He adjusted his grip on the Daemon and fired into the drone's eye. Akeso recoiled at the press of the trigger, and Caleb fought past the overwhelming urge to collapse to the ground and surrender. The drone, however, was unfazed by the strike as it prepared to fire a second time.

A shower of dust drifted down between them, and he glanced up. The façade on the right had crumbled in several places, and a large section of it teetered upon a long, wide crack. He swung the Daemon up and fired on the crack.

A huge chunk of wall tumbled free and landed on top of the drone, smashing it into the ground. Caleb didn't loiter to confirm the kill; instead he took off running into the network of interlocking alleys that wound behind the buildings.

He didn't stop for what felt like four blocks or so, but finally he stumbled to a halt and sagged against another crumbling wall in another alley, out of breath and out of practice. It was full dark now, but a half-revealed moon cast silvery light into the shadows of the alley, and he reluctantly peered at his left arm. The drone's beam had taken off a sizeable chunk of flesh, exposing torn meat and muscle, but it hadn't cut all the way to bone. His eVi medical routines must still be functioning, because while he'd been running, a hazy numbness had replaced the shooting pain. The archine blade dangled loosely in his hand, and he returned it to its sheath, lest he drop it without realizing it.

He slid the backpack off his shoulders and dropped to his knees to open it up and retrieve the smallest medwrap he'd brought that would cover the wound. He wanted to keep as many supplies as possible available for use should Marlee need them.

The sight of the Rasu flinging her through the air to crash into the sidewalk flared in his mind. As with the pain, he grabbed hold of the memory and used it to create the strength he needed to rise to his feet. Medwrap secure on his arm and backpack situated, he set out with renewed urgency.

CONCORD

17

AKESO
URSA MAJOR II GALAXY

Alex flopped into her cockpit chair on the *Siyane* and started up the Caeles Prism. Destination: home.

Abigail said it was going to be another eight hours before her mother woke up in a brand-new body on the Presidio, and once that happened she wasn't planning on leaving her mother's side for a while. Therefore, she should take the time to shower and change clothes—neither of which she'd done in far too long—and pack a bag.

Thank you for taking care of the Siyane *for me, Valkyrie. For getting her out of a warzone and safely home.*

There is no need to thank me, for she is and will always be my heart.

Alex smiled to herself. *And mine.*

She was so busy adding to and annotating the list of things she needed to do before heading to the Presidio that she hardly paid any heed to the Caeles Prism traversal—then jerked in surprise when the *Siyane* shuddered sideways. Driving rain and hail pelted the hull at a forty-five-degree angle, driven by a vicious wind. Lightning ripped across the turbulent sky, its flashes revealing roiling black thunderclouds racing low across the horizon.

What the hell? Akeso almost never stormed, and in fourteen years of living here, she couldn't recall one so ferocious as this. She concentrated on carefully guiding the *Siyane* down onto its landing pad and was relieved when the clamps locked into place.

Outside, the trees behind the complex whipped themselves into a frenzy, and smaller limbs lay strewn across the pad. All right, then. She went into the main cabin and retrieved a jacket she kept on board, tugged it on and stepped outside, letting Valkyrie close the airlock for her as she made a beeline for the house. Twice, large pellets of hail whacked her in the head as she dashed across the meadow. The stone path had already been overtaken by muddy rivulets, and she slipped and fell to her knees halfway to the porch. Ugh, perhaps the shower would be best performed once she was back on the *Siyane*, because no way was she making it out of the house and to the ship without getting soaked. She climbed to her feet and trudged forward, fighting gusts of wind as well as the mud trying to drag her into the earth.

Finally she stumbled through the door. Warm, welcoming and most of all dry air greeted her, and she leaned against the foyer wall to catch her breath. She wiped mud off her cheeks and was about to strip her filthy clothes off right here in the entrance when the glow of a detached aural floating above the kitchen counter caught her attention.

Dread snaked up her spine as she warily approached it. Caleb had left to go to Mirai and confer in person with Nika about the situation on Namino hours earlier, but had he come home briefly before leaving? Even if he did, why did he leave her a message instead of just pulsing her?

Multiple paragraphs shimmered above the marble surface, which caused the dread to spike. The last time he'd sent her a message this long, he'd promptly died after sending it. A shrill ringing in her ears grew to drown out the howling wind buffeting the house.

She placed both hands on the counter and began reading the message, until the words blurred together. Started again...and buried her face in her hands. *No*, priyazn.

But she should've realized. If she hadn't been so distracted by grief and worry and hope about her mother's fate, she would've seen what was staring her right in the face.

And he'd counted on her distraction, hadn't he?

A tree branch crashed against the side of the house, and she sprinted upstairs to spread her hands, palms open, upon the wide glass wall spanning the front of the house, where she gazed outside with wiser eyes.

Her heart broke into a thousand shards and spilt upon the floor. The storm? It was Caleb's consciousness manifested in raw, primal form.

"Oh, Akeso. He's not dying, is he? He's killing."

RW

THE PRESIDIO

CHRISTOPHER RYCHEN MEMORIAL WING
MILKY WAY GALAXY

Alex felt stretched thin, as if her soul were being twisted and warped by a torture rack. She ached for Caleb; her heart pounded in distress with worry for him and sorrow that he was now suffering beyond her reach. Yet hope laced with terror flooded her chest at the prospect of her mother rejoining them, miraculously alive and whole. The human soul was not equipped to hold so many contradictory emotions aloft at once, and she was surely going to crack wide open any second now.

She strode into the private waiting room outside the military regenesis lab and dropped the two bags she carried on the floor, then collapsed into one of the cushioned chairs. Caleb was now on the other side of the Rasu's quantum block, which meant she couldn't so much as get a message to him...so she had to focus on her mother for now. She *had* to.

The door opened to let her father inside. "Good, you're here—" he rushed over to crouch in front of her "—*milaya*, what's wrong? They haven't told me about any problems with the procedure."

She shook her head wearily. God but she was tired. "I talked to Abigail a few minutes ago. Everything's fine with Mom."

"Then what is it?"

Maybe if she shared the burden, she wouldn't break for a while longer. This was what family was for, right? "Caleb went to Namino to try to find Marlee and rescue her."

Her father stood and took several steps back, toward the center of the small room. "I know."

"You...what?"

"I know he's gone to Namino."

She slowly stood, her limbs heavy and her soul burdened. "Dad, *what have you done?*"

"Everything in my power to give him the best chance to survive and succeed in his mission."

"What the *d'yavol* does that mean?"

"It means I used Richard's authorization codes to help Caleb steal a Ghost—the new CINT stealth reconnaissance craft. It'll enable him to sneak past the million Rasu at Namino and, assuming he can find Marlee, sneak her back out and come home."

She closed her eyes to belay fresh tears, for all the good it did. "How *could* you?"

"I've seen the look he had in his eyes before. I've carried that look in my own eyes. He was going to Namino, with or without my help. So I thought it was best for everyone if I helped."

"Why didn't you tell me? Why didn't you *ask* me?"

He offered her a sad, too-endearing smile. "To spare you the pain and worry you're feeling right now for as long as possible. I'd hoped your mother would be awake before you found out."

She lunged out and shoved him in the chest; he did her the courtesy of tripping back a step before steadying himself. "You don't get to decide what I do and don't know about my own husband, dammit! How dare you!"

"*Milaya*, I'm sorry. I only wanted to protect you a little, for a moment."

"Don't make this about you missing my adolescence. Neither of us is ever getting those years back, so stop fucking trying." She retreated to the chair, utterly exhausted all over again. "Did you pause to consider what this is going to do to him?"

"Did you consider what it will do to him if Marlee dies?"

"She could already be dead, and you and I both know it. Now his attempt to save her could kill him, too."

"Come on now, you know Akeso won't let him die."

"Oh, don't patronize me. Putting aside how not even Akeso can save him if the Rasu slice him up into a thousand tiny pieces, you're not comprehending what I'm saying. The Rasu might rip him to literal shreds, but killing other living beings will rip him to psychological ones. His mind could very well shatter. I just came from home, and Akeso is a literal hurricane. The whole damn planet is tearing itself apart. Do you understand what that means? *So is he.*"

David sat in the chair next to her and leaned over intently. "I realize they share a deep connection, but Caleb is not Akeso."

"Yes, Dad. He *is*. He's as much Akeso as he is himself. Now he's taking up the mantle of savior—of killer—again, and those two aspects of his nature are going to war with one another."

She pressed her head into her hands as fresh despair welled up in her chest. There was no outlet, nowhere for it to escape, so it took up residence to fester away at her heart. "And there's nothing I can do to help him."

18

THE PRESIDIO
CHRISTOPHER RYCHEN MEMORIAL WING

"What makes you think you have the skills and mettle to excel in the military?"

It wasn't as if Miriam had expected a supportive reaction from her father to her announcement that she would be entering the Naval Academy in the fall. She squared her shoulders and lifted her chin. "My track record at everything I've accomplished in my life so far, for one. Did you notice the part where it says I've been awarded a scholarship to attend? Were you paying attention when I won the Regional Tennis Championship last year? Has it slipped your mind how I was accepted into the Accelerated Program at twelve years old, then graduated Salutatorian of my class?"

"Second place never won a war."

The words hit her like a punch to the gut, but she was her father's daughter, and she didn't flinch. "I'm sorry you feel that way, but I worked hard for every single mark."

He put aside the report he'd been pretending to read and stood opposite her, his expression no more cold and affectless than on any other day. "You're not tough enough to survive in the military. It will break you, then you will run home in tears, begging your mother and me for sympathy. Better to never attempt it at all. Go to a so-called respectable college and get a respectable paperwork-pushing job. Visit us on holidays and tell yourself you've succeeded in life."

She tried so hard to steady it, but her voice trembled nonetheless. "No. I can do this. I will prove you so, so wrong. When I do, I *won't have to rub your nose in it, because you'll know. And though you'll never tell me so, you'll go to your grave regretting not having faith in me."*

RW

Miriam stopped at the door to her tiny apartment; she didn't move to enter the code in the keypad, instead letting her gaze rise to focus on David Solovy's too-enchanting face. He'd thus far made good on every one of his rash declarations. He'd taken leave time to stay on Perona after the Leninist radicals were subdued and shipped off to either the brig or the morgue, depending. He'd picked her up at the station and taken her on a picnic lunch before depositing her back at work on time. Then he'd waited for her shift to end and treated her to dinner at the most expensive restaurant on Perona.

He was funny, charming and occasionally ridiculous. Everything she was not. And while both meals had been more delightful than anything she'd allowed herself to experience in several years, she still couldn't figure out why he was here. She was proud of all she'd accomplished in her life, but there were literally billions of vivacious, exciting and gorgeous women out there for him to waste his time with. Why her?

"Thank you for dinner, though I wish you'd let me pay for my half of it."

"Nonsense. One of the locals mentioned that there's a bakery down the street famous for its orange danishes. Can I interest you in breakfast before work tomorrow?"

"I've been there. The danishes are delicious, but the blueberry scones are even better."

"Wonderful. We'll have those."

"Why?"

"When I was a kid and visited my aunt and uncle in Rybinsk during the summer, they had blueberry bushes growing all around their house. I'd stuff my face full of them and ruin my shirts with the juices. I'm a big fan of blueberries."

She dropped a shoulder against the door and rolled her eyes. "No, I mean...why breakfast? Why breakfast with me? Don't you want to spend what's left of your vacation on a beach somewhere wooing a singer or model or wealthy heiress?"

His brow furrowed. "I can't imagine a worse fate. How horribly dull must such people be?"

"And I'm not dull?"

"Bozhe moy, no. You're fascinating. I've scarcely begun to un-ravel the mystery of how your extraordinary mind works—and of why the left corner of your mouth twitches every time I compliment you."

Her skin flared hot. Dear god, was she blushing? The mischie-vous twinkle in his gray irises suggested she was.

"Exactly like that. Right here." He reached out and touched the crease of her lips with a fingertip, and the heat spread to other, less visible places. He must be able to sense her pulse racing just beneath the skin.

More fingertips joined the first, and they skimmed feather-light across her jaw. "Permission to kiss you, Major Draner?"

Her renowned good sense abandoned her entirely beneath the tsunami of his touch. "Permission granted, Captain Solovy."

RW

The doors to the womb center opened, and a medical officer emerged carrying a tiny bundle swathed in a thick beige blanket.

She and David both leapt to their feet and hurried forward, but Miriam abruptly stopped several meters short. What if there had been a problem with the delivery? All the tests ahead of time said the baby was healthy and normal, but what if...?

The medical officer smiled. "Are you ready to meet your daughter?"

"Yes."

"Yes!"

Their responses overlapped, and David squeezed her hand. "Go ahead, Miri."

She took what felt like the most fateful three steps of her life and accepted the bundle into her arms.

Bright gray eyes gazed up at her from beneath feathery lashes, surrounded by delicate, pale pink skin. An impossibly small thumb fumbled its way into a mouth. Her daughter blinked at her.

She felt David at her shoulder, but she didn't dare divert her focus in his direction. "She looks just like you."

He reached over and nudged the blanket back a little, revealing wispy tuffs of burgundy locks. "Not only me, dushen'ka. *She's going to have your beautiful hair."*

She could hardly think, dumbstruck with awe that she and David had somehow created this miracle cooing in her arms. She adjusted the bundle against her chest and reached up to touch her daughter's cheek. "Hello, Alexis. Welcome to the world we've made for you."

RW

Miriam opened her eyes and stretched her arms over her head. "Goodness, did I fall asleep during the imprint? I'm sorry about that."

A hand grabbed hers as she lowered her arms, and she looked beside her to see David offering her a brilliant smile. "Hi, Miri."

"David? Why are you here? Has something happened?" She began sitting up. "Do I need to get to Command?"

Another hand, from the other side, urged her back down onto the cot. "Let's take it easy for a few minutes."

She frowned as her attention shifted to the speaker. Dr. Canivon? Whyever was *she* here for a routine neural imprint backup?

Behind the doctor, Alex rested against the wall of the clinic room, both hands at her mouth to cover a cry.

Something was badly wrong. She broke free of Dr. Canivon's gentle grasp and sat up. "Tell me. Whatever it is, tell me this instant."

David motioned Dr. Canivon off and wound his fingers through hers, forcing her attention to return to him. "That's my Miri, issuing orders from the first second. There was a battle against the Rasu, over in the Asterion Dominion. The Rasu boarded the *Stalwart II* and, in order to prevent them from accessing the records stored on the ship and learning about Concord, you activated the ship's self-destruct mechanism."

"A…how has there already been a battle against the Rasu? And what…" the words that *weren't* spoken made their way past her assumptions into her brain "…I died. This is regenesis. This is…." She lifted her left arm and regarded it curiously. New skin, unmarked by the vagaries of life.

She sucked in a sharp breath, unaccountably afraid her lungs no longer functioned. What if the body was defective? The imprint? Her mind? "When?"

"Four days ago."

"No, I mean how long since the imprint? How much time have I lost?"

"Two weeks. No time at all."

"No time? It's so long…." A thousand thoughts competed for dominance, and dizziness overtook her. What about—how could—but no—

One of David's hands pressed into her cheek while the other held her right hand in a vise grip. "Hey, hey. It's okay. You're okay."

She stared at him, uncertain of everything except the calming reassurance on his face and the solidity of his touch. She opened her mouth, but no words won the battle to reach her lips.

"I know what you're feeling right now. Just breathe deeply and let yourself settle into being alive."

He did know, didn't he? She blinked past inexplicable tears and looked around again. "Alex?"

"I'm here." Her daughter yanked a chair over, plopped down in it and took her other hand. Trails of recent tears glistened on her cheeks. "Welcome back."

"I don't…." What did she want to say so badly? Her brain wasn't working correctly. Her thoughts darted from Concord military protocols to memories of her disastrous tenth birthday party to meeting David and holding Alex in her arms for the first time. The Rasu? How could they have boarded the ship? It didn't make any sense. Was she truly here at all? Was this Heaven or, depending on how things went from here, Hell? Was she comatose from some catastrophic incident and dreaming all of this?

She let go of David and Alex's hands and sat up straighter. "Doctor, you need to run a thorough battery of tests on me. I think something went wrong."

Alex's countenance darkened in concern. "What? No, it didn't. You're *fine*. Waking up is a little disorienting, that's all."

"It's a great deal more than a little disorienting." David refused to stop touching her, reaching up to caress her face. "You *are* fine, but I understand why you're afraid to believe it right now." He glanced past her. "Doctor, run your tests."

RW

Dr. Canivon's placid, professional countenance hadn't wavered in the last hour. "Your husband is correct, Commandant. You are 'fine.' The imprint we used was as close to perfect as they get, and it grafted onto your neural structure without complaint. Your body is new, but your mind is precisely as it was two weeks ago."

Miriam massaged her temples. "Then why do I feel this way?"

"What way?"

"Like I'm not really here. Like this is a dream or…something worse."

Dr. Canivon's attention flitted past Miriam. "Why don't we let you and Professor Solovy talk alone for a few minutes. Alex, I expect you want a bit of reassurance as well. I'll be happy to review the test results with you."

Alex gazed back at her, a deluge of emotions cascading across her features. "I'll be right outside if you need me."

"Of course, dear." The affectation rolled off her tongue without thought; this was a good thing, wasn't it? She remembered what to say.

When they'd gone, David urged her up. "Come, off the evil cot. Let's sit."

She followed him over to the two guest chairs in the clinic room. Though she'd never admit it to him, she was shocked when her legs remembered how to maneuver one foot in front of the other.

He sat opposite her, then leaned forward and grasped both her hands in his. "Be glad you only lost two weeks and not twenty-five years—" his breezy demeanor vanished "—no, that's not fair of me. I won't minimize a second of what you're going through right now. You feel as if your body isn't your own. You worry your limbs won't work properly. You wonder if you're a shell, a golem, a soulless imitation of yourself. You fear you'll dissolve away into dust the first time a breeze hits you."

She nodded wordlessly, and he brought their hands together between them. "I crossed planes of existence—entire universes—for you, Miri. I know you like no one else ever has, and I promise you here and now that none of it is true. You've come back to me, just as I came back to you. I also realize words won't make what you're experiencing magically go away. But know that when you feel like you're dissolving, I'll be here to keep you solid and real."

She gasped in air and struggled past threatening tears, because her previous self did not cry. God help her if this incarnation did. "Thank you. I'm certain I will be back to normal as soon as the disorientation passes."

"It'll be okay if you're not."

"No, it won't be." This time she drew in a suitably controlled breath and stood without assistance. "I want to see the recording of what happened on board the *Stalwart II*."

19

THE PRESIDIO
OPERATIONS WING

Blood and viscera splattered across the corridor outside Engine Control, and Miriam recoiled at the sight of the carnage. But she forced herself to continue watching, because her previous self was not squeamish, and these were people under her command dying.

The final minutes of the *Stalwart II* and her own life played out quickly after that, a blur of split-second decisions and the crushing rush of inevitability.

When the transmissions from Thomas finally ended, she steepled her hands at her chin and silently fought down waves of nausea. "It was the correct decision. It was the only decision. It was necessitated by a stupid, thoughtless earlier decision on my part that got my ship trapped in the first place, but once there, I had no other option."

"This was a brand new, never before seen tactic on the enemy's part. You had no way to know what the Rasu vessel was going to do."

"Yes, I *did*," she snapped. "It's called extrapolating from available knowledge on hand. Obviously a vessel made of shapeshifting metal can and likely will shapeshift into whatever the hell it wants to."

David gave her a patient expression and didn't try to reach for her. "Even so."

"Even so." She inhaled through her nose and willed herself calm. Her nerves felt frayed and prickly, as if they hadn't finished connecting yet. "Thomas, thank you for everything you did. I know the situation couldn't have been easy for you, either."

"We both performed to the best of our abilities in an impossible situation, Commandant."

The Artificial stalked the meeting room on the Presidio in the representation of a mighty lion. His backup was stored at Concord HQ—one of the many precious items David had been protecting during the coup attempt—but he must be experiencing his own somewhat shorter time gap, same as her.

"I've no doubt that you did, though I fear the same can't be said for me."

"Mom, don't beat yourself up. You were extraordinary."

She didn't look over at her daughter, who paced with jarring and disruptive intensity behind Thomas. "Alex, you are wonderful and talented in many ways, but you are not a qualified judge of military tactics in action. What about the crew?"

Thomas responded. "Eighty-eight percent of them are scheduled to undergo regenesis in the next few weeks. For evident reasons, you were first."

"Why only eighty-eight percent?"

"Two percent were found to have faulty imprints. This is still a new process for everyone involved, and there will be errors at times. The remaining ten percent had "No Regenesis" clauses in their wills."

"Oh." She'd been aware of some people, mostly but not all religious believers, adding such clauses to their wills once the news spread that the Regenesis Extension Project was being proclaimed a success for humanity. However, she'd been foolishly ignorant of the reality that this included members of her own crew. Death never stung so bitterly as when it could be conquered.

"I see. Let's review the memo I wrote."

Frustration appeared in the tight creases around David's eyes. "Why don't you slow down and absorb one thing at a time?"

"Thomas, the memo, please."

Thomas dutifully displayed the message she'd distributed minutes before blowing up her ship, and she read it twice before motioning for it to go away. "How are we supposed to do any of this?"

David offered up an encouraging smile. "We'll figure it out. We always do."

He was trying to keep her from getting upset. She'd permitted him the indulgence during the perilous first minutes of her reawakening, but she couldn't allow him to coddle her now. "That's not a good enough answer." Her gaze went to Alex, who she desperately wished would stop with the pacing. "Alex, what does Kennedy say about the seamless adiamene?"

"She's…working on it."

"Tell her to work faster. Has anyone prepared new engagement protocols for Rasu encounters? We can't allow our ships to be trapped in such a manner again." She exhaled harshly in disgust—at what, she couldn't say. "There's nothing in my new messages about such protocols. I need to get—"

David's hand landed firmly on her arm. "Miri, it's been a *polnyi pizdets* of a day. You might have just woken up from a nice, long nap, but we're all exhausted. Let's go home and get some rest. The Rasu can wait until tomorrow."

"And what if there is no tomorrow? What if they show up with an armada of millions and it all ends an hour from now?"

He took her by the shoulders, refusing to let her escape. "There will be a tomorrow, and one after that as well. I swear it to you. You need to give yourself time."

Behind David, Alex stood—finally not pacing—staring at her. Her face was an open book, displaying a turbulent mix of emotions but most of all frantic concern. Did her daughter think she was crazy? A broken facsimile of herself? Was she?

She closed her eyes and breathed in the slightly stale recycled air of the station…and longed for the crisp, cool air of the woods surrounding Buntzen Lake. "Okay. We'll go home. But I am back in my office at HQ by zero six hundred tomorrow."

"Whatever you want, Miri."

RW

EARTH

GREATER VANCOUVER

Miriam stood in a river of blood, sticky and viscous. It painted violent streaks along the corridor walls, where the edges dribbled down in a slow drip...drip...drip. The corridor glowed a florid crimson hue, for gore had splattered across the row lighting above.

She looked down to see a severed arm wash up against her foot as the river's current grew more forceful. She tried to step away, but her feet were stuck to the floor.

She couldn't move from this spot. Couldn't elude all this death.

From out of the blood swirling at her feet rose inky aubergine tentacles. They wrapped around her ankles and slithered up her legs. No matter how hard she fought them, their grip only tightened. She reached for the Daemon at her hip, only to find it had become a third tentacle winding around her waist. It squeezed, denying her air, as more tentacles reached her neck, then her face. Liquid metal poured into her ears, nose and finally her mouth.

"You think you are alive, but you are mistaken. You never left us. We will never let you escape—"

Miriam gasped in air, clawing at her throat in a desperate attempt to yank the tentacles free. But they were already inside of her and—

"Hey, hey."

She jerked away from resurgent tentacles, frantic to escape the Rasu's clutches, and fell onto a hard, dry surface. She was free! She scrambled backward, searching blindly for an exit—

Something strong gripped her shoulders. "Miri, wake up. You're safe."

She tried to free herself once more, but their grasp was too powerful. She blinked, then blinked again, grew cognizant of air reaching her lungs...and finally the blood-soaked walls faded away, replaced by moonlight-hued slate ones. Hardwood flooring beneath her.

David's gray eyes studying her in desperate concern, his hands warm on her bare shoulders.

She was at home. In her bedroom. Safe, just like he'd said.

She breathed in fresh, untainted air and let him wrap her up in his arms.

"It's okay, *dushen'ka*. I've got you. You were having a nightmare."

She buried her face in the crook of his neck and tried to calm her ricocheting pulse. She *was* safe. She'd stopped the Rasu from capturing her on the *Stalwart II*, at the temporary cost of her life. Yet she couldn't shake the vivid sensation of liquid metal slithering through her veins. *Be logical, Miriam! Do not let fear and hysterical panic destroy you.*

She drew back a little. "I was. Thank you."

"A bad one, I'd daresay."

"But it wasn't real."

"No, it wasn't. This is real." He took her hand and laid it flat on his chest. "Feel my heartbeat. Feel yours, and be here with me now."

20

CONCORD HQ
COMMAND

M iriam inspected the smooth surface of her desk and the way her fingers splayed comfortably across it. It was cool to the touch—had she ever noticed this before? Probably not, as she rarely took the time to notice those sorts of details. Always moving relentlessly forward, taking charge, imposing order, keeping things functioning, holding entropy at bay. Such had been her life's work.

But this was a new life now. Or was it? She still couldn't tell, and no one had written a guidebook to inform her. When David had returned, he'd certainly treated it as a new life. But he'd been gone for twenty-five years, whereas she'd lost a few short weeks. The Anadens, on the other hand, treated regenesis as no more consequential than a long night's sleep; they made no distinction between the 'before' and the 'after.'

The lost weeks shouldn't matter, as she could have just as easily been in a coma. No one questioned the continued authenticity of a person when they awoke from a coma, did they? Perhaps if she thought of her…intermission…in such a way, this would all begin to make sense.

It seemed like only yesterday that neural imprints were a mere scientific curiosity. People were born, lived and died. They held funerals and wakes for those lost; those rituals were painful and heart wrenching, but also cathartic and healing. In her heart, she was glad a day waited on the horizon when there would be no more funerals, no more goodbyes. But without death at its end, did life have meaning?

She sighed and pressed her fingertips to her forehead. If she didn't stop wearing a thousand-meter gaze and murmuring spiritual questions with no answers, more people than her were going to start questioning her authenticity. Behaving in such a manner was not her way, which was part of the problem. The very fact that she questioned the qualitative state and realness of her soul made her...question the qualitative state and realness of her soul. She'd maneuvered herself into a proper Gordian Knot now.

An alarm rang in her eVi to remind her of the first of many scheduled appointments today. The list of people who wanted an audience with her, either to express their happiness at her resurrection or to get a good gander at her and try to decide if she was the genuine article or a simple golem, was long. With inter-species fires raging on multiple fronts, she would not be allowed an opportunity to ease back into being alive. Which was for the best. The only way through was forward.

Dean Veshnael and Pointe-Amiral Thisiame were her first guests, and the easiest, for the Novoloume leaders were long accustomed to Anadens returning from the dead with regularity. In fact, they both hoped to join her in the experience one day, and given the success of the Novoloume part of the Regenesis Extension Project, they likely would.

Next came Pinchu, who mostly stared at her oddly, periodically shaking his head and muttering about how peculiar humans continued to be. But he'd been forced to accept greater impossibilities than resurrection in the last fourteen years, so after probing her with questions for a few minutes, he seemed to accept the situation and departed willing to take orders from her.

She appreciated the warmup the other leaders provided her, because now came the thorny part. Her professional relationship with Field Marshal Nolan Bastian had improved little in the last fourteen years, possibly deteriorating a bit after he was passed over for the AEGIS Fleet Admiral position in favor of Malcolm. It hadn't been her decision, not technically, but there was no question that her preference had carried great weight, and he knew it.

Now Malcolm was dead—properly so, unlike her—Bastian was the leader of humanity's military, and she had no choice but to make it work.

As the man strode into her office, she experienced a vivid flashback of her striding into Eleni Gianno's office to plan a counterinsurgency against her own government, and a wave of nostalgia washed over her. But Eleni wasn't here; because the woman had died fifteen years too early, she never would be.

Miriam stood and prepared herself to return the salute...that never came. Bastian regarded her warily as he took up a parade rest stance in the center of the office. "What do I call you now?"

"Commandant Solovy remains the order of the day."

"Does it? Has the Concord Senate confirmed your position yet?"

"They will meet later today to discuss the matter, but it is a mere formality. Here in Amaranthe, resurrection is a reality. I thought you understood this."

"Doesn't mean we're any good at it. Your daughter turns herself into a synthetic hybrid. Your husband magically returns from the afterlife. Now you blaze the trail of our newly minted regenesis miracle. I wonder...are any of you Solovys real?"

"Field Marshal, of all the people I desire to discuss philosophy, religion or metaphysics with, you aren't even on the list. If you have a qualm to voice, voice it."

"Hmm. Maybe you are the same as you were. Nevertheless, several of the AEGIS political representatives have concerns about your...situation. Senator Requelme has expressed her support for you, but she's not exactly in an ideal state of mind at present, so I'm not convinced the rest of us should follow her lead."

"If the political leaders of the Earth Alliance, Senecan Federation or IDCC wish to interrogate me, they are welcome to make an appointment to do so. Otherwise, everyone needs to stop gossiping and do their jobs. AEGIS does not possess the power to decide my status with Concord, and we are facing challenges on multiple fronts. We all have a great deal of work to do, and we should see about doing it."

"But AEGIS does have the power to decide whether to follow your orders."

She arched an eyebrow. "Oh, are you planning to follow the Anadens' lead and try to secede from Concord? Do you imagine you will defeat the Rasu on your own? Or the Savrakaths, for that matter?"

"Concord *is* humanity. I submit we have a great deal to say about who runs it."

"Field Marshal, do not do this. Do not make the Anadens' argument for them and bring everything we've built here crashing down. If we splinter apart now, we will all fall—to the Savrakaths, to the Rasu, to the next enemy on the horizon. Most of all, to our own failings."

He stared at her, intense eyes trying to peel back the layers of her skin and see if anything real existed on the inside, or if she was just an empty shell. Finally he nodded minutely. "I'll toe the line for now. But I will be watching you."

"When have you ever not? Thank you. Now, if there's nothing else, I am, as you noted, expected at the Senate shortly. Oh, and you'll be receiving a new strategic plan regarding Concord defenses and Rasu scenarios to review later today."

His head tilted a fraction. "Indeed."

When he'd left, she drew in a deep breath and closed her eyes. It was possible the verbal sparring had rekindled a tiny spark of fire in her belly. *Better.*

She should have some tea.

While she waited for a cup to brew, she sent a message to Kennedy Rossi requesting a meeting as soon as possible to discuss the details of building her a new ship—of building Concord a new flagship vessel, that was.

The response arrived as she brought the teacup to her lips, savoring the steamy aroma, just like she had a hundred thousand times in her life.

> *Commandant Solovy,*
> *I thought you knew. David commissioned you a new vessel less than an hour after the coup attempt was quelled. As such, it's*

already over twenty percent complete. There's still a little time to make interior changes, though, so let me know soon if you have any ideas for improvements over the old design. Oh, and welcome back!
—Kennedy Rossi
CEO, Connova Interstellar
Design Consultant, Concord Command

In the privacy of her office, Miriam laughed. Of course David had. He'd have realized she wouldn't be truly whole again until she could stand on the bridge of her ship. No Solovy was.

RW

Later in the evening, she sat in the conference room at the apex of Concord HQ with everyone she'd sent her report to in the final minutes of the Namino battle. The final minutes of her life. Thisiame, Pinchu, Richard, Kennedy, Alex, David. Everyone except Malcolm, which made for a stark reminder that she shouldn't whine even to herself about her struggles with rebirth. Bastian replaced Malcolm at the table; in the smallest boon, his demeanor suggested five percent less antagonism than he'd displayed this morning.

"Richard, thank you for acting so quickly to update Concord security protocols and for coordinating with SENTRI to do the same for AEGIS protocols. I don't believe the Rasu had an opportunity to obtain any Concord or AEGIS intel, but it's better to respond as if they did."

"Of course. The updates needed to happen in light of our Anaden problem in any event."

"Yes. While we face a lot of challenges in that arena, this meeting isn't about the 'Anaden problem.' We failed spectacularly in our first encounter with the Rasu. Platitudes will and have been given on how we couldn't have anticipated the nature and extent of their combat capabilities. This is undoubtedly true, but also irrelevant. We will face the Rasu again, as our alliance with the Asterion

Dominion stands. We failed them at Namino, and we can't let it happen a second time. We need to do better. Further, the Rasu now know we exist, and I expect they will come hunting for us."

Somber countenances ruled the table—except for David, who kept tamping down a smile while his eyes never left her. She loved him for it, but now wasn't the time for sentimentality. "So. Let's talk about weapons. Field Marshal?"

"We're working toward tripling the production capacity of negative energy weapons at the AEGIS Crux II Field Manufacturing Facility. Most AEGIS vessels are capable of launching negative energy missiles from any of their launch tubes, and frigates and larger vessels can carry a full loadout of them. We'll increase our supply of the weapons by two hundred percent for all standard patrols, to guard against the possibility of an unexpected Rasu encounter. In an expected one, by next week we should be able to increase the supply by an additional order of magnitude." He glanced around the table. "And of course, we are happy to provide the Khokteh and Novoloume militaries with a portion of our supply until they're able to ramp up their own production."

"Excellent. Thank you, Field Marshal. Now, let's talk about nukes. So long as the Rasu are located at least two megameters outside any planetary atmosphere or distant from any space station, I think long-range tactical fusion nuclear missiles should be our opening salvo in every encounter. Our shields will keep the resulting radiation from reaching crew members for the length of any practical encounter. This way we can hold the negative energy missiles in reserve for when we've closed to a range that makes nukes impractical. Does anyone disagree?"

A couple of uncomfortable looks were exchanged, but no one spoke up. Part of her was glad no one was leaping up to challenge her proclamation as to the color of the sky, but she didn't want them donning kid gloves, either. "Please, if anyone has concerns, I want to hear them."

Thisiame tilted his head in a ripple of iridescence. "I dislike nuclear weapons. They are dirty, crude instruments of destruction.

But I concede to the science. They will kill Rasu, which is what we must do."

"Yes, we must. Increasing the use of negative energy and nuclear weapons is the easy part, relatively speaking. What additional tools do we have in our arsenal, or need to add to it?"

Richard spoke up. "Special Projects is hard at work on iterative improvements to delivery mechanisms for all manner of negative energy explosives—"

"We don't need *iterative* improvements—we need new weapons. Weapons that give us a fighting chance against these...." She fought back a wave of frustration-induced vertigo. Why now? "Against this enemy. I'm sorry. I'm sure anything coming out of Special Projects to aid us in this fight will be most welcome. But I want them to think so far outside the box that there need not be a box at all."

"I'll pass along the recommendation. Devon and his people will rise to the challenge."

"I have every confidence they will." She was fairly certain this was what she would say in this situation, yes? "Next, we require new, comprehensive rules of engagement for our military forces to follow when facing the Rasu. Guidelines about when to run so as not to be..." her vision swam briefly "...captured. Instructions detailing what tactics are most successful on the battlefield and which ones most definitely are not. Rules for safe use of unconventional weaponry. I'll address these as time allows, but I want high-level bullet points distributed to all ship captains and fleet commanders immediately.

"Frankly, we need to approach space warfare from an entirely new angle if we want to entertain any hope of defeating the Rasu in combat. We need to reassess every assumption and examine every convention."

David cleared his throat and leaned forward slightly. "If I may? I realize I'm no longer active-duty military, but this sort of wargaming sounds right up my alley. Above and beyond all the strategizing the military leaders will be doing, I'd like to work on the project.

Then you all can review whatever I come up with. Toss out as much as you want and keep the rest."

"It's a good idea, and I...welcome your input." Too personal? Not everyone in the room was a friend. Rather than tie herself up in greater knots over a small slip in decorum, she forced herself to redirect her attention to the others around the table. "Ms. Rossi? What can you tell us about improving the security of our adiamene hulls? Can we make them seamless?"

Kennedy glared at the ceiling. "Adiamene by definition is seamless. The problem arises when parts of a ship have to move like gears. I'm working on modifying the ship designs to eliminate all unnecessary joints. We can also make more of the components out of adiamene—weapons housing, for instance.

"But the weapons themselves—the crystals, the rare earth elements, the lasers, the power supplies—are not adiamene, and this leaves an unbridgeable gap. Any module that needs to move, to open and close or change position, can't be seamless. It just...can't be. Now, we can write adaptive shield routines to reinforce the shields around any modular area, or on direct command—"

Alex stopped trying to bore a hole through Miriam's forehead with her stare to speak up for the first time. "What about the double shield the Machim Imperiums use? It's virtually impenetrable from the outside, yet allows the Imperium weapons to fire."

Miriam shook her head. "Unfortunately, no Imperiums fought at Namino to test the theory that it's impenetrable to Rasu incursions. But given that it *does* operate without any gaps, I have a hard time believing the Rasu will be able to slither through it."

Kennedy sighed. "I agree. But we've never been able to fully crack the shield's operation. The Anadens have spent the last fourteen years refusing to share the technology with us, and...."

"And I told you we weren't going to push them on it, because with adiamene on our side we didn't need the extra shielding. Perhaps that was a mistake, but it is what it is. Ms. Rossi, keep attacking the seams in our hulls, and I'll add to Special Projects' workload by asking them to strengthen our standard shields in every way they can engineer. We haven't needed to rely on shields for a long time, but now we must do so once again."

R̪W

After the military leaders and Kennedy had departed, Miriam gave David, Alex and Richard an honest, weary smile. "One hurdle cleared."

"You were perfect." David reached over and squeezed her hands atop the table. "Kennedy said your new ship will be ready in a week or so. What are you going to call her?"

"I hadn't really considered it. The *Stalwart II* redux? *Stalwart III*, I suppose? If that isn't getting too absurd."

David snorted. "'Stalwart' my ass. We might as well have called them 'ships that blow up Solovys.' I say it's time for a new name."

She chuckled lightly, and it elevated her mood so much she decided she should try to do more of it. Alex, though, regarded her in abject horror. She should tell her daughter that she wasn't a glass figurine who would shatter at the slightest touch. And she would do so as soon as she was confident of it herself.

"You may have a point. I'll think on it."

Richard had been sitting there unusually quietly; he'd refused to joke with David, or so much as look at him…and she did not have the mental bandwidth to consider why this might be. "Richard, what do you have for me on the Anadens?"

"Ferdinand and his *elasson* friends are holed up at the Kyvern Primor's former compound on Epithero. He's got twenty-five to thirty *elassons* on-site, though we can't rule out the possibility that additional supporters are situated elsewhere. Still, it appears his supporters number less than half of the *elassons*, and all indications are it's not going great for him so far. To the surprise of no one at this table, the *elassons* are bickering with one another over how to proceed. So far, they haven't decided on a clear direction for their rebellion."

"How do you know all of this?"

"I'm a spy, remember?"

"I do. However, that is not an answer."

"The aide to one of the Kyvern *elassons*, Taiv ela-Kyvern, was an anarch. Because he acted as a mole for Sator Nisi, none of the *elassons* ever found out he was an anarch. Now, he works for CINT on the side as an informant."

"Brilliant. What's Casmir's status?"

"He's being held in...I'd call it 'house arrest.' He's not restrained in a cell, but he doesn't have much freedom of movement and he hasn't been allowed to participate in the strategy sessions. My informant believes he's refusing to take part in any actions taken against Concord interests."

Miriam exhaled in relief. It hadn't always been easy to deal with the man, but truth be told, Casmir's betrayal would have stung. "With multiple Machim *elassons* on Ferdinand's side, they're dangerous from a military perspective. We should keep the alert levels at all facilities at their current heightened level. Meanwhile, we'll take advantage of their indecision to strengthen the security and solidarity of Concord institutions..." rhythmic nods answered her every word, and she paused to huff a breath "...which you all have already been hard at work doing in my absence. Forgive me. I owe you everything."

David reached across the table to squeeze her hands again. He was indulging in physical affection too often, but she couldn't bring herself to stop him. Not yet. "We were just doing what we could to try to protect everything you've built."

"Everything *we've* built. Okay. I'm confident we can respond to and defeat any attacks on Concord citizens or property, but this conflict is about more than who has the stronger military. What can we do to destabilize Ferdinand's rebellion before it gets its sea legs and begins to disrupt basic Concord functions?"

ASTERION DOMINION

21

NAMINO
CAMP BURROW

Marlee sat cross-legged on the floor opposite Xyche'ghael. The Taiyok was idly weaving a thick, coarse material into a rope with his hands while he entertained her inquiries and let her practice her Taiyoken.

"Do many Taiyoks live on Asterion worlds?"

"A few thousand have chosen to settle on their planets. The majority who have done so came here, to Namino. The climate and the work done here suit us."

"It's honorable for so many of you to serve as ambassadors to your ally."

The Taiyok made a low, rumbling sound deep in his throat. "Some, yes. Others are not viewed as such."

She sensed she'd hit on a touchy topic, but as usual, her mouth moved faster than her brain. "Is this why you dug the tunnels? Because not every Asterion wants to run into Taiyoks on the street?"

Xyche stared at her sharply. "Your young eyes see much, *laiti'manu*. It is not quite so... 'cut and dried,' I believe is the phrase. Less that some don't want to run into us, more that we do not enjoy enduring their open gaping and inconsiderate curiosity. Our culture is not theirs, but most Asterions have never bothered to learn anything of our practices or traditions."

"What a shame. I find alien cultures fascinating, and I can't imagine ignoring the culture of your neighbor and ally." Xyche merely lifted his folded wings in a shrug of sorts, which probably meant he'd said everything he intended to on the subject. "Do you miss home?"

"Every day. To sail amongst the towering forests and alight upon their limbs amid the falling dusklight? But it is not to be. I cannot go home."

"What do you mean, you can't?"

His compound eyes reflected the harsh light of the bunker like a prism, while revealing nothing of the thoughts hidden behind them. "That is a tale I will reserve for a later time."

"I understand. I didn't mean to pry."

"Hey." Joaquim showed up to crouch beside them. "Xyche, we can take the tunnels all the way to the Curio Market, can't we?"

"Indeed."

"Great. One of the drones did a fly-by of the sector, and the Rasu haven't bombed out the Market yet. I want to raid it for supplies—the sort of supplies your shop offers."

"Offered, I believe you mean."

"Yeah, sorry. But all isn't lost if we can put your inventory to good use."

Xyche set aside his rope-in-progress. "I accept this logic. What do you have in mind?"

"Disguises and traps. I was thinking…there's no reason why morph tech won't work on the Rasu, right? It manipulates EM waves, which has to be what they use to 'see.'"

"Joaquim, appearing to be someone other than yourself will not save you from the Rasu. They do not care what you look like."

"I *know*. I was thinking of disguising inanimate objects—drones, light poles, benches, whatever—as Asterions to draw Rasu in. Then we spring a trap and shred them into tiny metal pieces."

Marlee piped up in interest at the notion of fileted Rasu. "Shred them using what?"

"Improvised bombs packed with archine blades and an electrical blast."

"Ooh, sounds awesome. Do we have enough blades?"

Joaquim laughed. "I am shocked to report that Panetier has agreed to send out scouting parties to the rest of the bunkers. If they find people, excellent. If they don't, they'll bring back the food and other supplies stored there—especially archine blades. We should have hundreds by tomorrow." He nodded at Xyche. "So what do you say? Permission to raid your shop?"

The Taiyok exhaled ponderously, the soft feathers at his neck ruffling as if disturbed by a non-existent breeze. "Granted."

RW

BENEATH NAMINO ONE

The maze of underground tunnels was turning out to be far more extensive than Marlee had initially appreciated. The bunkers were built off the tunnels at strategic locations tied to surface access, but the passageways themselves wound beneath the entire city.

With her eVi's positioning system down, she reluctantly admitted—only to herself—that she was completely lost five minutes into the trek to this Curio Market. Thankfully, she wasn't the navigator. Selene had a map of the tunnel network and locations of all the bunkers; she was able to project it in the air so everyone else could view it, but without quantum communications she had no way to share it more permanently.

Xyche may or may not possess a similar map, but he moved through the tunnels with the confidence of one who had trod them many times before.

How odd, for winged creatures who could soar among the clouds to choose to travel these dark, claustrophobic paths buried beneath the bedrock of a world.

She thought about Xyche's enigmatic explanation, and decided to seek out the other side of the story. As the tunnel curved to the left, she slowed her steps to fall in beside Grant. "Is it true the Taiyoks used these tunnels to get around the city?"

"That's the rumor."

A bit of annoyance flared, as yet again he was giving her a flippant, evasive answer. "But is it true?"

"For the most part, yes."

"But why? Before the attack began, it looked as if there was a perfectly functional street, levtram and shuttle network on the surface."

"The Taiyoks are naturally secretive creatures. They prefer to operate in shadow rather than light. And, truth be told, the Taiyoks here on Namino haven't exactly integrated into our society. Officially, we are allies all day long. And we are. But our cultures don't meld well. I suspect many Taiyoks are more comfortable using the tunnels than enduring the stares of the people."

On this much, it appeared Xyche and Grant agreed. "It's horrible how they've felt compelled to hide."

"That's life—imperfect. Don't you have a bunch of species living together in Concord? Are their cultural idiosyncrasies all treated with equal respect?"

She wanted to snap back with a snarky response, but it was a childish desire, and she was doing everything in her power to convince Grant—and the others, of course—that she was not a child. "It's a complicated question. Us humans didn't know *any* aliens until fifteen years ago, when we encountered the Kats. Then we got dumped—in the best way possible—into the middle of an ancient, flourishing society comprised of dozens of species. So for many humans, all the aliens are weird and incomprehensible, but they're kind of all equally so? Except for the Efkam. They're weirder and more incomprehensible than the rest. But they're glowing gelatinous blobs, so."

Grant chuckled. "So they would be. Sure. But you don't act nonplussed in the slightest by the Taiyoks."

"Well, I work for the Consulate. Interacting with aliens is sort of my job. And I always wanted to do it, from the time I was a little girl. Each species is fascinating in its own way, and I—"

Joaquim and Xyche came to an abrupt stop at the front of the procession, and she could practically hear Joaquim scowling. "Are we here? I don't see a way up."

"Yes." Xyche walked straight into a solid stone wall—and through it.

Joaquim laughed. "Nice camouflage!" He motioned them forward. "Through the stone, everyone."

The stone wasn't actually there, obviously. It was some sort of projection, though Marlee discerned no equipment powering it, and it provided no resistance when she stepped through it. On the other side was a lift built into the earth.

Joaquim gathered the group around him at the lift. "Standard high-risk operating procedure once we're above. Assume Rasu could be anywhere, so stay quiet and move carefully. Grant, you know the type of materials we'll need and you're familiar with the Market layout, so you and Marlee investigate the other shops. Ava, go with them and watch their backs. Xyche and I will empty out his shop, Selene and Dominic will stand guard and keep an eye on the horizon, and we'll meet back at the lift in fifteen minutes."

No one voiced any objections, and once Joaquim gave the all-clear, they followed him up the lift.

It felt like ascending into a well-preserved tomb. No lights brightened the hallways of the building, and since they were above-ground they didn't dare risk using lights themselves. Everything was cast in dull flint and muted amber. The halls were wide and tall—again, Taiyok construction—and a dry wind wafted in through jagged holes in the exterior façade. She didn't see any windows...they could have all been blown out, but given what Grant had said about the Taiyoks, the most likely conclusion was that the Curio Market contained none.

The odor of rotting flesh greeted them when they rounded the first corner, and her hand reflexively came to her mouth. A few meters ahead, the shadowy outline of a Taiyok corpse lay sprawled beneath broken chunks of wall, its wings spread wide, as if it had been preparing to take flight. She hurriedly turned down her olfactory receptors and gave the body a wide berth.

Grant took her hand in his, which was *nice*, and guided her through a doorway on the left, while Ava took up a defensive position at the door. What minimal light had existed in the hallway from the moonlight vanished, pitching them into near-total darkness. She increased the infrared filter in her ocular implant, so she was at least able to make out the outlines of furniture and equipment.

Grant appeared to be able to see a lot better—she shouldn't really be surprised—as they moved to a floor-to-ceiling stack of drawers along the back wall. He set his bag on the floor and opened it up, then studied the drawers for a moment before pointing up and to the right. He leaned in close to her ear to whisper, sending a tingle racing up her spine. "Empty the second, fourth and fifth drawers from the right, third row from the top."

It was with a great deal of reluctance that she stepped away from him and started opening drawers. As near as she could tell in the dark, they held fibers, wires and small objects of unknown use.

Her bag was half full when Ava backed into the room, her gun arm trained on the door. Grant grabbed Marlee's arm and dragged her behind Ava; Marlee leaned out to peek around the tall woman's shoulder.

Beyond the door and a gaping hole across the hallway, two aerial drone-looking Rasu cruised past. Their darting violet irises crisscrossed the landscape before swinging around to sweep over the Market.

Marlee held her breath, every muscle frozen, as the beams passed over the broken structure…and kept going.

She sensed Grant relax beside her as he picked up his bag. "Finish emptying those drawers, then we should go, before they decide they need to investigate more closely."

22

NAMINO
CAMP BURROW

The trip back to the bunker passed in silence, as the roving Rasu drones and decomposing Taiyok corpses had everyone a little rattled. Once they were again ensconced behind their camouflaged door, Grant and Joaquim dumped the spoils of the field trip out on one of the workstations and sorted the items into piles in preparation for building some bombs.

Curious about what the design and assembly of an Asterion bomb entailed, Marlee leaned against the wall a meter away and watched them work. She had a thousand questions, but she'd learned that Joaquim got cranky if you peppered him with inquiries while he was working on a project. It wasn't a problem. She could figure out most of what they were doing by careful observation.

Abruptly a rapping noise resounded from the other side of the door, and Selene, Joaquim and Ava instantly had weapons in their raised hands as they cautiously approached the door. Grant nudged her and several other people into the hallway and out of line-of-sight of the door. A hush fell over the bunker.

As Marlee understood it, the code for the doors and how to access them had been widely shared among the residents of Namino in the hours before the invasion, but it was conceivable that someone hadn't received all the necessary information. Also, a Rasu wouldn't bother to knock, right?

She positioned herself at the front of the hallway and peeked around the corner in time to see Joaquim jerk a nod to Selene. The woman approached the door, reached in from the side and opened it, then quick-stepped back to train her weapon on the opening.

A deep voice murmured something unintelligible, and a man half-covered in blood and soot stepped through—

—her heart dropped straight through her chest as she leapt out of the hallway and shoved past Grant into the open space. "*Caleb?*"

The instant his gaze landed on her, he rushed forward, and she let herself be swept up into his embrace. "You're alive."

"I am," she mumbled into his neck. He was squeezing her almost as hard as Pinchu did, and she wiggled in protest until he set her down. "What are you *doing* here?"

He regarded her with shining sapphire eyes and a big smile. "Rescuing you, of course."

"What?" Her hand came to her mouth to fail at muffling a sob. Why was she crying? She laughed as tears streamed down her face. "You...." Then she was in his arms again, and it sure sounded like he was crying, too.

"I was coming for you when all the wormholes shut down, and I had to take the long way instead. I'm sorry it took me so long to get to you." He pulled back to hold her at arm's length. "Are you hurt?"

"No." She shook her head roughly. "I mean, I was, but Grant and Selene and the others took care of me. I'm fine now. But what about you? You're covered in blood."

A shadow passed across his features, and he shrugged with forced mildness. "Had a few Rasu encounters on the way here. Nothing too bad."

Given his state, she shuddered to think of what a 'bad' encounter would entail. She suddenly noticed Grant, Joaquim, Selene, Ava and half the occupants of the bunker gathered a respectful distance away ogling them. She choked out a teary laugh and gestured to the room. "Everyone, this is my Uncle Caleb. He came to find me, because he's a badass."

Caleb wiped his cheeks with the back of his hand and offered a general nod to the room. "Thank you all very much for taking Marlee in and looking after her. I, um...." His voice trailed off and his face blanched, almost as if he were seeing a ghost.

She swallowed back renewed sobs and motioned him over toward a free couch. "Come, sit. Do you want water? You must. Food? You look exhausted. And, again, very bloody. We have a shower, too, whenever you want to get cleaned up."

"It's been...yeah." He eased down onto the couch. "In a minute. Sit with me first. Tell me what happened to you."

RW

After spending twenty minutes listening to and trying to absorb Marlee's story, which was alternately astounding and surprisingly mundane, Caleb finally stood to stretch and take her up on her offer of food...which was when he realized the numbness had faded, and his left arm hurt like a son of a bitch.

He didn't want to take the medwrap off in front of her, though, so he needed a distraction. "How about some of that food you mentioned? Now that I've finally stopped moving, I'm famished."

"You bet." She stood, then frowned darkly. "You *did* get injured!"

He glanced at his arm; the ragged hole in his shirt revealed part of the medwrap and a fresh trickle of blood. "It's nothing. Merely a scratch."

She studied him suspiciously for another few seconds before disappearing down a hallway on the opposite side of the bunker from the door. Once she was gone, he dug into his pack and retrieved a more robust medwrap before removing the existing one from his arm. In the bright lighting of the bunker, he was able to take in the full extent of the singed flesh, torn tendons and glimpses of bone. He didn't see any signs of infection, but normally a wound such as this one would be well on its way to knitting itself together by now.

He checked the medical readout from his eVi while he secured the new medwrap. It insisted the wound *was* healing, but at a regular human rate at best. In other words, Akeso was not currently pitching in. He rubbed at his jaw. *Fine, then. Just pout.*

"Here you go." Marlee stood over him, offering him some sliced chicken and cheese on rye bread.

She looked so fantastic—all her limbs attached and unmarred, her hair wild with untamed curls and her eyes dancing with vivacity. He allowed himself to relax a little bit. Only for a minute.

He accepted the sandwich from her and patted the seat beside him.

She plopped down on the couch, but instantly zeroed in on his re-bandaged arm. "Are you sure you're not badly hurt?"

"I am. But it is ugly out there."

"Oh, I know. Joaquim let me go with them on a supply raid to the Curio Market this evening. It was intense."

He hunted around for the man she'd earlier identified as Joaquim, a righteous tirade poised on his lips…but he let it go for now. He wasn't going to be the grumpy uncle who was no fun at parties—or insurgencies.

"Then I'm glad you made it back here safely. We'll stay here for a few more hours—I admit I could use a nap—then head out. Darkness will provide us some added cover, and if things go well, we can reach the Ghost by sunrise."

Her eyes hooded, and she gazed deliberately around the bunker before returning her focus to him. She reached out to grasp his free hand, and her shoulders rose. "I'm staying."

"You're…*what?*" He hurriedly set the plate on the floor and turned all his attention to her. "No. I came all this way just to save you. This is a deadly warzone—a bloody killing field—and we need to get home."

"I know it is. I know we do. But these people? They're facing what seem like insurmountable odds, but they've been wonderful to me anyway. They need help—they need *your* kind of help, or else this cavern is going to become their grave. We can't leave them to that fate."

"I sympathize with them. With everyone on this planet, believe me, I do. But Marlee, be reasonable. What about your mother? She thinks you could be dead. And if we stay here for much longer, she might be right."

"Mom." Marlee let go of his hand to cover her face. "I realize she's worried sick, and I feel *horrible* about it. But a couple of days won't change our eventual happy reunion for her, while they can make all the difference for these people."

"A couple of days? I don't think the Rasu are planning on leaving anytime soon."

"We—they, but also with my input—have been trying to pin down the source of the quantum blocking field. If we can zero in on it, Joaquim wants to mount a mission to take it out. Then we can call in the cavalry."

"Marlee, I'm not certain there *is* a cavalry. The battle wiped out the Asterion fleet and cut a huge swath through the Khokteh, Novoloume and Taiyok fleets."

Selene had hinted at the same thing, but Marlee had chosen not to believe it. "Pinchu?"

"He's alive and still in command."

"Whew. And the AEGIS ships held out, didn't they?"

"Sort of." He hadn't wanted to break the news to her. He chose to believe that back home, Miriam had by now woken up well, whole and completely her old self. But here on a besieged planet, where thirty meters over their heads a cold and callous enemy laid waste to a civilization, it no longer seemed inevitable.

"What is it?"

He forced himself to meet her gaze. "The Rasu learned how to squeeze through cracks in our adiamene hulls. During the battle, they boarded several AEGIS vessels."

"Boarded! What happened?"

"The AEGIS vessels self-destructed to prevent the Rasu from taking prisoners or gaining vital Concord intel."

"What aren't you telling me?"

"The *Stalwart II* was one of those vessels. Your Aunt Miriam—"

Marlee fell back with a gasp. "She didn't—is she—"

"Going to wake up in a new body via regenesis. I expect she already has by now. She'll be fine. I'm certain of it."

"Oh no! Poor Gramps. And Alex...I can't even imagine what they've been suffering through. But you..." she regarded him oddly "...you left them to come here and search for me anyway?"

"I did. I love you, and I will always come to rescue you. No matter what."

She reached out and hugged him, inadvertently squeezing his wound. He didn't care; he'd take this kind of pain any day. "I love you, too. I'm sorry if I've been a bitch to you recently."

He chuckled. "Neither of us has been the best versions of ourselves lately. I forgive you. Will you forgive me?"

"Of course I will. I...." She drew back to stare at him somberly. "Gosh, this is so hard for me to say. But here it is: I'm still staying. I hope you will, too."

"I'm not leaving without you, but—"

"I know all your 'buts' before you say them. And you're not wrong on any of them. I feel awful about what I'm putting Mom through, and Gramps, and Alex, and Mia—oh god I bet I am totally fired now—and I desperately hope Aunt Miriam is all right. But this has become my fight, too, and I can't abandon it now. Please join me in it."

He dropped his head into his hands. As strong as he'd made the wall between them, Akeso still roiled through his veins with renewed outrage and despair. He didn't blame his esoteric companion. Could he do it? Could he go back out there on the streets and fight these creatures? Could he do it and keep Marlee alive as well?

He felt as if he were being ripped apart from the inside out. He needed Alex, so badly. She was his center, his soul, his lodestar, and he was utterly lost without her. He needed Akeso, needed to subsume himself in its peaceful nurturing. He needed to protect Marlee from this vicious, cruel enemy...

...but she needed him to believe in her.

He took in the hopeful, pleading yet defiant expression animating her features, and admitted to himself that maybe he had the wrong of it. She was brave, and giving, and hardheaded...and not a child any longer. She hadn't been whimpering in a dark corner since being trapped here; she'd taken up the fight alongside these people. She was strong, talented and fierce. He *did* need to protect her, but maybe the best way for him to do that was by teaching her. By guiding her into her strengths and helping her become the woman she was determined to be.

He wished the training ground wasn't an active warzone. He wished he were better prepared for this trial, wished Akeso understood why he needed to make *this* choice. But here they were. He nodded slowly. "If you insist, we'll stay. But there will be rules."

She grabbed him in a bear hug. "Thank you! Yeah, sure, rules, whatever. Thank you."

"And as soon as the quantum block is down, we're going home."

"Yep. More or less."

"Marlee? It's called compromise."

"Right." She tried to look serious. "We'll set that as a goal, okay?"

He threw his hands in the air. "*Okay.* Now, if we're staying, I should shower and get cleaned up. Then I think you'd better introduce me properly to the people in charge."

23

NAMINO
NAMINO ONE

P arc Eshett pressed against the alley wall so hard he'd probably sink into it and disappear if the molecules would simply give way and allow him passage. Which would be better—better than dying to the Rasu for the second time, better even than the suffocating terror of trying to stay alive on the streets of Namino One.

His left leg shrieked in pain at his slight movement, and he glanced down to see renewed rivulets of blood seeping out of the wound and cutting trails over his knee. He'd tried suppressing all the pain receptors in his leg earlier, then had promptly fallen on his ass, which served only to tear open the gash yet wider. Apparently the damage was so extensive that cutting off the pain receptors also cut off fine motor control. This left him with a couple of choices, none of them ideal: suffer in breathtaking agony, risk destroying his leg entirely and rendering himself completely immobile, or give up, huddle on the ground and wait to die.

When the Rasu had appeared above Namino, he'd been delving the Makers Market for dyne components, trying to put together a kind of...gearhead gift basket for Ryan as an apology. Thanks to his twin on Mirai, he'd known about the attack long before the Rasu breached the atmosphere and began blowing the city up. But because he was an idiot, he hadn't fled for safety. No, he'd continued fucking *shopping*. And by the time the ships showed up in the city to wreak their havoc, it was too late to escape.

He'd holed up in a series of seemingly safe harbors that inevitably lost their status as the Rasu rampaged across the city. With every move, he saw fewer survivors; it had now been half a day since he'd come across any living Asterion. The injury to his leg had happened while he caught a fitful few hours of sleep inside an abandoned light manufacturing plant. He'd awakened to the high-pitched scream of a Rasu laser beam cutting through the walls. The beam missed him, but a giant shard of glass fell from a window above him to impale his left thigh. The artery shut itself off before he bled to death in the first five minutes, and he'd fashioned a tourniquet out of his shirt, but his leg was a ruined mess.

The heavy thuds of bipedal Rasu footsteps grew louder on the street outside, and he held his breath, willing himself not to flinch. A shadow overtook the alley entrance, a harbinger of two Rasu striding by the opening with all the grace of hauler dynes. Then they were gone.

Air escaped through pursed lips in a weak, narrow stream until his lungs were empty. He waited for another one…two…three seconds, then gulped in fresh air and sank down the wall to the ground.

The next thing he knew, he was hyperventilating. The harsh, antiseptic lights of the Rasu lab strobed through his mind. Whirring tools of torture descending from above to slice into him—

Get it together, man. The surest way to get himself killed by the Rasu for the second time was to panic. Damn but he wanted to panic, and the struggle to wrestle his pulse under control left him exhausted.

He'd seen people get taken prisoner, rounded up by roving gangs of Rasu and herded onto transports that soon breached the clouds and vanished. He comprehended full well what awaited the prisoners at the destination. He *couldn't* suffer through that again. So he vowed not to allow himself to get captured. If such a moment arrived, he'd self-destruct his OS and suicide.

Honestly, he should just go ahead and suicide now, right? His memories and experiences were synced in real-time with his Plex twin, so this incarnation could be created again easily enough.

But some deep-seated and little-used sense of honor and duty—likely Ryan's fault—stopped him. He might be the only functioning Plex with presences on both Namino and Mirai. One instance had a front-row seat to the attack and, in theory, should be able to relay the situation on the ground, and the other instance had a free pass into the halls of power at the Initiative. He needed to tell someone what was happening here, even though it would mean revealing his Plex secret and facing the consequences of doing so. Which was going to suck.

The sound waves from a distant explosion boomed off the narrow walls of the alley. The explosions were getting more infrequent, so perhaps the Rasu were mostly done blowing shit up. Now they were crawling through the wreckage and carting away anything that was still intact. Learning all the Asterions' secrets. Their strengths and, more importantly, their weaknesses.

He made for a crappy spy, though, considering how he could hardly move. His OS worked overtime to manage the wound and speed up the healing process, but then he kept insisting on walking on it and bollocksing everything up. With all the soot and dirt and death hanging thick in the air, the gaping hole in his leg was already infected beyond his OS's ability to treat it. He needed shelter—shelter that managed to stay standing for longer than a few hours.

The Initiative had prepared a series of underground bunkers around the city as part of Project Guerilla, but damned if he knew where any of them were. Beneath DAF Command seemed like one possibility, or beneath the central transit hub, or Namino Tower. But they'd been working with existing tunnels and the surrounding geography, so it was more likely the bunkers were located wherever the underground environment cooperated. When the attack had begun, the public nex web had broadcast all sorts of instructions, including directions to numerous bunkers...but he'd suffered an instant PTSD-induced panic attack and hadn't paid attention to the details.

So now here he sat, busted up and bleeding in an alley somewhere in the southwestern region of the besieged city.

He wasn't going to last much longer out here. It was time to go fess up and share what he knew, and maybe get some directions to a shelter in return.

24

MIRAI
MIRAI ONE

Parc tried for the third time to stand up from the couch; when asked to support his weight, however, his left leg immediately buckled. He frantically grasped for the arm of the couch for support, then fell back onto the cushions.

This was ridiculous! His body was perfectly functional and undamaged.

But his mind refused to accept it. Overwhelmed by the pain and debilitating injury bleeding across linked kyoseil strings from his *other* body, his brain was busily transferring those electrical signals to this body. Maybe Asterion brains weren't as adept at multithreading disparate experiences as he'd once thought. He could certainly use a little separation about now, but there was no ceraff to disconnect from—he *was* the ceraff.

He closed his eyes, scrunched up his face and tried again to stand. *You are fully capable of walking. So walk, dammit!*

Pain shot through his left thigh as he took a step forward, but he *did* take a step forward. Then another—

—the sound of the door to the warehouse apartment opening distracted him, and his other consciousness surged forward to overwhelm his present mind and send him crashing to the floor beside the couch.

"I just came by to get a couple of—gods, Parc, what's wrong?"

He peered up to see Ryan hurrying across the apartment to his side. Ryan hadn't been here in days, having vacated in a huff over Parc's continued Plex antics, and all his messages to the man had gone unanswered. Despite the absurd circumstances, he was thrilled to see his onetime lover's face. "Here you are, finding me a crumpled disaster on the floor yet again."

"You should probably stop doing stupid shit that turns you into a crumpled disaster on the floor, then."

"Yep."

"Are you hurt? I don't see any blood or jutting bones."

"No. Yes. I mean...."

"Oh." Ryan stood, took a step back and crossed his arms over his chest. "Another version of you is hurt, is that it?"

Parc shrugged weakly. "I'm afraid so. On Namino. The Rasu—"

My chest is flayed open, the folds of skin held back by clamps. The cavity revealed glows hot like steel fresh out of a kiln. But I can't peer inside at my own insides, because my head is locked in place by something hard and unyielding. My eyelids are held open by more unforgiving clamps. My eyes are dry, scratchy, sandpaper scraping over unfinished wood. I haven't blinked in...I can't say.

Time has blended together into an endless series of brief respites between the pain.

He grimaced through the flaring memory, pressing his fingertips to his temples until the worst of it faded away.

Ryan propped against the arm of the couch. "Well, shit."

"Listen, I know you're angry at me, and I know I don't have any right to ask for your help. But I need to get to the Initiative, and it doesn't look like I'm making it there on my own. I have information Nika will want to hear."

"Why don't you simply send her a message?"

"Because it's a lot of information, and it's complicated, and there's a chance I can become an ongoing conduit for information between the siege on Namino and the Advisor Committee. But to do it, I've got to stay alive there, and to stay alive there I need shelter. And I don't have a clue where the underground bunkers are."

"So you need someone at the Initiative to tell you where to go. I knew it would all come down to you saving your own ass."

He hated the acrimony in Ryan's voice, hated how badly he'd fucked this whole thing up. "That's not fair. The best way for me to save my own ass would be to straight up die on Namino. But I'm staying alive, despite being in intense physical pain and suffering panic attacks every ten minutes in *both* bodies, entirely so I can be that conduit between worlds."

Ryan stared at him intently, suspicion and distrust darkening his normally quite handsome features. Finally he rolled his eyes at the ceiling. "All right, I'll help you get to the Initiative, but I'm not doing it for you. I'm doing it for all the other people trapped on Namino. For Joaquim and Ava and Dominic and everyone else."

It wasn't the answer he'd wanted, but under the circumstances it might be a better one than he deserved. "Good enough. Thank you."

Ryan crouched beside him, wrapped an arm underneath his left shoulder and helped him stand. "I'm not carrying you, either. I'll keep you from falling on your face every five meters, but you're going to have to put one foot in front of the other and walk."

RW

OMOIKANE INITIATIVE

"Dashiel, did you hear what I said?"

He jerked his attention back to Nika and offered her an apologetic shrug. "I'm sorry."

"What's on your mind? Other than the obvious, I mean."

"Merely trying to think my way into a solution that will keep the Rasu out of our ships. Somehow. What was it you were saying?"

"Miriam Solovy is back among the living over in Concord, which is good news. They've squashed the Anadens' coup attempt for the time being, though the instigators are still on the loose...."

A minor commotion at the lift drew her attention away, and she looked up in time to see Parc and Ryan stumble into the

Initiative. Ryan appeared to be actively holding Parc upright while Parc sweated profusely, his face a worrying ashen.

She leapt up and hastened over to the lift, nudging past several people to reach them. "Here, let's get him to a chair." She grabbed Parc's free arm, and together she and Ryan eased him down at one of the cubicles.

He collapsed into the chair in visible relief. "Thanks."

She studied him in concern, noting the complete absence of blood or burns. "What's wrong? I don't see any open wounds."

"He doesn't have any."

She glanced at Ryan, taken aback by the dry acerbity in his tone. "Then what happened? Parc, did you catch another virutox?"

"Very funny." Parc pushed himself up higher in the chair and grasped onto the lip of the desk for support. "I have a confession to make."

RW

Nika dropped her chin onto her hand. "Of *course* you're a Plex. If anyone in the Dominion would be a Plex, it would be you. I should have guessed it instantly."

"Yeah, yeah. Lecture me if you want, but trust me, I am reaping what I bloody sowed right now."

Behind Parc, Ryan snorted. She vaguely remembered Perrin mentioning something about the two of them going through a rough spot, but then the Rasu had attacked and all other considerations had faded to the background.

She leaned forward to focus on Parc. "Because you're once again trapped by the Rasu?"

"My own personal hell on an endless loop. Good times."

"I'm sorry, Parc."

"No, I most decidedly brought it on myself. But why don't we table my just desserts for a little while and concentrate on more important things, like the situation on Namino?"

She leapt up so dramatically her chair tumbled over. "No."

He frowned in confusion. "Um, okay, but—"

"I mean, no, the specifics of the situation on Namino aren't the most important thing about you being here while also being there. Don't you see? This means kyoseil can circumvent the quantum block."

Parc and Ryan's unexpected arrival had attracted the notice of several of the Advisors, and a small group had gathered around the cubicle to hear his tale of woe. Adlai was one of them, and now he shook his head. "But we don't think it can. We've tried to contact Selene through the Justice Advisors' ceraff multiple times. We tried several others as well. No one we know was on Namino is answering."

Parc shrugged. "Maybe they're all dead, because let me tell you, there are a fuckton of people dead on Namino."

Nika flinched away. She wanted to bury her face in the crook of Dashiel's shoulder and weep for hours, but instead she forced herself to project strength she did not feel. Parc's duty here was to tell the unvarnished truth, and her duty was to weather that truth and find a way to turn the information into a plan. "Or maybe it's something else. Maybe only connections between the *same* kyoseil are strong enough to get through the block. A normal ceraff is simply a central connection point for different people to temporarily join, but Parc is literally the same person both here and there. A Plex kyoseil link must be much, much stronger."

"It makes sense. My link is definitely…" Parc winced "…strong. So I'll be your conduit for so long as I can stay alive on Namino. I might last longer if you would be so kind as to point me toward one of the underground bunkers."

"Adlai?"

"We can do that. I'll pull up the map now. The question is, Parc, do you know where *you* are?"

The muscles around his eyes tightened, and for a second he looked as if he was about to pass out. "Near Cornwall and Leeds. I've been trying to make my way toward DAF Command."

"Good. You've got about nine hundred meters to go to reach the nearest tunnel entrance."

"Is that all? Piece of cake." His head lolled onto his chest; he wrenched it back up.

Nika took both his hands in hers. "You can do it. I believe in you." *Please, Parc. I desperately need to know there are people alive in those bunkers.*

25

MIRAI
OMOIKANE INITIATIVE

They had barely gotten Parc situated in a makeshift enclave in a relatively quiet corner of the Initiative when the air around Nika brightened via the introduction of a thousand points of light. She took a second to muse to herself how this war had driven her to consort with strange bedfellows indeed.

"Mesme?" She'd yet to meet another Kat, but she was too tired to be surprised by anything any longer.

The lights wavered in front of her. *It is I again. In our previous meeting, I told you we hoped to contribute additional measures to the defense of Dominion worlds. Today I bring you the first of those contributions.*

"Oh?" She perked up a little, though hard-earned caution tempered her response. Every passing hour brought with it the increasing prospect that the Rasu would send forces to invade other Axis Worlds. The possibility loomed like a specter over her every waking step and sleeping nightmare.

Indeed. When this measure is activated, the Mirai proximity sensors will be tripped. Might we avoid an unnecessary panic by alerting military officials beforehand?

"Of course. Let's go see Commander Palmer."

Mesme's manifestation trailed her down the lift and across the hall to the large meeting room they had converted into temporary DAF Command Headquarters. Lance stood with Brigadier Johansson and two other officers poring over a bank of charts and data tables.

"Lance, can I speak to you for a minute?"

He did a double-take upon seeing Mesme. "I was going to ask if it was urgent, but I see we have an esteemed guest."

"Yes. The Kats want to bring…something…to Mirai to aid in our defense in the event of a Rasu attack. Let's not shoot it down, okay?"

"That depends. What is it?"

A device similar in function to the Humans' Dimensional Rifter.

"What the hells is a singularity in space going to do for us?"

Quite a lot when one considers how the singularity in space will envelop the entire planet of Mirai.

So this was what Lance looked like when genuinely caught off guard. She made a note.

"You're kidding me."

I rarely 'kid,' Commander Palmer. Please, allow us to activate the device and demonstrate its capabilities to you.

She made an insistent waving motion at Lance, and after a beat he acquiesced. "All right, we won't shoot it down. Don't make me regret it."

You will not.

"Sir, sensors are picking up a small foreign object entering Mirai's atmosphere."

"Already? Your people move fast."

Indeed. Nika spun to Mesme. "Wait, I thought it was going to be positioned in orbit above the planet?"

No. Full effectiveness requires it to be situated on the ground, but it does not matter where. We have provisionally selected a location twenty kilometers outside the borders of this city.

She shrugged weakly. She wasn't comfortable ceding their protection to these bewildering, cryptic aliens, but they desperately needed the assist right now. "Understood. We'll worry about security once the demonstration is complete."

Military drone cams followed the spherical object throughout its descent. No propulsion mechanism was visible, but once it broke through the cloud cover, it slowed until it settled gently to the ground in an agricultural field. The metal outer shell split open and fell away, revealing a porous lattice constructed of an obsidian metal.

A tiny, golden ball of energy manifested at the center of the lattice, spinning faster and faster until it grew to encompass the structure.

Now, if you will turn your attention to our superdreadnought located at the coordinates I am providing to you.

Coordinates popped into her head like a spontaneous thought, which was a bit disconcerting. Lance shot Mesme a suspicious glare, then went over to the officer managing the orbital sensors and muttered something in his ear.

An image of one of the Kats' fearsome vessels orbiting Mirai appeared on a new pane.

Please pull back as much as possible for a more fulsome perspective.

The viewpoint withdrew until the hazy outline of Mirai's mesosphere shone in the lower-left corner of the pane.

Thank you. A moment.

Five seconds passed while they waited. Then abruptly the superdreadnought fired a tremendous crimson beam toward the planet below.

"You traitorous bastard!" Lance started to lunge toward Mesme, though what he planned to do with his balled fists she couldn't imagine—and stopped when the beam vanished. One instant it was streaking toward Mirai; the next instant it was simply...gone.

As you can see, the device will consume any physical object or energy that is directed toward the planet.

Nika stared at the once-again peaceful scene on the orbital view. To wrap an entire planet in some sort of singularity bubble...the Kats' level of technology defied comprehension. Honestly, it frightened her. But it was what they needed if they hoped to ever defeat an enemy so formidable as the Rasu. "Where did the beam go?"

We are able to exercise a great deal more control over the location where the rift reemerges than Humans currently can. As such, I chose a location I think you will appreciate.

"Where's that?"

The center of Mirai's sun.

Nika cackled, allowing genuine optimism to flourish in her chest, even if for just a minute. "Brilliant."

We will provide you with a signal for friendly ships to transmit in order to pass through the barrier and reach the surface. However, it may be wise for us to power down the device until Rasu signatures are detected, as we would not wish to cause unnecessary death.

Her brow furrowed. "No, we wouldn't want unnecessary death. But can I count on you to activate the device on no warning, at any time? No, wait, don't answer that question. Instead, teach me how to activate it."

To do so will not be practical at this time. I give you my word that I will be available immediately upon notice should the device require activation. Is this acceptable?

It represented yet another step toward being dependent upon the Kats for their defense, for their very survival. She didn't like it. Asterions had always exuded pride in taking care of themselves. And for all the Kats'—or at least Mesme's—gracious entreaties, formidable warships and now clever technology, she still resisted trusting them fully. Their notable absence at the Namino battle remained unexplained. Also, the condescending frostiness of their treatment of Asterions, and of her specifically, while they hid behind the guise of the Sogain for the last two hundred millennia had left a bad taste in her mouth.

But she was in no position to refuse aid such as these aliens could offer. "Your word that you will be here when we need you?"

My word and my oath.

"Then accept my thanks for this gift. I pray we never have to use it."

RW

Nika retreated to an empty room on the third floor for a spell of solitude. By any objective measure, today had brought a deluge of genuinely good news, and she felt as if she needed to stop for a minute and reorient her attitude.

Mirai was now protected from the Rasu. Mesme had promised the imminent delivery of additional rift devices, so soon, the other Axis Worlds would be as well. This was *huge*.

Pridefully, she still wished they'd found a way to protect themselves. One day, they would no longer be at the mercy of mysterious, secretive, ethereal aliens. But for this day, it was the protection that mattered, not where it came from.

Then there was the revelation about kyoseil's ability to penetrate the quantum block, at least for Plexes. Her mind went back to the tickle of an idea she'd had when she'd realized what Parc's mere existence both here and on Namino meant. If there was a way—

Nika, the Anaden wants to speak with you.

Thank you, Katherine. I'll be upstairs in a minute.

The Supreme Commander and his granddaughter had been given free rein of Mirai, though not unsupervised. Their security detail reported that they'd strolled the streets of Mirai One for an afternoon and taken several meals at local restaurants, but had spent most of their time on board their ship.

She took a deep breath, drawing on the surfeit of good news for the strength she needed to cordially interact with a man who had once been her mortal enemy. Then she headed back into the fray.

RW

Nika sat opposite Corradeo Praesidis at one of the small meeting tables behind a shoji screen, giving them the illusion of privacy. "What can I do for you today, Supreme Commander?"

"You can begin by not calling me that."

She didn't respond directly to the request. "What else?"

He steepled his hands atop the table. "I recognize that I have stumbled into a crisis for your civilization. For my own personal reasons, as I mentioned earlier, I am predisposed to despise these Rasu, separate and apart from the horrors they've inflicted on your people. And after further consideration, I find I strongly wish to...help you."

It was one hells of an admission from him, even if his reasons for doing so remained selfish. "What help can you offer?"

"A valid question. Nyx and I encountered something troubling during our travels that...well, she believes it might point toward a weakness in the Rasu you can exploit, though I fear the trail for discovering it is cold."

"Forgive me, but a hundred items would benefit from my attention, and I don't have time for obfuscation or mysterious declarations from you. I already get plenty of those from the Kats. What did you encounter?"

"Many millennia ago, I spent a period of time with a species called the Ourankeli. They were impressively advanced—far more so than either your or my people. I took Nyx to meet them, only to find their civilization in ruins. Moons and habitats destroyed, their splendid solar halo ring wrent apart, their cities smashed."

"You think the Rasu attacked them?"

"I think the Rasu annihilated them. Which, considering the Ourankeli's level of technology, implies only dire contemplations about the Rasu's capabilities. But this is not why I bring up their fate. While we were there, our equipment—our environment suits, our weapons, our ship itself—came under passive assault. Multiple seals and connections became corroded and weakened in a matter of hours. And we were thinking...what if the Ourankeli devised a weapon to combat the Rasu? Something intended to prevent them from changing shape, or possibly from solidifying at all."

"If they did, it didn't work. You said they were annihilated."

"Indeed. Perhaps they didn't develop it in time to change the course of the conflict. But the Rasu left behind teratonnes of advanced materials and resources in the system. Why, unless they were forced to abandon it?"

It was a good point. "It's worth looking into. Unfortunately, right now we can't spare a single ship to do so. It sounds like it could be up Alex and Caleb's alley, but neither of them is in a position to investigate it either." She sighed. "Will you provide us the location of the Ourankeli's system? Once things settle down a bit, if they ever do, we can send a team to delve into what happened there."

"Absolutely. We'd return and investigate the scene in greater depth ourselves, but at present we lack the resources to do so. As I said, our ship began taking damage soon after arriving in the system."

"I'll make sure whoever investigates the system takes proper precautions. Unless it's...." She fisted her hands beneath her chin. She had no reason to trust in his veracity, but it didn't hurt to pose the question. "Can I ask you something?"

"Of course."

"What's your opinion of the Katasketousya?"

"Ah. They are quite enigmatic, aren't they? You want to know whether I think you can trust them."

"At present I have no choice but to trust them. But I am curious as to whether I *should*."

"I'm afraid my first-hand experience with the Kats is somewhat limited. They might have been an ally to the anarchs long ago, but a bevy of misconceptions and differences of opinion kept us from working together for a long time. Once the Humans entered the picture, however, they stepped up in a notable manner. In fact, I'd go so far as to say that without their assistance, the anarchs and the Humans acting together would not have been able to topple the Directorate. I have come to accept that they are speaking the truth when they say they want to protect sentient life whenever possible. However, I continue to suspect they have their own private agenda for doing so."

His answer made her feel a little better, though it didn't really add much to the equation. "Thank you for speaking honestly. I also appreciate your desire to help us defeat the Rasu. Your business is your own, but if you want my opinion on how you can best contribute to our fight, then I will give it to you.

"As I understand the situation back in the Milky Way, the Anadens are busily trying their damnedest to fuck up Concord. And since Concord remains our only genuine hope of standing against the Rasu, it is in all our interests—including the Anadens, even if they don't realize it—for Concord *not* to fall."

192 | G . S . J E N N S E N

She sighed. "I seem to recall you were a superb military commander, to the detriment of my people. I'm told you weren't responsible for the cruel turn the Anadens took after we departed, and in fact that you were forced out precisely because you argued against following such a path. I'm also told you were an inspirational rebellion leader. I hope you learned something valuable from the experience.

"My advice? Go home, *Supreme Commander*. Get control of the Anadens before they destroy all of us and leave our tattered corpses for the Rasu to pick through. Reclaim your name and your position. Bring your people together if you can; bring them to heel if you can't. With my worlds currently on fire, I frankly don't care much which one you do. But bring them to this fight, and see to it they line up on our side of the battle."

A troubled, almost haunted glint passed across his arresting sapphire irises. When she'd known him before, those irises had glowed the blood red of the *diati*. He opened his mouth and started to speak, then drew back, exhaled and began anew. "I'm not certain the Anadens remain the same people I once led…and I'm not certain I remember how to lead them."

She leaned forward across the small table. "*Try.*"

RW

Nika stared at the lift for several minutes after Corradeo Praesidis departed. Talking with him was surreal, almost like a waking dream-memory. Based on what her journals about the SAI Rebellion conveyed, he bore scant resemblance to the man who had driven her people out of the Milky Way. He was reasonable and thoughtful; he listened and discussed issues without violence or the threat thereof.

Yet in just as many respects, beneath the surface he *was* the same man. Quietly confident, profoundly charismatic, utterly unflappable. Those characteristics had served him well in the Anaden Empire—too well from her perspective. Maybe now they would do so again.

CONCORD

26

EARTH
CHICAGO

A frigid wind whipped off Lake Michigan to howl down Chicago Avenue. Alex rubbed at the arms of her black wool dress and pushed onward, one foot landing deliberately in front of the other.

The Holy Name Cathedral loomed large and somber over the next block. One of the oldest standing churches in Chicago, it had nearly been destroyed at least five times in the last four hundred years but was saved every time—its parishioners would say miraculously so.

She knew all this because Malcolm had shared the church's history with her on the two occasions she'd accompanied him here. Once for a Christmas Eve service, when their relationship had grown newly serious and she was genuinely trying to make a go of it, and once for his father's funeral almost a year later.

Funerals. They circled around her now like a haunted, taunting mob, outstretched hands intertwined to ensure she couldn't escape their torment. Beshai, Cosime, now Malcolm...who might be next? Marlee? Caleb—no. That wouldn't happen. If she screamed into the void, 'no more funerals!' would the void listen?

She knew she didn't have a proper right to vent or complain. In every instance, others suffered the loss far more acutely than she did. For Beshai, Jaisc and every Taenarin who knew the woman. With Cosime's death, Eren lost everything he held dear. Today, Mia mourned alongside Malcolm's mother and sister. Alex, however, had been spared the despair of mourning her mother, and

Caleb...Caleb was going to come back. Broken and in need of healing, but he would come back, and he would bring Marlee with him.

She climbed the stairs to the cathedral entrance alongside her mother and father, just ahead of Kennedy and Noah. Behind them, a steady stream of attendees filed in through the doors. Inside, the air felt cool but mercifully wind-free. A towering ceiling loomed above them, framed by a series of dramatic arches. Dozens of colorful stained-glass windows should have rendered the sanctuary radiantly lit, but on this cold and overcast day, only meager light filtered through.

Because her mother was scheduled to speak during the service, they were seated on the third row. Mia sat on the front row beside Malcolm's mother, sister and the sister's husband. Alex had never actually met the sister's husband, since her thoughtless refusal to attend their wedding brought a dramatic and abrupt end to her and Malcolm's relationship. It had been a terrible thing for her to do, even if the outcome was the correct one.

She hadn't seen Mia since those tear-drenched moments on the floor of the Consulate office. Mia looked frozen, as if she'd been petrified in place—her olive skin blanched pale, her jade eyes coldly bright but not sparkling, her hands clasped into tight fists on her lap. Whispered tendrils of her pain leaked through the Noesis into Alex's mind, and she hurriedly reinforced the block. Doing so made her a coward and a selfish one, but her heart was exhausted, and she simply couldn't bear any more grief right now.

A line of priests followed a man in traditional Catholic garments—the actual Archbishop of Chicago, she'd been told—in from a side hall to the altar. An enormous picture of Malcolm in full military dress hung in front of the altar, because of course there was no body and thus no casket. The Savrakaths probably desecrated it then chucked it into the swamp—

She closed her eyes until the wave of nausea passed, and with it budding tears. The rich strains of an organ filled the sanctuary, everyone stood and a hymn began. She hadn't known the words to any of the hymns on either of her previous visits, and she certainly hadn't learned them since. Her father was raised Eastern Orthodox, her mother's family practiced no religious traditions, and Catholic burial rituals were nearly as much a mystery to her as Taenarin and Naraida ones.

The Archbishop read several passages from the Bible in a deep, booming voice, then David squeezed her mother's hand as she stood and went to the altar. Because to the world, Malcolm was a military leader and a war hero, the family had chosen Miriam to deliver the eulogy. Apparently eulogies weren't a traditional part of Catholic funeral liturgies, but if a person was noteworthy enough, exceptions existed for every rule.

Her mother had never been comfortable speaking in front of crowds, but she'd gotten quite good at it with frequent practice over the years. The speech was solemn yet touching, suitably reverential and occasionally even a little funny. For those few minutes up at the pulpit, her mother showed no hint of the immense strain she operated under, gave no sign of her continuing struggles with dying, skipping her own funeral and returning to life.

The Catholic Church's official position was that regenesis was an abomination, but today the Archbishop treated her mother with the utmost respect—which was to say, he didn't gasp and back away from her while clutching his rosary and performing the sign of the cross or grasping for the holy water.

Miriam rejoined them in the pew, and only the involuntary twitching of the muscles along her jaw betrayed how difficult standing up there and giving the speech had been for her. Her mother wasn't okay, not yet, and Alex found herself at a loss as to how to help her become so. It seemed like maybe her father knew how, though, for obvious reasons. And while she remained angry at her father for 'helping' Caleb behind her back, right now they needed to hold tight to one another as a family, lest the cosmos notice they shouldn't exist and rectify the error.

More hymns, recitations and readings of scripture followed, and it all felt so formal and pointless and ineffectual, though she realized Malcolm would have taken comfort from it. But funerals weren't for the dead, they were for the living, and none of this was giving her any peace whatsoever. Only a growing frustration with a callous and capricious universe.

When the service concluded, she excused herself from her parents to go speak to Malcolm's mother and sister. She hadn't seen them in years, but a proper upbringing had taught her it was the polite thing to do, and for once she followed the rules. After a few stilted condolences she placed a hand on Mia's shoulder, but the woman just stared straight through her. Alex nodded in understanding, though she deeply hoped that she never did, turned and hustled down the aisle to catch up to her parents.

She couldn't take this any longer—this submissive acceptance of tragedy, this reacting instead of demanding. She needed to *do* something. Something to staunch the bleeding and the carnage, something to force the universe to right itself and resume spinning in the correct direction.

27

SAVRAK
MILITARY HEADQUARTERS

General Kuisk Jhountar's thick tail whacked the side of his desk with every livid pivot. "Concord cannot simply have their way with us! If we let them invade our sovereign territory at their every whim, we've already become nothing more than indentured servants."

Brigadier Akhar Ghorek snarled a retort; unlike most officers, he refused to blindly kowtow to Jhountar's power. It was, he suspected, why he was in the room. Jhountar made a show of expecting unconditional obedience from his subordinates, but even he recognized he needed someone to occasionally call him on his bullshit. "General, it is fair to say that Concord has thus far been restrained in their behavior toward us. They possess the fleets and weapons to destroy our military and civilian infrastructure, yet they have not done so."

"They are afraid of our antimatter weapons."

"No, General, they are not."

"They will be if we begin utilizing them on soft targets."

Ghorek blinked. Jhountar had always been a ruthless leader, but not a sadistic one. "General, I hope you are not suggesting—"

"No, not at present, though I refuse to remove the option from our arsenal. But the fact remains that we cannot allow these incursions to go unopposed, else we might as well surrender to our new overlords."

"What do you propose?"

"They have made the mistake of handing us poorly protected military targets right on our own soil. It is time we remove them."

RW

AFS TRINSKY

AEGIS Flight Lieutenant Adam Goodwin carefully guided the Rescue and Recovery transport vessel *AFS Trinsky* toward the landing pad at the Savradin spaceport. His eyes scanned the horizon for threats, then the ground below for the same.

This was his third Godjan refugee retrieval mission undertaken on Savrak. The first two had been met by much bullying and threats from Savrakath officials, but no violence. Still, the air crackled with tension and animosity. The Savrakaths did not want them here; they wanted to let go of their Godjan slaves even less and were doing so only under the threat of a full-scale Concord invasion.

Though it technically belonged to the military wing, AEGIS' RAR Division's purpose was to conduct humanitarian relief operations. They did so armed because such missions often took place in unfriendly territory. Such was the case today, where RAR acted under Concord's banner, per the Consulate and Command's decree that any Godjans who wished to leave Savrak under Concord's protection would be welcomed and granted refugee status.

The landing gear touched down on the pad. Goodwin performed the standard arrival checks before motioning to the operations officer, Lieutenant Fowler, who sat beside him in the cockpit. "Open the ramp and prepare to receive passengers."

Fowler stood and disappeared into the belly of the ship.

Flight Lieutenant Goodwin (AFS Trinsky): "Savrak Transportation Northern Spaceport, this is the AFS Trinsky. We have landed at Pad #5C and are ready to receive Godjan passengers. Please open the doors."

Savrak Transportation: "We will not aid a Concord incursion. Open them yourselves."

The passive resistance they'd encountered since beginning relief efforts was petty blustering, but it got tiresome. He leaned around the cockpit chair so his voice projected into the hold. "Specialist Figueroa, confirm Lieutenant Fowler is ready to receive, then get the doors from the spaceport open. Stay at the entrance to assist anyone who needs it. And take your sidearm."

"Yes, sir." Figueroa also headed to the back. A minute later, he emerged on the landing pad below and approached the double doors leading to the interior of the spaceport. Thus far Savradin security had allowed a number of Godjans to enter the spaceport and depart on the RAR transports, though Adam couldn't say what gauntlet they might have forced the refugees to endure to arrive here.

As before, the doors opened to reveal a throng of the small, bipedal yet disturbingly frog-looking aliens. Most wore little more than rags and carried bags stuffed full on their backs and shoulders.

Figueroa directed the refugees toward the extended ramp, where Fowler waited to get them processed and situated. To a one, the Godjans obeyed the AEGIS officers' gentle instructions as if they'd been delivered over the barrel of a gun. It wasn't Adam's place to make moral judgments about other species, but it sure seemed as if the Savrakaths had cowed the Godjans into meek submission on a societal scale.

The sounds of movement and quiet mutterings in Savrakan began to fill the transport hold behind him. They had room for two hundred ten passengers, and judging from the line that extended into the spaceport, it would be another full flight.

Another ten minutes of steady progress brought the hold to half capacity. Many of the passengers had never experienced spaceflight, and getting them calmly situated took a great deal of patience, which was why Fowler was in charge of doing so rather than Adam. The man had raised four children on his own after his wife died in a hurricane on Demeter, and he displayed the patience of Job when it came to the fragile and the helpless.

Motion in Adam's peripheral vision caught his attention. The doors to the spaceport had abruptly slammed shut.

Goodwin: *"Specialist, what's the situation with the doors?"*

Outside, Figueroa pressed repeatedly on the control panel. *"Sir, the controls aren't responding. The doors may have been locked internally by security."*

Another petty attempt to make their job as difficult and unpleasant as possible. *"Acknowledged. Keep trying. I'll reach out to Savrak Transportation."*

Flight Lieutenant Goodwin (AFS Trinsky*): "Savrak Transportation, this is—"*

Two fiery streaks emerged from the horizon to burn hot across the sky—in their direction. Missile launch? Fuck! *"Figueroa, Fowler, get on board and close the ramp now! We are being targeted."*

But there was no time. He'd barely shouted the order when both streaks slammed into the broadside of the *Trinsky*. The force of the impact sent the ship skidding across the landing pad, and one piece of the landing gear sank into the mud beyond the pad. A wave of searing heat billowed through the hold, and the door behind him slid closed a nanosecond before the wave blasted into the cockpit to burn him alive.

Goodwin: *"Fowler, Figueroa, report!"*

Nothing.

Flight Lieutenant Goodwin (AFS Trinsky*)(AEGIS Operations Channel): "AEGIS Central Command, this is the* AFS Trinsky. *We are under attack at the Northern Spaceport in Savradin, Savrak."*

System warnings flashed across the HUD and his virtual vision. The adiamene hull had held, but because the ramp was down when the missiles hit, the explosions had ripped apart the inside of the ship.

AEGIS Central Command (AEGIS Operations Channel): *"AFS* Trinsky, *vacate your location ASAP. Is your Caeles Prism operational?"*

Flight Lieutenant Goodwin (AFS Trinsky*)(AEGIS Operations Channel): "Affirmative, Command. Will vacate as soon as everyone is on board."*

He peered out the viewport, where a line of charred corpses led to the spaceport doors, ending at Figueroa's prone and burnt form. Flames consumed the body and licked hungrily at the entrance.

Acid burned in Adam's throat as he jumped up, reopened the cockpit door and hurried into the hold. The stench of roasting flesh assaulted him, but sporadic cries meant some Godjans were alive. In the smoke and confusion, he didn't see Fowler anywhere, but the lieutenant had been at the bottom of the ramp, and the bottom of the ramp was piled high with...he gagged, bent over and vomited. He was a trained medic, but no amount of training or experience prepared one for this.

Adam straightened up even as his stomach continued to churn, then felt his way along the hot wall until he reached the control panel. He fumbled the entry, and it took him two tries to activate the ramp to close. As the bright midday sky narrowed then vanished, he sprinted back to the cockpit and initiated emergency liftoff procedures. More missiles could be inbound this second, and he had to get what survivors remained offworld.

His eVi belatedly released nanobot-aided adrenaline to keep his hands from shaking as he pulled the ship up hard and accelerated away.

28

CONCORD HQ
CONSULATE

Mia stood at the viewport in her office. Outside, thousands of ships arrived and departed, while tens of thousands more sat docked along the pinwheels stretching out from the colossal station. Ships Malcolm should be commanding.

When this perishable nature has put on imperishability, and when this mortal nature has put on immortality, then the words of scripture will come true: Death is swallowed up in victory. Death, where is your victory? Death, where is your sting?

The Archbishop's commanding voice taunted her every waking thought. If she ever slept again, it would surely lie in wait for her in her nightmares. Where was Death's sting? *Where was Death's sting?* It could be found in the bottomless pit of sorrow now residing in her chest and in the desolation drowning Malcolm's mother's eyes. It poisoned the permanent chasm which had been engraved in the firmament.

Stop this, Mia. You are torturing yourself.

I expect I'm torturing us both, Meno.

I will manage, but I fear you will not. Grief is a natural process, but do not destroy yourself with it. I need to believe that you will one day be mended. Let me help you, if I can.

The notion of a world in which she might be mended existing in the multiverse made her laugh bitterly. Damn Malcolm for making her love him so, for making her *depend* on him. Damn him for refusing to come back to her. Damn the monsters who extinguished his life so carelessly, who had now denied her his touch for eternity.

Nature abhorred a vacuum. And so deep in the abyss now carved into her soul, something stirred to fill the emptiness. It was dark, twisted and ugly, and Malcolm would never approve. But Malcolm was gone.

RW

Mia welcomed Richard into her office. "Thank you for coming—and for coming to the funeral. Malcolm would've...appreciated it."

"Of course. There was never a question...." He paused. "Senator Requelme, shouldn't—"

"Please, it's Mia. We've known each other for fifteen years."

"All right, Mia. Shouldn't you be at home, or spending time with friends and family? No one will ever fault you for taking a few days off. Weeks. However long you need."

"In the middle of a coup attempt and two flaring wars? I don't think so. Besides, I don't have any family, and my friends are diligently working on defusing said coup attempt and two flaring wars. I can do no less."

He dipped his chin. "It's not my place to lecture you, so I won't speak any more on it. What can I do for you?"

"You have an agent in place with Ferdinand on Epithero, correct?"

"More of a part-time informant than a formal CINT agent, but yes."

"Excellent. I need to get a message to Casmir."

"Not to Ferdinand?"

She scoffed. "I can send a message to Ferdinand whenever I wish, but it will go unanswered and, in all likelihood, unopened. His practicing of diplomacy was always a farce at best."

"I'm not surprised. What is it you need to tell Casmir?"

"Does it matter?"

Richard clasped his hands behind his back and planted his feet shoulder-width apart; like most present and former soldiers, he reverted to a military stance when uncomfortable. "I recognize that in most Concord matters, you outrank me, as it were. But I won't ask my informant to take any action I'm not comfortable with."

"A noble sentiment. My sense, from what I know of the man, is that Casmir is on our side. We can use him to further our own purposes while maneuvering him into a position where he can disrupt Ferdinand's rebellion."

"What do you intend, exactly?"

It was easy to forget that Richard's mild-mannered demeanor did not make him a pushover. She sent him the message she'd prepared.

He reviewed it briefly. "Does Miriam know about this?"

"I think she would approve of this tactic."

"But does she know?"

"I haven't discussed it with her, no, as her plate is quite full."

"You realize I have to run it by her."

She didn't want to see Miriam, didn't want to be reminded in flesh and blood how the woman lived again when Malcolm did not. How Alex and David had seen their treasured loved one returned to them, while she found herself forever alone. But no one had said walking the path of vengeance would be easy or gentle. "Fine. Let's go see her. Right now."

COMMAND

Miriam motioned them into her office, then rested against the front of her desk and crossed her arms over her chest. "Do the Anadens have the right of things? I've spent the last fourteen years balancing peace on the head of a pin. Now, despite all my best acrobatics, I find myself surrounded by war."

Richard frowned. "I don't think—"

"Never mind." Miriam offered a dismissive wave and went around behind her desk. "If you haven't heard by now, you will shortly. The Savrakaths just attacked an AEGIS RAR vessel that was receiving Godjan refugees."

Richard stopped short. "What do you mean by 'attacked'?"

"According to the pilot, two missiles struck the vessel and the landing pad it resided on."

"Casualties?"

"Two AEGIS officers and as many as one hundred fifty Godjans."

Callous murderers and savages, all of them. Mia pressed her hands together at her lips. "Then this meeting is all the more timely, and my proposal all the more urgent."

Richard shot her a look, as if to say *not now*. "How do you plan to respond? Will you cease refugee flights?"

Miriam's eyes were a little bloodshot, and she seemed unusually jittery. Mia had heard tell that the path back from regenesis wasn't necessarily a smooth one. But the priceless gift it bestowed.... "I haven't decided yet. Future missions might paint a target on innocent Godjans, but if we leave them to their fate...." She shook her head roughly. "I need to think on it."

Mia took a step forward. "Commandant, please. I have an idea for how we can deal with the Savrakaths while also gaining an advantage in the Anaden situation. I'm sending you the proposal now."

"Very well." Miriam read through the prepared message. It wasn't long, and with a portentous sigh she leveled a weary gaze on Mia.

Mia spoke up before the woman had a chance to voice an opinion. "We are at war against the Savrakaths. Anything we can do to hasten the end of the war will benefit us."

"I understand the logic behind your proposal. But this isn't about logic, is it?"

She didn't flinch. She couldn't. "My personal motives don't matter if the logic is sound—and it is."

"With respect to the Savrakaths, perhaps, but not with respect to the Anadens, who we are always fighting a war against. A cold war, thus far, but a war nonetheless. Historical precedents tell us the Anadens will not distinguish military targets from civilian ones. The death toll they will inflict will be astronomical, and most of the lives lost will be innocent. I'm sorry, Mia, but I cannot give the Anadens carte blanche to do anything except stand down and surrender peacefully."

"But Miriam—"

"Mia, I have been where you are right now. I understand, I truly do. But sating this bloodlust you're feeling won't bring him back, and it won't give you peace. I'm sorry, but my answer is no. We will handle the Savrakaths ourselves."

Righteous anger ran free through her veins, and it was all she could do not to pitch a fit here in the middle of Command.

Mia, she has walked this path, and she is correct.

I'll walk my own path, to its end.

The diplomat's mask fell across her features. "I see. Thank you for your time." She spun rigidly and strode out of Miriam's office.

RW

SPECIAL PROJECTS

Mia lurked in the atrium outside Concord Special Projects. The shift change currently underway created enough activity that no one took enough notice of her to realize who she was, especially since she was dressed in casual gray pants and a black sweater, her hair bound back in a low tail. No accoutrements of office gave her away.

She waited another ten minutes before it finally occurred to her that what with the brewing Rasu crisis, Devon was probably working long hours these days. Her mind felt fractured, split apart by wide crevasses, and they made it so hard to hold a train of thought for long.

She scanned herself inside, pulsed her ID to the security officer who challenged her, and barged into the Director's office.

Devon Reynolds stood behind his desk in an office decorated in giant frames of Emily's art and an assortment of incomprehensible gadgets. His gaze was unfocused as he reviewed unseen proposals by mad scientists, but he stopped mid-stride on seeing her. "Mia. I am so sorry. I wanted to speak to you at the funeral—"

"Hush. If you're genuinely sorry for my loss, you'll shut up for five minutes then help me with what I need."

To his credit, he went with it. "Okay, talk to me."

"I need you to break into CINT's secure server and spoof a message from Richard to his informant at the Anaden compound on Epithero."

His eyes widened, if only a little. "What?"

"Exactly what I said. I need to get an officially sanctioned message to Casmir authorizing him to take command of the Machim fleet and pursue a full-scale bombardment of Savrak. Miriam won't approve the order, because she refuses to give the Anadens a centimeter of leeway, and Richard won't send the message without her approval."

"CINT servers are locked up tight. I should know, since I wrote most of the security protocols."

"Excellent. Then you can get around them. Now, Marlee's installed a backdoor routine into the CINT servers—yes, she's already that good—so you can use it as a jumping-off point. But it's only a listener and isn't written to modify anything. She might be able to expand its functionality, but she's...not available. I took a look at it myself, but it's been aeons since I hacked a government-grade security system, and my skills are too rusty. But yours aren't. You can do it."

He eased into the chair behind his desk wearing a pained expression. "At the cost of my job and a fairly important friendship."

She blanked on what he could possibly mean.

I believe he is referring to Richard's friendship.

Of course. How had she forgotten? Crevasses. "And what of my friendship?"

"That's not fair, and you know it. What we share? It's closer than any friendship. But what you're asking...."

Maybe they had once shared something closer than friendship, shared a constant stream of thoughts and intentions bubbling beneath the surface of their existence, but it was long in the past. Like Alex and Morgan, she'd largely shut out the Noesis in recent years. It was so damn loud and unceasing, and as her public stature had grown, so had the value of her privacy.

"It won't come back on you. If anyone finds out, I will take all the blame—at the cost of my job, yes, but I really don't care. Devon, what if it was Emily the Savrakaths had killed? I saw what almost losing her did to you all those years ago. If it was her, wouldn't you go to any and all lengths to make them pay?"

"I would." He smiled to himself. "When you frame it that way, it will be my honor to help you exact some vengeance." He glanced around his office, wheels spinning behind his luminescent amethyst eyes. "Not from here, though. It's too easily traceable. Let's go to my house."

"No, let's go to mine. This way if they do trace the incursion, again, I take the blame."

"But—"

"No 'buts.' I've got the equipment you'll need." She forced a smile. "And Devon? Thank you."

29

CONCORD HQ
CINT

When he finally reached his office, Richard sank into his desk chair and dropped his head into his hands. It had been a brutally long two days filled with sorrow and frustration. And though he was only on the periphery of both, he felt their weight nonetheless. If Will were here right now, his husband would say it was okay to take a break, to go easy on oneself. But Will wasn't taking his own presumed advice, as he was currently hard at work setting a trap for Ferdinand's informant in CINT.

They all felt a driving need to get in front of the spiraling disasters that had wrecked the last week. To halt the spiral, then get ahead of events and find a way to wrest control of their fates. For him, this meant ensuring Concord strongholds remained in Concord hands while gaining actionable intel on Ferdinand's plans—

His door signaled an entrant a split-second before it opened; he'd obviously forgotten to lock it behind him. He looked up to find David standing in the open doorway.

"Go away, David."

"You're upset with me. I understand. But—"

"I'm not upset with you—I'm angry with you. There's a difference."

David nodded in apparent understanding, then promptly sat down in one of the guest chairs, like Richard *hadn't* just asked him to leave. "Fair point. I'm sorry I betrayed your trust."

"Forget the breach of trust. You stole the access codes of the Director of CINT—me. It's called a crime."

214 | G.S. JENNSEN

"Not so much 'stole' as...kept them around in case I needed them. I have Miri's, too, if that helps."

Richard regarded him incredulously. "How can that possibly help?"

"Because it proves I only have them so I'll be able to help the people I care about in an emergency, which is exactly what I did by using Miri's access codes during the coup attempt to lockdown Command. See?"

"The circumstances were different. Miriam was...incapacitated. I've been right here at HQ this whole time—seriously, I can't remember the last time I slept in my bed at home. You could've asked me for access to whatever you wanted at any time."

"Would you have given it to me, knowing what I planned to use it for?"

Richard pressed his fingertips to his temples. "Possibly. I don't know. I wouldn't have let you or Caleb steal a Ghost, but I might have been persuaded to loan one out for a sanctioned rescue mission."

"You understand I couldn't take the chance."

"No, David, I don't understand."

"It was for *Marlee*. This is family we're talking about. I couldn't go after her myself because I knew Miri was going to need me very soon, but I had to give Caleb every possible chance to rescue her. Is this honestly a surprise to you?"

"No, of course not. Doesn't make it right." Richard sighed. "Your entire life—both of them—you've always acted as if the rules don't apply to you. You simply do whatever you want, with no respect for boundaries. It's been entertaining to watch from the sidelines over the years, but now? Your contempt for the rules has become contempt for me."

David leaned forward, clasping his hands at his chin. "No. Never."

"Can you blame me for thinking otherwise?"

"Yes! You've known me for...I can't even guess how to count the years, but a damn lot of decades. You know I have never, *ever* treated you with anything but respect."

"I thought so, but here we are."

David's brow knotted up in consternation, which was at least an improvement on blasé conceit. "You're not going to forgive me for this, are you?"

Richard wished he had a better answer. He didn't want to alienate his oldest friend, but a line had to be drawn somewhere. As he'd told David not long after the man had returned from the dead, he wasn't the sidekick any longer, and he couldn't allow that to change now. "Not for a while, no."

David nodded thoughtfully.

"This is the part where you leave."

"No…it isn't. I need you to do me a favor."

"Oh, you have got to be kidding me. Is there no limit to your hubris?"

"Fine, don't do me a favor. Do Miri one. Do Concord one. Ferdinand still has a plant in CINT, doesn't he?"

"The leaker? We believe so. Will's trying to pin down their identity, and in the meantime, I've locked down all CINT intel under the guise of the coup. Well, it's less a guise and more a legitimate reason."

"I want you to unlock one piece of information and see that it gets to Ferdinand."

He cast his eyes to the ceiling. He was a patient man, but his wit's end was five seconds away at most. "What information?"

"The location of the two remaining Savrakath antimatter facilities."

"Why?"

"I heard about the meeting with Mia today. Miri's correct—we can't give the Anadens free rein to take out the Savrakaths. They'll do as much harm as good, and possibly more. But so long as the Savrakaths possess antimatter weapons, they *are* a threat to us. Command is otherwise occupied at the moment, which means we have to let the Anadens take out those antimatter facilities, for all our sakes. As a bonus, you can use the opportunity to put a trace on the intel. Identify the leaker and, after they've passed it on, fire and arrest them."

Frustration morphed into anger once again. Had David heard a damn word he'd said? "So now you're going behind Miriam's back as well? Doing what *you* think is best instead of letting her—letting any of us—decide for ourselves."

David spread his arms wide, his expression veering toward a glare. "I have to do *something*, Richard. Miri is overwhelmed simply trying to...*breathe*, to exist again in this world. We are all hanging by unraveling threads here, and I have to find some way to help hold everything together."

The anger faded as swiftly as it had flared. David had several flaws, but a lack of sincerity had never been one of them. All these bull-in-a-china-shop actions of his were intended to ensure they didn't lose anyone else.

"I appreciate the sentiment, I do. But this is not the way. You convince Miriam to allow the leak of this information, and I'll do it in an instant. But not before then. I won't betray her trust, or the chain of command for that matter." He dragged both hands down his face; it was possible he really did need a good night's sleep. "Maybe your actions the other day will save Marlee's life. Or maybe they'll get her and Caleb both killed. Either way, the people you're claiming to want to help? By cutting them out of your decisions and charging ahead with your own ideas about what's best for everyone, you're hurting them instead."

30

CONCORD HQ
CONSULATE

Mia darted around her office in a frenzy. Her limbs lurched to and fro, out of sync with the muscles controlling them and driven by a primal, vengeance-fueled energy that might be the sole thing keeping her upright and functioning.

Devon had helped her send the message under Richard's name to the CINT informant on Epithero, who hopefully would cooperate in making certain it reached Casmir. But it could be days before she'd learn if Casmir had received the message, much less if he'd agreed to the directive it contained, succeeded in convincing Ferdinand of his sincerity and managed to return to the bridge of an Imperium. Each of those days stretched ahead of her like a literal eternity.

She wanted to watch Savrak burn, and she wanted to watch it burn now.

"Senator? The Godjan girl is here to see you."

Mia jerked to a halt, surprised out of her reverie by the Consulate receptionist's comm. The Godjan girl…. Oh, Vaihe. Right.

The words to send the girl away hovered on her tongue. She was in no condition to play gentle, supportive diplomat to a frightened refugee. But so long as she resided in this office, it remained her job to do so, and for some tiny part of her conscience, this still mattered.

"Send her in."

The door opened a moment later, and Vaihe peeked inside, as if unwilling to commit herself to entering.

Mia motioned to her. "Please, Vaihe, come on in. Let's sit, shall we?"

The girl wore a loose-fitting jumper in a bright clover-and-citron floral pattern and woven slippers. Had she made the clothes herself?

Mia sat down on the couch and waited until Vaihe joined her, then shifted around to half-face the girl. "How have you been doing? In Marlee's absence, I told you to contact me if you had any troubles or concerns, but I haven't heard from you until now. Is there a problem?"

"No, no problems. I mean, everything's so strange, but people are being nice to me. Helping me. I wanted to ask you…Miss Marlee…I haven't seen her for so many days. Is she okay?"

Mia froze her expression in place rather than let it broadcast the wave of guilt and despair that rushed up to drown her, which would terrify the girl into hysterics. There had been no word from Caleb since he'd left for Namino and no constructive word from Nika about the situation on the ground there. Best case, Marlee was scrambling to survive on an alien planet under siege by monstrous, nearly unkillable invaders. Worst and most likely case, she was dead…and Mia had hardly thought about her in days. Her heart couldn't be broken any more thoroughly than it already was.

But Marlee had risked her life to save this alien girl, and Mia owed it to her to continue to protect Vaihe for as long as she was able. "Marlee's doing fine, don't worry. She's on an extended mission for me, and unfortunately she can't comm home while she's gone. But she did tell me to let you know she is so sorry she had to leave you for a little while, and she hopes to be back home soon."

A huge smile broke across Vaihe's face. "Good! I miss her. She's so kind to me—" her eyes widened in horror "—you are, too, Senator Miss Requelme. So sorry if I offended."

"You didn't, Vaihe. You're doing wonderfully, and you don't need to thank me." She struggled against a resurgent need to pace and scream and cry. "Is there anything else I can do for you today?"

The Godjan fidgeted on the edge of the couch. "I am not brave. I am not a fierce warrior like you and Miss Marlee are. But I want to help my people. I've been talking to the others you rescued from the Okshakin, trying to help them understand how they're safe now, and how the people here are nice. But I want to do more. Is there a way for me to do more?"

"Vaihe, you *are* brave. You were brave to escape Savrak with Marlee. You've been brave every day of your new life here."

"I don't feel brave. But I do feel...lucky. Please, I want to help."

Mia's ears burned as shame washed over her. Here she was fixated on blood-soaked vengeance, while a simple refugee girl with no family and no home was determined to save lives. This might be the last productive, positive act she undertook in this job, but the least she could do was help the girl in her quest.

The problem was, she still hadn't heard whether or to what extent Miriam intended to continue with the RAR refugee transports. If blowing the transports up was the new Savrakath modus operandi, it was foolish and counterproductive to continue them. And if her message to Casmir worked...she was forced to concede that Miriam was correct about the Anadens' approach to warfare. Machim warships and troops would not stop to distinguish between military and civilian, between Savrakath and Godjan. So if she and Vaihe intended to save more Godjan lives, they needed to do it soon.

She leaned forward to gaze at Vaihe intently; the girl shrank away, and Mia hurriedly softened her body language. "Do you know of places around Savradin, or even outside the city, where many Godjans congregate? Live or work together in large numbers?"

"Of course. We live in our own villages, so as not to bother the Savrakath masters with our...." Her voice trailed off, and her shoulders rose a notch. "They forced us to live apart from them. I know of many villages."

"Excellent. If I showed you a map, could you point out some of these villages to me?"

"Um, a close-up map, maybe? I know how to get to the villages, but I've never seen them from the sky."

"That's fine. I'm sure we can create a good map for you." Her mind raced...how best to accomplish this? "If I were to open a...path between here and one of the villages, would you be willing to briefly go through it and convince the people living there to return here with you, through the path?"

"Like what Miss Marlee did in the swamp? You'll make a hole in the world?"

So *that* was how Marlee had gotten Vaihe off Savrak. But Marlee wasn't a Prevo, so she must have redirected an existing wormhole somehow. "Yes, like Miss Marlee did—so you know it's safe."

"People will not believe me. They will be afraid."

"Aren't they already afraid? Afraid their Savrakath masters will kidnap and torture them? Or worse?"

Vaihe's enormous eyes widened into giant orbs, and her throat worked for several seconds. "This is a good point. They are...and I can maybe offer them hope for a better life." She nodded resolutely. "Yes. I wish to try."

31

SAVRAK
UNKNOWN LOCATION

M alcolm extended a gloved hand to Mia, who sat at the dignitary table at the front of the ballroom entertaining all manner of politicians. "May I dance with the most beautiful woman in the room?"

Her lips curled up into a little smile as she murmured an apology to the man sitting next to her—the governor of Atlantis, Malcolm thought—then accepted his proffered hand and stood. "It would be my pleasure to accompany the guest of honor to the dance floor."

That was him: the guest of honor. Earlier tonight he'd nodded and blushed his way through excruciating speeches by three separate political heads of state praising him. Many handshakes had followed, and finally the pinning of a modest pewter star beneath his rank bars to signify his new status as the AEGIS Fleet Admiral. The first true AEGIS Fleet Admiral, in point of fact.

Though he'd never shirk the responsibility that accompanied the title, and he appreciated the power it should grant him to get important work done, the fawning and general ass-kissing the promotion brought made him deeply uncomfortable.

They reached the periphery of the dance floor, and he rested one hand at the small of Mia's back while holding the other outstretched to the side. Dancing also made him deeply uncomfortable, but at least a gruff drill sergeant had taught him how to do it properly in officer training school a lifetime ago.

"How do you suffer all this overwrought praise and flattery, Senator Requelme?"

"I return it when required, then banish it from my mind and go about doing my job, Fleet Admiral Jenner."

"You make it sound easy, because for you it is. For me? Not so much."

She effortlessly followed his lead as they glided across the dance floor while dodging the other couples. "You'll be fine. Just issue some orders and bask in how everyone obeys them without question."

"That will be nice, I admit. But I prefer my men cursing me to curtseying me."

Her laugh rippled sultry and melodic, and he suddenly wanted to be somewhere far more private. She truly was the most beautiful woman in the room, and it wasn't a close call. Her jade satin dress shifted across her curves with every graceful movement, and her ebony hair was swept up in a pearl ornament to expose her slender neckline.

He leaned in closer as they passed a twirling dervish that might have been the Earth Alliance Assembly Speaker and his wife. "So, how much longer do you think we need to stay here?"

"Oh, no. You're not getting off so easily this time. You're the star of the party. You can't abandon your admirers now."

"But..." he pressed his palm flat at her waist, drawing her tight against him "...I only care about one admirer."

"Good." Her lips found his ear. "Then let me tell you all about what we're going to do when we can finally retire to the hotel room."

Malcolm jerked awake to the sound of raucous activity outside and to the left of his cell, and the blissful haze of the memory evaporated. Multiple heavy footfalls accompanied barked but muffled commands that sounded unusually rude even for the Savrakaths. Were they delivering a new prisoner to a nearby cell?

He waited quietly, maintaining his dejected pose slumped against the wall. It wasn't hard. His shoulder was actually healing fairly well at this point, as the antiseptic had provided the healing boost his cybernetics had needed to get a handle on the infection. He didn't intend on letting his captors know this, however, and he had every reason to believe the cell was monitored. If he started looking fit and spry—relatively speaking—his captors were apt to engage in further enthusiastic interrogations, which he would just as soon skip.

Additional orders were barked in the direction of the adjacent cell, but all Malcolm was able to make out was "—back for you soon." One of the guards strode down the hall, stopping in front of his cell to snarl in his direction. Malcolm let his chin loll to his chest and remained silent. After several seconds, the guard opened the small hole in the force field and tossed a wrapped package through it. The package bounced across the floor and landed next to his leg. The force field closed, and the guard disappeared.

He waited through another thirty seconds of silence before gingerly reaching out for the package. His left arm remained chained up, and while he'd regained minimal range of motion in his right arm, every movement he demanded of it sent pain radiating through his body.

He fumbled the package open using one hand to find a lump of…bread? Possibly? They were feeding him barely enough to keep him alive, presumably in case they found some use for him. His eVi could finesse his cybernetics to keep him alive without food for several months, assuming he had water, which they provided only slightly more regularly than food. But under the assumption the Savrakaths didn't know the finer points of modern human physiology, he made a show of hungrily devouring the dry, stale starch before nudging the wrapper off to the side.

Then he shifted around in an ostensible attempt to get comfortable, but in such a way that his head faced toward the left wall. If the new prisoner worked for Concord in any capacity, and if the comm block was a bubble instead of a field, a directional/vicinity comm signal should reach them. He closed his eyes, feigning sleep.

Are you there?

No response arrived.

I'm in the cell next to you, to your right. Who are you?

Silence continued, which likely meant one of his two assumptions was false. Dammit! He craved friendly contact, and he was desperate for any information about what was transpiring in Concord.

Who are you?

He mentally jumped to attention...then hesitated. Not all prison mates were created equally.

I'm an AEGIS Marine. I was captured during a mission to rescue imprisoned Godjans. My name's Malcolm. You?

Torval elasson-Machim, Navarchos of the Imperium Delta.

Malcolm groaned aloud, hoping it sounded like a groan of pain to any listening devices. His limited interactions with Torval over the years had not left him with a positive impression; the man was arrogant, boisterous and reckless. Plus, more recently, a murderer and seditionist. He was also supposed to be locked in a different cell at Concord Detention.

How did you get here? Did Concord give you to the Savrakaths?

No, Command is far too cowardly to pull such a stunt. Some Idoni fop kidnapped me from Detention and handed me over to them.

Eren Savitas, no question. Torval was responsible for the death of his girlfriend and teammate, and Eren had always played by his own rules. No one deserved the punishment of a Savrakath gulag, but Malcolm could understand how Eren might judge it fitting for the man.

What's happening at Concord? I've been cut off for a week.

No idea. I've been cut off for longer, ever since that cunt Solovy pitched a tantrum and threw me in a cell.

Malcolm recoiled at the vile insult the man had casually hurled at Miriam. Thus far, his earlier impressions were proving to be spot-on, and the man hadn't even brought any news to offer up as compensation. The brief surge of hope evaporated, and he let dark thoughts consume him.

What have they done to you? What can I expect from the torture?

Malcolm didn't particularly want to engage any further with the murderer, but it had been so long since he'd talked to anyone other than his captors.

I've got a shoulder wound they've exploited for pain purposes. Food and water deprivation, a couple of shock baton hits. Nothing I can't handle.

Dammit. I suspected they were all bluster, but I need them to be rougher with me. The Idoni warned them not to kill me, but the Savrakaths are violent and reactionary, so I intend to provoke them into doing exactly that at the soonest opportunity. Then I can wake up in a Machim lab back home. Humans have regenesis now, don't they? You should do the same.

Malcolm sighed. *It's not quite so simple for me.*

Huh. Your loss. I don't intend to be here for long.

For the thousandth time since he'd woken up in this Hell, his thoughts drifted to the 'no regenesis' clause he'd included in his will. For better or worse, if he died here, there would be no reawakening for him.

Both intellectually and spiritually, he continued to believe in the rightness of his choice. He didn't look down upon those who disagreed with him and had already taken advantage of this new 'miracle' of immortality. He respected and trusted David Solovy and, when they were trustworthy, the Anadens with whom he worked. It was not his place to pass judgment on the state, presence or absence of anyone else's soul.

But for himself, he believed that he'd been granted one solitary soul, and when he died, God willing, it would depart for a peaceful afterlife. Thus any clone of his would by definition be something...lesser. A hollow shell of a human being. But the promise of a second life was so damn tempting—and never more tempting than at this moment. To be able to return to Mia's arms, to not leave her to face an uncertain future alone, to be able to hug his mom and sister again, to keep fighting to protect his people....

It was a good dream, but it was only a dream. Still...if he were able to go back in time and make a different choice, would he?

What harm could there be in allowing a golem copy of himself to go on living his life after he died? If the copy was convincing enough, it wouldn't need a spiritual soul to bring Mia and his family many years of happiness.

He shuddered. No. Hedging his bets was the coward's way out. The ultimate dark temptation, but he couldn't go against what he believed.

Which brought him full circle to his singular goal: since he wasn't going to be reborn, he needed to stay alive and escape. His wounds were healing; another few days and he thought he'd be able to overpower the guard. He'd watched the procedures they followed for the force field, and if he timed his moves perfectly, he could get out while it was down. It was time to start planning his escape in earnest.

He considered the left wall of his cell with deep reluctance. Two trained soldiers stood a far better chance of escaping than one, if they worked together. He sent another message.

They haven't let me out of this cell since I got here, but it sounds like they're planning to move you elsewhere.

For special torture, no doubt. The Idoni made sure their General Jhountar knew the full extent of my transgressions against the Savrakaths.

Sorry to hear it. But if they do move you around, keep an eye out for any weaknesses we can exploit. Maybe together, the two of us can manufacture a way to escape.

What makes you think I'll help you escape, Human?

Malcolm blinked in disbelief. God, the man really was a first-rate asshole.

We're on the same side, Torval.

Don't be so certain of that.

I see. Good luck to you then.

32

***

CINT VESSEL 23A-X
VICINITY OF SAVRAK STELLAR SYSTEM

A stygian darkness roiled across the landscape. Eren ran, and the darkness chased.

Flames roared up out of the depths of a fissure in front of him. He turned away, seeking another path of escape, but the fire spread in a circle to surround him. To trap him.

The ground shifted beneath his feet; he looked down to see it had transformed into a pit of viscous sludge. A terrible itching sensation spread up his legs, as if spiders scurried along the underside of his skin. They raced up his chest in a mad skittering dash for his heart. Panicked at the thought of the creatures spinning a web around his heart, his nails dug into his chest, desperate to get them out—

Eren's eyes popped open at the surge of self-inflicted agony. His vision swam, blurry and cobweb-coated. His gaze dropped in a panic, certain he would find spiders pouring out of a hole in his chest. But there was nothing save several thin lines of blood welling up out of deep scratches beneath his collarbone.

"You're awake."

He jerked in surprise at the sound of a voice…a familiar voice, no less. He rubbed at his eyes until the blurriness resolved into a force field. On the other side of it, Drae Shonen ela-Machim sat on a crate of supplies and studied him. How?

He tried to think through the raging pain splitting open his skull. He'd been plunging headlong into Savrak's sun, seconds away from a blissful and final death, then…nothing. Nothing until the nightmarish hallucinations began.

He dragged a hand down his cheek, and it came away soaked in sweat. Now he was in the hold of his own ship, restrained by the same force field he'd used to keep Torval locked away. "Drae, you bastard. What did you do?"

His friend and teammate frowned, apparently not liking what his inspection of Eren showed him. "Your Kat pal, Mesme, showed up in the middle of the CINT offices. It was most worried about your mental state, and I agreed to let it spirit me onto the ship here. I knocked you out before you could suicide us both into the star. I just got out of regenesis, and I did not fancy suffering through that gauntlet again so soon."

"I don't want your help. You can take the ship, I don't care. Shoot me out of a torpedo tube and go home."

"The ship doesn't have any torpedo tubes, remember?"

"Not really." His face scrunched up in a grimace as the creepy-crawly sensation flared between his toes to race up his left leg. He grabbed for his calf, nails scratching and digging into the skin. If he could only get to the spiders before they ate him from the inside out!

"Hey, calm down." Drae stood and approached the force field. "I've got one more dose of *immade* for you. It should ease those *dialele* withdrawal symptoms for now."

The tiny part of his brain that retained a tenuous hold on rationality remembered the litany of risks that came with taking *dialele*. Objectively, the spiders were a figment of his tainted imagination. But the aftereffects of the hypnol had him in their clutches now, and the louder part of his brain, where insanity had already taken root, did not care to listen to rationality's whispers.

"And what about later?"

"You'll have to tough it out. I'll pin your arms up in those restraints if I need to do it to keep you from clawing your skin off, but I'm not going to let you die."

Eren banged his head against the wall behind him as his fists clenched from the effort of not chasing the maddening itch snaking through his body. "*Arae*, Drae, why not? Please. Let me go. I'm so…tired. I'm so…*done*. Without Cosime, I've got no more reason to fight and nothing left to hope for. I just want it all to stop. I want peace."

"Too bad." Drae crouched in front of the force field to gaze at him with a mix of sadness and frustration. "I know you're hurting right now, I do. It's called grieving. But it won't last forever. One day, you'll thank me for helping you."

"I will not."

"I say you will, but we'll see. For now, let's concentrate on getting you detoxed."

RW

The subsequent hours passed in a haze of brutal pain and terror. The malevolent gloom returned; the viscous pit consumed him, stringing him up like a ritual sacrifice to be fed to the spiders. They scurried through his veins and into his brain, and he was powerless to stop them.

On finding them shut, Eren opened his eyes, blinking against the harsh brightness of the force field. Drae was nowhere to be seen, but his *former* friend had made good on his threat, as both of Eren's arms were secured in cuffs and chained to the wall.

He jerked at the restraints, panic giving strength to his muscles, but they refused to give way. He'd secured them too damn well in order to ensure they kept Torval imprisoned. Now the prison was his own. His fingers convulsed, clamoring to gouge his eyes out and set the spiders free.

A wave of nausea boiled up out of his stomach, his prison lurched sideways, and he succumbed to the torturous darkness once more.

33

EPITHERO

Casmir sat perched on the edge of the small couch, his hands folded fastidiously in his lap. Waiting, and thinking.

Ferdinand had seen to it that his every need was taken care of. The suite included a stocked kitchen, a full bath and a spacious bedroom in addition to the living area, and supplies were brought in by a Machim *asi* loyal to Otto whenever requested. He was, in all material respects, quite comfortable.

But such comforts only served to strip away the veneer painted atop his imprisonment. He was prevented from leaving the suite; all communications were denied him, and his sole visitors were Ferdinand and the *asi* guard. He believed his location to be the former home of the Kyvern Primor on Epithero, but he had no way to know who else might be in residence or what destructive activities they might be pursuing.

He could speculate, of course. Ferdinand had attempted a coup of Concord, half-assed in the execution as per usual. Casmir assumed the attempt had failed, else a lot of things would be proceeding differently now. The identity of his guard suggested Otto was a participant in Ferdinand's schemes and likely operating out of the building, which meant the Machim *elassons* loyal in practice to Otto—three to four of them—were on board as well.

So a conclave of *elassons*—possibly a quorum, but it would be a close call—were gathered together to see if they could manufacture a future for themselves (and their Dynasties, eventually) without anyone, whether it be the Directorate or Concord, telling them how to do it.

He didn't hold out much hope for the endeavor. He was a poor excuse for a leader, but at least he'd actually *led* on occasion. The people he imagined squabbling and shouting upstairs right now? As *elassons*, they were uncommonly intelligent, clever and resourceful, but millennia of serving as the Primors' favored children meant they were also arrogant, headstrong and uncompromising. They were bullies, and if Ferdinand's increasingly foul moods during his visits were any indication, they were blowing a fair number of gaskets upon finding it impossible to out-bully one another.

Casmir didn't relish the thought of being in that room, but he wanted out of this one even more. Machims did not sit idly by while the world burned. Which, between the Rasu and the Asterions, the Savrakaths and the coup attempt, he must infer it was currently in the process of doing.

He'd be able to overpower the *asi* easily enough and confiscate the man's weapon. But he had to believe Ferdinand had Vigil officers stationed every ten meters, and without a detailed layout of the building he would be run to ground soon enough.

He was standing to go make some coffee when the door to the suite opened. The visitor was neither Ferdinand nor his *asi* guard, however. Instead, a Kyvern man, an *ela* by the cut of him, stood in the doorway.

"Can I help you?"

"A message for you, sir." The man held out a case enclosing a tiny Reor slab.

Casmir approached him warily. "From whom?"

"I'm sure I don't know, sir. I was instructed to deliver it to you."

"Instructed by whom?"

The man simply stared at him, hand and case extended.

"I see." Casmir took the case and turned it over to check it for tripwires or tiny explosives. When he looked up again the man was gone, the door closing behind him.

He sat on the couch and activated the slab.

Navarchos Casmir elasson-Machim,
    We thank you for your continued loyalty to Concord. We recognize that acting at odds with your fellow elassons *cannot be an*

easy path for you to walk. The current disagreement between Concord and certain members of the Anaden leadership remains in a state of flux, but we hope to resolve it without further bloodshed.

In the meantime, Concord is now in a state of war against the Savrakath government. Accordingly, on behalf of Concord Command, we authorize you to lead such Machim fleets as are at your disposal against any and all Savrakath military targets. Fire at will, and help us end a pointless war before more Concord citizens die.

— Commandant Miriam Solovy
Concord Command

He set the slab on the table and stared at it while he connected the dots. The Kyvern *ela* was a Concord spy, clearly, reporting back to CINT Director Navick on everything that transpired here. And now acting as a conduit from Command to Casmir.

He allowed himself a minuscule smile as something akin to hope blossomed in his chest. The only way out of this trap was to maneuver past it, and he'd just been handed a key to the first door.

Before he got too carried away with dreams of freedom and honor restored, he forced himself to refocus. First, the message.

The request made sense. If he knew Commandant Solovy at all, and he'd like to think he did, she would desperately want the Savrakath problem to disappear so she could direct all resources to the Rasu problem. He suspected she very much wanted her Anaden problem to disappear as well. And perhaps if he got himself out of this room and into the one upstairs, pretending to play along while building trust with the other Machims, he might in time be able to help with that as well.

He'd need to lie—only a little, which was lucky considering he was a terrible liar. But what if everything depended on it? He decided to assume it did, so lie he would. Only a little.

The smile returned. It felt good to have a purpose and direction. If he were honest with himself, it felt good to be given orders he could follow.

RW

Ferdinand acted distracted as he strode into the suite displaying yet more agitation than on previous visits. "You wish to have a word with me?"

Casmir nodded soberly. "I do. I'm concerned about what's happening here. You and I will never see eye to eye, but I want our people to be protected. To thrive and succeed. Will you tell me, how are the Machim fleets currently being deployed?"

Ferdinand peered at him in suspicion, hesitating.

"You lose nothing by telling me. But I am a Machim *elasson*, and I need to know."

"To the extent they are being deployed at all, it is in a defensive capacity—here, Machimis and the other homeworlds."

"We're not attacking the Savrakaths? Or the Rasu?"

"No. Nor are we attacking Concord, which is the question you didn't ask. Your brothers and sisters are having some difficulty reaching agreement among themselves, never mind among the rest of us, as to the best course of action."

Color him not surprised. Machim *elassons* excelled at executing on battlefield tactics, but the Primor had always conceived of the broader strategies underlying those tactics.

He tried to make a show of engaging in deep, soul-searching thought. "That's unfortunate, but not surprising. Maintaining resilient defenses of all our homeworlds is an utmost necessity, but it leaves us with many idle ships. In my considered opinion, the obvious choice is to use them to dispose of the Savrakaths forthwith. They are the easiest target, and their antimatter weapons represent an unacceptable threat to our people."

"Are you willing to attempt to convince the other *elassons* of the wisdom of this plan?"

"No, but I am willing to order them to execute on it. Ferdinand, release me from this lockdown, and I will lead our forces against the Savrakaths for you—but solely against the Savrakaths. I refuse to attack any Concord interests."

"And you will not betray us to those Concord interests?"

"I will not betray you to anyone."

Ferdinand regarded him inscrutably. "I confess that while Hannah, Otto, Ulrich and the others speak with much gusto around the table, none of them seems capable of…."

"Leading?"

"To put a fine point on it."

"Then allow me to lead them."

Ferdinand's expression softened; the man would never admit it, but he too craved direction given by someone who acted as if they deserved to issue it. "Why have you changed your mind?"

"The Rasu are an enemy worthy of respect. The best strategy at present is for us to dispose of the Savrakath annoyance as quickly and efficiently as possible, so that we may focus our attention on what represents a genuine threat."

"The Rasu are barely on the horizon and—"

"Ferdinand, do not try to be a military strategist. It doesn't suit you. As a Machim *elasson*, I am telling you the Rasu are a formidable threat to every Anaden."

"Fine. We can argue over them and Concord at our leisure once the Savrakaths are…how did you put it? 'Disposed of.'" The man clasped his hands in front of him. "I accept your offer. Do not make me regret it."

"I won't, and thank you." He made sure to look stern. "I'll need a ship."

"You will find your Imperium in orbit here above Epithero, waiting for your return."

34

AKESO

Tree branches scraped against windows relentlessly pelted by arrows of driving rain. Alex pulled the bedcovers up over her head...but after a few seconds she shoved them back down again. She didn't truly want to silence the storm, for it told her Caleb was alive. More than this, it offered her a glimpse into the state of his psyche. Was every lashing of a branch synchronized to him slicing a blade through Rasu metal? Every clap of thunder roaring in time to the slamming of his fist?

It might not be quite so literal as that, but the dual message was coming through loud and clear: Caleb continued to fight and kill, and Akeso's objections to his actions continued without respite.

The creek was overflowing its banks, the meadow had devolved to a sludgy mud pit and the shredded limbs from hundreds of splintered trees littered the landscape. Another day or two of this temper tantrum, and she was going to need to worry about the house flooding. In fact, she should pick up a crate of pop-up water barriers tomorrow...she checked the time...later today.

Ugh. She'd been lying awake for hours now, her mind traipsing through a recap of Malcolm's funeral, the *Stalwart II* exploding, the attack on HQ, her mother miraculously waking up...she couldn't recap Caleb leaving because when she'd turned around, he was simply *gone.* But she'd witnessed what he'd seen before the wormhole to Namino collapsed through Mia's eyes, so Marlee tumbling through the air after being mauled by a Rasu enthusiastically participated in the slideshow.

Sleep was not going to join her tonight, so she sat up and rubbed at her eyes. She'd spent the last week running herself ragged trying to help her mother, and by extension, Concord, and by further extension, the Asterions. Her mother remained stubbornly resistant to coddling or being fussed over; Alex took comfort from this, for it surely meant Miriam had emerged from regenesis fundamentally herself. But it made performing her chosen role as hyper-supportive daughter a mite challenging.

So she should maybe concentrate her efforts to help on an area where she was actually qualified to act: ships. Protecting the people inside them while using them to defeat the enemy.

Kennedy had ginned up a number of improvements to their ship designs that reduced the number of hull seams. But the Rasu only needed a single seam to effect their insidious incursions, which meant their ships remained at risk of being swallowed whole and boarded by the enemy. Increased Rifter use could mitigate the risk, but only if battles were fought outside the buffer zone of a planet or station, and she doubted the Rasu would be amenable to polite requests for a change of scenery. The impenetrable double-shielding used on Imperiums *should* keep the Rasu out, but the Machims had hoarded the secrets of the shielding for fourteen years now, and considering they were currently in political revolt, they weren't apt to agreeably hand it over now.

…Wait. She knew something. In her quest to overnight become a Concord power player just so she could help her mother, she'd reviewed volumetric tonnes of information, enlisting Valkyrie to collate and catalog the reams of data into a semblance of order. Now she called up the data stores and began sifting through them with renewed urgency. What did she know…?

Right, that. She climbed out of bed and went to the sink to splash water on her face, then tied her hair back in a messy tail.

> *Dad, are you awake?*
> *How did you guess?*
> *Call it a suspicion. What about Mom?*
> *Your mother left to go to the office an hour ago.*
> *Has something happened?*
> *Not in the way you mean. She merely…needs to work.*

Is that healthy?

Probably not. But have you ever tried to stop your mother from doing something she has decided she will do?

Good point. Get dressed, and I'll pick you up in five minutes.

Oh? Where are we going?

You seem to be highly skilled at stealing ships, so let's go steal a ship.

RW

EARTH

GREATER VANCOUVER

"We can't steal a ship from the Machimis Military Annex. They won't even let us land there, and given the current conflict, they'll likely fire on us the instant we show up on scans."

"Much as I'd like to see them try, the Imperium in question isn't at the Machimis Military Annex, but instead at the Concord Dry Dock in MW Sector 9. The damage it suffered in the Savrak battle wasn't severe, and they mainly needed somewhere to park it long enough to complete internal repairs. But then Mom gave Casmir a new Imperium, the crew transferred ships, and this Imperium remained in dock. It originally belonged to Torval, and he's not available to retake command. All the other Machim *elassons* have their own Imperiums, so it's sitting there idle, forgotten by anyone who might have authority to claim it."

David regarded her speculatively from where he sat at the kitchen table in her parents' house. He looked as if he'd been getting about as much sleep as she had, but at least his hair was brushed and his clothes unwrinkled, unlike hers. "The Sector 9 Dry Dock, huh?"

"Yep."

"It's still a military facility, and one now controlled by Machim forces."

"Sure, but it'll be far less guarded than the Annex, and all the infrastructure is Concord. The only reason the Machims got hold of it was because no AEGIS vessels were docked there at the time of their so-called rebellion. Besides, it's not as if we'll be knocking on the front door asking to be let inside." She jingled the tiny Caeles Prism on her wrist.

"Okay, that gets us on the bridge. Is the ship flight-worthy? What's the status of the repairs?"

She shrugged. "It flew into dock. It can fly out of dock. We're not taking it into battle, so everything except propulsion is window dressing."

"True. Do you think station security is just going to let us undock and abscond with a Machim command ship?"

"No, I do not." She opened the refrigerator and hunted for an energy drink; she'd forgotten to bring one from home, and despite her frayed nerves and rest-deprived body, she didn't expect to be sleeping anytime soon. Finally, she spotted one in the back and dug it out. "I figure if you have Richard's access codes, you have Mom's as well. Don't you?" She tried to keep any acrimony out of her voice, but she didn't entirely succeed.

"As I explained to Richard, I only pilfered them for use in a 'worst-case scenario' situation. I never had nefarious intentions."

She took a long sip of the energy drink. "You sound like Caleb."

"How's that?"

"Did I never tell you the story about how not long after we met, he secretly had Mia use Meno to crack the *Siyane's* security measures and grant him flying rights? When we were on Portal Prime, he used those rights to fly the ship to a location from where he could rescue me from Mesme's evil clutches. Well, not evil as such, but they felt evil at the time."

"See?" David spread his arms wide. "There are times when we have to do things that aren't technically 'proper' in order to save the people we love."

"Which is why you used Richard's access codes—to help Caleb save Marlee."

"Yes!"

But what about saving Caleb? She pursed her lips to keep from voicing the question aloud, for in her heart she recognized there was no good answer. Sometimes every choice hurt someone.

The conversation lulled into an uneasy silence, and she finished off the energy drink before shooting him a light, if forced, smile. "You *do* have Mom's access codes, don't you? Wait, never mind. You had them during the HQ attack."

"She changed them as soon as she woke up—not because of me, because of the Rasu. But yes..." he had the decency to act mildly chagrined "...I have the new ones."

She couldn't fairly fuss at him when she'd counted on precisely this. "Good. I'm playing a bet that the provisional Machim station security hasn't thought to change all the underlying ship authorization protocols."

"Because if they haven't, Miri's access codes will allow us to cancel the ship's lockdown and clear it for departure."

"Correct."

"I hope you're right. Can I assume you know how to fly a Machim warship?"

"Please, Dad. I've known how to fly a Machim warship since I hacked into the Machim Central Command Complex servers fourteen years ago. Or Valkyrie's known, anyway."

"I am officially out of holes to poke in your plan." He stood and grabbed his jacket. "What are we waiting for? Let's go steal a ship."

RW

MW SECTION 9 DRY DOCK (OWNERSHIP CONTESTED)

The Imperium's bridge stretched almost twenty percent larger than the bridge—former and soon again bridge—of her mother's flagship vessel, and it conveyed none of the warmth of the *Stalwart*

II. Of course, the warmth had always originated more from the occupants than the structural design. Due to the docking angle, the wide viewport displayed only the curving chrome metal of the station's hull.

David gestured grandly around the empty bridge. "I cede the floor to you. Tell me when you need me."

She fished her trusty Reor block—a universal decryption key to the secrets stored in other such blocks—out of her pocket and held it aloft in front of her. "Work your magic, Valkyrie."

'A moment.' The voice echoed disembodied through the bridge, as Valkyrie had elected not to instantiate her virtual form here. It required a lot of her processing power to instantiate, and so would her activities for the next few minutes.

'Navarchos Casmir's personal command codes are stored on a Reor block contained within the server bank inside the rear wall. I have the codes.' A multitude of screens and stations lit up throughout the bridge.

Alex stepped up to the bridge overlook, where the primary control panel waited for instructions, and gave it a sharp frown. Casmir's command codes gave her control, but if she didn't want to accidentally blow up the ship, she needed some guidelines on systems operation. When she'd said she 'knew' how to fly a Machim warship, she'd meant it in the loosest sense.

"We don't have time to parse every single file through the Reor strings. I'm brute-forcing this." She jogged over to the wall that protected the bridge server and internal systems hub, where she took out her plasma blade, activated it and cut a half-meter square out of the wall, then wiggled it out and set it on the floor.

"Done this before, have you?"

She shot her dad a smug look over her shoulder. "Not this *exactly*, but yes." She paused and glanced back again. "Watch this."

She turned to the open square and studied the interior. An intricate matrix consisting of hyperfine traces of darkness divided the light in a rigid, ordered pattern. Deeper, the circuits fed into stacked slabs of Reor. The Anadens were nothing if not set in their ways. She plunged her left hand inside.

"*Milaya….*"

"It's fine." Her voice came out tense from concentration, and also because her whole body had just absorbed a nasty wallop of both data and electricity, but in her world this counted as fine. "Valkyrie, go to town."

'Going to town.'

Alex removed her hand, mercifully free of singe marks, and returned to the overlook as a steady stream of legitimately useful data began scrolling up the control panel. Power systems and atmospherics, nominal. Engine status…nominal. Most excellent.

'I have control of the bridge.'

"Yes, you do." Her fingers flew across the control panel. "We're in luck. Since the ship is officially undergoing maintenance and repair, it's hooked into the station's network. I'm tunneling through the network to the automated station systems. The last thing we want to do is get into an argument with a Machim *ela* supervisor entertaining delusions of promotion." She raised her hands in triumph. "Aha! As I thought. The core Concord infrastructure is intact. Dad, if you would do the honors?"

Her father appeared at her side to study the blinking cursor.

Authorization required for undocking request:

He scratched at his head, sighed and punched in a complicated string of letters, numbers and symbols.

The floor shifted smoothly beneath her feet. "Valkyrie, confirm the clamps have released."

'Confirmed.'

"Terrific. Start up the engines and ease us away from the station."

The station began receding in the viewport, revealing a suitable tableau of stars beyond it. "Take it slow. No need to draw unnecessary attention to us—"

Dry Dock 9 Security to CCOV-14C88V: "Your departure is not authorized. Cease all activities immediately and allow a Security squad to escort you back into dock."

She groaned. "I knew this was too easy."

"I thought you said we weren't taking the ship into battle?"

"Very funny. Valkyrie, how long until we can superluminal out of here?"

'Fifty-two seconds.'

"That's too long—" Something slammed into the hull, and the bridge canted fifty degrees to port. She grabbed for the railing too late; her fingers slipped across the slick metal as she landed hard on her shoulder and skidded head-first into the far wall.

Her father was at her side the next second. "Alex!"

"I'm all right." She let him help her to her feet, wincing as she worked her shoulder around. It wasn't dislocated, but *owww*. "Valkyrie, get that vaunted shielding operational. Dad—" she waved her good arm toward the weapons station "—start shooting at things."

"I thought you'd never ask." He studied her for another beat, gaze brimming with parental concern, then pivoted and hurried to the weapons station.

By the time she reached the overlook and had strapped into the chair, belatedly, he was muttering half-formed phrases as his hands flew over the controls.

A wide cadmium-hued beam shot out from beneath the viewport and slammed into the broadside of the station. Cracks spread out from the point of impact in an expanding web, and faint wisps of atmosphere seeped out into space. "Damn, this is a powerful weapon. I might recommend stealing more than the shield tech."

"I say we take whatever the hell we want." A second blast knocked the ship hard to starboard, but the restraints held her in place this time. "Valkyrie...."

'A moment...shield operational.'

A prismatic shimmer rippled across the viewport, and Alex's shoulders sagged in relief—first that they wouldn't shortly be blown to bits, and more generally at the confirmation the Imperium's shielding was functional and this little adventure hadn't been an exercise in futility.

Beyond the shimmer, two missiles swept in and shattered against the force field. The bridge didn't so much as vibrate. There was a reason why they needed the shielding.

"Taking out the defense drones, which almost seems like a waste of one impressive weapon." David glanced over his shoulder to wink at her. "Almost."

He was amazing on the bridge of a ship, just as she'd always suspected. She understood the many reasons why he'd never returned to active service, but it was the military's loss.

'Ready to engage the superluminal drive in five seconds.'

She slid the control panel closer and punched in destination coordinates. "Take your last shots, Dad, then we are in the wind."

'Engaging.'

The damaged station and an incoming swarm of fighters blurred away and vanished beyond the superluminal bubble.

RW

CONCORD HQ

Kennedy dragged into Connova Interstellar's satellite office at Concord HQ still rubbing at bleary eyes. She'd been here at the office until well after midnight the night before, then had arrived home to find Jonas and Noah camped out in the lavatory, Jonas vomiting up pink gunk because he'd eaten a Dankath 'delicacy' while at the market. His starter eVi insisted a visit to a hospital was not required, merely a lot more vomiting to fully eject the unwanted substance.

Braelyn was gleefully taunting her brother's misery from the open lavatory door, so after a soulful plea from Noah, Kennedy had scooped Braelyn up and carried her off to bed, then fallen asleep curled up next to her daughter.

And now she was here at the office once again, as ready as she was capable of being to spend this day, like the last several days, trying to accomplish the impossible. Untold lives depended on her finding a way, so she needed to inhale another cup of coffee before—

Hey, I brought you a present.

Alex? What?

Look out your viewport.

Too tired to ask why, she went to the viewport and peered out—then almost screamed in surprise. Hovering above the daisy chain of ships docked closest to her office was a Machim Imperium. No alarms were pealing through the halls of Concord HQ, which suggested Security wasn't deeming the vessel an immediate threat, which suggested…. Wariness gave way to resurgent hope.

Are you on board the Imperium?

Yep. Where do you want me to park it?

RW

Kennedy met Alex—and David, it turned out—at the airlock of the Imperium, which she'd directed to the closest open docking port to her office. She laughed when she saw them together. "Did you two have a fun daddy-daughter date?"

"If getting shot at by station defenses is fun?"

David nudged Alex in the side. "Come now, *milaya*. We had a smidge of fun, no?"

Alex rolled her eyes. "We did. How could stealing an Imperium out from under the Machims' noses not be fun?" She laid a hand on Kennedy's shoulder. "You understand what this means, right? Get inside this ship and figure out how the double shielding operates once and for all. If you can't replicate its functionality in less than a day, rip the modules out of this ship and install them on Mom's new one, but make it work."

Kennedy nodded eagerly, all thoughts of sleep deprivation vanishing beneath the excitement of finally wrestling this beast to the mat. "Oh, I will. Count on it."

PART III

THE TIES THAT BIND

ASTERION DOMINION

35

NAMINO
CAMP BURROW

They sat in a semi-circle on the floor near the center of the bunker, with new cam feeds from the roving drones hovering in the center.

Caleb silently considered those assembled, for he was still trying to get a proper read on the players. Marlee sat beside him, practically vibrating with eagerness and enthusiasm at whatever they were about to learn. Beside her sat Selene, the no-nonsense cop, then Joaquim, the rebel with a renewed cause and more than one rough edge. Ava, the walking weapon with attitude; Xyche'ghael, the reticent and reserved Taiyok; Rogers, the soldier out of his depth; Grant, the…Caleb wasn't certain how to characterize him. A good-hearted man in search of purpose, maybe? But if his planet being invaded by rapacious aliens didn't provide him with sufficient purpose, then nothing would.

The leaders of the group had welcomed him into their midst with the intensity of the desperate. Most of those trapped here weren't fighters, which meant he represented a weapon they could use. They'd quickly armed him with additional archine blades and one of their Glasers, an electricity-based gun not dissimilar to Alex's conductivity lash, modified to target and disrupt Rasu electrical signals.

In his heart, he wanted to dissuade them from their notions about his nature, but it would be a lie. The harrowing journey across the city to reach the bunker had stripped away the last soft, comforting layers of Akeso's peace and tranquility, leaving the raw nerves beneath exposed. If he stayed here much longer, there might be nothing left of him except the weapon.

But Marlee needed him to stay. And she wasn't wrong; these people needed him, too. The old him, the man who excelled at killing without hesitation to protect others.

Three virtual screens flickered to life—apparently they'd lost one drone to the Rasu—to display live feeds from various parts of the city.

It took only seconds to classify the scenes relayed by the drones as uniformly devastating. People being rounded up, herded into cages and ferried into the sky. A massive Rasu compound expanding in height and breadth on the outskirts of the city. The few structures of any size that still stood being ransacked and pillaged before being reduced to rubble. Three Rasu leviathans, dozens of cruiser-sized ships and a host of smaller vessels watching and directing it all from the sky.

"Well, shit. Things have not gotten any better."

"That's not a helpful attitude, Lacese."

Joaquim scowled at Selene. "No? How would you characterize what's happening outside?"

"I only mean…if you're going to be fatalistic, at least keep your voice down. We have to keep spirits up in here."

"With *what*?"

"With—"

Grant interrupted their bickering. "Hey, wait! On the third screen—that's near here, isn't it?"

Joaquim shot Selene another withering glare before checking the small virtual panel in front of him. "About six blocks away. Why?"

"Because I just saw people. Three, or maybe four, stumbling into here." Grant pointed at the blown-out windows of a corner business. A restaurant, perhaps, or a shop, once upon a time. "Rewind it."

"This is a live feed."

"Are you telling me you're not recording it?"

"I am, but I'll have to pull it up separately." Joaquim entered several commands on his panel. The third screen flickered, then again displayed the feed from a few seconds earlier. Sure enough, several shadows scurried around the corner and climbed through the broken storefront windows.

Selene nodded sharply. "Good eye, Grant. We need to go retrieve them if we can. Lacese, Ava, Rogers...." She shot Caleb an arched eyebrow.

"I'll go. And..." he checked beside him to see Marlee had already stood and was latching one of the archine blades to her pants "...so will she."

"Thank you. Everyone gear up. We leave in five."

Caleb stood and placed a hand on Marlee's arm. "You stay behind me, do you understand? And if we see any Rasu, you run all the way back here to the bunker."

Her face screwed up at him, so like the way it had when she was a little girl and he'd said something silly. "What would be the point of me coming on the mission if I ran away at the first sign of trouble?"

"The point of keeping you alive."

Her lips quirked around in defiance as she stared at him, unflinching.

Dammit. "Just stay behind me."

NAMINO ONE

The voluminous dust and debris generated by the Rasu's bombing out of the city had settled into a persistent low cloud layer, turning everything a charred gray in color. It was dusk going on night, as near as Caleb could determine, and the shadows were long.

He let Selene and Joaquim take the lead. They knew the neighborhood far better than he did, and they both seemed to be capable warriors, even if they approached the world in vastly different ways.

His skin prickled painfully. Nerves on edge, straining to act yet recoiling at the psychological pain they knew would inevitably follow. His arm still hurt, as the wound was annoyingly reluctant to stitch itself together. But his eVi retained enough functionality for him to load the Rasu-specific signature as a visual filter, and he focused on detecting movement cast against the dusty fog and monochrome environment.

Marlee's hand touched the small of his back, and he flinched more overtly than he meant to.

"Are you all right?"

"No, and I won't be all right until we are safely back underground."

She didn't snap a retort, instead scanning the street ahead. Good.

Thanks to the quantum block, none of them had any way to communicate except verbally, which made their progress slower, not to mention more dangerous.

At the next intersection, Selene waved everyone ahead, and they dashed across the street. When they reached the block where the survivors had been spotted, she crept forward, flattened against the building and peeked into the blown-out windows—

—laser fire shot out from the interior. She jumped away, then risked raising her voice. "Friendlies! Cease fire!"

A voice answered from the darkness. "Sorry!"

She turned and indicated for them to advance. "We're coming inside now."

Selene entered with her hands high in the air. Joaquim did the same behind her, though Caleb noted he had a grenade cupped in one of his hands. "Is everyone all right?"

"Joaquim? My man...you are a sight...."

Joaquim scrambled over to the source of the comment. A man lay sprawled on the floor, both hands clutching a bloodied and bandaged leg. "Parc? The hells are you doing here?"

"Nothing good, for certain."

"You're hurt."

"Yeah. These people—" the man gestured weakly to a couple talking in anxious whispers to Selene "—found me a couple of hours ago. I told them there was a bunker nearby, then promptly fainted before I could share the directions. A lot of good that did. Woke up in time to stumble in here when some Rasu passed nearby."

"We're from the bunker. You were almost there."

"Yay me...." The man's voice trailed off, and his head dropped to his chest.

"Ava, get over here and help me carry him. We need to get him to the bunker before he bleeds out."

Selene whipped around toward Joaquim. "Wait. We all move together."

"Then we all move now."

"In ten seconds. We need to check the perimeter first."

This sounded like a job for him. Caleb started to return to the street, then searched around in a sudden panic. Where was Marlee?

He spotted her stepping through the blown-out window, weapon at the ready. *Checking the perimeter.* He sighed, recognizing she was far too much like him for her own good, or his. He moved to join her—

—a menacing shadow lurched off the sidewalk to cross the street, its caster a bipedal Rasu easily three meters in height. Time careened to a stop as the Rasu veered toward them. Caleb sprinted forward, both hands grasping for his blades.

"Wait!" Marlee planted her feet and stood directly in the Rasu's path. "We don't have to kill one another. We can learn from each other, if only we understood what you want from us."

The Rasu halted, and a low, screeching sound emanated from it. Caleb's translator deciphered the shrill sound waves while he moved.

"To give up your secrets, then die."

The Rasu pointed an arm toward Marlee, and the metal comprising it slipped and slid and transformed into a gun—

—Caleb flanked the Rasu, dropped one arm low and raised the other, and scissor-cut the weaponized arm off with dual slices of the archine blades.

The Rasu jerked its body toward him, its other arm swinging. He dropped into a crouch as the arm swept above him, brought both hands tight together and yanked upward through the center of the alien's body. The archine blades cut through the metal like butter, splitting the creature in half.

He kicked one half as hard as he could, sending it skittering down the street, then spun toward the half that teetered off balance but remained standing. He grabbed the stub of an arm with one hand and cut diagonally through what approximated a shoulder, down and out through the severed torso. The motion tore open the wound in his arm, but he filed the surge of pain away for later.

The Rasu's head and neck toppled to land at his feet, and he hurled the mass of metal down the street in the opposite direction from the other half—

—sprouting limbs stretched out from the torso and leg that remained to claw insidiously at him. He slashed blindly, a whirlwind of finely honed blades slicing through every appendage and sending chunks of Rasu flying through the air like confetti. The grasping limbs finally stopped moving, and the last disparate pieces fell to the ground…and as soon as they landed, melted into pools and began slithering toward one another. Christ, were the Rasu truly unkillable?

The world began to rush back in around him—the low rumble of distant buildings collapsing, the closer gasps, shouts, and insistent footsteps. He worked to find his voice and project it above the chaos. "We need to move before this monster puts itself back together."

Marlee gaped at him from the sidewalk, her eyes wide and mouth open. "Oh my god. Everything they ever said about you is true!"

He gasped in short, raspy breaths. "Are you hurt?"

"No. Are you?" She leapt forward and put her hands on the flush, sweat-soaked skin of his neck. "You're burning up."

"I'll be fine. Let's get everyone together and move."

Behind Marlee, Ava was blasting the half of the Rasu he'd severed and kicked away with her weaponized arm, which packed an impressive punch. Joaquim had gathered his friend's limp form across his shoulders while Selene urged the other two survivors out of the false safety of the shop and into the street. "We don't have kamero filters for them, so we're going to need to forget stealth and move fast."

"Don't get any on your boot!" Marlee pointed to the expanding pool of Rasu a meter away and closing.

He tried so hard to laugh for her, but it came out as more of a cough as he took her hand in his, guided them well afield of the Rasu pool and willed the others to *move already*.

RW

CAMP BURROW

"Quick, let's get him hooked into the repair bench!"

Marlee urged back the anxious onlookers who had gathered at the door to clear a path as Joaquim hurried over to what the Asterions called a 'repair bench'—in actuality a fully equipped medical station, robotic nurse and pharmaceutical dispensary—and dropped to his knees beside it. Ava and Selene reached out, took his charge by the arms and legs and rolled him onto the 'bench' part of the station.

"Hook him up to the IV. I'll see to his leg."

Ava wound out a long tube with a needle at the end from the station, then hunched over the man—Marlee thought Joaquim had said his name was Parc—and jabbed the needle in where his head met his shoulder. Next, she guided a thin cable with some kind of interface on the end to the base of his neck. Meanwhile, Joaquim cut off the shredded, blood-soaked material of the man's left pant leg and tossed it to the side while Selene grabbed two pads from the repair bench and secured them on either side of the now exposed and quite ghastly wound. Almost instantly, a mechanical appendage extended out from the bench, hovered above the wound and fired a tiny laser into the mangled tissue.

Joaquim stood and took a step back, panting from exertion. "He needs a tank."

Selene adjusted a couple of settings on the bench's console. "We don't have one, so we'll have to make do." She shot Joaquim an inscrutable look. "You handled this like a pro."

"Not the first time I've had to evacuate the injured and triage combat wounds."

"Right." Selene glanced toward the entrance, where the other two survivors had huddled up next to the door, looking exhausted and shell-shocked. She sought out Marlee wearing a weary grimace. "Marlee, can you get our new guests situated while we see to Parc?"

"You got it." Caleb had disappeared down the hallway as soon as they'd arrived, presumably to clean himself up, so she readied a friendly smile and went over to the couple. "Hi. Sorry for the commotion there, but thank you for helping our friend. Welcome to Camp Burrow!"

The man's brow furrowed in confusion, creating deep, dirt-filled creases along his forehead. "You're not an Asterion."

She sighed breezily. "No, I'm a human. Got trapped here with everyone during the initial attack. My name's Marlee. If you want to come with me, I can get you some cots and show you where to find food and a shower."

RW

Twenty minutes later, she'd finally gotten the new residents set up in some improvised free space along the far wall and left them to catch their breaths and absorb the reality of their new, marginally safer environs. She peered around the bunker to gauge the state of affairs. The panic around Parc had died down, though the man remained unconscious and Joaquim was watching him closely while the repair bench robot did its work.

Where was Caleb? Had he never returned to the main room? She wanted to gush over his mind-blowing moves against the Rasu.

There weren't a lot of places that provided solitude and privacy here—basically only the lavatory and the supply room. She headed down the hallway and opened the door to the supply room. The lights were off, and she started to close it...then hesitated. "Caleb, are you in here?"

"Hey, muffin." His voice sounded pinched and strained.

She increased her thermal vision and spotted him hunched against a bare spot of wall, his knees drawn up to his chest and one arm braced atop them.

She shut the door and went over to crouch in front of him. "Are you okay? Did the Rasu hurt you?"

"No."

She put a hand on his arm above the wrist. He was shaking, his skin sopped in hot sweat. "Then what's wrong?"

His throat worked, and his eyes briefly shut. "Akeso and I are having a minor disagreement about my chosen course of action. Coming here, and...basically everything since then."

"Akeso didn't want you to rescue me?"

"Of course it did. Akeso cares about you. It's...complicated. Akeso abhors violence, so much so that me committing it makes us both physically ill. It's gentle and kind and treasures all life. And that's the problem."

Dammit, she'd *known* something was wrong from the minute he'd arrived. He mostly managed to put on a good act, and she'd tried to chalk it up to him being upset with her, plus the whole death-and-destruction-everywhere, but in her heart she'd known. He wasn't okay. And it was her fault.

"What can I do?"

"Nothing. It'll pass in a little while."

"This isn't the first time this has happened?"

He shook his head, then flinched as if he'd been struck. "No. Which is how I know it'll pass." He reached out and patted her hand, though it seemed a tremendous effort for him to complete the small action. "So tell me. What were you *thinking* trying to negotiate with a Rasu?"

She shrugged sheepishly. "I don't know. Language is what I do. I thought if we talked to it like the intelligent beings we are, it might recognize we're worthy adversaries, capable of reason and understanding. I guess that was pretty foolish, huh?"

"No. Well, it was foolish to run out in the street and confront the monster instead of getting behind me like I told you to, but it's not foolish to seek a peaceful solution to war. I'm just afraid the Rasu aren't interested in listening. Or in peace."

"Probably not."

His gaze drifted toward the door. "Are things calming down out there?"

"They are. That Parc guy is still unconscious, but he's not dead so far, and I got the new people settled in." She sat down, scooted beside him and rested her head on his trembling shoulder. "So I'll stay here with you until you're feeling better."

36

NAMINO
CAMP BURROW

Marlee watched on in keen interest as Joaquim and Grant stuffed bundles of cloth with a bunch of archine blades wrapped around an explosive material they'd gotten from the DAF armory, all connected to a small module they called a 'morph.'

Joaquim hefted one of the bundles up and tossed it in the air a few times. "Thanks for the help. Ava, Dominic and I will head out and set some traps."

Grant nodded. "Shall I let Selene know?"

"Up to you." Joaquim arranged the makeshift bombs in a large bag, stood and strode off to enlist his friends.

Marlee took half a step forward, intending to offer to go with them; then she stopped, her gaze drawn to where Caleb sat talking quietly to Selene. It had taken more than an hour for his shakes to subside enough that he was comfortable leaving the supply room. He'd taken a shower, eaten a sandwich and resumed projecting an air of normalcy. But now she'd seen behind the curtain, and she knew it was an act. She wanted so badly to help him, but she didn't—

"Your uncle loves you very much."

She turned back to Grant, who was cleaning up the mess he and Joaquim had created, and shrugged weakly. "I suppose he does. He did come all this way for me."

"You're not close?"

"We used to be. Not so much for the last several years. But I guess family is family, no matter what."

Grant didn't respond, and she studied him more closely for a minute, working it out in her head. "Asterions don't have families, do they?"

"Not in the way you mean, no. But we do have people with whom our bonds have grown strong over the millennia—stronger than those between any mere family."

She regarded him curiously. She really enjoyed spending time with him, but she was tired of getting the constant runaround from him. "Can I ask you a question? I realize it's a sensitive subject since you keep deflecting, but I'm asking anyway: exactly how old *are* you?"

Grant leaned against the front of the workstation with a sigh. "Old enough that you need to stop looking at me with an intrigued glint in your eye."

She shrank back, mortified. "Excuse me?"

"Listen, Marlee. You are courageous and bright—you're running circles around me with languages, combat and possibly even programming, as promised—and very, very pretty. But you've scarcely begun to live your life, and I've...let's just say I have houseplants older than you. Or I did. I expect the Rasu have pulverized the plants and the house by now. I'm going to try to make sure you get to live a lot longer than my houseplants, but I can't.... The point is—"

"Oh, I get the point just fine." She stoked the anger rising in her chest and quelled the stinging hurt his words inflicted, taking care to ensure her bottom lip did *not* quiver. "As if I could ever fall for a coward like you."

"A coward? That's not fair."

"You should be raging in fury at what's happening to your home. You should be *fighting*, the way Joaquim and Ava and Selene are. Instead you're simply...hanging out. Doing what they tell you to do and fiddling with electronics, but nothing else. Don't you *care*?"

His jaw locked, and she decided she'd struck a nerve. "I fought for my home once. It didn't help."

"So you try again. Fight for this one."

"I *did*. I spent the last two months designing a fleet of warships that got themselves blown to smithereens by the Rasu in a matter of hours. See, whatever I do, it doesn't make a difference. So, yes, I'm thinking I'm going to hang out and fiddle with electronics."

"Well, I'm not." She shot him a dark glare then marched off with whatever semblance of pride she could muster.

Selene had gone to check on Parc, and Marlee threw herself onto the couch beside Caleb in a huff.

He was inspecting one of the kamero filter modules, but when she arrived he looked over in concern. "What's wrong?"

"Why does anything have to be wrong?"

"Because your lips are puckered down just like your mom's always do when she's upset."

She cast a sideways glance across the bunker. "Grant called me a child."

Caleb opened his mouth—

"I swear, if you say 'but you are a child,' I will...I will...punch you in the arm so hard!"

He chuckled faintly. "I wasn't going to say that. You like him?"

"No. I mean, I thought I might. He's ridiculously cute, and he seemed funny and kind at first. But it turns out he's an asshole and a coward."

"He risked his life to save yours."

"Ugh. Okay, maybe he's not a coward. But he's not a fighter, either."

"Is that what you want in a...?" His voice trailed off.

She leaned in to whisper in his ear. "*Lover*. The word you're searching for is 'lover.'"

Caleb squeezed his eyes shut in an exaggerated grimace, and she laughed.

"Fine, fine. Is that what you want in a..." he exhaled dramatically "...*lover*? Someone who's also a fighter?"

Well this conversation had taken a more serious turn than she'd intended. She cast her mind back to her growing list of discarded girlfriends, boyfriends, fluidfriends and unrequited crushes.

"I think so, yeah. I do." She paused. "It's all your fault, you know. I idolized you growing up."

"Until you didn't. Which is on me."

Deeper and darker still. Oops. She shrugged with intentional mildness. "We could split the blame and get fairly close to the truth."

"Deal." He sighed. "The thing is, I never wanted this kind of life for you."

"I appreciate it. I do. But I get to decide what kind of life I want for myself."

"You do." He shot her a smirk. "I'm still telling your mother about all of this."

"Unh!" She jabbed him in the shoulder, and he flinched visibly. "I'm sorry, did I hurt you? But…." Suspicious, she reached over and peeled his sleeve up to reveal a large, blood-darkened medwrap. "I thought you said the Rasu didn't hurt you."

"The one today didn't. This is from before—from the trip here."

"Why aren't you healing? Akeso should have had this patched up in an hour or two at most."

"Akeso's not necessarily focused on healing at the moment. I assume. But Akeso's also not talking to me right now, so I'm guessing here."

"But even without Akeso, the medwrap and your cybernetics should have taken care of the wound by now."

"And yet." He slid the sleeve back down over the medwrap. "We were talking about Grant, weren't we?"

She rolled her eyes, surreptitiously checking to confirm blood hadn't started seeping down his arm. She hadn't meant to *hurt* him, dammit. "We don't have to. Unless you have any wise uncle insights you want to share?"

Caleb scooted closer and lowered his voice to a murmur. "The thing you need to understand is, every Asterion in this room is ancient by our standards—they've all lived thousands of years longer than any human. And I suspect a few of the people in this room are ancient even by Anaden standards. Your friend Grant is one of them."

"He's not my friend."

"He saved your life, so he probably ought to be."

"And a mature person who definitely isn't a child would move past any perceived slight, right? I hear what you're saying about their ages, and Grant's for certain old. But at some point the number of years a person has lived doesn't matter any longer, does it? We've seen it with many of the Anadens we know."

He nodded thoughtfully. "True. But let me ask you this: why would you want to be with someone who's seen and endured so much that they've lost the capacity to experience wonder?"

She opened her mouth to argue, but he made a good point. Damn him for being so perceptive. She didn't think most Asterions she'd met were so depressingly jaded, but she couldn't deny Grant's ennui—

A small commotion broke out by the repair bench. "He's waking up!"

They fell silent to watch in interest as the injured man stirred, moaned and tried to sit up, only to be eased back down by Selene and one of the other women.

She'd heard a number of interesting things about this Parc guy in the hours since he'd arrived here unconscious, most notably how he was supposed to be some sort of tech wonder-genius. With him here and now awake, perhaps their fortunes would start looking up.

37

MIRAI
RIDANI ENTERPRISES

Dashiel pressed his palms together at his chin and studied the chemical formulation for adiamene, much as he'd done for the last...many hours. The molecular structure was a work of art—but for all the strength and resilience of the finished product, the structure was also delicate. Tweak one bond, add or remove one electron, and the whole formulation disintegrated. This feature of the material threatened to make his chosen goal impossible.

Still, he stared at the symbols and interlocking chains until his eyes glazed over. Then he sank back in his chair, blinked his failing eyes several times and adjusted his neurotransmitter output for a jolt of concentration. At this rate of abuse he was going to fry out this body in record time, but it was fine. So long as the Rasu kept their shapeshifting hands off the rest of their worlds, he could order a new one. And they were far more likely to retain ownership of those worlds if he solved this godsdamned problem.

But juiced-up attention and clarity of vision refused to yield any further answers. Honestly, adiamene shouldn't exist, which had to be part of the reason why tweaking it was an exercise in futility. Unless...what if the answer lay in its creation? Emboldened by the head-rush of a new idea, he sent a comm request to Alex Solovy. Somewhat to his surprise, she responded immediately.

"Alex, I'm sorry to bother you. Do you have a minute to answer a few quick questions?"

"If they involve how to stop the Rasu, absolutely."

"They do. I'm hoping for some information on how adiamene was originally created, and Ms. Rossi has indicated you're the person to talk to about that."

"True enough. So Caleb and I got into a firefight in the Metis Nebula—"

"With each other?"

"Yes. We had a...misunderstanding. I blew up his ship, but not before he ripped a hole in the undercarriage of the Siyane. We both ended up stranded on this total shitshow of a planet—I landed, he crashed—without any way to call for help, because the Kats were blocking all quantum communications—wait, I should've thought about that. Is anyone poking into how the Kats did it and if it can help us circumvent the Rasu block?"

"I, um, believe someone is, yes."

"Good. Still, I ought to talk to Mesme. Anyway, we used amodiamond scrap from his ship to patch up the carbon metamat hull of the Siyane. The metals were similar enough for us to straight weld them together. Within a day or two, the patched section of the hull started changing color and, it turned out, began morphing into what we now call adiamene."

"A chemical reaction occurred between the two materials?"

"Yes."

"But the entire hull eventually transformed, right? How long did that take?"

"It happened slowly at first, then suddenly all at once."

"Do you have any explanation for why the process sped up?"

"Well...there was one thing. A few weeks after we did the patch job, we got into another firefight—"

"With each other?"

"Ha. No, not this time. With several Kat swarmers. Their weapons fire grazed the Siyane's undercarriage. The hits didn't do any damage, because that section of the hull was already adiamene. But after the encounter, it only took a couple of days for the transformation to consume the ship."

"You think the energy from the weapons fire accelerated the transformation?"

"I think there's a temporal correlation between the two events. But causation? I haven't the slightest clue."

"Of course. Thank you for your time. Oh, one last question. Do you happen to be able to find out the nature and energy output of a swarmer's weapon?"

"Thirty-two kilotonnes of tight-beam laser energy per second."

"I kind of expected you to need to ask someone, such as a Kat or possibly a military historian."

"I'm a Prevo, remember? It was relevant information for our final battle against the Kats, back when they were the enemy."

"Understood. Thank you again. I won't take up any more of your time."

There was a long pause on the other end. *"No news from Namino?"*

"I'm sorry. I wish there were."

RW

RIDANI ENTERPRISES TESTING FACILITY

Dashiel met Vance Greshe at Ridani Enterprises' outdoor testing facility near Mirai Two. By the time he arrived, Vance had secured a six-by-three-meter sheet of adiamene onto a vertical frame like a range target. And for the moment, it basically was one.

Two techs were finishing up the assembly of their makeshift power source, which had been hastily designed to mimic the output of a Kat swarmer vessel. It was an ugly, oversized block of cobbled-together components and cables, but it didn't need to be pretty. It just needed to work once.

Dashiel rubbed his hands together to warm them against the frigid winter wind as he joined Vance. "You're a miracle worker, as always. Did you run into any problems with the setup?"

"The only open question is the angle of impact, if you think it matters."

"Hells, anything could matter. She said the fire 'grazed' the hull, so let's set things up for a sideways glancing blow."

"Yes, sir." Vance went to confer with the techs, and they rolled the firing assembly to the left until it was situated at a twenty-two-degree angle from the sheet.

"We're ready when you are, sir."

"All right. Let's output a three-second burst, then wait and see what happens."

Vance reached around the rear of the assembly and flipped a switch—it really was that rushed of a setup. A beam of crimson light shot out to skim across the surface of the adiamene sheet before flickering off.

Dashiel jogged up to the sheet for a closer look. It remained completely unmarred. Not so much as a faint scorch mark. But it also continued to sit placidly and silently, as a proper metal should.

He took a few steps back, crossed his arms over his chest, and waited. Seconds ticked by, then minutes. Nothing happened.

Finally, he sighed. "Dammit."

"Sir, perhaps the problem is that it's all already adiamene. It has nothing to turn *into* adiamene, which as I understand events is what happened the first time."

"Good point. So, what? We graft strips of carbon metamat along the edges for it to feast on?"

Vance shrugged. "It's an idea."

"Before we take the time to scrounge up more material, let's think this through. If your idea does work, what would this tell us? Our ultimate goal is to create protective shells over the parts of a ship that require seams—engines, weapons, exhaust ports, airlocks. To do this, we'd have to install retractable covers over those areas made of the metamat, then when needed, activate the covers and direct an energy surge into the adiamene adjacent to them."

Damn, he wished Grant were here to tell him if any of this was remotely feasible or, more likely, as ludicrous as it sounded. The skeptical expression on Vance's face, though, got close enough.

He ran fingertips pensively along the flawless sheet of metal. "But say all this works, and we end up with a seamless, impenetrable shell of adiamene over the area in question. How do we retract the cover once it's no longer required? Any seam defeats the purpose, but you can't break adiamene. That's the point of using it."

Abruptly he spun away from the sheet, shaking his head. "Vance, I'm sorry for wasting your morning."

"It's no trouble—and also my job."

"To entertain my fanciful and wholly impractical ideas?"

"As well as the practical ones, sir."

"Right. I ought to try to come up with more of those." He turned and started to leave...then pivoted back to reconsider the test setup. "But what about...?"

"About what?"

He shook his head. "I'm not sure. I'll be in the kyoseil lab if you need me—no, scratch that. I'll be in the adiamene lab. Or, both."

"Yes, sir."

RW

RIDANI ENTERPRISES

The threads of kyoseil glittered within the chrome molten metal like strings of stars woven through a nebula. The metal had been carefully painted in a thin sheet upon the kyoseil lattice; as it began to harden, it took on an almost plaid appearance. A kilt of precious, life-infused and life-saving material. Maybe.

Standing here waiting for it to cure wasn't going to speed up the process, so he tracked down the Adiamene Project Lead in the adjacent prototype assembly lab.

"How's our experiment look, sir?"

"So far so good, but we haven't truly accomplished anything yet. As soon as the test sheet finishes curing, I want it subjected to every single test we initially ran on the first sheets of adiamene. If the composite material isn't as strong and flexible as the pure adiamene, this will be the second wasted endeavor of my day."

"And if it passes those tests?"

He hesitated, reluctant to voice another ludicrous proposition. "Then we see if we can talk to it."

RW

The idea had come to him when he'd started talking about 'retracting' the hypothetical adiamene covers. An image had flashed in his mind of the Reor responding to a harmonic wave by softening and retreating to set its kyoseil fibers free from their protective armor. Only now did he fully appreciate how it wasn't the Reor controlling the response, but rather the kyoseil. He knew from millennia of experience molding it into products that kyoseil was highly adaptive, but it was easy to forget that, however mysterious and arcane kyoseil remained, it was also alive.

If the kyoseil and adiamene played nice with one another, and *if* their blending didn't weaken both, then *maybe* they could use the kyoseil to expand and retract adiamene on command by using its native language: harmonics and resonance.

It shouldn't work. But adiamene shouldn't exist and kyoseil shouldn't be sentient, and they desperately needed something to break their way.

38

MIRAI
DAF MILITARY SERVICES CENTER

C onstruction cranes and assembly mechs created an air of purposeful activity along the perimeter of what had been, until a week ago, a barely staffed adjunct military center in Mirai Two. Operating under the reasoned assumptions that DAF Command on Namino was going to remain inaccessible for the foreseeable future and the Initiative floorspace was never going to suffice as a military command center, Lance's third act after reawakening was to order the immediate expansion of the center here. His forces needed a dedicated space to train, organize and grow.

He exchanged salutes with the members of the officer corps he passed on the way to the auditorium at the center of the facility, then strode directly to the podium at the center of the raised dais. Once there, he focused his attention on the sea of faces gazing up at him with rapt attention.

Three hundred sixty-four special forces ground troops—the entirety of the ground forces in the Dominion Armed Forces, save the twenty-eight who were on Namino when the Rasu attacked. DAF fielded no infantry, as the possibility of fighting a sustained ground war had always seemed unimaginable, even to him.

Perhaps he should have sent all these troops to Namino as soon as the Rasu attack began. Though based on what little they knew about the situation on the ground there, three hundred ninety-two soldiers stood no greater chance against the invaders on the ground than their warships had stood against the invaders in space. The scores of pilots lost in the rout at Namino were still being regened.

Enlistment was up, at least. Provided a tangible enemy, people wanted to fight. And Kat Rift Bubbles or not, Lance knew in his bones that one day soon, they would get their wish. He only hoped he'd have time to mold their growing ranks into a proper fighting force before the day arrived.

"Everyone, thank you for coming today. I know you've all begun training in earnest for ground combat against the Rasu. I'm happy to report that new weapons will soon be coming your way to give you an advantage in such combat. Killing Rasu takes unconventional armaments, and we're working hard to develop them, get them into your hands and train you on how to use them to destroy these metal motherfuckers. Now, given the current size of our special forces regiment, we must be strategic in how we think about taking the fight to the Rasu. We need to—"

A hand shot up in the front row. Lance frowned; he didn't care for being interrupted. "Yes, Lieutenant? You have something to add?"

"I volunteer to diversify. I want to help increase our numbers."

Another hand rose, on the left side of the auditorium. "Captain?"

"So do I. I always wanted a brother, anyway. Maybe two of them."

Shouts now began overlapping one another from throughout the crowd—all people volunteering to do the same.

Lance motioned for quiet. Those present being soldiers, they quickly complied. "Thank you, Lieutenant, Captain. A show of hands: how many of you are willing to diversify within the strictures of military personality profile guidelines, thus creating additional DAF fighting forces?"

A good forty percent of those present in the room raised their hands.

"You realize this is a permanent proposition. Once created, your sibling shards will have their own thoughts and desires. They'll follow paths of adaptation and improvement that you won't be able to control and might not approve of."

Four or five hands lowered, but no more. He did the math in his head. If everyone who volunteered created two siblings, which was the most common option, the number of special forces soldiers would double in a matter of days. If any of them created a greater number....

Lance was not a sentimental man, but the dedication to protecting the Dominion on display here made his heart do a little pitter-patter in his chest. He even smiled, briefly. "Thank you all for wanting to support our mission. I'll appoint someone to spearhead a formal diversification program, so we can track your new siblings and integrate them into our existing forces in an organized and swift manner."

Applause spontaneously broke out among those gathered, leaving Lance momentarily speechless. He cleared his throat and adopted a scowl. "That's enough. Now, later today, we're rolling out new modifications to our combat training program."

RW

Walking off the dais twenty minutes later, Lance spotted Dashiel waiting for him by the side exit. He diverted in the man's direction. "Ridani? What the hells are you doing here?"

"I need to show you something."

He spread his arms wide. "I'm waiting."

"Come with me."

"I don't have time to go on a field trip."

"Just down the hall. I've set everything up in one of the meeting rooms."

"Set everything of what up?"

Ridani looked almost gleeful. "You'll see."

It seemed today was bringing more than one surprise. Lance trailed Ridani out of the auditorium, down the east hall and into a small meeting room. Inside, a sergeant stood at attention beside a sheet of chrome metal laid out on the table.

"Thank you, sergeant, for guarding it for me. We're good now."

"Yes, sir." The sergeant saluted Lance and departed, while Ridani started fiddling with the metal sheet, attaching a small transmitter mid-way down one side of it.

"Is that adiamene?"

"Sort of."

"If this is supposed to be engineer humor, it's lost on me."

Ridani squinted at the tiny screen on the transmitter and made an adjustment. "Sorry. I don't have an official name for it yet, so let's call it 'enhanced' adiamene for now."

"Enhanced with what?"

"Kyoseil. Watch this." Ridani activated the transmitter, evoking a slight *thrum* in Lance's bones.

After a few seconds, the sheet dimpled in a line perpendicular to the transmitter. The metal thinned there, then gradually separated until the one sheet became two.

Ridani smirked.

"I thought adiamene was designed to be indestructible. How is this an enhancement?"

"Oh, I'm sorry. Let me show you." Ridani tweaked a setting on the transmitter and activated it again. The inner edge of the left sheet expanded until it touched the right sheet, and in seconds the two had re-merged into a single solid piece.

He arched an eyebrow at Ridani. "I don't get it."

"Don't you see? Kyoseil can control the shape and breadth of the adiamene! We can have seamless hulls when we need them—to keep Rasu out—and discrete components when we don't."

"Won't it break our ships if their hulls are randomly shrinking and expanding?"

"No. With a sophisticated enough oversight program, we'll enjoy a highly precise degree of control over what sections of the hull open and close. We'll semi-isolate those sections, so a properly designed ship won't suffer any stresses from the alterations."

"And who's writing the oversight program? You?"

"Yes. I should have it finished by tonight."

Lance dragged a hand down his jaw. "New hull designs? Now new materials? We can't keep starting over from scratch every time you get another brilliant idea."

"I know we can't. This will be worth it, I promise you. Not only will our ships be all but indestructible, they'll be impermeable to Rasu incursions. Let me build you a fleet of these ships, and the next battle will go very differently for us."

He stared at the reformed sheet of metal. "And when the pieces join back together, the material is as strong as it was before splitting?"

"Absolutely. This is what kyoseil *does*—bond with other materials to enhance their strengths."

"What's the transmitter for? How are you coaxing the adiamene to split apart?"

"Harmonic resonance wave functions."

"Fine, don't tell me." Lance jerked a nod. "Build me one ship and show me that it works in the field. Then we can talk about your fantastical notions for a new fleet."

"A prototype is already under construction. It'll be ready in thirty-six hours."

39

MIRAI
OMOIKANE INITIATIVE

"Hey."

Nika jerked out of her reverie to see Perrin standing in front of her. Perrin thrust out her hand, which held a steaming hot peach croissant. "You look like you could use a boost."

She gratefully accepted the croissant. "I've been meaning to go down to the cafeteria and get some breakfast, but I keep getting distracted..." she glanced around, only now remembering that she'd holed up at a workstation behind a shoji screen as soon as she'd arrived "...by my own thoughts, apparently."

"I've seen this expression on your face before." Perrin dragged a second chair closer, sat down opposite Nika and produced her own half-eaten croissant. "I need to tell you something, before my guilt eats me alive."

"What is it?"

"I knew about Parc being a Plex. Before he showed up here, I mean. It's how he was able to help me find and rescue Adlai from Ian Sevulch."

Nika set the croissant down on the workstation. "Why didn't you tell me?"

"Because he asked me to keep his confidence, and I owed him big-time, so I agreed. I'm sorry. I confessed to Adlai last night, too, which...well, it didn't go great, but I think I finally made him see my side, at least a little bit, and he didn't kick me out." She dropped her head into her hands. "I am a terrible secret-keeper, and I should never ever do it again."

Nika wanted to be angry. She *should* be angry. But her emotional processes had devoted themselves exclusively to obsessing over the destruction and loss of life on Namino and her own guilt for not being on the ground there. Besides, she'd hardly found the time to so much as speak to Perrin since the Rasu attack; when did she imagine her friend would have confided in her?

She forced a weak smile. "It doesn't really matter—or it didn't, until it did. I'm just glad Parc came forward and told us."

"You're not angry at me for keeping this from you?"

"Perrin, I...I don't know what I'm feeling right now, or even if I'm capable of feeling anything at all. I'm drained as dry as a gully in a drought. All I can do is keep putting one foot in front of the other and trying to move forward—"

"Hey, he's waking up!"

Nika and Perrin both leapt up at Ryan's shout from across the room. As one, they rushed over to the cordoned off space in the far left corner of the Initiative.

Parc had passed out not long after arriving at the Initiative and making his dramatic declaration. The onsite repair bench had been unable to identify any specific physical ailment that might explain his unconscious state, so they'd situated him on one of the couches in the corner and made him comfortable. The presumed source of the collapse must be his twin on Namino, which suggested nothing good regarding the health of said twin. If the twin hadn't been able to reach one of the bunkers before collapsing, then what did this say about the situation in Namino One?

But now he was awake.

Ryan knelt beside Parc on the couch, one of Parc's hands clutched in his. Despite acting demonstrably upset with Parc, Ryan had remained at Parc's side once he passed out. Nika wasn't sure what had happened to cause a rift between them, but it was a reasonable conclusion that it involved the Plexes. Their mere existence introduced a host of philosophical and societal concerns, never mind the very real, practical ones.

Parc moaned as his eyelids fluttered, and Ryan hurriedly dropped his hand and backed away, motioning for Nika to take his place.

Another few seconds and Parc's eyes fully opened. He grimaced and squinted around, his blurry gaze lingering on Ryan for a long beat before settling on Nika and Perrin. "Hey, you two." He struggled up to a sitting position, then inhaled deeply. "Damn, that sucked. But hey, I got rescued!"

"Wonderful!" Nika sat beside him on the couch. "What happened? What can you tell us?"

"Joaquim, Ava, Grant, Selene, Dominic, Josie? They're all okay. They're holed up with about fifty people in the bunker near DAF Command. Oh, and two Humans are with them."

Relief flooded her pathways until her head swam from dizziness. By gods, all was *not* lost. She reached out and grasped Parc's hands in hers. "Please, tell me everything."

"Yeah, yeah. They have a lot they want me to tell you, believe me. But first, do you know someone named Alex?"

"I do. Why?"

"Because this Human here—there—named Caleb has a message for her, and he won't get out of my face until I pass it along."

RW

Getting the Advisors back around a table on half an hour's notice had taken a herculean effort. Nika suspected it was due in part to a reluctance to be confronted with another avalanche of bad news, when instead they could be concentrating on trying to make their own little corner of bad news a little less bad. She didn't blame them for it. But organization, planning and an overarching strategy were thus far all that was keeping the Axis Worlds from descending into anarchy. Besides, she was actually bringing *good* news to this meeting.

She projected an upbeat demeanor as she passed around a replenished basket of fresh peach croissants. "Good morning. I realize we're all busy, so we'll work while we eat, and I'll try not to waste your time. First, I have some excellent news to share. We've got people alive on Namino. Selene, Grant, several former NOIR members and many others, as well as our missing Concord representative."

Katherine frowned, looking suspicious. "How do you suddenly know this?"

Nika sighed; Katherine could sour the most festive of occasions. "Because Parc Eshett is a Plex, and his twin is currently on Namino. He managed to reach Bunker #3 near DAF Command, which Selene and Grant are using as a base of operations."

"Has Selene arrested him? Plexes are against the law."

She glared at Katherine in disbelief. "Um, no. Everyone's concentrating on staying alive. Spencer's debriefing him—our Parc here—regarding everything he's learned on Namino, but he's not planning on arresting this version, either. Besides, Parc is a valuable asset. He believes he can find the origin point of the quantum block on Namino. If he does, we will stand a chance of taking it out."

"Then what?"

"Then we fight. But we're not there yet. Dashiel, however, has more good news for us on that front."

"I do. The kyoseil-adiamene fusion works. It works fabulously, in fact."

She already knew the answer, but she asked the question for the group's benefit. "So we can now build starships made of adiamene that also feature impenetrable hulls?"

"Even better. We can build them so they're impenetrable only when they need to be. It's all about flexibility and responding to the needs of the moment. Our new starships will be able to morph and alter themselves—no, not like the Rasu, but enough for our needs."

"It sounds as if you're talking about building 'living' ships."

He opened his mouth to respond, then smiled. "Perhaps I am. As far as we know, kyoseil has neither the ability nor the inclination to fly such ships themselves, so for now we still need pilots. But the possibilities are intriguing."

"Incredible work, darling."

He almost blushed. "Thank you. There's a lot more work ahead transforming the concept into an entire fleet of ships, but I think this is going to make a real difference, and soon."

"It will." Her lips pursed. "And the Rasu virutox?" The word still tasted foul on her tongue, but a virutox wasn't evil in and of itself; it only became so when malicious people imbued it with evil purpose.

"The Conceptual Research ceraff members believe they've finalized it. Based on everything we've learned about Rasu programming, when injected directly into one of their systems, it should corrupt the system's functionality within a few seconds."

"Excellent. Now we merely need a target in which to inject it. Perrin? What's the status of the refugees?"

Perrin lifted her chin and adopted an overly serious expression. Nika knew she wasn't comfortable being included in these Advisor-level meetings, but she deserved to be there. "As of yesterday, no one is camping in the streets any longer. Much of the housing we've set up is designed to be temporary, but it is providing roofs, warmth and running water to the refugees. Now..." she checked with Katherine uncertainly "...we estimate there are almost two hundred thousand people who are refusing to evacuate from the Adjunct Worlds."

Lance groaned. "I have a bunch of soldiers sitting around twiddling their thumbs waiting to fight the Rasu. Declare martial law, and we'll move them out posthaste."

"No one is going to declare martial law." Nika glowered at Lance. "We've made it crystal clear to everyone living on the Adjunct Worlds the nature of the risk to their homes and lives and explained how at this time we can't adequately protect them. If, armed with this information, they choose to stay, that is their right. Perrin and Katherine, just make sure they know that should they decide to leave at any time, we will take care of them."

Perrin relaxed in her chair. "Will do."

"Next, we need to decide where to send the next Kat Rift Bubble, which I'm told will be available for deployment in a few hours."

"Synra, obviously. It's our oldest and most populous world—"

"Kiyora, without a doubt, as vital military and manufacturing infrastructure is located there—"

She held up a hand to silence everyone. "Every Axis World has a solid claim to be the next in line. But I want to offer a different suggestion: Chosek."

Adlai stared at her in shock. "What? You would put the Chizeru ahead of our own people?"

She dropped her chin to her chest. "No. But without kyoseil, we have no people. It's regened bodies for all those who have died on Namino and all who will sacrifice themselves in the battles to come. With Dashiel's breakthrough, it's the ships that will protect our military crews and help defeat the Rasu."

"But we're getting literal tons of kyoseil from Concord now."

"Regrettably, Concord remains in a somewhat precarious situation. I'm hopeful they will be able to regain control over the Anaden rebels and other disruptive elements in their midst, but we can't plan our future based on hope. We need to maintain our own supply."

Lance snorted in disgust. "Never underestimate the ability of Anadens to get what they want. She's right. We can't rely on a friendly and generous Concord."

Adlai shook his head. "I still don't like it."

"Mesme says it'll only be a few days before another Rift Bubble is ready. Then another. Trust me, I wish we didn't need to prioritize lives this way. I am stricken at the thought of leaving *any* of our people unprotected. But we have to think strategically. We *have* to."

Maris, who had been subdued throughout the meeting—and ever since the invasion began—clasped her hands formally atop the table. "I have a question."

"Of course."

"We can assume that by now the Rasu have captured and analyzed zettabytes of government data from Namino. There's zero chance they don't possess the locations of every Dominion world. Why haven't they attacked us somewhere else yet?"

An uneasy silence answered Maris. Nika was reluctant to break it, but hiding from the truth did them no good. "Because the Rasu don't fear us."

Dashiel frowned at her. "But we destroyed their entire presence in this galaxy."

"We did. And by now, they realize that we accomplished it using smoke and mirrors and are unlikely to be able to replicate the feat anytime soon. They don't fear us, which means they can afford to take their time, methodically dismantling our civilization block by block, then planet by planet."

Lance arched an eyebrow. "Then we need to make them fear us again."

"We do, and I believe we will. Everyone, keep plugging away. We are starting to get our feet back underneath us. From a position of strength, we can move forward and defend our people."

She remained seated as the others filed away, absently drumming her fingers on the table. Parc's collapse then reawakening kept running through her mind. It was disturbing, watching him as he physically experienced events happening to him on another planet in real-time. But the mere fact of this experience held deeply profound implications.

Kyoseil's interconnectivity ran deeper than any of them had previously understood. It wasn't limited by distance, dimensions or quantum fields. No wonder the Rasu were so desperate to unlock its secrets and use it as a weapon of control and domination.

But maybe she could use it as a weapon, too.

40

CHOSEK
GENNISI GALAXY

D ashiel watched Nika draw open the plush curtains of the embassy meeting room to let in the light, then gaze pensively out at the craggy Chosek landscape. Her mind was parsecs away, as it had been every minute since Namino fell. He couldn't blame her, for his often was as well. Still, he felt the yawning chasm between them growing with each passing hour. They should seek solace and comfort in one another, but she refused to just *stop*, even for a moment, and allow herself to receive any solace. Instead she bore the weight of this crisis on her shoulders like a badge of honor, as if they weren't all carrying the same weight.

He rested a hand on her shoulder. "Nika—"

"What if this is the wrong decision? What if Synra gets attacked tomorrow and millions die?"

"Then we'll need kyoseil to regen them in new bodies. There's no perfect decision here, but this isn't the wrong one."

She shifted to half-face him and placed her hand atop his. "Okay. Thank you for the reassurance."

"You don't have to—"

The doors opened to admit Shoset and his delegation. Instantly she plastered on a breezy countenance and knelt to greet the Chizeru leader with open arms.

The leathery-skinned, diminutive alien hurriedly waddled over to her. "Our extra work did good for Nika-friend?"

"Yes. You helped save a lot of my people. You have my deepest thanks." She nodded to Dashiel; he took the cue and retrieved the gift they'd brought from where it rested against the wall. "We brought you a present to show our appreciation."

He unrolled the long rug across the floor beside them. Crafted of thick, soft yarn in royal purple and crimson, the pile stood a good three centimeters thick.

Shoset's eyes widened in delight. He leapt onto the rug, jumped up and down a few times, then crouched down to run his rough fingers through the material. "Ah! Softest I've ever felt!"

"It's for your home. Or wherever you want to display it."

"My bed!" Shoset laid down on his back and wiggled around, eliciting the first genuine smile from Nika that Dashiel had seen in many days.

"As I said, wherever you want."

"Most pleased!" Shoset climbed to his feet and went over to hug Nika's legs, then Dashiel's as well. Dashiel rolled his eyes dramatically at Nika over Shoset's head, but the Chizeru's open, honest affection left him genuinely touched.

Nika waited until Shoset disentangled himself before clearing her throat. "Shoset, there's something else. The bad thing we told you about is still out there, in the stars, and we want to protect you from it. We've brought another present—a different kind of present—that will ensure the bad thing never comes here to hurt your people."

"Good. Most good. Shoset has thanks."

"I'm glad. Now, here's the thing about this present: it's a little scary. It's kind of similar to the ships we visit here in. It runs on powerful technology, but don't be afraid. It's here to protect you."

Shoset peered at her suspiciously. "Scary thing will protect us?"

"That's right. Now, shall we go outside and see it?"

RW

They'd identified a crater carved into the mountainous, rugged landscape as the best location to situate the Rift Bubble. The area offered a wide, flat expanse protected by the surrounding mountains far from any settlement—far enough away to discourage curious Chizeru from making the trek to see the strange alien device.

Nika knelt behind Shoset on the hard-packed dirt and placed both hands on the Chizeru's shoulders. "Don't be afraid. We're here with you."

All eyes went to the sky as, much like the one on Mirai had, a circular object was released from an unseen superdreadnought in orbit and descended through the clouds to land gently on the surface. The casing fell away, revealing the obsidian lattice and dancing golden center of the Rift Bubble engine.

Shoset gasped and stumbled backward, but Nika held him steady. "It won't hurt you. See? It's just sitting there glowing."

"Like the sun." He pulled his attention away from the lattice to regard her curiously. "What else it do?"

"Well, the glow is generating a shield of sorts. A shield extending all the way up into the sky to protect all Chizeru from the bad thing."

"How long it last?"

"As long as it's needed. Now, no one should get close to it. It'll zap you, like a shock stun. Understand?"

Shoset's gaze drifted back to the lattice and the spinning orb within it.

"I tell you what. If it's okay with you, we're going to send some friends here to put a fence around the device. To make sure and keep your people safe."

"Okay. Children be reckless and too curious."

"That's a good point. We don't want any children getting hurt trying to touch it."

"Need to care for present? Clean it?"

"You don't need to do anything. Maybe check on it occasionally, and let us know if it's stopped glowing or looks as if it's gotten damaged. That's all."

Shoset's attention darted between the device and Nika. "Will appoint an Official Shiny Orb Checker." He shifted his stance from one leg to the other. "The bad thing in the sky...it is most evil?"

She glanced up at Dashiel, the weight of her burden shining brightly in her stunning teal eyes. "It's the evilest thing I've ever encountered. But I won't let it get you."

RW

MIRAI

DASHIEL'S FLAT

Dashiel stirred awake. His hand instinctively reached for Nika beside him—and found her side of the bed empty. Their lovemaking earlier had gone beyond passionate to frenetic, tinged with desperation, as if they were outracing an accelerating clock. And maybe they were.

He opened his eyes to see her standing naked at the window. A bolt of lightning streaked across the night sky to silhouette the curves of her body and cast them upon a canvas of light.

The wave of déjà vu was so powerful it choked off the air in his throat.

I didn't enjoy seeing her troubled, particularly since in this instance I was the cause of it, in a way. I had shared my concerns with her and, lacking any obvious path forward for myself to follow to resolve them, had allowed her to involve herself in them. Had I told her in the secret hope that she would in fact involve herself? Shame flared at the thought, but perhaps.

I wound my hands behind my head and relaxed against the pillow in false casualness. "This brooding is unlike you. What are you stewing over so intently?"

"The outpost on SR27-Shi? It isn't the only outpost to disappear recently. In the last two years, four other exploratory world outposts have become ghost towns, each one seemingly overnight."

I hadn't expected this answer, and I abandoned the relaxed pose to sit up straighter. "Five outposts gone? How is it that no one has noticed? Have the Guides not noticed?"

The next day she'd vanished, and he'd lost her for five desolate years. He climbed out of bed, determined they would not suffer the same fate a second time. He sidled up behind her to press against her bare skin, draping his hands on her hips and letting his lips caress her neck. "You should get some sleep. You can't keep going like this without rest."

"I caught a nap." She looked back to kiss him lightly. "I need you to do something for me."

He ignored the warning twinge in his gut that whispered how history was surely intent on repeating itself. "Of course. Anything."

"You should hear what it is first." She shifted around in his arms. "I need you to design me a new body, one soaked through from head to toe in kyoseil."

It was the last thing he'd expected her to ask of him. "I'm not a biologist."

"I know. You'll want to work with a regen expert, I assume. But you are our foremost expert on kyoseil. Here's my reason for asking: kyoseil is not hindered by the quantum block. I suspect this means kyoseil should protect whatever is encased within it from the quantum block as well. I need its encasement to be *me*. I need to be able to transport, protect and deliver the virutox your people have developed into a Rasu system without the block interfering with the transmission."

"The virutox? But the only Rasu systems are..." the twinge grew into dread "...you're intending to go to Namino. But Nika—"

"I know there are several details to work out. Reaching the surface, then reaching our friends in their bunker, then choosing a worthy target and fighting our way to it. But now we know the others are alive and where they're located, which is so much more than we knew yesterday. Dashiel, it's time for me to go. But first, I need you to create a version of me that can succeed in my mission once I get there."

So be it. He locked his jaw in resoluteness. *We are forever.* "I'm going with you."

"No, you're not. You're staying here with me."

"What?"

"I'm going to Plex this. One version of me will stay here. They—I—will be in constant communication with the version who goes to Namino. More than communication, I'll see and hear everything they do. I can coordinate our actions, provide intel to everyone here, and plan our next moves on both planets."

"Nika...."

"I'm not crazy about the idea either. I didn't enjoy splitting myself into 8,000 shards on the Rasu stronghold. But this will merely be two shards, so." She shrugged, adding a falsely lighthearted smile. "Now that Parc—on Namino—is healed up and marginally protected by Joaquim and Selene, I firmly believe he will be able to pinpoint the source of the quantum block. But wherever it's located will be heavily defended, and they'll probably have to take out massive Rasu defenses in order to reach and disable it. This virutox can do exactly that, faster and better than any other tool we can wield. I need to get it to Namino, because if we ever want to reclaim our world and rescue our people, we *have* to disable the quantum block."

Her hand came up to drift along his jaw and down his neck. "So what do you think? Can you create what I need to make this happen? *Will* you?"

He took her hand in his and brought it to his lips. "You know it's almost impossible for me to refuse you. I wish Forchelle were still alive, as he could do a superior job of it in a quarter of the time. But I have the notes he left behind detailing his work creating the first kyoseil-infused Asterion bodies, and I worked with Dr. Takeda to expedite your 8,000 copies. I'll contact him first thing in the morning...which is about an hour from now." He paused, searching her gaze and finding only steadfast determination painted atop desperation. "If you're sure."

"I'm sure." She wound her hands into his hair and drew him into her arms. "Thank you. I love you beyond words."

"Even if I couldn't produce you a kyoseil-laden body on demand?"

"Even if...but it doesn't hurt that you can."

CONCORD

41

CONCORD HQ
COMMAND

"Let me see if I understand this correctly. The Machim Imperium that shot up a Concord station temporarily under Anaden control was actually piloted by *the two of you?*"

Alex swung her legs casually off the edge of the table she'd hopped on, while David wandered around the office rubbing his hands together. He glanced over at her, and they reluctantly met Miriam's incredulous glare. "Yep."

"You realize I was about five minutes away from formally declaring war on the Anadens for firing on Concord assets."

David pivoted and raised his hands in the air. "We did realize this, belatedly, and thus rushed here to correct the record. I mean, we were *going* to tell you, obviously—" he checked with Alex, who hurriedly nodded agreement "—as soon as you had some free time."

"Oh, *obviously.*" Her mother's stern, disciplinarian countenance was such a spot-on match for the expression that had dogged Alex's teenage years, any last traces of worry about the state of her mother's soul faded away. This was definitely Miriam Solovy standing here scowling at her. "You could have been captured. Both of you."

Her father's brow furrowed, while Alex shrugged mildly. "Nah," they answered in unison.

Her mother's scowl held for a solid two seconds—then broke to allow an amused chuckle to escape her lips. "Galaxies should tremble when the two of you team up. It was still a reckless stunt, and you're both still in trouble." She glared at the ceiling rather than at them. "Was it worth it? What does Kennedy say?"

Alex hopped off the table wearing a self-satisfied grin. "Yes, it was. She's currently ripping out the shielding module to install it in your nearly finished ship to save time, but she's also confident she can manufacture new ones. You, and soon everyone, are going to have impenetrable shielding protecting indestructible hulls. No more Rasu ship infiltrations."

Her mother's gaze fell away to fixate on the floor, and she didn't immediately respond.

"Mom?"

David was reaching out to touch Miriam's shoulder when she looked up, eyes glistening and a radiant smile lighting her face. "No more infiltrations. This is a most welcome development." She arched an eyebrow. "I suppose you'll be expecting official commendations? Possibly medals?"

"Eh, we're good—"

A priority message arrived from Nika, and the subject line sent Alex stumbling backward to fall into one of the guest chairs. Time and her heart stopped in unison while she opened it.

Her father was kneeling in front of her even before she'd finished reading the message. "What is it? What's wrong?"

She laughed through an aborted sob and shook her head. "Not wrong. Good." She splayed her fingers wide to peer at her father. "He's okay. For now, anyway. Marlee, too."

David rocked back on his heels, then stood as Miriam joined him. "*Milostivyy menya*, this *is* good news. Most excellent news."

Her mother reached out and patted her knee. Alex responded by leaping up and grabbing her mother in a hug. Was it possible the universe had, however grudgingly, ceded to her demand that she not lose anyone else? She didn't want to get cocky, as Caleb and Marlee remained in terrible danger, but...

Miriam returned the embrace before stepping back a little. "I am so glad to hear it. But how do you know?"

"Apparently one of the Asterions on Namino figured out a limited way to communicate through the quantum block. He's with Caleb and Marlee and a bunch of other people in one of the bunkers near DAF Command. Marlee was injured in the initial Rasu attack, but the Asterions helped her, and she's healed up now."

"That's fantastic. Can we use this communication method to coordinate with the people on the ground there?"

"Um..." she pulled the message back up to reread it, as most of the content had blurred away in favor of words like CALEB and ALIVE and TOGETHER "...not easily, no. Nika didn't share the details, but it seems to be an Asterion-specific solution and, as I said, limited. But Nika can talk to this guy, and vice versa. So that's something."

"When are they coming home? Caleb and Marlee?"

She kept reading...and her heart wrenched into knots all over again. "It sounds as if...not right away. The group they're with is trying to pinpoint the originating source of the quantum block. They want to try to take it out—which would be awesome—and Caleb and Marlee have decided to stay and help." She pushed off the chair to stride across the office in an explosion of movement and emotion. "Goddamn him!"

David sighed. "Something tells me it's more like 'goddamn *her*.' Marlee has found herself a righteous cause now, and I'd be willing to bet she's refusing to give it up. And after going to such lengths to reach her, Caleb can't exactly leave her there."

Alex retraced her steps in growing agitation. "I guess she's too old for him to grab around the waist and carry kicking and screaming back to the Ghost, huh?"

"Also might attract unwanted Rasu attention, what with the kicking and screaming."

"Good point." The pacing continued, until finally on her third pass around the office, her father blocked her path. "Alex, what are you thinking?"

"What? Nothing. Everything. Mostly I'm glad he got to her, they're both okay, and they have a place to shelter, safe from the

Rasu." Her mind flashed back to the continuing maelstrom consuming her home on Akeso…'okay' was clearly a relative term.

Her mother stepped up beside David and took Alex's hands in hers. "You should go."

"Go where?"

"To Namino. Use the *Siyane* to get past the Rasu. Now that you know where they are, get to Caleb and Marlee and help them take out the quantum block. Save millions of lives—save *their* lives."

A tumble of words caught in her throat. "Mom, no. You need me here to help you—"

"I do not. In point of fact, you are driving me insane with all your hovering and constant well-meaning questions and suffocating kid-glove treatment. I'm *fine*, Alex. It was an iffy first couple of days, I admit, but I'm doing much better now. And I won't stand here and watch you drive yourself mad like this any longer. You have been incredible, and I couldn't ask for a more wonderful daughter. I mean it. But now it's time for you to go and do what you do best. Get the quantum block down, so I can redo that godforsaken Namino battle. Better this time."

Her limbs felt frozen in place, while her heart and mind were being torn asunder, pulled to the breaking point in opposite directions. "Mom…."

Her father laid a hand on her arm. "Alex, she's right. I can't believe she all but ordered you to sneak into an active war zone, but she's right. I wish I could go with you, but your mother genuinely *does* need me here."

Miriam tilted her head in agreement, an almost smirky smile dancing on her lips.

Which meant it just might be true. All of it. She breathed in deeply and made the decision for herself. The rending ceased, to be replaced by a dizzying lightness of spirit. "All right. I'll do it." She hugged her mother tight, then reached over and hugged her father as well. "I love you both so, so much. Thank you."

RW

Alex's muscles vibrated, blood pushing rapidly through her veins to spur her on to greater speeds. The temptation to leap into the *Siyane*, wormhole across five megaparsecs of space and touch down on Namino inside the hour was so powerful she could *taste* the anticipation.

But she'd only get one shot at this, and she owed it to Caleb, Marlee, her mother—to basically everyone—to calm down and do it properly. So she started making a mental list, then quickly converted it into a real list...then stopped in the middle of the hallway, moved out of the flow of traffic and concentrated on imposing order on the slapdash list. She still wanted to leave as soon as was humanly possible, so she needed to attack the list with efficiency and economy of motion.

Finally satisfied with her plan of action, she sent a message detailing everything she knew about Caleb and Marlee to Isabela and a similar one to Mia. Then she set off for Special Projects.

42

CONCORD HQ
SPECIAL PROJECTS

Alex was busily reordering her list for the third time as she walked into the enormous wing of HQ devoted to Concord Special Projects—

—she bumped into an unmoving object. "Pardon me, ma'am."

She looked up to meet the suspicious stare of a tall Novoloume man with iridescent rose skin. "I'm sorry. I wasn't watching where I was going."

"As is evident. May I inquire where you intended to be going? Special Projects is not open to tourists."

She was too distracted to be offended. "I know. I have an appointment with the Director." An appointment she'd scheduled approximately ninety seconds earlier, but whatever.

"I'll let him know his appointment has arrived, if you'll wait here."

"I won't take another step."

"See that you don't. Many of the objects in here do not respond favorably to getting knocked around."

Wasn't he just a bundle of joy. Alex made a show of crossing her arms over her chest and planting her feet in a wide stance as he disappeared around the corner.

Every surface of Special Projects shone and gleamed. Opaque glass walls divided the large main room into sections and obscured the mad-scientist work occurring behind them. Security doors on the left, right and rear sealed off even more secret areas, for the protection of the experiments as well as the thousands of people on the station.

"Alex!"

Devon Reynolds jogged toward her, and she readied a polite greeting. She bumped into him every few months or so, but the truth was he belonged to a part of her life she'd left behind after The Displacement. Left behind until now.

He clasped her shoulder in a side-hug, then backed away. "Have you talked to Mia recently? She is not in a good place right now."

"I know. When did you see her?"

"You're not the only Noetica Prevo suddenly in need of my rarified services. My feelings should be hurt that it takes mortal danger and gut-wrenching loss to bring you all to my door."

"But?"

He shrugged and motioned for her to follow him through the maze. "I get it. It's not like I made a point to go visit you guys, either."

"Nope. Listen, I'd like to catch up, but I am in one ferocious hurry."

"I understand. You want Rasu-killing weapons."

"Not for the *Siyane*. Weapons I can use on the ground. Ideally ones that destroy Rasu, yes, but I'll take slowing them down if that's what's available."

"Then you're lucky creating such weapons has been my driving focus for the last few weeks. I can hook you up with some outrageous shit."

RW

Devon removed one of three small ring-shaped modules from a carbon composite case. "First off, you'll want this."

She studied the ring, but its exterior gave no hints as to its purpose. "What is it?"

"Our newest defensive shield tech protecting against physical blows. If a Rasu takes a swipe at you with one of its sword-hands, this ought to hold it off from cutting through you long enough for you to scurry out of reach."

"*Scurry?*"

"Or whatever you do to get away. It'll provide decent protection from energy blasts as well—better than whatever you currently have on hand."

"Great." She pointed to the case. "I need the other two modules as well."

"But those are all we've made. The new model's not scheduled to go into full production until next week."

"Do you expect a ground force squad consisting of two people to be facing Rasu in hand-to-hand combat in the next week?"

"No, but—"

"Then I need them."

"All right, fine." He reached into the case, retrieved the other two modules and handed them to her.

She dropped all three into her bag. "What else do you have?"

He motioned her out of the cubicle and strode toward the opposite side of the room. Three times he got stopped by employees, and by the second time she was tapping her foot impatiently.

Finally he scanned them through the left-side security doors. Beyond the doors waited a long hall with many windowless doors; he unlocked the last door on the left.

As soon as they stepped inside, she felt the suffocating silence of heavily shielded walls. "Welcome to our lab for weapons that will destroy everything they touch, including us."

"Is it a good idea to have such a lab here on the station?"

"It's perfectly safe. The safety measures in place will contain any explosion to the area inside these walls."

"If you say so. What's in here?"

"So much." He went over to a worktable positioned near the door. On it sat a long box made of polycrystalline alumina glass, which held some sort of device in a soft, velvety casing. "For you, this."

She leaned down and peered at it more closely. It vaguely resembled a handgun, if only because the lower half consisted of a fairly traditional grip. The rest of the body, however, was a sort of smushed orb ending in a tiny opening. "Is it a gun?"

"A gun? Ha!" He chuckled to himself. "Well, yes, but not just any gun—a negative energy gun. We're calling it the Rectifier."

She eyed him dubiously.

"What? One of the biggest advantages of this job is that I get to make up cool names for dangerous objects, and everyone has to use the names."

"True enough." She frowned. "Is it fragile? I don't think carrying it around in this case is going to be practical where I'm headed."

"No, no, this is merely for show." He opened the case and reverently lifted the gun out of its velvet shroud. "Now, don't ask for two more of these, because this is literally the only one in existence—at least until tomorrow."

She took the weapon from him, turning it over in her hands and letting her fingers run across its length. Unusually for a handgun, the metal shell was coarse and rough to the touch, almost dimpled. "Talk to me about how it works."

"It fires a tiny capsule from the chamber that disintegrates when it impacts anything at a speed of 1,000 kph or higher—and I do mean anything. This exposes a bundle of negative energy particles packed inside which…well, you know what happens next. The detonation should be large enough to disintegrate one of the bipedal Rasu—a normal-sized one, not a giant one, assuming they…yeah, they probably make those—or two Rasu if they're standing next to one another. The effect will fizzle out after about three meters or so, depending on the density of the object it hit, so make sure there aren't any people or valuable items within three meters when you fire it—including yourself."

"Got it." She dropped the gun into the bag to join the shields. "Anything else for me?"

Devon rolled his eyes at the ceiling. "Not for ground combat, no. Not yet. I've been trying to set up research collaborations with the Asterions, since it's stupid for us to be separately banging away at this problem, duplicating a bunch of each other's work and missing out on opportunities. We almost had a working structure when the Namino invasion happened, and since then they seem a little out of sorts, but mostly not interested in taking my comms."

"Can you blame them? Of course they're out of sorts. But I'll try to kick up a response for you, because you're right. We do need to be working together." She nodded sharply. "Okay. Thank you for letting me abscond with all your toys."

"Call it field testing. Once you live to return home, stop in and report back on how they performed."

"Will do—the living and the reporting."

"Good. So, should I expect Morgan to walk into my office next?"

"No." She laughed wryly. "But I am about to walk into hers."

43

CHALMUN STATION ASTEROID
LARGE MAGELLANIC CLOUD

Alex knew a little about Chalmun Station due to Eren's grand stunt here on behalf of the anarchs back at the height of the war against the Directorate, as well as the Kats' clever protection of the asteroid in the aftermath of Nisi's speech. She'd never visited it, however…and as she departed the hollowed-out hangar bay for a series of claustrophobic tunnels, she decided that had been the wiser course of action.

It took her a minute to pinpoint what was odd, other than a generally shady nature, about the patrons who brusquely moved past her in the passageways. She'd yet to see a single Anaden. Plenty of Barisans and Naraida, a healthy dash of Dankaths, the occasional Novoloume and even one or two Khokteh. But no Anadens. No humans, either, but this wasn't so surprising, as humanity had brought its own wretched hives of scum and villainy with it to Amaranthe.

She assumed there must be a few Anadens skulking around in the shadows, but this appeared to be the most eclectic collection of species in Concord space. The fact that a large majority of them were criminals of a greater or lesser sort served as pointed commentary on the lasting damage the Directorate's boot on the necks of these species had inflicted.

No map existed for the layout of Chalmun Station. The guard at the hangar bay had muttered something to the effect of 'if you can't find what you're looking for, you probably shouldn't be looking for it.' She reached an intersection of five tunnels and stopped.

Growing frustration set her nerves on edge as her internal mission clock raced ahead.

Abruptly she realized in her rush to steamroll her way to Namino, she was being an idiot. *Valkyrie, a little help here?*

Take the tunnel located at thirty degrees, then the third tunnel on the left, then the next right.

Thanks.

With the benefit of directions, she reached her destination in less than a minute. A shingle hung over the door, the name '*Purgatory*' chiseled into it like some manner of stone-age carving.

Before going inside, she paused to send Nika a message.

Your note means more to me than you will ever know. Thank you. So, do you want a ride to Namino?

The response arrived almost immediately.

More than you *will ever know.*

Excellent. I'll pick you up in ten hours.

Hang on. I might need a little longer than that.

Now that she was committed to a course of action, she didn't want to delay a minute longer than she must…but she would seriously benefit from Nika's expertise once she got to Namino.

No guarantees. Try to hurry.

She took a deep breath and strode through the door to *Purgatory*. Inside, the space opened up considerably. The establishment was dimly lit, but so far as she could tell, also immaculately clean. Two Novoloume women danced on a raised stage along the back wall, surrounded by flickering lights and a hint of smoke, to the hypnotic sounds of Novoloume trance music. To the left ran a lengthy bar stocked with the choicest poisons for every species.

The open space in the middle was dominated by round tables seating between four and eight people. Over half of them were occupied, where a variety of competitions played out: games of chance, virtual tabletop strategy games and multiple games of *skalef*, the Anaden version of poker.

At one of the occupied tables near the left wall, Morgan Lekkas stared down the Barisan man sitting opposite her. Morgan had cut her chestnut hair into a chin-length razor-straight style, and it fell across her face to obscure one glittering amethyst eye.

Alex made her way across the room and propped against the wall behind the table to watch for a minute.

"Boros, unless you've got something new to sweeten the pot with—anything but your firstborn, please—you're out."

The Dankath to Morgan's left ground his chitinous jaw in agitation for several seconds, which made a grating sound akin to metal scraping across concrete. Finally his pincer hands sliced through the air, and the pattern of lights arrayed in front of him scattered and vanished. "It seems I am out."

"That's what I thought. Eafe?"

The Barisan on her right tossed a claw-extended hand at the table, and their pattern vanished as well. "You're too expensive for me."

"Now you know. Linoke?"

The Barisan opposite her snarled. "Call."

"Call it is." Morgan dropped the shield in front of her, revealing an intricately lit pattern of blue and gold.

"Bullshit! You cheat."

Morgan reached out to retrieve a thin film sitting at the center of the table; she placed two fingers atop it as she glared at this 'Linoke.' "Careful, there. If you can't lose like a proper gentleman, you won't be gracing us with your presence here in *Purgatory* in the future."

"But this is next month's rent!"

"Then you really should not have bet it." Morgan motioned dismissively. "That's it for me tonight, boys and girls. Off you go."

The others grumbled and hissed and clacked, but they all gathered up their drinks and retreated into the depths of the bar.

Morgan studied the thin film, presumably checking the sums it held. "Go away, Alex."

"Can't." She pushed off the wall and sat in the seat vacated by Linoke. "I need your help."

"Don't care." Morgan waved at someone over Alex's shoulder, and the next instant a server drone appeared with a glass of rich, amber liquid. Morgan took the glass off the tray and turned it up, downing half its contents in one sip, then glowered at Alex over the top of the glass. "You're still here."

"I'm not one of your marks you can simply shoo away when you grow bored of them."

"Unfortunately. What do you want?"

"I told you. I need your help."

"So?"

Alex had hoped six years of self-imposed exile had softened Morgan's outlook, but no such luck. And she did not have time to delicately woo the irascible woman. "I can offer you something I suspect still means a lot to you—maybe the only thing that still does. The opportunity to fly again."

"I have a ship. I fly all the time."

"Not like this, you don't. Not against worthy enemies."

"Nope. I am not getting involved in Concord's spats with the Anadens or the Savrakaths. Whoever's asking—Concord, AEGIS, the IDCC—I don't give a shit. They took everything that mattered from me, and I don't owe them a goddamn thing."

"I realize they did. I'm not asking on behalf of my mother or any institution. I'm asking for me. This is personal. Caleb and his niece, Marlee, are trapped on a Rasu-occupied planet in the Asterion Dominion. I'm taking the *Siyane* straight into that hellhole in a few hours. Once there, I'm going to have to leave it in as safe a place as I can find in order to go on foot into a Rasu-occupied city. I need you to stay with the ship while I'm gone. At some point, I'll need you to pick me up, as well as Caleb and Marlee I hope, and maybe other people, too, at an undetermined location at an undetermined time."

"That is the most boring piloting assignment I have ever heard."

"Not if Rasu are shooting at you the whole time, it isn't. Do you know about the Rasu? Highly unpleasant shapeshifting metal—"

"Of course I know about the Rasu. I'm brooding, but I'm not a hermit."

Alex gazed pointedly around the bar. "Oh, this is brooding?"

"Fuck you, Solovy."

"Uh-huh. Morgan, *please*. They're trapped on this planet behind a quantum block, so this might be the only chance they have to escape. To survive."

"A quantum block? You mean I won't have Stanley to entertain me on this boring-ass frolic?"

"Is Stanley still in there?"

"Afraid so. Couldn't get rid of him a second time."

"Good. There's hope for you yet, then."

The muscles around Morgan's mouth twitched; her gaze fell to the table. "No, there isn't."

Alex wasn't connected to the Noesis, and she suspected Morgan wasn't either, but she didn't require a supradimensional quantum field connecting them to sense the woman's pain. Regardless, the only thing she could do for Morgan right now was put her in a cockpit and give her an enemy to shoot.

"Well, it's not for me to say. But this is why I need you. Valkyrie won't be able to pass through the quantum block, either, so she can't fly the ship for me. I won't be able to land anywhere close to where Caleb and Marlee are holed up, which is smack in the middle of a metropolitan hub under siege. And at some point after I arrive, I suspect I'm going to need the *Siyane* to show up behind enemy lines to rescue all of us. For this to happen, a damn good pilot is going to have to be at the controls, and you are the best pilot I have ever seen fly."

Morgan finished off her drink silently.

"Do it for the adrenaline rush. When was the last time you had a good one of those? You'll be surrounded by oversized and overpowering enemies. Lots of opportunities for hide-and-sneak and very possibly lots of shooting—and *not* getting shot in return."

Morgan motioned toward the bar. A Novoloume man arrived a few seconds later, placing a fresh glass in front of Morgan then sitting in the empty chair to Alex's left.

"Solstan, if I were to be absent for a couple of days..." she glanced at Alex in question, and Alex shrugged in response "...or weeks, would you be comfortable keeping things running for me?"

"Certainly, ma'am. I'll make sure the lights stay on and the drinks get mixed."

"I believe you will, but thank you for the reassurance. I'll let you know."

The man stood. "Forgive me, ma'am. Can I get you anything to drink?"

Alex shook her head. "I'm only dropping by."

The man returned to the bar, and Alex shot Morgan a dubious look. "Are you telling me you *own* this place?"

"Won it from the former proprietor in an all-night game of *skalef* four years ago. I'd have thought word would've gotten around by now that I can kick anyone's ass at the game, but patrons keep paying me to relieve them of their credits. I guess there's a sucker born every day, and two on Sunday." She groaned. "The question is, am I one, too? Am I a sucker if I take you up on your offer?"

"No. You're a fighter."

"Not any longer. But..." Morgan sighed dramatically "...what the hell does it matter anyway. Fine. But one flight only. When we get back, I'm heading straight here, where I will resume swindling gamblers out of their not-so-hard-earned credits. Understand?"

"Loud and clear. You live your life however you choose."

"That option's no longer on the table for me. So I make do. When do we leave?"

44

AKESO

Alex sprinted through the driving rain and around the new pop-up water barriers to reach the warm and so far dry house. Once she was inside, a wave of sentimentality rose up to make her heart ache, but she didn't have time to entertain feelings that would only slow her down. She quickly packed two bags—one with several changes of clothes for herself (plus extra for Marlee) and Caleb, one with every weapon and tool they owned. The *Siyane* was always stocked with provisions and first aid supplies, which freed up much-needed space.

Satisfied she'd grabbed everything on hand that could help on her mission, she set the bags down beside the front door, stripped down to her underwear to avoid ruining more clothes, and stepped out into the raging thunderstorm. Rain pelted her like a swarm of tiny needles, and the wind whipped her hair around her face and neck like a binding knot. Her toes sank into the mud as she trudged across what used to be a meadow toward the line of trees at the creek. To *the* tree—the gateway to Akeso that had once cured her of a poisonous infection and later bonded inexorably to Caleb in order to bring him back to life, and to her.

She only hoped it could do so one more time.

The hanging vines danced like marionettes in the wind, and it took her three tries to grab hold of one. She held tight to it using one hand while she removed the blade from her pocket, then with a quick cut sliced her palm open. Raindrops spilled across her skin to turn the blood pink and wash it away.

She clenched her fist around the leaves decorating the vine. "Hear me, Akeso. I want to bring an end to this madness and to bring Caleb home to both of us, but I need your help to do it. If you understand me at all—if not my words then the true longing of my heart—deepen my connection to you and, through you, to him. Show me the way."

The storm vanished from her perception and was replaced by the shattered profile of a ruined city. Heavy, dark shadows crept across empty streets, cast by Rasu cruisers soaring far overhead. Whispered voices echoed around her. Within her, a heart thrummed, each beat driven by pain and turmoil.

She gasped and let go of the vine to stumble backward. Tears streamed down her cheeks and were carried away on the rain; her chest hurt with every breath. The distressing scene faded in intensity, but if she allowed her vision to blur, she was still there, standing on a broken street on Namino. Only it wasn't her standing there—it was Caleb.

"Thank you."

RW

A few minutes later, showered, clad in dry clothes and her hand bandaged, she sat in the cockpit of the *Siyane* while the storm raged on around her. She closed her eyes once more and listened for a heartbeat...and felt a stirring, weak and thready, inside her, as if a string winding across space and time tugged her toward the soul at the other end of it. It wasn't a giant red arrow pointing to Namino, but it might as well be.

She reopened her eyes and forced herself to focus on the practical. Before she left to pick up Morgan and shortly thereafter Nika, did she have everything she needed?

Who knew what she was going to need? She had everything she'd been able to pull together in a few hours, and she could only hope it was enough to guarantee everyone came out the other side alive.

"Valkyrie?"

'I am here.' The voice originated from the *Siyane's* speakers, then transitioned to a spoken voice as Valkyrie's virtual avatar materialized in the chair beside her. Caleb's chair, though Valkyrie had more right to claim it than anyone.

"You realize where I'm going, you can't follow."

"I regretfully do. I have been quiet, because you would not have benefited from another distraction, but I sensed when your decision was made, and I have been following your progress since then."

"I assumed as much. Allow me to preemptively apologize for any damage Morgan inflicts on our ship."

"Nothing we can't buff out, I'm sure."

"I'm not as sure, but hopefully so. This is my personal mission, but we have to keep pushing forward on all fronts—against the Anadens, the Savrakaths and most of all against the Rasu. I want you to do something for me."

Valkyrie's Nordic features brightened into a warm countenance. "Anything."

"Be careful what you wish for. While I'm gone, I want you to go speak to the Ruda about the Rasu...or rather, about shapeshifting metal and ways they may know to melt it, or alternatively permanently solidify it, or interrupt its functioning in some useful way."

"But you don't want me to explain to them the reasons for my inquiry."

"Not if you can help it. The Ruda trust and respect you above everyone else. They always have. But they're still quirky as all hell, and I don't completely trust them. If they learn of the Rasu, they'll be desperate to make contact with a species so similar to their own nature. And that is a spectacularly bad idea, so I need you to make up a story about why we're asking for the information."

"I wish I didn't have to lie to them."

"I know you're not comfortable lying, and I'm sorry to ask you to do so."

"No, it's the prudent choice."

"It is. Whatever you learn, relay it to my mother and to Devon and Annie."

"And to you."

She managed a faltering smile. "When I get back, of course. But don't wait for me."

45

CONCORD HQ
CONSULATE

Mia studied herself in the mirror of her office lavatory. She'd taken care with her appearance today, as befitted the stature of her guest this morning. She wore a black turtleneck crafted of Novoloume silk, what felt like an utterly useless miniature Caeles Prism draped over the cowl, and flowing burgundy pants. Her hair was slicked back in a tight tail secured at the base of her neck. Her makeup routine displayed perfectly, and it *almost* fixed her pale, blanched skin and bloodshot eyes. Meno was also tending to the bloodshot eyes, though his ameliorative measures only worked until she cried again. But this was the best mask she could don for the world.

She returned to her office, where objectively good news waited for her. Assisted by an AEGIS Rescue and Recovery squad, Vaihe had successfully brought over five hundred Godjans from three villages to Concord soil. Marlee was going to be so proud—because Marlee was *alive*. Alive and in Caleb's capable care. She wished so very badly that the knowledge brought more light to her world than it did, but even the brightest lights flickered weakly beneath the shadow of Malcolm's death.

Her guest arrived a few minutes later to save her from further descent into suffocating melancholy, and she welcomed him into her office displaying proper grace. "Sator Nisi, it is so good to see you alive and well. Welcome back."

"I am Sator of nothing. Please, call me..." his expression flickered "...Corradeo, I suppose. To reclaim the name feels strange on my tongue, but it is mine, for good and ill."

"Oh. Of course." Was his visit to the Concord Consulate something more than a mere formality? Why had he returned now, when they faced their greatest challenge since The Displacement? She tried to work up the will to care, but her wellspring was flat dry. Still, she should be able to fake it for a few minutes, she thought.

She motioned toward the meeting table by the viewport. "Please, join me. I understand you were instrumental in giving the Asterions several hours' advance warning of the Rasu attack. I'm..." Marlee flying through the air off the arm of a Rasu flashed through her mind—but it was fine, for she was alive "...certain they're very grateful."

"Some more than others. I confess my sudden appearance in their midst was not without conflict."

"Did you expect anything else?"

He looked at her in surprise. She was trying to keep control, but the rough edges continued to lash out here and there. "To the extent I expected anything at all, no. I was a bit surprised to find they count among their number people who haven't forgotten me, but I can't fault any of them for holding a grudge. The Asterions have done well for themselves, and it saddens me to find them threatened by an enemy as fearsome as the Rasu." He settled formally into the chair. "But this is not why I am here. I understand Humanity's peaceful coexistence with Anadens has hit a rough spot."

"Is that what we're calling it?"

He frowned. "Are you feeling well, Senator Requelme? You seem...more on edge than I remember."

She should resign her position this instant, go home to Romane and curl up in a dark corner for a year. Let Miriam and Dean Veshnael try to save Concord from itself, if such a thing were possible.

"Forgive me for my rudeness. Matters are difficult on multiple fronts at present. Yes, the Anaden leadership, to the extent the term 'leadership' can be applied to those involved, reacted to the Senate's approval of an alliance with the Asterions by coopting Machim military and security forces and attempting a coup. The attempt failed, but we have every reason to believe a breakaway group of *elassons* continues to foment insurrection among their ranks."

"Ferdinand elasson-Kyvern represented the Anadens in the Concord Senate, correct?"

"He did."

"I'm familiar with him. A sniveling bureaucrat, as I recall. Who are his allies?"

"We believe Hannah, Otto and Ulrich Machim are supporting him, and possibly one or two other Machim *elassons* as well. Casmir has been leading the Machim military forces for Concord, and so far as we know, he remains loyal to Concord. Ferdinand has persuaded at least four Kyvern *elassons* to support him, as well as between three and five from most of the other Dynasties—but not a majority. In fact, quite a few *elassons* have contacted us to declare their continuing allegiance to Concord." She smiled thinly. "Which we greatly appreciate."

"What about the Praesidis?"

"The Praesidis *elassons* are gone."

He flinched, almost as if she'd reached out and slapped him. "Gone? What do you mean?"

"Three were killed—permanently—on Solum during the…well, you were there. Three others disconnected from the integral and committed suicide during the first year after The Displacement, we assume due to the loss of their *diati*. I understand Nyx has been traveling with you, so this leaves five *elassons*. To be blunt, we don't know where they are or what's become of them. Perhaps they are living out lives of quiet reflection on garden worlds."

"Or it could be that we Praesidis have always been lone wolves. Never much for joining."

"Only for leading?"

He shrugged silently.

"It's a fair point, I admit. But the fact remains that we have no idea of their whereabouts or if they are alive at all. Ferdinand might, but he's not in a sharing mood—not with me, in any event.

You may enjoy better luck with him. There are also two Praesidis *elas* working for Concord Intelligence. They profess not to know the whereabouts of any *elassons*, but given your...unique stature, they could be more forthcoming with you."

"I see. Thank you." He stood and moved to the viewport, and she recalled that he had always enjoyed gazing pensively out the viewports of his mobile command fortress, if only for the impression the pose created. "This Concord—it's worked well these last fourteen years?"

"As well as we imagined possible. No members have gone to war against one another. We've worked hard to share our collective wealth, resources and technology with all member and allied species. It hasn't been perfect, but has it worked? Yes."

"Yet the Anadens remain lost and adrift without the Primors and the guidance of their integrals, just as I feared."

"We've tried to help them where we could. If nothing else, we've tried to provide a good example for them to follow. And we have succeeded, here and there. Many are embracing their freedom and individuality."

"But many are not."

The metaphorical cracks in her mask grew wider, and she found herself wondering whether Casmir had trained his weapons on Savrak soil yet. "What do you want me to tell you? That the despotic Primors ruined your species? Turned them into dull drones incapable of independent thought or action, of drive or curiosity? Because maybe they did. But Anadens can still adapt, recover, move on or grow past their failures. If they are us and we are them, then they carry within them the capacity to do so.

"But they have to want to do it, and this has been the trouble. Their cursed genetic determinism has trapped them in an infinite loop of indecision and uncertainty, and few have found a way out."

He nodded deliberately. "What do you suggest I do?"

"You, personally? Sator Danilo Nisi, leader of the anarch rebellion against the Directorate? Or Corradeo Praesidis, father of the

Praesidis Dynasty and former Supreme Commander of the Anaden military?"

A shadow passed across his face. "Perhaps it is time I accept that they are one and the same."

"Or you can choose the best traits of both and create a new persona. Whatever suits you. The point is, you were alive—you were a leader—long before the integrals, before the Dynasties and the Directorate and the genetic manipulation. Remember who your people once were, and show them the path they must walk to become so again."

"This will not be an easy matter to accomplish."

"Nothing worth doing is ever easy."

RW

Corradeo rented two adjoining rooms at the hotel adjacent to the Consulate. While he waited for Nyx to finish her errands, he fixed himself a bourbon on the rocks and sat on the edge of the bed.

It was strange…this world he'd returned to was not so different from the one he'd left, but it was as if all the lights had brightened by two levels. With the Rasu on the horizon, people had much to fear, but this didn't include each other or mad, immortal leaders. The Humans had done an extraordinary job of filling the chasm left behind by the Directorate with reasoned judgment, purpose and fairness. The Novoloume had also risen to the challenge of leading, as he'd always assumed they would. This magnificent station, the mighty ships that protected it and the energetic commerce that brought it to life were all testaments to what could be achieved through peace and openness.

Seeing it warmed his heart even as it eased his guilt over having left fourteen years ago. They had done just fine in his absence. But now his people were in trouble. And no matter how many times in his life he'd tried to walk away from the burden of leadership, he always found himself answering when its call grew loud enough. With or without *diati*, with or without title, he was Praesidis, and leading was in his blood. No scientist had artificially sculpted leadership into his DNA, but it resided there nonetheless.

He didn't want it. He'd seen so much death, so much loss, at times he could scarcely breathe thinking about it...but running away hadn't stopped the carnage. The Ourankeli, the Hoan, now his long-lost brethren-turned-enemy-turned-ally the Asterions. If he didn't step in and save the Anadens from the sins of their mothers and fathers, his own people might be soon to follow.

He ran a hand through his hair, finished off his drink and stood. So be it.

RW

By the time Nyx rang at the door, he'd showered and changed, and he greeted her wearing a smile. "Is everything settled with the *Periplanos?*"

She took in the room and his demeanor with a quick, practiced eye. "It is. We can stay docked here for as long as we like. How was your meeting with Senator Requelme?"

"Informative." He took her hands in his. "I want you to do something for me. Five Praesidis *elassons* are missing. Lost out there in the void, believing they are alone in this world. I want you to find them. Seek out your brothers and sisters, and bring them home."

She pulled away. "But grandfather—"

"I realize you were not close. I understand well the solitary nature of an Inquisitor. But they are our family nonetheless. They need us, and now we need them."

"What do we need them for?"

"To be whole again. To be Praesidis once more and, in time, to set an example for our people."

"You're talking poetic nonsense. What did the Senator say to you? What are you planning?"

He chuckled a bit wistfully. "You have gotten to know me so well during our travels, haven't you? I can't hide behind platitudes and flowery axioms with you. Very well.

"I plan to seek out Ferdinand elasson-Kyvern and his cohorts. I plan to bring an end to this madness of a rebellion he is stirring up, one way or another. Anadens are a proud species, but we cannot allow that pride to destroy a peaceful society full of people trying to do the right thing. Now, when all of civilization is most vulnerable, we have to stand up and be strong for everyone.

"What did Senator Requelme say to me? She confirmed to me that what I feared most would happen has in fact come to pass. The death of the Primors and the removal of their will expressed through the integrals has caused our people to lose their way. Now someone has to show them the way back."

She gave him a pained grimace, worry straining at the edges of her features. "You are wise, grandfather, and a true leader. I'm confident that if anyone can accomplish such a task, you can. But I should be at your side when you confront these rebels, not off on some sentimental quest for wayward souls."

"My dear granddaughter, I have lived for a million uninterrupted years. A Kyvern bureaucrat is no threat to me."

"A Kyvern bureaucrat and a cadre of armed Machim *elassons*."

"All the same. I will be fine. Please, Nyx. You have indulged my every fancy for fourteen years now. Indulge me one last time. Find the other Inquisitors and bring them home."

46

EARTH
GREATER VANCOUVER

S *he reached for the Daemon at her hip, only to find it had become a third tentacle winding around her waist. It squeezed, denying her air, as more tentacles reached her neck, then her face. Liquid metal poured into her ears, nose and finally her mouth.*

"You think you are alive, but you are mistaken. You never left us. We will never let you escape—"

Miriam's eyes popped open in a panic, and she choked off a cry in her throat. But she'd been here before, and lucidity returned more swiftly every time she awoke. She stared at the ceiling of their bedroom, inhaled deeply and worked to slow her racing heart. Beneath her, the sheets were soaked in sweat yet again.

Finally she sat up and rubbed at her eyes—and jumped half out of the bed at the sight of a shadowy figure sitting on the chaise opposite the bed. "David?"

He sat with his elbows on his knees and his hands fisted at his chin, watching her. "You're still having the nightmares?"

She nodded.

"I'm so sorry. For me, they stopped after about a month. Mostly."

"It's okay. I'm adjusting." She took a sip of water from the glass on the nightstand. "What are you doing up?"

"I have something I need to tell you."

She curled her legs beneath her and gathered her hair up off of sweat-damp shoulders. "You mean you've been sitting there ruminating on the best way to tell me what you need to tell me."

"Correct." He sighed. "First thing: I used Richard's CINT access code to help Caleb steal a Ghost to take to Namino."

She hadn't given much thought to the details of the specific manner in which Caleb had reached Namino. Too many selfish cogitations had taken precedence. But it made sense. "That's why Richard is cross with you."

"No, that's why Richard *was* cross with me. He has a new reason now." He started to stand, then eased back onto the chaise. "You know that everything I do, I do for you. I will go to the ends of the universe in order to ease your burdens."

"David, you have been amazing since I...since the regenesis. I don't have the words to properly thank you for everything—"

"Stop, please. There's more, so best to get it all out in one go. I've been going behind your back to act on your behalf. I pled your case to Bastian and to the Earth Alliance Prime Minister. I also asked Richard to leak the locations of the remaining Savrakath antimatter facilities to the Anadens, so they could destroy them for you. To ease your burdens."

Her gaze fell to the bedcovers, and she absently bunched them up in her hands. For a moment they resembled someone else's hands, cast as they were in shadows and silvery moonlight...but no. They belonged to her, and she was real. "He said no."

"He did, both before and after sharing his uncharitable thoughts about my recent behavior. Probably for the best...in retrospect, I was wrong to suggest it. But did you know? Did he tell you?"

"No. Richard is treating me with kid gloves nearly as soft and gentle as yours. Which needs to stop, but it's a conversation for later."

"You don't seem surprised. And you're not using 'the voice' on me."

"I may yet. No, I didn't know this, but I do know Richard. He is fiercely loyal to me—to an even greater extent than he is to you, it turns out."

"The two of you had to look out for each other for a long time. Without me."

"We did. As for why I'm not surprised?" She smiled haltingly. "You are and have always been an open book to me. Your strengths overwhelm me, and your weaknesses...sadden me. But I accept that I can't change your instincts. I've ventured down that maze of a road before, and it dead-ends just short of a cliff."

Now he did stand, rushing over to fall to his knees next to her side of the bed. "My *instincts* are to protect you with every fiber of my being. No, you can't change those."

"And I suppose I shouldn't. So somewhere along the way, I decided that except when your actions threaten my ability to do my job, I have to let you run wild. You see, you are my weakness—my Achilles' Heel. Don't tell the Rasu. Or the Anadens or the Savrakaths. Definitely don't tell Bastian."

"On my oath." His throat worked as he reached out and wrapped his hands over hers atop the covers. "So you're not angry?"

She laughed; it sounded frayed at the edges, which she blamed on the lingering ghosts of the nightmare. "I am angry—angry that you feel you need to clear the road for me. Angry that those closest to me are treating me as if I'm brittle and frail—"

"No, we don't think you're—"

"Absolutely you do, because I *have* been brittle and frail, not to mention half insane. I'm lucky you haven't committed me to a padded room. I expect the only reason you haven't is because you have walked this path ahead of me, and you have faith I'll come out the other side."

"You will."

"I wasn't certain at first, but, yes, I believe I will. So I forgive you for protecting me, while begging you not to go behind my back again, while realizing you will always do what your heart and conscience demand of you."

He climbed onto the bed in front of her and retook hold of her hands. "I love you, *moya vselennaya,* and I am sorry for not trusting in your intrinsic strength enough to come to you with my wishes first. To counsel you rather than manage you."

"Well, you are both the first and only person to ever successfully 'manage' me, so I can understand why you would choose to go this route."

"No. It wasn't right of me. I shouldn't 'bull in a china shop' my way through your life and everything you've built, but I get frustrated when I feel helpless. Doesn't everyone appreciate how you will burn down the world to protect them? How no one could ever do a more extraordinary job of protecting them than you?"

"Now you're just flattering me."

"Is it working?"

"Did you miss the part about where I said you were my weakness?"

They moved at the same time, their mouths meeting with a flood of passion driven by fear, desperation and resurgent hope. His fingers wound into her hair, and she smiled against his lips. "The truth is, I need you. I let Alex go, because I had to—because Caleb needs her and she needs him—but I'm not ready to believe I can do this alone."

"You will never be alone."

Her heart swelled, pushing aside any last remnants of anger. All these years, and her renowned good sense still abandoned her entirely beneath the tsunami of his touch. "I hope not." Her lips danced over his cheek and across his forehead. "But you are not Richard's Achilles' Heel, so you might want to buff up your apology a bit before trying it out on him."

"Trust me, I know it." He chuckled throatily, his chest rumbling delightfully against hers. "Any chance you could put in a good word for me?"

"Don't push it."

"Of course, *nastoyatel'.*"

RW

CONCORD HQ

For the first time since she'd woken up in a regenesis lab, Miriam didn't experience a crippling tightness in her chest and throat when she stepped through the Caeles Prism onto Concord HQ.

She wasn't normal quite yet; perhaps when the nightmares finally stopped, she would begin to feel like her old self. Perhaps she never would. But existing in this world no longer felt akin to stumbling through a dream—or on occasion a nightmare itself.

People bustled purposefully around her, several of them stopping long enough to salute her, and today all the activity brought her comfort instead of a burgeoning panic attack.

David had said it was merely going to take time, and maybe this was all there was to it. Time to settle into this new skin of hers, time for thought and bones to get used to one another.

She glanced down the hallway toward the levtram leading to CINT before turning in the other direction to head to her office. Despite her mild rebuke to David, she actually did intend to talk to Richard about what had happened. Not to excuse David's actions, but to talk through them with a friend, because…she checked herself…*yes*. She was anxious, and possibly a little excited, to wrest back control of her life for herself. But first, she had an appointment—one that would hopefully confirm she was in fact ready to do so.

RW

Dr. Canivon roved a scanning device over Miriam's chest, pausing several times, then brought it up to circle her head. Next, she attached a module to Miriam's eVi ports for several long, silent and judgmental seconds before removing it. Finally she set aside her tools, took a seat opposite Miriam's desk and crossed one leg elegantly over the other.

"You continue to exhibit moderate signs of physiological stress, but I suspect you already knew this. And it's possible you have always exhibited those signs, given your line of work. Otherwise, you are..." the woman shrugged faintly "...fine. Do you feel fine?"

"More so today than yesterday, which was better than the day before."

"But not fine."

"Not yet. Almost. I think I've spotted 'fine' on the horizon. However, I do want to recommend that our regenesis protocols include psychological counseling for those who undergo it. I fear we are not sufficiently anticipating the mental and social disruption returning from the dead elicits."

"I'll file the recommendation. Do you want to schedule an appointment with a therapist?"

"Oh, no. It won't be necessary—not for me. I'm...I have David to talk to when things get challenging, and since he's been through something similar, he understands most of my hysterical rantings. I suspect you might understand as well, though I don't recall you experiencing any obvious difficulties when you returned to the world."

Dr. Canivon pressed her fingertips together at her lips, an uncommon shadow flitting across her normally poised features. "Like you, I prefer to keep my challenges to myself. This does not mean I didn't experience them."

"Forgive me for assuming." Miriam sighed. "The time gap is in some ways the worst of it. It's almost as if...I got yanked out of my own timeline and dropped into someone else's."

"The gap being years in my case made this part easier, I think. I'd been gone for so long, and the universe literally changed both location and composition while I was gone, so I had no choice but to accept my rebirth as a new beginning. For you, I imagine you've been expected to simply...continue."

"Yes. And it's all I want to do—continue. The actual doing of it has proved more problematic than I'd hoped, but I'm grateful that nearly everyone is willing to let me try."

"You've met resistance from some people? In a world steeped in frequent Anaden regenesis, I must say I'm surprised."

"We haven't lived here in Amaranthe long enough to internalize what regenesis truly means for individuals, for our society and for our beliefs. Many people aren't ready to accept it. And I honestly don't blame them. It's going to change us all more than we anticipate. But as one of the first to venture forward on this new journey, I need to show people how it's also going to save us. Show them I'm still the same person on the other side of regenesis."

Dr. Canivon's gaze drifted off. "I confess I often ask myself the same question, even twelve years later. Do you believe you are the same person?"

"That's what I intend to find out."

47

CONCORD HQ
COMMAND

Miriam greeted newly minted Fleet Admiral Bastian, the Tokahe Naataan and Pointe-Amiral Thisiame with the individualized salutes traditional in their militaries. "We'll join the Command Operations staff in the briefing room momentarily, but first I need to share with you some classified information, and an assignment.

"A Ghost squad has identified the locations of two additional Savrakath antimatter development facilities—one in a rural region on Savrak and one on its satellite. Fleet Admiral Bastian, please prepare a mission plan to destroy both facilities. Stealth-heavy, precise strikes are preferable, as I do not intend to turn Savrak territory into a full-scale warzone. I want the mission completed by 0800 CST tomorrow."

Bastian didn't argue. "Understood, Commandant. I'll see it done."

She pushed aside the whispering insecurity that came with the knowledge David had pressured the man to accept her continued leadership. For now, it was more important that he *did* accept it. "Thank you, Fleet Admiral. While we can't say how many antimatter missiles are in the field, we can ensure the number will go no higher.

"In additional good news, Connova Interstellar, working closely with Special Projects, has replicated the technology behind the double-shielding on the Machim Imperiums. Within the week, we should be able to adapt it for installation on all command vessels. If field tests confirm its viability on those ships, we'll begin gradually rolling out the shields to all vessels in our fleets capable of supporting the hardware."

"We've never been able to crack the secret of their shielding. How did we suddenly replicate the technology now?"

She met Bastian's hard stare without flinching. "We stole it. Is that a problem?"

The beginnings of a frown tugged the Fleet Admiral's mouth down, but he shook his head. "No. We need it."

Pinchu puffed out his chest. "This will prevent the Rasu from boarding our ships, yes?"

She smiled, keeping it professional and measured. "Yes, it will. What happened to too many ships at Namino will not happen a second time." She gestured toward the door. "Now, if you will accompany me."

RW

All two hundred ten employees of Command Operations were gathered in Briefing Room A. They included representatives from every Concord member species, including forty-eight Anadens. She'd be lying if she said she was one hundred percent comfortable with their continued presence, but none of them had betrayed Concord yet. If they had chosen to follow her rather than a motley assortment of *elassons*, then she would make it work.

As Miriam approached the podium, Bastian, Pinchu and Thisiame following behind her, she noted David sitting way in the back, in the far right corner.

Doesn't everyone appreciate how you will burn down the world to protect them? How no one could ever do a more extraordinary job of protecting them than you?

She resolved then and there to find a way to be worthy of his boundless belief in her. She lifted her chin minutely, and the chatter in the room quieted down. "Thank you all for coming today. The last several weeks have tested our mettle and our resolve, but we—you—have persevered in the face of many daunting challenges. I am proud of the work Command has done. I am proud of you.

"First, let me review the status of the current conflicts we are managing. The Savrakaths remain under a red-flag designation. The procedures for dealing with a red-flagged species are well established, and our forces will continue to obey them. After the Savrakath military callously bombed an AEGIS R&R vessel on a humanitarian mission, we have implemented alternative methods for evacuating Godjan refugees from Savrak, and this work continues apace.

"Regarding the ongoing dispute with the Anaden Senator and certain other Anaden *elassons*: the Senate has opened a recall proceeding to strip Ferdinand elasson-Kyvern of his position on the Concord Senate. Criminal charges have been filed against him commensurate with his actions, which include the suspected kidnapping of Navarchos Casmir elasson-Machim and the orchestration of the recent attack on Concord HQ. If other Concord personnel are discovered to have participated in Senator Ferdinand's crimes, they will be dealt with accordingly."

The door to the briefing room opened, and Richard and Will quietly slipped inside. Shortly before her meeting with the fleet commanders, she'd gotten word they had identified and arrested Ferdinand's CINT mole this morning, a Kyvern *ela* who worked as a shift supervisor in network security. One more obstacle overcome; one more path cleared. One more way she owed them both a greater debt than she could ever repay.

"But the actions of a few rogue *elassons* are not the actions of the Anaden people. Every Anaden in this room today has reaffirmed their commitment and dedication to the cause and mission of Command, and I take each of you at your word. Know that you are welcome here.

"However, we need to acknowledge the reality that a good portion of the Machim fleet is under the control of Ferdinand elasson-Kyvern and those who support his revolt. Therefore, any Machim

336 | G. S. JENNSEN

warship approaching Concord HQ will be quarantined and detained while its captain is interviewed and the purpose for its presence determined. We will not fire first on any Anaden vessel, but we will defend our stations, our worlds and our people from aggression.

"In addition, heightened travel restrictions are in effect for Anaden civilians. No one will be prevented from accessing Concord property, but anyone not previously cleared will be watched. I regret the need to take these actions, but the blame for their necessity lies at Ferdinand elasson-Kyvern's feet."

She worked to soften her countenance just a touch. Everyone here now knew she was not invincible, and to pretend otherwise would only serve to alienate them further.

"Finally, and most importantly, we need to discuss the elephant haunting the corners of our rooms: the Rasu. Our first battle against this enemy took a heavy toll on us all. It took a heavy toll on me personally, and I am grateful to be standing here before you once again. Thank you for your continued trust. I will endeavor above all to never let you or the great people of Concord down.

"All servicepeople who lost their lives in the Battle of Namino will be receiving posthumous Concord Stars, in recognition of their heroic sacrifice." She gazed to her left, then her right. "Tokahe Naataan, Pointe-Amiral, your ships and your people bore the brunt of the Rasu's savagery. Please, accept my heartfelt condolences and deepest sympathies, on behalf of everyone at Command."

After their acknowledgments, she returned her attention to the room. "The fight against the Rasu is just beginning. They are unlike any species we have ever encountered, but this will not keep us from defeating them. Doing so will require much of us. But as my friend Aristide Vranas once said at a crucial moment in humanity's history, we did not come this far by being afraid. So we must not be afraid now—instead we must be clever and stalwart, ingenious and resolute. We must transform our concept of what it means to engage in warfare. We must develop new weapons, new defenses and new tactics and use them to defeat this new enemy.

"The first steps on the road to accomplishing such feats have already been taken. A lot of hard work yet lies ahead of us, but know that we *will* accomplish our goals. We will match the Rasu on the field of battle and emerge victorious, however many times it takes to vanquish the enemy and protect our citizens." She nodded sharply. "So let's get to work."

48

IMPERIUM ALPHA
SAVRAK STELLAR SYSTEM

C asmir strode down the Imperium's bridge to the overlook, a bounce *almost* livening his steps. The bridge of a warship had always been his true home, but now it offered added benefits as well. He was relieved to escape from the alternating isolation of his confinement and the relentless bombardment of sniping and bickering among the other *elassons.*

For the first time in many days, he felt a taste of...freedom. If he wanted to, he could take the Imperium and run. Leave all this madness behind.

His ingrained, genetic sense of duty compelled him to remain, however. He was lucky, for unlike the other *elassons*, he'd received that which he most craved: orders from a superior officer. Ferdinand would wreck a room upon hearing it, but Casmir viewed Commandant Solovy as the supreme military leader in this corner of the universe. Standing on his own against Ferdinand, against Otto and Hannah and the other *elassons*, had been exhausting, but having the commandant's implicit if secret blessing gave him the strength to endure it.

Still, it *was* exhausting, and it pleased him to leave it behind for the familiar embrace of the Imperium bridge and the purpose of a new mission. The Savrakaths had overstayed their welcome by a fair amount and proved themselves unworthy of civilized society; they were nothing more than a failed Kat experiment foolishly let out of the lab, and they needed to be brought in line or, if necessary, annihilated.

He'd start by wiping out their unearned technology and weaponry, then destroying their remaining military capability. Finally, if it proved helpful, he'd send in ground troops. He found himself almost missing the Ch'mshak, as they were uniquely suited for such cleanup operations, but Machim soldiers were fully capable of handling the job.

He doubted it was going to be necessary to send them in, though. The Savrakaths were paper tigers, all snarl and spittle and no backbone. They tossed about their new antimatter weapons with no appreciation for what it meant to wield weapons of such destructive power. And without those weapons, they were nothing but backwater lizards only half-crawled out of the swamp.

As he studied the tactical profile he'd developed for the mission, he found himself wishing he knew the locations of all their antimatter labs, for they needed to be his first targets. Then again, if he eliminated every military installation on the planet and in space, he'd surely take them out along the way.

The yellow-and-green silhouette of Savrak came into view as they decelerated, but his attention quickly shifted to the barren satellite orbiting the planet. "Target all structures on the lunar surface, starting with the location marked Target A1 on the tactical map. Fire when ready."

RW

Six hours later, all Savrak lunar facilities lay in broken ruins, naught but debris floating off into the void. So, too, did the military headquarters on the northern outskirts of Savradin and the three shipyards situated a hundred kilometers into the swamp.

Only the headquarters had put up more than the most token of resistances, and it involved a few dozen conventional missiles and a handful of hastily launched fighter jets. All were disposed of without fanfare. No antimatter missiles had been directed their way yet, which likely meant the entire supply was loaded on warships—warships sure to now be frantically speeding home from patrols. This should not present a problem, for Casmir had some ideas on how to negate the antimatter advantage as well.

But next up on the target list was a facility outside one of the smaller Savrak cities. It had been labeled 'military training' by Command analysts, though whether the Savrakaths provided the name or this had been Command's reasoned judgment, he couldn't say. But it was a trivial matter to destroy it. A single laser fired from the Imperium would suffice.

"Prepare to fire on Target C3 on my—"

A roiling plume of flame rocked the low, sprawling structure in the distance. Had the weapons officer jumped the gun? No. Did one of the other ships in his fleet take it upon themselves to fire? A quick check of their constantly updating status negated this possibility as well.

Had the Savrakaths blown up their own facility rather than allow it to be destroyed? Absurd and pointless. "Report!"

His XO studied three separate screens. "We're picking up multiple small fighter-type vessels in the vicinity."

"Savrakath in origin?" Was it possible they *had* blown up their own facility?

"Checking, sir." He leaned over to study the XO's visuals, which displayed three fighters crisscrossing above the structure as they fired upon it a second time. He squinted to make certain...AEGIS fighters?

*Lochagós Garon (*MVC 814*): "Targets acquired. Firing."*

*Navarchos Casmir (*Imperium Alpha*): "Belay that, Lochagós! We are not to fire on Concord vessels!"*

*Lochagós Garon (*MVC 814*): "They're AEGIS fighters. Firing now."*

The same difference...which Casmir recognized constituted the crux of one of Ferdinand's biggest complaints about Concord—that Humans controlled it in all practical respects. But now wasn't the time for semantics.

Garon's cruiser engaged, but the fighters spiraled upward and fanned out, deftly evading the initial volley.

Navarchos Casmir (Imperium Alpha): "Lochagós Garon, you will stand down this instant, or I will fire upon you myself."

Lochagós Garon (MVC 814): "Sir!"

Navarchos Casmir (Imperium Alpha): "You have your orders."

No further response arrived, but no further fire originated from the cruiser, either.

Dammit, that was too close. When larger, more formidable AEGIS vessels didn't appear on the horizon to escalate the encounter, he studied the tactical map with one eye, the viewport with the other. The AEGIS fighters had done a fine job of destroying the facility; it took them longer and required greater firepower than he'd have needed to accomplish the task, but the result was the same. So why were they here? Why would Commandant Solovy authorize him to attack Savrak if she intended to order AEGIS to do the same? It didn't make any sense.

Should he expect to bump into Concord forces at other sites now? He'd do what he could to keep his ship captains reined in, but the fog of war meant mistakes were bound to happen eventually. Of course, as he was now free, if only in the most technical sense, he might simply send the commandant a message requesting clarification or updated orders…

…but with the Savrakaths all but disposed of, she would likely then order him to return to Concord HQ with the ships and men he oversaw. And that wasn't his deal with Ferdinand. If he did it, he'd be signing the final seal on his betrayal of his Dynasty and his people. And try as he might, he just wasn't ready to do it. Not yet. He still believed he could carve a path through this crisis that preserved both Concord and the solidarity of the Anaden people.

"Should we proceed to the next target, Navarchos?"

He checked the tactical profile, grateful to need to focus on the here and now. But there *were* no more known military targets. In a single day, his fleet had eliminated their short- and long-term military capability. As Machim fleets did. The Savrakath vessels currently on patrol were going to find themselves in a predicament when it came time to land somewhere.

This left civilian targets, and he found himself hesitating once again. When the mission was to Eradicate an enemy, Machim fleets did not distinguish between military and civilian targets. But the last fourteen years had taught him that Concord fleets *did* so distinguish. Commandant Solovy's message authorized him to attack military targets. While his Primor would have ordered every building over ten meters tall flattened before calling in a Theriz Cultivation Unit, Commandant Solovy would stay her hand here.

Which kind of leader did he want to be? Which kind was he capable of being?

Perhaps, as a first step, he could split the difference. He prepared a message to be delivered to General Jhountar, then returned his attention to the tactical profile.

"I'm marking a heavy industrial distribution center in the city of Pakrak as our next target."

EPITHERO

Lochagós Garon ela-Machim entered the converted military situation room, stopping just inside the door to salute Casmir. "Sir, you wished to see me?"

Casmir had been reviewing the updated scans of Savrak with Otto and Hannah, searching for any signs of military activity needing to be stamped out, but he diverted his attention from the scans to fix a cold gaze on Garon. "Yes, I did. You're fired."

The man blinked twice, and the rigidity of his formal stance evaporated. "Excuse me, Navarchos?"

"Fired. Relieved of command. You are no longer captain of a cruiser, or of any vessel for that matter. You disobeyed a direct order in the middle of a live combat situation. Therefore, you can serve as a junior officer on a frigate until you learn how to obey orders and respect the chain of command. You'll be issued a bunk at the Machimis Military Annex until I determine your next assignment. Dismissed."

Garon stood there, jaw dropped, gaping at him.

"I said *dismissed*."

The man shook his head roughly, pivoted and stormed out of the room in a fit of outrage. Once the door had closed behind Garon, Casmir turned back to the other Machim *elassons* and met their equally disbelieving stares with projected resolve. "It's called discipline. In the absence of the integral, we need to enforce it ourselves. We should have begun doing so fourteen years ago, but we can begin today. In time, the people serving under us will learn to respect the chain of command, but orders such as this will send an unequivocal message to our soldiers that we will not tolerate insubordination." He recalled Commandant Solovy's admonition and decided to crib it. "And fear will suffice as a workable substitute until we can instill a tradition of proper discipline."

Otto frowned. "Relieving soldiers of their posts is not a concept which exists in our Dynasty."

"Then it's time we introduce it. Am I being clear?"

Somewhat to his surprise, no one else argued. It was possible that, much like him, they were simply looking for guidance and leadership. He didn't know if he was up to the task of providing it in the crisis scenario they now faced, but dammit, he had to try. Uncountable lives might depend on him changing the course of this debacle of an insurgency.

Ferdinand blasted them with an urgent summons then, saving him from having to fumble his way out of the awkward silence lingering in the wake of his grand declaration.

RW

This communique is addressed to Ferdinand elasson-Kyvern and all Anaden elassons *who are supporting or cooperating with his actions.*

If Machim warships fire on Concord-affiliated vessels again, Concord will view it as a declaration of war. You have been warned.

The Senate has voted unanimously to strip Ferdinand elasson-Kyvern of his Senate position. The Anaden seat will remain open until the Anaden people choose a new senator to represent them in Concord affairs. If the Anaden people wish to withdraw from Concord, they may do so by popular vote. Until such time as this occurs, we will continue to treat the Anaden people as full and equal citizens.

Furthermore, charges of treason and abuse of office have been filed against Ferdinand elasson-Kyvern and a warrant issued for his arrest. He is requested to report peaceably to Concord Security for processing. If he does not promptly do so, measures will be taken to effect his arrest.

Any elassons *who wish to disavow Ferdinand elasson-Kyvern's actions and surrender to Concord Security will be granted pardons, absent evidence of prior actions on their part that threatened the lives of Concord citizens.*

The offices of Concord Command, Senate and Consulate wish to resolve this dispute peacefully. However, we will answer any acts of violence or threats of violence or coercion against Concord citizens or property in the strongest possible terms.

— Commandant Miriam Solovy, Concord Command
— Senator Mia Requelme, Concord Consulate
— Concord Senate
> *Senator Mia Requelme*
> *Senator Pinchutsenahn Niikha Qhiyane Kteh*
> *Senator Daayn Shahs-Ian*
> *Senator Onai Veshnael*
> *Senator Tasme Chareis*
> *Senator Bohlke'ban*
> *Senator Ahhk-sae*

Ferdinand tossed a hand in the direction of the message floating above the table. "Rubbish, all of it! How dare they threaten to arrest me! They haven't the right. I've only ever acted in the best interests of our people."

His eyes narrowed as he scanned the others in the room, perhaps not finding the reactions he was expecting. "I hope no one is considering taking them up on their pardon offer. Consider your responses carefully, for if you surrender to Concord, you will lose all authority of your Dynasty."

Basra practically snarled at Ferdinand. "You don't have the power to make such a determination, brother. I am an *elasson* of the Kyvern Dynasty by blood and genetic destiny, and you cannot take that from me."

"Do you want to see me try? I can ruin every person in this room with a few well-placed comms. See, this is what Concord is hoping for! They want to sow discord among us. They want to tear us apart, and you are letting them."

"We're already torn apart, Ferdinand." Rachele elasson-Theriz spread her arms wide, as if to draw everyone in. "Less than half the *elassons* are here supporting you, and no one new has joined us in days. We have torn *ourselves* apart. So I come back to the first question I asked: what is it you want to do? Do you want to go to war with Concord? Withdraw and form our own government? Or are you merely interested in throwing a month-long temper tantrum? Because if it proves to be the latter, I am out."

Ferdinand sputtered and fumed, and Casmir had to wonder exactly how close the man was to losing all control. "This is *not* a temper tantrum. I believe that we should answer to no one but ourselves. We need to create a structure where we are beholden to no authority but our own."

"Athena's grace! Then stop grandstanding and *do* it, for fuck's sake."

Casmir forcibly bit his tongue. Many of those present, Ferdinand included, still viewed his 'conversion' with suspicion, and rightfully so. If he spoke out in favor of Concord now, he risked losing what meager goodwill he'd built up. That being said, he made a note to have a private conversation with Rachele and possibly Basra later.

Diplomacy was not part of a Machim's skillset, but he was starting to think he must be better at it than Ferdinand. Maybe genetics weren't everything after all.

49

SAVRAK
UNDERGROUND MILITARY BUNKER

General Kuisk Jhountar,
*   Your military capability is decimated. Lay down your arms and surrender all remaining military weaponry and interstellar-capable vessels, military or civilian, within the next Concord Standard Day. If you do not, your population centers will be annihilated in the hours that follow. By next week, you will not have a population. The choice is yours.*

*   Your surrender can be directed to Navarchos Casmir elasson-Machim at this address.*

"Arghhhh!" With a deep growl Jhountar slammed his hand into the bronze urn resting atop his desk and sent it flying across the room. It had hardly crashed into the wall and tumbled to the floor when he'd upended a guest chair and hurled it at the door. The chair broke into pieces on impact; the door did not.

"Sir—"

He spun on Brigadier Ghorek with a vicious snarl. "Is it true? Is Northeast Military Command gone? The Lunar Forward Maneuvers Center? The Arctic Strategic Base?"

Ghorek kept his distance, one conniving eye on the exit. "All those locations, as well as six additional military bases, are offline and not responding to communications."

"That tells me nothing. What does Reconnaissance say?"

"Reconnaissance is unable to provide any information, as the satellite network is down, sir. Likely destroyed."

Jhountar's blood rushed hot through his veins, and he searched around for something fresh to inflict abuse upon.

Ghorek stood calmly, though he'd retreated nearer to the door during Jhountar's rampage. "We are dispatching our fastest ships to the affected locations to assess the damage. We should know more in an hour or two."

"We do not have hours to spare, as they have only given us a day to respond. If this Navarchos' claims are true, I must know it now. Send additional vessels."

"Yes, sir. You're considering complying with the demands and surrendering?"

"Never. But we need time to regroup and prepare an appropriate response, one which will teach Concord we are not to be trifled with."

"I see." Ghorek's tail swished deliberately. "What response might that be?"

Jhountar ignored the question to go to his desk and call up the visual from the interrogation room at the top-secret Akasav facility. The Anaden prisoner lay strapped to a table, his arms and legs restrained and pulled wide apart. Bruises dotted his pale, squishy flesh, and blood dripped to the floor from multiple locations—the toes of one foot, a long cut along the left section of his stomach, his nostrils and a portion of his scalp. His eyes were closed, his breathing shallow.

The man's heart had nearly stopped twice during the morning's interrogation, according to the onsite doctor. The warning provided by the Anaden deviant who delivered the prisoner had proved accurate: the man was making it exceedingly difficult not to kill him. He hurled insults and spat in the interrogators' faces, screamed and flailed, and generally took every action available to him other than providing actionable intel on Concord.

The Savrakaths were not a gentle people, but the tortures they'd subjected the prisoner to gave even Jhountar pause—or had done so before Concord warships wrecked a host of military assets a century in the making. Now, he wanted to travel to Akasav and slit the man's throat himself, one slow millimeter at a time.

The unpleasant truth was that they had nearly run out of inventive torments to subject the prisoner to. Their most creative efforts had not broken the man. As a murderer of Savrakaths, he deserved the punishment all the same, but in his single-minded quest to die and be reborn, he was determined not to give them the information they craved.

But perhaps he could still be of some use as a bargaining chip. And if he failed to serve this purpose as well, they retained one more prisoner in reserve. They'd kept his capture secret in the hope that he might be a long-term source of actionable intel, but it turned out the Human was only a grunt soldier, possessing no noteworthy intelligence to be tortured out of him. Jhountar nevertheless kept him alive for now; if a public demonstration became necessary, the man could serve as a useful example of why it was unwise to go to war with the Savrakaths.

He hoped it wouldn't come to that. First, a lifeline and the beginnings of a plan.

Jhountar pivoted to Ghorek, who had slid yet closer to the door while his focus was elsewhere. "Order all antimatter materials and weaponry in the field to be delivered to a central location—somewhere remote that won't attract Concord attention."

"Yes, sir. It will take longer than a day to collect and transport everything."

"I'm aware. Do it as quickly as possible, no matter the expense. I have an idea of how to buy us the time we need."

50

CINT VESSEL 23A-X
VICINITY OF SAVRAK STELLAR SYSTEM

For the first time in uncountable ages, Eren didn't wake to the sensation of spiders stealing around carving rivulets through the muscles and tendons beneath his skin.

Drae had removed the wrist restraints while Eren slept, and his arms now hung limply at his sides. His left cheek ached from spending hours pressed against the cold, unforgiving floor of his prison. Most other parts of his body ached worse, as though every muscle had been clenched tight as he lay there. Possibly they had been.

He breathed in—and promptly decided the spiders were the better option. Bolts of pain ricocheted around his skull to stab him behind the eyes and rip apart his jaw. Pressure on the inside of his skull made it feel as though the bones were about to burst apart. He needed to release the pressure somehow, this instant. A needle through the ear, or through the eye if necessary.

His ears popped as the pressure became unbearable, and his hands gripped his horrifically bare head in a vise-grip. What was this fresh form of maddening torture? His eyeballs swam in their sockets, bulging in preparation for being forced out of his skull.

Something bumped against his foot, and he forced his eyes open to see a syringe lying to his left. On the other side of the force field, Drae stood with his arms crossed over his chest, regarding Eren dubiously.

Eren hissed through clenched teeth. "Whatever's in there, is it enough to kill me?"

"No, you ass. Just enough to knock you out for a little while longer."

"Up the dose." He struggled to gather his legs beneath him—then abruptly he lunged toward the force field, taking perverse pleasure in the shock of electricity that cascaded over his body when he collided with it even as the charge knocked him back to the floor. "If you have ever been my friend, kill me—or let me loose so I can do it myself."

Drae's expression hardened into grim resoluteness. "No. I know you'll find this hard to believe right now, but you're doing better. Almost done."

Eren picked up the syringe and tried to focus on it as his vision blurred from tears. Tears of agony, or possibly from smarting due to the jolt of electricity. Almost done with detox, maybe, though at present it felt more like the endless beginning than the unreachable end. But on the backside of recovery waited only sorrow. The loneliness of a bleak universe stripped of color and joy, for its brightest star had been snuffed out forever.

Then the pressure in his head exploded anew. He jammed the syringe into his neck and let the darkness engulf him.

RW

Drae collapsed in the cockpit chair and let it spin him around as he rubbed at his face. He needed sleep, but he hadn't dared leave Eren unattended for longer than a few minutes at a time. The dose of *ferusom* ought to send his patient into a calm, dreamless sleep for four or five hours at a minimum, however, so now was his opportunity.

He kicked the chair around in another lazy circle. Was he doing the right thing? Should he have taken Eren to HQ Medical, where he could receive proper treatment from qualified professionals? No, his friend would simply shut down and bide his time until he could escape and finish the job of his slow suicide.

Should he let him go? As stubborn as Eren was, he would find new and inventive ways to frustrate Drae's best efforts until he got what he wanted anyway. What was the point of saving a man who didn't want to be saved?

He blinked in surprise as a wave of ice-blue lights filled the cabin. Random, unannounced visits from Kats were not part of his normal existence, but this was a damn weird week.

"Mesme?"

It is I. I have but a moment, but I wanted to learn how Eren is doing.

"He is miserable and wretched, but it's actually looking as if he's going to survive the detox. After that? I don't know. I can't keep him locked up once he's regained his lucid mind."

You worry he will pursue a renewed attempt at suicide.

"I do. He's hurting right now, and I don't mean from the detox. The only cure anyone has ever found for grief is time, and he's refusing to allow himself that time."

Caleb believed it was important to save Eren. That he was worth saving. I believe he is worth saving. Do you believe he is worth saving?

Drae sighed and rolled his eyes at the ceiling. "I do."

Then we must ensure we save him.

ASTERION DOMINION

51

KIYORA

KIYORA ONE GENERATIONS CLINIC

The form on the medical cot glowed the color of honey dipped in a pool of stardust. It was due to the kyoseil, of course, for this body included almost three times the amount of the mineral they normally used in Asterion bodies. The kyoseil spun through every vein, every bone, every tendon.

As requested.

The med tech nodded to Dashiel, and he approached the cot as this new version of Nika stirred. Her lashes fluttered, a harbinger of her eyes opening to reveal gilt-flecked luminescent teal irises. Her lips curled up on seeing him, even as she blinked furiously. "This is…" her throat worked "…whoa."

He frowned in concern that threatened to plummet toward panic. What if he'd done it wrong? What if the formula Asterions had relied on for hundreds of millennia existed for a reason, and throwing the balance out of whack had brought ruinous results? "Are you all right?"

"I am…it's just…." She pushed herself up to a sitting position and gingerly draped her legs over the edge of the cot, then reached out to grip his arm for stability as she swayed unsteadily. "I can see all the kyoseil wavelengths in my normal vision. An endless rainbow of energy flowing through everything." She shot him a pained grimace. "This is way too disorienting. I need to work out a way to tune out, or at least tone down, all these…we've been calling them 'strings,' but in this volume they're more akin to pervasive waves."

"I'm sure we can tweak your ocular programming to filter some of it out. Can you stand?"

"I think so." She eased off the cot until her feet touched the floor. After a long, deep breath, she let go of his arm and slowly turned in a circle. When she returned to facing him, she was smiling. She brought a hand to his cheek. "Ceraff with me for a minute. See what I'm seeing."

"Absolutely." He switched on the visual k-band and followed the string weaving across the scant centimeters between them—

"Damn." He stumbled backward, fumbling for the wall to brace himself. "You're right. This is disorienting. Yet...."

"Beautiful."

"Yes." He gazed at her, at the shimmering waves of color dancing around her body, and the words caught in his throat. "So beautiful. Do you feel any different?"

"I feel like I got dosed."

"Okay, but other than that?"

"I feel as if...these insanely powerful emotions are welling up inside me. I'm bowled over by our incredible interconnections, by the power flowing—"

The door opened and Nika—the original—burst into the room. "—in and through us." The words left both their lips simultaneously.

The original stared at them for a split-second, then came over and wrapped her arms around them both.

Because he was in a ceraff with one, he effectively was with the other as well, for they shared a mind, to a far greater extent than he'd appreciated until this moment.

He shook his head roughly, stepped out of their embrace and hurriedly severed the connection to the ceraff. "Sorry. That was a little too much to absorb. How are you going to function like this?"

"Once we dial down the visual stimuli—" They cut themselves off in unison, giving one another identical looks of consternation. "We should try to—ugh! Hey, has our nose always curled up crooked on one side?"

He laughed, shaking his head in wry amusement. "Yes, it has."

"Great. What we're going to do is...." One of them—the original—backed toward the door. "We're going to not be in the same place at the same time doing the same thing. I'll, um…Dashiel, I'll see you at the Initiative in a little while."

Because *she* would be staying here, at his side. He watched the door close behind her…then pivoted toward her twin. Gods, his head already hurt. "But you're still experiencing whatever she's doing now?"

"Walking down the hall, muttering to herself about our crooked nose and making a new, better-informed list of questions to ask Parc."

"And she's experiencing whatever you're doing?"

"Yes."

"Even this?" He cradled her face in his hands and pressed his lips to hers. "Am I kissing two of you at once?"

She grinned against his lips, gilded teal eyes dancing in amusement. "In all the ways that matter, you are." She dropped her forehead to his, and he felt her sigh in his arms.

Then she backed away and gave him a sharp nod. "Come on. We've got a lot to do and not much time to do it in. Alex will be here soon."

RW

Perrin fidgeted in the clinic waiting room, for no good reason. Nika's procedure was for all intents and purposes a simple regen, only in an extra body. While also keeping the existing body. Plus, with an overdose of kyoseil. Okay, so it wasn't a *simple* regen. But it posed no risk to the original, so she had no reason to be worried. Except for the risk inherent in being a Plex….

She watched Parc cross the breadth of the waiting room for the third time in less than a minute. He acted as anxious as she felt, on top of carrying around so much responsibility for what was soon to come, never mind whatever other crazy notions routinely ran amok in his head.

"Parc, you're making me dizzy. Sit with me."

He glanced at her in surprise, almost as if he'd forgotten she was there. "What? Sure." He came over and plopped down on the couch next to her, then immediately began tapping his feet on the floor. "So, Ryan's gone again. He vanished from the Initiative as soon as I was up and walking around."

"I know. I'm sorry. But he stayed by your side the entire time you were unconscious. I had to bring him food up from the cafeteria and everything."

"He did?"

"Yes. He cares a great deal about you."

"Not enough to stop being angry at me, apparently." He groaned and sank lower on the couch.

The doors leading into the clinic remained closed and silent. "Parc, he's not angry at you. He's hurt."

"Oh, trust me. He's *definitely* angry at me." The fingers of his left hand began drumming a beat on his thigh. "What do you mean, 'hurt'?"

"Well, I'm merely speculating here, but—"

"But you understand people. How they think, what they need. Speculate away."

She wished she had as much faith in her abilities as he seemed to. "I suspect he's hurt because to him, when you became a Plex, it felt as if you were saying he wasn't enough for you. As if you created a copy of yourself to go out and experience all sorts of thrills and adventures in the world that he wasn't giving to you."

"No, that's not at all why I did it!"

"Then why did you do it?"

He stared at her strangely, blinked and looked away. "Because it was there to be *done*. It's the bleeding edge of technology and our evolution as a species. It's exciting and dangerous and new, and I couldn't resist the lure of it. Basically, why I do everything I do."

She laughed, though it came out a little stilted. "Did you talk to Ryan about it beforehand? Explain what you wanted to do, and why?"

"No. I just...did it. You know, like everything else." The drumming intensified. "So do you think if I tell him he's enough for me, he'll forgive me?"

"I think it would be a good start, but you're probably going to need to *show* him, too."

"How?" His expression darkened. "By killing off my copy? I don't...I can't. He's *me*, as much as the me sitting right here with you." Abruptly he leapt up off the couch. "Ask Nika what it's like."

Perrin spun around to see Nika—*a* Nika—emerging through the doors to approach them. She looked the same physically, but the mysterious, thousand-meter glimmer in her eyes told a different story. Transformed, yet again...and with the act, Perrin's closest friend fell further out of her orbit.

An aching, empty sorrow welled up in her chest. A part of her had known way back when Nika discovered her true identity that one day she would lose her friend. Nika's world was so big now, populated by intergalactic allies, immortal power brokers and monstrous enemies. Perrin had no doubt Nika would do anything to save their people, no matter the cost to her personally. No matter if it meant becoming something *else*, something greater, something Perrin could never understand.

She covered up any sadness behind a bright smile as she stood and met Nika halfway. "Did it work?"

Nika's gaze blurred and unfocused. She brought a hand to her lips. "It did."

52

NAMINO
CAMP BURROW

J oaquim dropped to the floor beside Parc; a trickle of blood seeped from a cut on one temple, and his shirt was soaked through with sweat. "All right. We managed to retrieve another drone from the armory, get it in the air and send it to the Rasu's processing center on the outskirts of town, all without getting killed. I hope our trouble was worth it."

"It will be." Parc regarded Joaquim dubiously. "Do you want to spend a few minutes at the repair bench, or maybe the shower, before we get started?"

Selene dropped to her knees across from them, looking little better than Joaquim did. Her lower lip was busted and flyaway strands of once-blond hair appeared to be singed.

Parc considered feeling guilty for asking them to so blatantly risk their lives for what was scarcely more than a hunch...but his hunches were hardly ever wrong. Besides, Nika would soon be on her way here, and she was counting on him to have answers when she arrived. The clock was ticking.

Joaquim shook his head as other people—Grant Mesahle and the two Humans, Marlee and Caleb—joined their growing circle. "Nope. I'm good. Let's take a look." Joaquim's wrist flicked, and a pane instantiated between them.

"Hells. This place got bigger."

The drone hovered near the sprawling Rasu compound on the northwest periphery of the city. It almost resembled a traditional fort, complete with a defensive barricade bounding a series of circular structures that surrounded a towering spire at the center. The uniformity of the aubergine Rasu metal made it difficult to distinguish many individual features or assign them a purpose.

The apex of the spire was another matter, however. A violet glow leaked out through a dense, orb-shaped matrix situated below a needle-like cap.

Parc scratched at his left leg while he scrutinized the visuals; the skin was so new it glistened, and also itched something fierce. He'd caught several glimpses of the distant compound during his torturous trek across the city, noting the heavy traffic to and from the area and the frequent visits by patrolling Rasu vessels. The compound was important, and he had a *hunch* as to why. "The violet glow is one of their power vortexes, similar to what Nika encountered on the stronghold platform. My guess? It's powering the needle."

Grant studied the image. "Those vortexes generate a ton of power. So far as we know, only one thing they can be running here would require so much fuel: the quantum block."

Selene frowned. "But we don't know that for certain. In fact, they could be running hundreds of high-energy devices. For one, they're clearly doing *something* with all the material they're hauling into this compound."

Parc let the debate fade into the background while he focused in on the needle at the spire's apex. "Show the scene in infrared."

Joaquim entered a command on the module in his lap, and the view flipped to a heat map of the region. Cardinal filaments spilled out of several heat blocks to wind through the concentric circles at ground level.

Parc gestured to the streaks of cardinal flowing through the compound. "No, there's power everywhere, fueling whatever they're doing in all these buildings. Zoom into the apex."

Joaquim silently complied, and a raging ball of crimson spewing upward like an erupting volcano filled the screen.

"See? All the power from the vortex is flowing up into the needle. But the needle is just...sitting there looking pretty." Parc crossed his arms over his chest. "It's generating the quantum block."

Joaquim rolled his eyes at the low bedrock ceiling. "But the quantum block was activated long before this tower ever existed."

"They probably kept it stowed on one of their ships until they could build it a more permanent home."

"But why bother? Why would it need a more permanent home?"

"I don't..." his head twitched "...oh. Nika says it might be similar to those Rift Bubbles the Kats are handing out like candy. For whatever reason, they apparently work better when situated on the surface of a planet rather than in orbit."

Grant narrowed his eyes at Parc. "I'm not going to lie. It's a little weird, you talking to Nika back on Mirai."

"You should *be* the one talking to Nika back on Mirai. Anyway, maybe it's as simple as the closer it can get to the center of the field the device is projecting, the better it functions. Or maybe it uses the planet's interior to spread the interference pattern. The reasons don't matter." He jabbed a finger toward the pane. "That's the quantum block."

"All the power is getting drawn in by a massive engine for *some* purpose." Selene conceded the point. "It's a reasonable assumption."

Joaquim nodded. "Great. So how are we going to take it out?"

Selene pulled her singed hair out of its tail and ran a hand through it, then frowned as several pieces came away with her hand. "We don't have any weapons powerful enough to blow the needle up, assuming we can get anywhere near it."

Grant shrugged. "If we can take out the vortex powering it, it will kill the block for a minimum of a couple of hours, which is time enough to get a lot of survivors off the planet and a lot of soldiers onto it."

The Human, Caleb, spoke up for the first time. "The first question needing an answer is this: are the Rasu so arrogant in their superiority that they haven't bothered to implement proper security protections at this compound? Or are they paranoid to a fault, in which case nothing is getting inside there. Not weapons, and certainly not us."

Joaquim scowled. "The mere existence of the quantum block implies they're...if not paranoid, at least thorough. But it's a good point. We need to find out for sure."

Selene matched him scowl-for-scowl. "How? In case you haven't noticed, our resources are severely limited."

Parc butted into their sparring—or flirting, he wasn't sure which. "Can you program the drone to kamikaze into the compound, then watch to see what manner of defenses respond to the incursion?"

"Nope. Quantum block, *remember*? I can't remotely reprogram the drones, and I can't call them home to alter the programming, either."

It was easy to forget how much of their daily lives—their tools, their weapons and even their bodies—relied on quantum programming. In fact, if not for the kyoseil woven into their bodies providing them some protection, every Asterion would probably have dropped dead the instant the quantum block was switched on.

"We'll have to get close enough to the compound to test the defenses ourselves. And by 'we' I mean all of you." Parc pointed to his still-healing leg stretched out stiffly in front of him.

Selene shook her head. "But then they'll know someone is out here, fighting back."

"Good!" Joaquim threw his hands in the air. "It's about time they felt threatened."

"Guys, if whatever we send in is innocuous enough, it could be mistaken for leftover tech, flying around blindly with no master to direct it."

A devious smile grew on Joaquim's lips. "Or, it could be the opposite of innocuous." He twisted around and shouted toward the left corner of the bunker. "Rogers, the DAF Command armory has shoulder-fired SALs in stock, doesn't it?"

The colonel's brow furrowed up, but he nodded.

Selene dropped her head into her hands. "Again? We just got back from the armory and nearly lost our skin escaping."

Joaquim was already climbing to his feet. "This is worth one more trip. A couple of SALs will take out that power vortex from two kilometers away."

"If the defenses are weak."

"Right. So let's find out how strong they are."

RW

Marlee guzzled a bottle of water while she watched the others step through their usual pre-mission routines. Selene secured a tactical belt over her hips then motioned for Grant to join her outside the supply room. "Grant, you're in charge while we're gone. And if we don't come back, it's up to you to take care of these people until help arrives."

"I'll look after them. You have my word. But come back in one piece so I don't have to, okay?"

Marlee chuckled to herself. It wasn't the first time she'd noticed Grant joking about shirking responsibility, as the insults she'd hurled at him earlier demonstrated. Once she'd gotten past her wounded pride, however, she could admit that he was an honorable man. In addition to risking his life to rescue her, he'd never hesitated to act to care for any person here in need.

But not only was he not a fighter, he also wasn't a natural leader, and being forced into the role seemed to make him intensely uncomfortable. Which didn't make sense to her, because he genuinely *was* kind, clever and resourceful. Yet whenever allowed to do so, he quickly slipped into the background. The spark of attraction might be fading after their spat, but he remained a puzzle she longed to solve.

Caleb approached her carrying a tactical flak jacket identical to the one he wore. "Have I expressed to you how strongly I want you to stay here?"

"Only seven or eight times. I understand, I do. But I can't sit here waiting helplessly to get slaughtered, not when they're something I can do to possibly help end this nightmare for these people."

"But we—"

She took the jacket from him and slipped it on. "Come on, Caleb. I'm going *crazy* down here. I feel like I can't breathe, like I can't move without colliding with a rock, a wall or a dejected shell of a person. But what I can do is fight. You know I can."

"You can. You have a lot to learn—things I can't teach you right now—but you have exceptional natural reflexes."

"I got them from you."

"We do have good genes…." His voice trailed off, and a troubled expression darkened his features. Then he shook his head roughly, and the pall vanished. "Still. If I could force you to stay put, I…wouldn't do it. Pay attention, because this is me accepting that you're an adult, and that I can't control your life or the choices you make."

"Thank you! It means a lot to me." She reached out to hug him, and was taken by surprise when he wrapped her up in his arms and squeezed her tight. She laughed haltingly into his neck. "I won't let you down."

"I know you won't." He stepped back to scrutinize the fit of her jacket. "Will you at least promise me you won't try to engage in polite diplomacy with any Rasu we meet?"

She rolled her eyes for dramatic effect. "I promise."

DAF COMMAND

A warm, dry breeze wafted in through the blown-out front doors of DAF command, and Marlee greedily drew the fresh air into her lungs. The bunker had only the most basic air filtration system, and the air really could get stifling in there at times.

She waited by the wall near the lift, sandwiched between Joaquim and Caleb, because Caleb had conned Joaquim into feeling as though he needed to protect her, too.

Silence hung heavy in the building; no rumbles or thuds echoed from deeper inside, and it appeared to be empty of Rasu. Selene, Ava and Colonel Rogers had headed into the depths of the DAF complex five minutes earlier, hoping to reach the armory and return before that situation changed.

In the absence of working comms, Joaquim had taken to muttering in short whispers when Selene and the others finally reemerged from the dark hallway opposite the entrance. He rushed to meet them, taking the long, thick cylinder positioned under Colonel Rogers' arm from him and crouching on the floor to inspect it.

"This isn't a SAL."

"No. All the SALs were damaged. It's a rocket launcher."

Joaquim glanced up at Rogers, one eyebrow raised. "Nice. This will certainly do."

Selene opened up her bag as Marlee and Caleb arrived. "Frag and electricity grenades for the taking. They might not stop a Rasu cold, but they should slow them down."

Caleb showed her how to hook a couple of grenades to the latches on her tactical vest, then proceeded to daisy-chain half a dozen off his belt. When she got home, the first thing she was going to do—after hugging her Mom and Gramps and getting a haircut—was acquire herself a military-grade tactical belt.

Joaquim returned the rocket launcher to Colonel Rogers and removed his Glaser from the holster. "Let's move."

53

SIYANE
MIRAI

The *Siyane* landed at a private spaceport on the outskirts of Mirai One. At the exit from the small terminal, Nika murmured unheard words to Dashiel Ridani, embraced him, then hefted a backpack over her shoulder and picked up a heavy bag in each hand. Weapons for the coming fight.

Alex extended the ramp and went to greet her newest passenger—which was when she realized Nika now full-on *glowed*, as if she were a sylphean, angelic creature.

She arched an eyebrow as the woman strode up the ramp. "Get some new upgrades?"

Nika shrugged as she passed Alex and headed into the main cabin. "I dosed myself with kyoseil to be better able to protect myself and the routines I carry from the effects of the quantum block."

"Hmm." Alex nodded thoughtfully. "I dosed myself with Akeso to be better able to find Caleb in the city."

Morgan peered at them from around the cockpit chair. "Can I dose myself with vodka to…be better able to endure this trial?"

"No." Alex gestured between the two of them. "Nika Kirumase, Morgan Lekkas."

Nika jerked a greeting and tossed her backpack on the worktable, then set the two bags on the floor. "Why is she here?"

"Because we're going to have to leave the *Siyane* behind on the outskirts of the city, but someone will have to fly it when the shit hits the fan, and Morgan's the best pilot in the universe. She'll get the *Siyane* where we need it when we need it, without the Rasu destroying it."

Nika's gaze drifted toward the cockpit. "Best in the universe, huh?"

"On a bad day…which she admittedly has a lot of."

"The amethyst irises…she's a Prevo, isn't she? I was under the impression Prevos were Humanity's best and brightest."

"Not just any Prevo, either. She was one of our original four who defeated the Kats when they invaded. But her partner was killed in a combat action six years ago, and since then…."

Nika's hands paused with the backpack flap halfway open. "Oh. I didn't mean to pry, but I know what such a loss can do to a person."

Alex folded her arms over her chest and leaned against the edge of the data center table. "No disrespect, but how could you know? Your people live forever."

"Not all of them. And sometimes, what survives isn't the same person who they used to be."

In the recesses of her mind, Akeso hummed in staccato notes, tugging her anxiously toward Namino. "Someone before Dashiel, then?"

Nika regarded her strangely. The woman's own eyes were now more gilded honey and silver than teal. Valkyrie had once described them as resembling luminescent oceans, but with the transformation they more closely resembled luminescent *galaxies.*

"There is no way I can answer your question that you'll understand, so I'm going to move on. The point I was trying to get to was, can we count on her?"

"Yes. She'll come through for us when we need her to, if only because she hates to lose."

"Okay. I trust your judgment."

"Thank you. Are we ready to go?"

"Yes."

Alex raised her voice in the direction of the cockpit. Reluctantly, she was allowing Morgan to fly from the start so the woman could get a feel for the ship while Alex was on hand to answer questions. "Time to depart, but don't jump us into Namino space quite yet."

Nika slipped off her flak jacket and folded it on the worktable, then removed several items from her backpack and spread them out beside the jacket. Beneath her snug tank top, the shimmer of a tattoo danced across the woman's back above and beyond the radiance of her skin.

"Your tattoo…is it a phoenix or some other bird of prey, or maybe a winged ray?"

"Maybe."

"You're not sure?"

The woman stared at her hands. It was possible their enhanced glow was rattling her a little as well. "When we first settled on Synra, it was a prominent constellation in the night sky. The star at the tip of the beak was the Milky Way."

Oh. If Caleb were here, he'd whisper to her how another layer of the onion that was Nika Kirumase had just been peeled away. "A map home."

"Symbolically. The constellation no longer exists, of course."

"Yet you've kept the tattoo through what must have been hundreds of bodies." Alex took a step back and tilted her head to the side. "You know, with the glow of your skin surrounding it, the pattern almost reminds me of—"

Morgan grumbled as the hull began to vibrate against the buffeting atmosphere. "Have Asterions never invested in a few atmosphere corridors? Damn."

Nika strapped a tactical belt over her hips, then began slotting a variety of blades and other weapons into it. "We mainly travel to other worlds by quantum d-gate, not by ship."

"What a tragedy."

RW

NAMINO STELLAR SYSTEM

They exited the Caeles Prism wormhole within sight of Namino, its quantum block and its patrolling Rasu armada. Nika stood with them in the cockpit, silently taking in the sobering tableau.

Alex had seen the armada on her last visit to the planet, so this time she studied Nika out of the corner of her vision. Tiny muscles in the woman's face quivered and jumped, and her throat worked visibly as her eyes narrowed in grim determination. Nika was here to save millions of lives; Alex was only here to save two, though the millions would serve as a nice bonus.

The woman gave nothing else away in her steely countenance, so Alex returned her attention to the viewport. There appeared to be about as many Rasu present as there had been during the battle, though their formations were more spread out now. Mini-clusters above several locations suggested they had moved on to sieging the smaller cities, but the greatest concentration by far remained above the northeastern swath of the largest continent. It was home to Namino One and the planet's military and political seat of power, though there seemed to be little left of either at this point.

Morgan groaned. "How exactly are you planning to kick all these monsters out of here?"

Alex shrugged. "No idea—that's my mother's department. But I do believe we can get many more people off the planet, right out from under the Rasu's metal noses. We simply need to take out the quantum block, even if only for a few hours."

"Most of the d-gates will have been destroyed by now. Hopefully the Initiative can find a few that are still operational. Otherwise, this ship can hold, what, fifty people? For a short while?"

Alex smiled. "You won't need your d-gates to evacuate people. Once we get the quantum block down, I can have a dozen wormholes open on the surface inside of a minute. In ten minutes, hundreds. Now, they'll send people to wherever the Prevo operating the wormhole is, which means all over Concord space, but—"

"No, that's fine. More than fine." Nika's lips quirked around. "We get past this crisis, and you need to teach me how to open wormholes on command."

Alex took a moment to enjoy the fact that for once, she held a technological advantage over an Asterion. "As I think on it, there's no reason why you shouldn't be able to do it, so it's a deal. But time's wasting, so let's get ready."

She went into the main cabin, retrieved a box of small, handheld devices, kept three out and put the rest in her backpack. She returned to the cockpit and handed two of them to Nika and Morgan.

They peered at the devices, then at her, in question.

"They used to be called 'walkie-talkies,' or so I'm told. They allow for communication over radio waves—no quantum signals required. Like this." She held hers up to her mouth and activated the recessed button. "Can you hear me?"

Her voice reverberated through both devices and echoed out of her backpack in the cabin.

Morgan frowned at the device. "Weird. Where did you get them?"

"A present from Devon."

"Makes sense. How's he doing?"

"He seemed well. Overlord of his own tech fiefdom."

"He must be insufferably happy. What about Mia?"

Alex stared at her in surprise. "You haven't heard?"

"Clearly not."

"Malcolm was killed on Savrak three weeks ago."

Morgan's gaze flickered to the viewport and back to Alex. "Well, have they made a new version of him yet?"

"No. He had a 'no regenesis' clause in his will."

Her eyes widened. "Ah, fuck. I mean, I never liked the sanctimonious bastard, but...damn. Mia doesn't deserve that."

"No, she doesn't." Alex drummed her fingers on the top of the pilot's chair—*her* chair. "When we get home, perhaps you should reach out to Mia. You've, um...been through what she's going through now. You could help her talk through some of it."

Morgan's expression shuttered. "I don't do 'sharing of feelings'—not even with one of us."

'Us' unequivocally meant the original Noetica Prevos, for though they'd drifted apart over the years, they would always share an extraordinary bond, one that ventured far beyond mere friendship.

"I understand. It's just something to think about." She clasped Morgan's shoulder, and to her surprise the woman didn't shrink away. "Say your goodbyes to Stanley. We need to do this thing."

Valkyrie, take care of yourself while I'm gone. Look in on Mom, please—but don't look like you're looking in on her. Make sure Abigail tells you if any problems pop up in her checkups.

I will do all of that and more.

I know you will. And stay alert, because when we break the quantum block, I may need you to perform a lot of stunts in a short period of time.

I will eagerly await the excitement. Now go, and bring our family home.

54

SIYANE
NAMINO STELLAR SYSTEM

They proceeded deliberately toward the planet below. Kat scouts had pinpointed the outer edge of the quantum block at eight megameters distant from Namino's surface, so it didn't come as a shock when they crossed the threshold and everything *dulled*.

Alex and Valkyrie didn't actively share mindspace nearly as often as they once had, but the void which opened up in her mind when the connection was severed felt vast and empty nonetheless. Silence, where there should be *presence*.

Morgan grimaced. "I'm going to miss the annoying prick. Don't tell him I said so."

"He'll be back pestering you soon." She glanced behind her. "Nika? How are you doing?"

The woman held out her arms and stared at them, but the enhanced glow had not subsided. Her eyes closed, and she inhaled deeply. "I'm...good, I think. Almost everything continues to function normally. I can't send messages, but otherwise I think the kyoseil upgrades are doing their job."

"Glad to hear it." Alex found her attention drawn inexorably back to the viewport. The Rasu blockade now filled the landscape, dark and forbidding. "Morgan, thus far our stealth has held up against the Rasu, but give them as wide a berth as possible anyway. Our destination is planetary coordinates 36.3° N, 72.4° W, but don't head straight down there, as that's where the thickest concentration of Rasu are located. Swing out to the west and adopt a—"

"Oh my god, Solovy, are you seriously trying to tell me how to fly?"

"I...*fine*. Get us on the ground in one piece and unnoticed by any Rasu." She muttered several curses on her way into the cabin, where she checked the contents of her backpack for the fourth time. Walkie-talkies, energy bars, water, a few grenades, all the med kit supplies she could stuff in there. The Rectifier was latched to her hip, next to an archine blade Nika had given her. She flicked her wrist to test the conductivity lash, and was relieved when a rope of white electrical power surged out of her bracelet into the cabin.

"Nice weapon."

She chuckled, remembering the scene with her father during the coup attempt. "I hope to hell I don't get close enough to a Rasu to have to use it."

"True." Nika joined her at the data center table. "Are you certain you're up for this? I don't mean it as an insult, believe me, but you're not a combat specialist."

"I don't have Caleb's skills, no—or yours, I imagine—but I've had to fight my way out of more jams than you might expect. I'm ready. And I won't be a burden to you."

"I didn't think you would be. But just in case, so I'm clear, if you die...?"

"Valkyrie will be able to provide a comprehensive neural imprint of my mind and consciousness, current as of about ten minutes ago. I'll wake up in a new body a few days later."

"Good." Nika's gaze flickered. "Dashiel says the tests on the adiamene-kyoseil fusion material I told you about are coming up spectacular. We'll only have a few of the new ships ready for this battle, but the next one will be a different matter."

"I thought you couldn't send or receive messages?"

"Oh, that's right, I didn't get a chance to mention this detail, did I? I'm not currently the only one of me walking around."

"Care to elaborate?"

"You remember how you watched 8,000 copies of me take on the Rasu stronghold? Somewhat to my dismay, some of our more enterprising citizens have taken the concept and run with it. They're called 'Plexes'—multiple physical instances of a single mind, all connected through kyoseil." She held out a hand and twisted it around. "I made a copy of myself—actually this is the copy—so I could stay in contact with everyone on Mirai while I'm on Namino."

Valkyrie would *love* this, and Alex made a note to tell her about it on their return. "That's fairly amazing. And potentially very useful."

Nika's countenance took on an odd pall. "That's why I did it."

The woman seemed to have mixed feelings at best about splitting her consciousness, but now wasn't the time to delve into such an esoteric topic. Instead, Alex retrieved yet another of Devon's last-minute gifts. She handed Nika a tiny black dot, then took one for herself and pressed it onto the skin behind her ear. "Non-quantum trackers. If you flip the walkie-talkie over, there's a small screen on the back. It'll display the location of the other trackers on a basic, and I do mean *basic*, map."

The hull vibrated once more as they began their descent to the planet's surface, and Morgan remarked over her shoulder, "Atmosphere corridors, Nika. They'll change your life."

Alex gave Nika a shrug, and they both returned to the cockpit to get their first glimpse at the current state of Namino One.

Nika had said the city was home to almost nine million people…and Alex's first thought when she saw the skyline was that most of them were dead. It looked as if a giant had stomped its way across the city with all the grace of a toddler plodding through a sandbox. Numerous fires raged, though they were grossly outnumbered by smoldering ruins. Multiple large Rasu vessels and many hundreds of smaller ones patrolled above the region.

The flat, arid terrain at least provided them plenty of options for landing, and they opted for an open area 1.2 kilometers from what had once been a levtram track encircling the city proper. The bunker where Caleb, Marlee and the others were located was almost five kilometers from the landing site, but parking any closer risked putting the ship directly in the path of regular Rasu activity.

Oh, how she hated leaving the *Siyane* behind. She fastened her flak jacket up, then checked with Morgan one last time. "Keep the walkie-talkie within arm's reach at all times. If any Rasu get too close, move if you believe it's the safest course of action. And—"

"And stay sober?"

"I wasn't going to say that. I assumed I didn't *need* to say that. Morgan, when this is finished, if you decide it's what you want, you can return to conning drunk bar patrons out of their credits, vehicles and retail establishments. I hope you'll choose differently, but it's your call. But so long as we are here, you will do everything in your annoyingly talented power to keep this ship safe and, when the time comes, bring it to our rescue. Understand?"

"Yes, ma'am." Morgan flung her a mock salute and kicked her legs up on the dash.

Alex forced herself to walk away. She slipped her backpack on, opened the airlock and descended the ramp. Nika followed her down. Between the woman's overstuffed backpack, hip pack, tactical belt and flak jacket, she appeared to be single-handedly preparing to go kamikaze on every Rasu occupying Namino. Which she was—but not single-handedly. "Ready?"

"Ready."

Alex activated the kamero filter Nika had provided her with. Allegedly, so long as they gave any ground Rasu a reasonably wide berth, the stealth mechanism should allow them to stroll straight through downtown.

They set their attention upon the apocalyptic wasteland due ahead and set off.

55

NAMINO
NAMINO ONE

U nder cover of night, the city looked as if nuclear winter had descended upon it. A coat of ash had settled onto the streets, sidewalks and the awnings that still stood; yet more hung in the air like snow too buoyant to fall. Soot and scorch marks darkened the crumbling façades like the scars of a war already lost.

But it wasn't lost, Marlee told herself. It was just beginning.

They had to trek across six kilometers to get in range of the Rasu compound. The Asterions' kamero filters gave them some protection from discovery, and the long night shadows provided the rest. The Rasu had taken out the electrical grid in the first two days, and the only light came from the massive vessels patrolling overhead and a sky full of stars.

Once they were moving toward their target, Joaquim and Selene battled for position and the right to give orders, which ended up meaning they took turns clearing blocks and waving everyone forward. But they both seemed smart enough to not let their simmering rivalry endanger the mission.

Several times they had to give Rasu patrols a wide berth, but during their journey they never saw a living Asterion. This didn't mean there weren't living Asterions in the city, of course, merely that they had gone to ground as instructed.

Nevertheless, since the last time Marlee had ventured outside, it felt as if the Rasu had claimed the city and made it their own. Now they—she, Caleb, their Asterion companions—were the invaders.

A kilometer short of their destination, the Rasu activity began to grow thick, and their progress slowed to a crawl. The compound was now the hub of Rasu operations in Namino One, no question.

After roving Rasu hauling their bounty into the compound drove the group into the cover of alleys three times in a single block, Selene motioned for them to gather around her, where they could all hear her furtive whispers. "We can't risk getting any closer. From this point on, Rasu are stationed every four meters all the way to the compound."

Rogers shook his head. "We don't have a clear shot from here."

Joaquim peered out of the alley for a minute, then rejoined their huddle. "Another block to the east, most of the buildings have been leveled. We should have line-of-sight from there."

Selene's gaze flickered between Joaquim and the street for several seconds. Finally she nodded. "All right. One block to the east."

They slow-hurried across the open, exposed intersection then pressed against one of the few remaining façades on the next block. As they tip-toed east, that structure soon crumbled away into ruins. But its absence revealed the menacing silhouette of the Rasu compound. A high wall obscured much of the interior, but a thick, tapered spire rose far above it to an apex lit by a brilliant violet glow.

Rogers set the launcher on the ground and opened a panel on its side. A smaller cylinder extended out from one end and locked into place. He hefted the device up onto his shoulder, pointed it and himself in the direction of the tower, and steadied it with one hand while typing a series of commands on the control panel with the other. "It's locked onto the upper quarter of the tower. Maybe we can take out the whole operation with one shot."

Joaquim placed a hand on the device, studying the control panel closely before locking his gaze on the spire. "Don't miss."

"I am a Colonel in the Dominion Armed Forces. I know how to fire a rocket launcher."

"I'm sure you do." Joaquim backed away, hands raised. "So don't miss."

"Asshole." Rogers returned his other hand to the cylinder, exhaled and activated the trigger. The payload shot out of the cylinder and streaked across the sky toward the tower, leaving a trail of cool blue fire in its wake. It crossed above the outer wall—

—four violet-hued lasers shot out of turrets ringing the wall and slammed into the rocket, disintegrating it in an instant.

"Motherfucker!" Joaquim spun and punched the closest wall high enough for his fist to impact.

"Quiet!" Selene buried her face in her hands for a single second. Then she snapped to alert and motioned everyone toward the next intersection. "They'll be searching for the source of the attack. We have to move now!"

Marlee glared at the glowing spire in resentment and growing rage—Caleb grabbed her by the hand and began dragging her away. After a few seconds she relented, turning and breaking into a jog to catch up with the others. "What are we going to do?"

"We will talk about it at the bunker," Selene hissed. "Focus on getting there."

The rumbling of nearing Rasu machinery rattled the broken street beneath their feet. Selene checked behind them, and her eyes widened precipitously. "Forget subtlety—run."

Rogers tossed the empty rocket launcher through a shattered window, and they all did as ordered. Even at a run, the Rasu shouldn't be able to see them from more than a few meters away, but they needed to escape the tightening noose of a Rasu dragnet sweep.

Dust and ash began to clog her lungs, and by the time they pulled up three kilometers from the compound, Marlee's chest was on fire.

Selene sagged against a blown-out doorway. "Okay, I think we're beyond the perimeter of their initial sweep. Now let's take special care the rest of the way. We don't want to lead any Rasu straight to the bunker." She pushed off the doorframe as swiftly as she'd landed on it. "Let's go."

They'd navigated another five blocks when Joaquim stopped everyone just short of the next intersection. He hugged a standing girder and peeked around the corner—then frantically motioned everyone backward as he joined them at a rapid jog.

A series of heavy thuds they'd come to associate with the largest bipedal Rasu boomed from around the corner, and Marlee's pulse raced in time with her quickening stride.

Caleb leaned over, his voice shockingly calm and controlled at her ear. "Get some grenades ready."

Right! She felt around for the latches on the lower part of her vest, then fumbled past freeing two frag grenades while trying to keep up with the others.

Ahead of her, Selene waved Rogers and Joaquim inside a mostly intact storefront. Marlee glanced behind her in time to see a giant Rasu barrel around the corner, plant a leaden 'foot' to change direction and accelerate toward them as two more of the aliens followed in its wake. She reared back and hurled the frag grenades into the chest of the lead Rasu. Beside her, Caleb did the same—then he grasped her arm with both hands and flung her through the open storefront.

RW

Two bipedal Rasu burst out of the broken windows of what looked to have once been an office building and accelerated in Alex and Nika's direction.

They can't see you, they can't see you.... Alex groaned under her breath. "Oh, *gavno*, I need to test this thing out anyway." She raised the Rectifier in front of her, steadied it and fired at the left-most Rasu's center of mass.

It was as if a hole opened up in the fabric of the universe. The air around her target warped and turned...gauzy, as if someone had spread petroleum jelly over it. The leftmost Rasu disintegrated into a fine mist, then evaporated into nothingness. The one on the right did as well, and also a meter-deep section of the road beneath them.

Air rushed into the vacuum the negative energy had left behind, and the tear in space-time healed itself. The two Rasu were gone as surely as if they'd never existed.

"Wow." Alex stared down at the weapon in her hand. "So it works."

Nika laughed a little wildly. "Can I place an order for ten thousand of those?"

"Right now there's just the one, but once we report on our successful field test I bet we can convince Special Projects to ramp up production."

"Yes, let's do that." Nika studied the remains of the buildings on both street corners. "Okay, the entrance to the bunker is six blocks to the west, then three blocks north—"

In the distance, high above what few buildings remained standing, four powerful violet lasers in a circular formation streaked toward a common target. When they met, an immense explosion burst across the sky.

"What the hells?"

They sprinted toward the next intersection for a better view, but by the time they reached it the lasers had left behind only a dispersing cloud of smoke.

Alex rested her hands on her thighs. "Someone's fighting back."

A smile grew on Nika's lips. "Yes, they are. Wait...Parc says a group from the bunker headed to test out the defenses on some Rasu compound. Joaquim, Ava, Selene and...."

"Caleb." Alex focused on the long, wide avenue leading toward where the explosion had occurred. An invisible thread pulled her insistently forward, a heartbeat pulsing louder and more ferociously in her ears with each step she took in that direction. "Why didn't they wait for us to arrive before going on a field trip?"

"Because I asked Parc not to tell them we were coming."

She whipped around in surprise. "What? Why?"

Nika shrugged weakly. "In case we never made it to the bunker. I didn't want anyone risking their lives trying to rescue us. Not when the point is to rescue *them*. I'm sorry, but it felt like the right call."

Alex had raced headlong from the decision to come to Namino to standing here now; along the way she'd made snap judgments when required and let the rest fall away. It had never occurred to her to make sure Caleb knew she was coming, because obviously she was coming. *Ipso facto*. A was A.

So she let any recriminations slide in favor of focusing on what the explosion meant. "Well, whatever they were trying to do, it didn't work. The attack was repelled."

"And now the Rasu will be coming for the attackers. Our people will be running, likely in the direction of the bunker, but they've got a lot of ground to cover." Her hand touched Alex's elbow. "Can you find him while they're on the move?"

"It'll be a bit akin to a game of Marco Polo, but I think I can."

"A game of what?"

"Hot and cold? I go in the direction that gets warmer?"

"Ah. That should work. Of course, a lot of Rasu are going to be swarming the same section of the city, so...."

So resist the urge to blindly take off running toward the heat and the heartbeat. She nodded in understanding.

They did move faster now, though, ducking inside blown-out buildings to evade passing Rasu patrols but otherwise weaving through an endless parade of streets and alleys. Alex's chest burned hot, the thread now yanking her onward so forcefully she had to consciously fight against it.

They approached an intersection thick with smoke and the acrid odor of burning electronics, and she leaned in to direct a whisper toward Nika. "Left here. We're close."

They were crossing the street when three Rasu came into view one block beyond. Far larger than the typical bipedal models, they towered over everything like giant, angry mechs.

Nika thrust out an arm to shove Alex against a wall and back around the corner, but Alex resisted. "That's where they are. I think those Rasu have got them pinned down in one of the stores on the left side of the street."

"Shit." They peered around the corner just in time to see several grenades impact the Rasu and explode. The strikes knocked two of the three to the ground momentarily, but they soon rose to their feet, showing little visible damage, and pivoted toward a torn awning above a row of broken windows.

A heartbeat not her own pounded in her ears. "Inside that storefront."

One of the Rasu began shoving aside debris the grenades had created to clamber through the windows, and Nika unlatched two of the special archine grenades she'd brought along. "Shields to max. Let's go."

They took off running down the street, kamero filters active but otherwise concerns of stealth forgotten. Thirty meters from their targets, Alex again raised the Rectifier. But two of the Rasu were now too close to the building for her to risk dissolving it and the people inside. She fired on the one that remained farther out in the street.

The weapon itself was nearly silent, but the other two Rasu must have sensed the supradimensional void tearing at the air behind them and jerked around to witness their comrade being vaporized.

Nika shouted, "Everyone take cover!" Then she palmed an archine grenade in each hand and launched them toward the enemies.

Razor-sharp slices of Rasu flew in every direction. One slice bounced off Alex's shield at the shoulder, while another sailed centimeters above her head. The slices shattered what few windows remained on the block and fell to litter the street.

Nika yelled something in her direction, but Alex was already running for the building, deactivating her kamero filter and holstering the Rectifier as she did. She stumbled through the storefront—and fell into the arms she sought. The disparate heartbeats merged into one.

"Alex?"

All the air left her lungs as Caleb squeezed her impossibly tight. Alive, walking, talking and so much more. "Hi, *priyazn*."

"Hi, baby." His hot breath caressed her neck. "How is it possible that you're here?"

Nika nudged her on the way into the store. "No time for hugging right now. We need to move. Those Rasu outside are busily putting themselves back together."

Marlee crashed into her side and added her arms to the hug. "Aunt Alex? I didn't know you were a badass, too!"

She laughed and caught sight of Nika hugging a copper-haired man, despite her earlier admonition. "Nika's right. We need to get moving."

Caleb drew back a fraction to study her, his face marked by disbelief and concern...and a *hardness* she hadn't seen on his features in a long time. "But how did you—?"

"I'll explain once we reach the bunker. Lead the way?"

56

NAMINO
CAMP BURROW

A fair degree of bedlam erupted on their return to the bunker. Nika, it seemed, had many old friends to greet enthusiastically. Parc demanded answers on how the test had gone wrong, and ultimately he and Grant cornered Marlee to get them.

Caleb watched Alex take it all in, her expression reserved, her eyes not so luminescent in the absence of Valkyrie but sharp and clear all the same as she absorbed the setting, the people and the activity and likely made some judgments about it all. About him?

"You can put your backpack over here, with our—with Marlee's and my—things."

She nodded vaguely and followed him to where their pop-up cots were collapsed beside a collection of personal items, then let her backpack slip from her fingers. Next she shrugged off her flak jacket and let it fall to the floor as well. He watched her shoulders rise; abruptly she spun around to glare at him. She'd never been any good at keeping her sentiments off her countenance, and whatever joy she'd initially experienced on finding him had been replaced by darker, more troubling emotions.

"We need to talk. In private."

"We do. This way." He led her down the hallway to the supply room, which he knew from experience provided a measure of solitude—at least until your bossy niece barged in and refused to leave. He was indescribably happy to see Alex, and terrified for her safety in this bleak, deadly place, and there was no way this conversation was going to go well for him.

He flicked the light on and closed the door behind them. "How's your mom doing?"

"She's a fucking train wreck, thanks for asking."

"Then you should have stayed. It must be an incredibly confusing time for her, and she needs you."

"And you don't?"

His skin felt flush—the beginnings of another post-violence breakdown. *Not now.* "That's not what I meant. But your family needed you, and mine needed me."

"They're supposed to be one and the same, dammit." Suddenly she was in his face, a finger jabbed into his chest. "You left me a goddamn *note.* Do you remember what happened the last time you left me a note waxing philosophical about life and love and duty? You died. So don't you *ever* do that again."

He only had to meet her gaze to see how much she had suffered because of his actions. Her lower lip quivered—but from hurt, or rage? "If I had told you what I was planning to do, you would have tried to stop me."

"Or possibly I would have helped you." Her shoulders sagged in a full-body sigh, and she dropped the finger at his chest to rub at her neck.

Despair mingled with Akeso's flailing angst to choke the air out of his lungs. What else could he have done? "I know, but I couldn't ask you to make the choice between your mother and me. It wouldn't be fair."

"Fair? *Fair?* Since when is the world fair? Instead you made the choice for me, and that is *not* okay. Don't you get it? It's supposed to be you and me against the universe. Come what may."

The brutal truth of her words hit him like a punch to the gut. Where had he lost his way? How had he forgotten? How many times did he need to learn this lesson?

His chest swelled with emotions he'd feared he'd never again experience, feared had been extinguished forever beneath an avalanche of violence and cold wrath. "Saving each other over and over again in an endless cycle."

"*Yes.*"

Two steps and he was pulling her into his arms. One hand came up to cup her cheek. His voice scratched past his constricting throat, emerging in a gravelly whisper. "I am so lost without you."

Concern quickly replaced anger on her features, and her expression softened; he must sound even worse than he'd thought. "I know the feeling. I've been..." her eyes glistened and shimmered "...it doesn't matter. I'm here now, so neither of us has to be lost any longer."

He wanted so desperately to believe her. He needed to cling to the hope that she could be his guide back from this madness.

Her nose crinkled up as she wiped something off his cheek. "You're covered in blood."

He forced a stilted chuckle. "Just like old times?"

"Not quite. But maybe it can be."

"I'd like that very much." His fingertips cradled her chin as his mouth finally met hers—

—she jerked away to stare at him strangely.

"What's wrong? I realize you're angry at me—"

"I can feel you."

"I don't understand."

"I can feel you *feeling* me. Through Akeso. See, I asked it for help in finding you. I sliced up my palm and opened myself up to its consciousness, and for the first time in fourteen years, Akeso spoke to me. Not in words, but it's stayed with me all the way here. Out on the streets, when you were pinned down by those Rasu, that's how we found you. Akeso showed me the way to where you were. And now, touching you, I can...." She closed the distance she'd briefly created and crushed her lips against his.

Need and desperation surged through her and into him, drawing his own need into a feedback loop.

"God, this is astonishing. Can you feel it?"

He pulled back without meaning to. "I've had to block Akeso as much as possible. It's not happy with my current behavior."

"Oh, believe me, I know. You should see what it's done to our home since you've been gone. But while you may not be listening to Akeso, Akeso is listening to you. I never could have found you otherwise. Caleb, Akeso wanted me to find you. It wants you to be well and safe. Please." Her lips brushed across his, tender and inviting, and her fingers slid past his damp skin to wind through his hair. "Feel me feeling you."

Every fear he'd ever harbored lay on the other side of the wall he'd constructed to keep the worst of Akeso's anguish at bay. Now, though, so did every desire, every longing. Dammit, fear would not keep him from this.

Please, give me this one thing, for this one moment. I beg you.

He clasped her face in both hands and fell through her wondrous eyes straight into her soul. Then he let go of the constant coil of tension maintaining the psychological barrier—

—a rampaging deluge of despair and confusion and torment knocked the breath out of him, and his knees weakened under their weight. But then the deluge vanished beneath a new avalanche of emotions: love, passion, fire, joy. *Alex.* He felt the rough pads of his thumbs on her cheeks and the soft curls of his hair caressing her palms.

His lips found hers anew in a hurricane of dizzying sensations. They roved over her jaw, down her neck, lingered at the hollow of her throat—it truly was as sensitive as he'd always suspected—and his own mind reeled as a double jolt of carnal need swept away every last coherent thought of his reasoning mind.

She grumbled into his lips. "Someone could come in."

"They could. But they won't."

He felt her nod into the crook of his neck, and her hands dropped to the hem of his shirt and lifted it up and off. Then both hands were on his chest, and he felt his skin burning beneath her palms. One fever exchanged for another, infinitely more pleasurable one.

Her hands trembled with urgency, and her craving reinforced his own. He fumbled with bunching the material of her tank top up and over her breasts before yanking it above her head. Skin met skin, and they both nearly passed out from the sensory overload.

She moaned haltingly as her hands found his belt, and he felt her growing pleasure as he kicked his boots to the side and hurriedly stripped his pants off. Then he was on his knees, his tongue dancing around her navel as his hands dipped inside the snug material of her pants and frantically tugged them down.

He had to know. His tongue darted out—

—every nerve in his body screamed in a burst of agonizing pleasure, and he fell back, landing on his ass on the floor. Delicious delirium engulfed him, and he touched a fingertip to his tongue. "Oh my god...."

Alex, naked and magnificent in the harsh, antiseptic light of the supply room, started giggling into her hand. "Shhh, quiet."

"Right, right." He climbed to his feet, then instantly shoved her hard against the wall, relishing in how his muscled body pressing on hers caused her desire to spike to new heights. Or was it his desire? There no longer remained a difference.

His hand gripped her thigh as her teeth scraped past his ear. "I may not survive this."

He laughed, his heart buoyed by a joy he'd believed beyond his reach. "If this is how we die, it'll be a good death."

She wrapped a leg around his hip, and he slipped inside her. The world exploded.

They held each other up, he thought, or perhaps they were on the floor. Or the table stacked high with crates that stood beside them. Where didn't matter. He was in her and she was in him and they were one and it was *everything*.

Five megaparsecs and many galaxies away, confident no one was apt to notice, a planet shuddered.

RW

They rested against the wall near the far corner, curled up in each other's arms on the floor. Breathing, touching, *experiencing*.

He'd never felt closer to her than he did right now—a truth in the most literal sense.

And it frightened him. Past the passion and the afterglow lay the tattered wreckage of his psyche. He didn't want her to see how weak he was, how broken and battered, struggling for the smallest gasps of air. But if she was the cure, if she was his guide back to the light, didn't he have to let her see everything? The blood, the pain, the darkness?

She murmured contented sounds into his neck. If she saw any hints of it, she wasn't flinching away. "How long will this last?"

He kissed the top of her head. "I'm not sure. How long has it been since you communed with Akeso?"

"About fourteen hours."

"Then it should last another day or two, I'd say."

"Or longer?" She lifted her head to meet his gaze; her face was still flush from a new manner of ecstasy. "Do you think Akeso will let me keep the connection?"

Come home. Heal. All must replenish you, must repair what has fractured.

He winced reflexively at the reappearance of the voice in his head. He was relieved beyond measure that Akeso had not forsaken him permanently. But while this rapturous interlude might have just saved his life, his trial wasn't complete, and it wasn't time to turn to healing. Not yet. "I don't know. I'm afraid I no longer speak for Akeso."

Her brow furrowed, and she reached out to touch the medwrap covering his upper arm. "Can I?"

He nodded silently, and she peeled it away…to reveal a patch of pink, healing skin. He chuckled quietly. *Point taken and lesson learned. I'll come home soon, I promise. But I'm not done here.*

"What are you thinking? I can *feel* you thinking, but the thoughts themselves…it's as if they're churning barely beyond my grasp."

He rested his forehead on hers, relishing in the soothing touch of her warmth, of her breath blending with his. "I have to put the wall back up now, as much as I'm able. I can't do what I need to do here with Akeso fighting me at every step. It'll get all of us killed."

"When you do that, you won't be able to feel me any longer, either, will you?"

He glanced away. But so long as the connection between them remained this strong, he couldn't escape the sorrow engulfing them both. "No, I won't. And it will be the greatest tragedy of my life."

She tried for a weak smile and failed. "Well, we made it work for fifteen years. We can do it again. I don't need supradimensional sentient microbes to feel you in my heart." A single tear hovered on her eyelashes before breaking free to trail down her cheek. "Besides, while the physical feedback loop is *yobanyi* fantastic, I can't handle the emotional one. We're both useless like this."

"Liar. Thank you." He lifted her chin and pressed his lips softly to hers, drowning himself in their mutual sensations for one last, perfect moment.

Then he closed his eyes and gathered up the scattered pieces of the makeshift wall he'd constructed then ripped apart and carefully refit them together. In the last few minutes Akeso's turmoil and angst had begun to grow loud once more, but as the last sections of the wall locked into place, they faded into the background in time with the fading of his connection to Alex. The walls shrank in around him, closing him off from everything he held most dear. But it was necessary. There was no other way.

He found he was shivering despite the warmth of her body still snuggled against his. "We should get dressed and get back out there before they send a rescue party for us."

"We should." She studied him warily as she disentangled herself from his arms and stood, and he watched her battle to bury the heartbreaking sadness behind her eyes. "Are you okay? Will you tell me if you're not?"

He was reaching for his shirt where it had landed on the floor; the material bunched up as his hand fisted around it. "No, I am not in the slightest bit okay. But I'm better now that you're here…or at least I can now imagine a future where I will be better. Because of you." He pulled on his shirt and took a deep, ponderous breath. "I ask this with the deepest of appreciation and love. Why *are* you here?"

"Caleb, I was always coming for you. But if you want a logical justification? If you all have located the origin of the quantum block, we have a plan to destroy it."

PART IV

THE WAY FORWARD

ASTERION DOMINION

57

NAMINO
CAMP BURROW

Nika wore a smile as she wandered among the throng of people gathered in the bunker, but it was tinged by sorrow. Her heart wanted to burst with joy at the realization that so many of her friends had survived the siege. But Selene said only a few of the other bunkers were occupied, which meant the total number of survivors in Namino One might be less than a thousand. The prospect of such a gargantuan loss was staggering, and merely thinking about it threatened to force her to her knees in despair. Then there were the innumerable people who had been taken captive and were being subjected to the Rasu's horrific experiments.

If the Rasu hadn't cracked the kyoseil puzzle in eight years, they weren't going to suddenly crack it now. Their torture of innocent souls was utterly pointless and all the more tragic for it.

But why *hadn't* they ever cracked the kyoseil puzzle? She switched off the visual filter Parc (on Mirai) had configured for her and let the prismatic kyoseil waves wash over and through her. The bunker burned bright from a tangled web of interwoven strings connecting every Asterion present.

It didn't make any sense for kyoseil to be immune to the quantum block, given the life form's supradimensional existence—it should by definition be quantum in nature. Yet her vision didn't lie. The key to unlocking the answer felt as if it was on the tip of her tongue, dancing just outside the reach of her arm. She stretched out her arm anyway, and the strings undulated happily through her skin. Unknowable and, thus far, uncontrollable.

As soon as Joaquim, Grant, Selene, Parc and a few others had joined her at what she'd been told constituted their official meeting circle, she issued a declaration. "We need to destroy the quantum block."

Joaquim protested. "Damn, Nika, you didn't need to travel all the way here just to declare the bloody obvious. Ask Selene, who I've driven quite insane with my insistence since day one that we need to destroy the block." Beside him, Selene cast a rueful glance at the ceiling by way of response. "I don't know if you saw the laser light show on your way in, but unfortunately the block mechanism is defended."

Nika dropped her elbows to her knees and brought her hands to her chin. "Then we'll find a way around those defenses."

"You know I have always appreciated your tenacity. But our potential weapons consist in their entirety of two rocket launchers, a handful of assault rifles and amped Glasers and a big pile of archine blades. I heard you brought some modified grenades that will fuck up a bipedal Rasu nicely, and we've devised improvised explosives to do the same, but against that compound they'll be like tossing pebbles into the side of a mountain."

Alex and Caleb joined them then, having finally emerged from their private reunion. From the complicated expressions they wore, she honestly couldn't guess what manner of reunion it had been.

They sat beside Marlee, and Alex caught Nika's gaze. "Those aren't your only weapons. We brought a stealthed, combat-ready adiamene-protected ship loaded with negative energy missiles."

"Are the negative energy missiles cloaked, too?"

"Of course not."

Joaquim spread his arms wide and shrugged. "Then they'll get shot down long before they reach the target, same as our rocket did today. I assume shooting negative energy missiles out of the sky will make for some fascinating explosions and will probably do a little peripheral damage, but I doubt they'll get close enough to take out the spire."

"This is why we brought one more weapon—me." Nika extended her arms in front of her and flipped them over. "This new aura of mine isn't solely for show. My body is soaked in kyoseil for a very specific purpose—to protect the virutox loaded into my OS. One of Dashiel's teams at Conceptual Research derived it from the Rasu's own programming language. When injected into a Rasu system, it'll do the same thing a virutox does to us—corrupt running programs, degrade the operating code and, hopefully, severely cripple the overall functionality of the targeted system. Quantum block or no, if I can get my hands on a Rasu system—literally—the additional kyoseil woven through my body means I can deliver the virutox and bring the system down."

She stood to pace deliberately around their circle. "I came here not knowing exactly how I might use this to our advantage, but now it's obvious. The lasers that took out your rocket fired off in response to some type of proximity alarm. This means automated defenses. Automated defenses I can cripple. Once those defenses are eliminated, the *Siyane* can fire its negative energy missiles at the spire, destroying the blocking mechanism and the power vortex fueling it. Then the quantum block is gone, and everything about this war changes."

Joaquim arched an eyebrow. "Great plan. I like it. But there's one problem. How the hells are you going to sneak past the compound's defenses and deliver the virutox in the first place?"

She winked at him. "I was thinking you'd get me in there."

RW

While Nika hashed out the details of their plan with her friend Joaquim, Alex took a minute to just...stop. Caleb had disappeared back down the hallway, saying he needed a quick shower. In truth, he probably more needed a minute or two of solitude to clear his head and internalize everything that had happened between them, so he could don the warrior's mask once more.

Everything that had happened between them.... She felt as if she'd lose her mind if she contemplated it too hard, and this wasn't the time or situation to be misplacing her wits. Though she could still sense his movements, not to mention the literal beating of his heart, without reciprocation it only deepened a bittersweet pang in her soul.

She sat on of the couches lining the side wall. Right now, at this moment, she ought to appreciate the win. She'd made it here. She'd reached them both, and everyone was in one piece. They had the makings of a plan to properly disrupt this godforsaken invasion. She hoped her mother was ready to swoop in with a few hundred thousand ships if—no, when—the quantum block came down. Ready with some proper protection insulating her command ship from the Rasu this time.

Marlee sat beside her and handed her a juice drink. "Here. It's actually good."

"Thanks." Alex sipped on it; it tasted a bit like pineapple guava juice. "It seems as if you've made a lot of friends here."

"They've been great to me. And Caleb..." her niece fell back against the cushion and threw an arm over her eyes "...I'm so sorry he had to risk his life to come for me. I feel terrible about it. Now you've gone and done the same thing for both of us. It means the world to me." She peered down the hallway with one eye. "Did he used to be like this, before Akeso?"

She didn't need to ask what Marlee meant by 'like this.' She started to obfuscate, but Marlee had spent more than a week in close quarters with Caleb, and there was no way her niece hadn't realized something was wrong. "No. I mean, in the heat of battle he was always...intense, focused and a whirling demon of death and destruction. But the rest of the time? No. He'd made peace with the necessity for violence and kept it separate from the person he was."

"But now it's eating him alive, isn't it? It's because Akeso abhors brutality and death, and they're so intimately connected."

"Their connection has always been complicated, and so far as we know, unique in this world. They've never been through a trial such as this one together. I'm sure it's not easy for either of them, but...." She didn't have a 'but.' She didn't have any idea what the other side of the gauntlet was going to look like for any of them.

Marlee abruptly leaned forward and dropped her face into her hands. "This is my fault. He came here to rescue me, and to do it he had to become someone he doesn't want to be. Then I made him stay and keep fighting, and now he feels as though all these people are turning to him for their salvation. He doesn't see a way out, because I didn't give him one. And it's destroying him."

Startlingly insightful of her. Marlee was growing up fast, and events were forcing wisdom beyond her years upon her. Alex placed a hand on her shoulder. "I won't lie—you were dumb not to leave when Mia ordered you to. But you were trying to save people, same as he is. I guess this particular brand of dumb runs in the Marano genes. But understand this, okay? We would all have come to rescue you, because it's what we do for family. But Caleb was, I'm a little ashamed to say, the only person who believed with all his heart that he could reach you. And he was right."

Marlee leaned around Alex to stare down the hallway once again. "How do we help him?"

Oh, how I wish I knew. "We get out of here alive. All of us."

58

MIRAI
OMOIKANE INITIATIVE

"*I was thinking you'd get me in there.*"

Nika gave Dashiel a distracted smile. It had taken a little time and practice, but she'd adapted to this new, dual existence, for the most part. The words, movements, even thoughts of her twin faded into the background much of the time, like the din of a crowded restaurant. But right now, the show was on Namino, and she forced herself to pay close attention as details were hashed out and logistics debated until they had a plan, one with a non-zero chance of actually succeeding.

Then everyone in the bunker was moving. Gathering weapons and belongings, dividing up into teams and preparing to depart their underground haven for the last time.

She looked up at Dashiel, bright-eyed and focused once again. "They'll be moving soon. We need to get the Advisors together and come up with our own plan for what to do when the block goes down."

He frowned. "Lance is on Kiyora with Gemina, and Spencer and Adlai are dealing with a kerfuffle at one of the refugee centers on Synra."

"No time to wait for them to return. We'll use the Advisor ceraff."

All the Advisors knew what she had done and where one copy of her had gone. Degrees of approval varied, as did skepticism that she could accomplish her goal, but at least no one had suggested arresting her. On the other side of this crisis, they were going to need to figure out what place Plexes would have, or not have, in

408 | G.S. JENNSEN

Asterion society. But first they had to save what they could of Namino.

Connecting to the ceraff in her current state was quite...odd. Her mind was now split three ways, yet in some respects not split at all. Voices swam through the edges of her perception like ghosts in the mist, and she had to concentrate to discern the ones speaking within the ceraff.

Nika: "I realize everyone is busy, so thank you for jumping on here for a few minutes. We need to prepare for the quantum block surrounding Namino to go down in a couple of hours. When it does, we have to be ready to move instantly on every front."

Lance: "How is it going to go down?"

Nika: "We—Alex Solovy and I, together with Selene's people on Namino—have formulated a plan to take it out. It should work. The details aren't important, though. We'll simply proceed under the assumption that the block will go down and get ready for it to do so."

Adlai: "We can prep to turn the d-gates back on, but...."

Nika: "I know—Firewall still applies. And much as it pains me to admit, it should, because there are thousands of Rasu crawling the streets. We need to hold off on opening the floodgates for now. We'll be evacuating the people at Bunker #3 via Alex's ship. For those we've confirmed are located at other bunkers, Alex will work with several Concord Prevos to open emergency wormholes at those locations. After that? We'll have to see how events progress."

Katherine: "Nevertheless, we'll prepare for an additional influx of refugees, wounded and otherwise."

Nika: "Most of them will be coming home by way of Concord."

Katherine: "Understood. I'll designate a central location for them to return to, so we don't end up with battered, hungry, frightened people wandering the streets."

Damn, this was almost considerate of the woman. Perrin must be wearing off on her. *Nika: "Thank you."*

Dashiel: "I think we ought to consider what our primary objective here will be. Is it to evacuate as many people as we can from Namino in the few short hours before the Rasu get a new quantum block up and running? Or is it to try to defeat the invading armada and free the planet?"

Nika: "Yes."

Beside her, his deadpan glare bore into the side of her head. Dashiel: "That's not a helpful answer. And we don't yet have the ships to do the latter."

A corner of her lips curled up in response. Nika: "I know, which is why I need to speak to Mesme, then Lance and I need to go see Commandant Solovy."

CONCORD

59

CONCORD DESIGN & TESTING SHIPYARD
MILKY WAY SECTOR 6

If there existed any seams in the sleek adiamene hull of the *CAF Aurora*, as Kennedy insisted there did, Miriam could not spot them. Two massive weapons bays sporting eighteen launch tubes and ten laser assemblies extended down from the main body of the ship to wrap the golden glow of the Zero Drive/Caeles Prism in a protective half-cocoon. The crew decks curved up and forward for a full eight hundred meters, leading to the semi-circular bridge at the apex. Most of the viewports had always been virtual, but now not a single pane of glass composite marred the lines of the hull.

The profile reminded her of a lion poised to pounce, and Miriam idly wondered if Thomas had contributed a few sketches to the design.

"She is incredible."

Beside her, Kennedy nodded. "I think so. I admit it was kind of fun to get to start from scratch on a flagship. The basic interior design will be very familiar to you, but even given the tight time frame, I was able to incorporate a lot of improvements we've developed in the last few years. For the most part, they should be invisible to you until you need them."

"And the Imperium shield?"

"Installed and rigorously tested. The power requirements for it are tremendous, but with a brand-new boosted Zero Drive, they won't trouble you." Kennedy gestured toward the airlock. "Are you ready to shake her down?"

"I do believe I am."

RW

CAF AURORA

Miriam strode onto an empty bridge, and though it was not quite the *same* empty bridge, a wave of déjà vu washed over her.

The bridge spun dizzyingly around Miriam, and she lunged for the railing extending out from the overlook to steady herself. Then she tried—tried so—to stand up straight and proud.

She sensed her daughter's shadow retreat out of view and watched as this...man...slowly lowered his chin in...respect?

"But it's not up to Alex to convince you I'm real. It's up to me, and I accept the challenge. I will do whatever I must, for as long as I must, to earn your trust. I've done it before. I can do it again."

He took a step toward her, and she fought the urge to flee. He sounded so like David, from the rolling 'r's of the accent he hadn't bothered to lose to the easy confidence lending affect to his voice.

She did not understand. She could not find a path that might lead to understanding. She'd never wanted to believe in something so tremendously in her life, but belief, no matter how strong it became, did not make something real. He was gone, so long gone, and nothing could ever bring him back.

Could it?

Fourteen years had passed, but the memory still shook her to her core. The day she had never expected, when everything had changed.

But it was a good memory, so she smiled and shook off the spell. "Thomas?"

'Welcome back, Commandant.'

"And to you. How does she feel?"

'Like a hand-knitted sweater, all warm and cozy.'

Miriam made a face. "Try again."

'Like a honed and buffed weapon, primed to destroy all enemies and, this time, return to tell the tale herself from the head of a galactic ticker-tape parade.'

"That's better. I trust you'll inform me if you encounter any issues we need to address."

'Ms. Rossi has involved me in the design and testing since the ship's inception, thus I do not anticipate any problems cropping up.'

"Still, it's a new ship. There are bound to be a few kinks to work out."

'Of course. Do you want to take her for a spin and see if we can find any?'

"We don't have any crew on board."

'We have you and me—and, should you deign to invite him aboard, Professor Solovy, who is currently in the observation lounge salivating all over the viewport at the sight of our prize command ship.'

She chuckled quietly.

You can come aboard if you'd like.

What? No, I was just...checking to make sure everything was going smoothly with the handover.

David.

Oh, fine. I'll be right there.

Less than a minute later, he peeked his head in from the airlock, his gaze immediately falling on her to the exclusion of all the details of the shiny new bridge. "Magnificent."

Her heart fluttered in her chest, and she shot him a smirk while she headed to the overlook. "Kennedy is right. It does seem to feel similar to the old *Stalwart II* in the ways that matter, though it is surely better in every material respect." She glanced his way as he strolled toward her. "Where should we go?"

He shrugged broadly. "Home?"

RW

A precious blue marble, Earth had been called. Unique in its perfection for nurturing humanity.

Even before coming to Amaranthe, hundreds of garden worlds capable of supporting human life had been discovered; here, they had learned of tens of thousands more such worlds. But none would ever match Earth. That precious, little blue marble. Home.

A hurricane swirled across the Atlantic, its outer bands tickling the Carolinas shore, as they exited the Caeles Prism wormhole and fell into High Earth Orbit above the Northeastern Seaboard Metropolis.

Comms lit up the instant they arrived.

Earth Terrestrial Defense Command: "Unidentified vessel, transmit your designation promptly or defensive measures will be activated."

CAF Aurora: "This is Concord Commandant Miriam Solovy of the CAF Aurora, authorization CZX-89Z33 Alpha Zulu Mark 1.0. There's no need for alarm. I'm merely taking the new ship out for a brief shakedown cruise."

Silence answered as the shift supervisor frantically contacted Command and triple-checked the authorizations.

Earth Terrestrial Defense Command: "Acknowledged, Commandant. Will you be needing docking privileges at any AEGIS facilities?"

CAF Aurora: "Not today. Thank you."

David wrapped his arms around her waist from behind. "It's odd sometimes, you know. Everything looks the same, but this space? It's not Earth's home. Earth's home is gone, and so is its ancestral planet that grew from hot nebular gases to come to life here in *this* space."

"True, but I refuse to believe that Earth isn't a better steward of this corner of the universe than Solum ever was. It's earned the right to be here, at the center of a multi-galactic civilization."

"It has." He nuzzled her neck. "Have you checked out your new stateroom yet?"

"David!"

"Okay, we'll save there for later. What about your new office?"

She rolled her eyes, shifted in his embrace and kissed him softly. "Thomas, take us on a gentle trip around Sector 1 and run the systems through their paces. While you do that, David and I will set about on an extensive tour of every deck, starting with my *office*." She stepped out of his grasp to run her hand along the railing of the overlook. "I need to see every centimeter of this ship before I can rightly call it my own."

60

CONCORD HQ
COMMAND

"Commandant, Advisors Kirumase and Palmer from the Asterion Dominion are here to see you."

Miriam had spent the hour since returning from their somewhat indulgent shakedown cruise reviewing fleet updates, and now she quickly finished scanning the latest report from the AEGIS Crux II Field Manufacturing Facility. Since dramatically ramping up production, more than 900,000 negative energy missiles and 120,000 negative energy bombs had been produced and shipped out to every vessel outfitted to carry them. Another twenty thousand such weapons now rolled off the production line every day. She allowed herself to smile a little; the Rasu were going to find themselves in a markedly different battle the next time they met.

Which made this meeting most timely. "Please send them in."

She stood and greeted them both, motioning for them to join her at the small conference table in her office. "Welcome, Advisor Kirumase. Commander Palmer, it's good to see you back up and among the living."

"You as well, I understand."

"Yes. I don't have as much practice at it as you do, but here we both are. You've come to visit me today because you have news— and possibly a plan to liberate Namino?"

Nika nodded as she sat. "First, I want to let you know that Alex is...well, I suppose she isn't 'safe,' but she did reach the DAF bunker where Caleb, Marlee and a number of Asterions have been hiding out. As of right now, they're all doing well."

"Thank you very much for the update. And you are correct. My daughter is rarely safe, and I have come to terms with this reality. Most days." She clasped her hands on the table and leaned forward intently. "So it's true that you've been able to bypass the quantum block and establish some form of communication with those on the ground?"

The two Advisors exchanged a brief but mysterious look. "A limited form, yes. Basically, a small number of Asterions are able to use our ceraff technology to communicate with others who are connected to the same ceraff. One—excuse me, two—of those individuals are at the DAF bunker, and two others are at the Omoikane Initiative on Mirai helping us talk to one another."

"Excellent. I assume Alex is not presently on her way home with Caleb and Marlee in tow, so what is their plan, and how does it dovetail with yours?"

Nika stared at her for a moment, then laughed. "You do get to the point, which I appreciate. The group on Namino has identified the source of the quantum block, and they believe they can disable it. If they're successful, this will give us a few hours at a minimum and ideally several days to evacuate most or all of the people who are still alive via wormholes. But we are hoping it will mean something more as well."

"You're asking me to send another fleet to engage the Rasu at Namino when the quantum block goes down. We failed you so completely last time, why would you entrust us with your people's lives a second time?"

Commander Palmer sighed. "Is 'because you're the only civilization with a fleet worthy of the title' an acceptable answer?"

Miriam leaned back in her chair and brought her hands to her lap. "Yes, it is. I hoped for a better one, but it's also the answer I deserve."

"In all seriousness, Commandant, I'm the commander of a measly few hundred ships. There's virtually nothing I can do to fight the Rasu right now, or for several months at the earliest. But I still want to fight for my people. The question is, do you?"

"I want to fight for *all* of our people, Commander Palmer—mine, yours and anyone else the Rasu threaten. It will not come as a surprise to you to discover that here in Concord, we are currently waging multiple internal conflicts. But they are merely background noise compared to the threat posed by the Rasu. If I did not properly comprehend this truth before the Namino battle, I certainly did upon waking up after it.

"We got our asses handed to us in that engagement. But when humans get kicked to the dirt, we stand up, dust ourselves off and return to the battle stronger and wiser. We've been working around the clock on new and better weapons explicitly designed to injure or destroy this rather unique enemy, as well as inventive methods to protect ourselves from the Rasu's particular...skills. I, for one, am anxious to see how these new tools perform in combat.

"Of course we will join you in the fight to liberate Namino. And this time, I promise you we will mean it."

61

EPITHERO

Casmir reread the message he'd just received with a measure of dismay. He'd hoped to receive a conciliatory response from the Savrakaths, but he hadn't expected this.

Navarchos Casmir elasson-Machim,

The Savrakath Legion has taken one of your own prisoner. He proclaims his name to be 'Torval elasson-Machim.' As a gesture of goodwill, we propose a trade. We will return the prisoner to your care, in exchange for a one-week cease-fire in our ongoing dispute. During this time, we will consider your previous proposal in greater depth and review viable paths of negotiation that might lead to a permanent cessation of hostilities.

If you refuse this offer, understand this: we will keep him alive until such time as he reveals all he knows. It is unlikely to be a pleasant experience for your comrade.

—General Kuisk Jhountar, Savrakath Legion Commander

It didn't make any sense. How had the Savrakaths gotten Torval? They'd been operating under the assumption that CINT had transferred Torval to a secret black-ops facility on a Human world. Ferdinand had touted this as yet another reason to despise and mistrust Concord. But what if it wasn't true, and instead the Savrakaths had somehow captured him?

And the Savrakaths knew enough not to kill Torval. The lizards might be cleverer than they looked.

But their request still seemed pointless. What could the Savrakaths accomplish in a week, beyond try and fail to prepare for the coming apocalypse his fleets would deliver if they didn't capitulate? Unless they were far along in constructing an additional antimatter facility, they couldn't rearm themselves with the deadly weapons fast enough to inflict any significant damage. Did they envision themselves planning some grand statement of a strike against a Concord target? They didn't need a cease-fire to do that. Besides, they'd shown no capability to execute any such strike, and Casmir had deprived them of the tools they would need to do so.

Perhaps they simply needed to lick their wounds, for those were quite deep indeed. The message was unsurprisingly bombastic, but beneath the tone, the words were begging for mercy.

He pinched the bridge of his nose and considered what to do next. Navigating this viper's nest of lies, deception and competing agendas on Epithero was requiring all his skills and several he didn't possess. But this was an opportunity to test his growing clout at the table, or at a minimum to judge where he stood with the others.

He readied himself for the coming battle, then called for an all-hands meeting in the conference room.

RW

Ferdinand frowned at the message displayed above the table. "What is this?"

"I sent General Jhountar a communique asking for his unconditional surrender. This is his response."

"How did he get Torval?"

"No idea."

"I assume Concord auctioned him off in a bid to appease the Savrakaths."

Casmir shrugged. "That's a big assumption. As I said, I've no idea. Regardless, they have him. And I think we should accept their offer."

Otto scoffed dismissively. "At the cost of a cease-fire when we have already driven them to their knees?"

"A brief one, yes. It's no secret to anyone here that I despise Torval, but he is my *elasson* brother, and we need to bring him home."

Ferdinand stared out the window, his back to those gathered. "I agree. He belongs with us. And once he's free, nothing will remain to stop us from doing as we like to the Savrakaths."

Casmir blinked. "Nothing except our word."

Ferdinand spun around, emboldened. "A word given to an enemy, and one who we know plays dirty. We have no responsibility to behave honorably when the Savrakaths do not."

Just when he thought he'd plumbed the depths of Ferdinand's callous amorality, the man revealed yet greater depths of depravity. "You're suggesting we should agree to their terms, retrieve Torval, then continue our bombing campaign unfettered?"

"No. I'm suggesting we increase our bombing campaign and send in ground troops. The Savrakaths are desperate, else they would not have reached out. We can bury them here and now, once and for all. You did say you wanted to dispose of them."

"To neutralize them as a threat, yes." Casmir sighed; the problem with his improvised power play was that it constantly pushed at the boundaries of both conscience and duty. *Which kind of leader do I want to be? Which kind am I capable of being?* "But I cannot in good conscience lie to this General Jhountar and go against my word."

Ferdinand's jaw locked. "I knew too much time spent among the Humans had infected you with their weakness and cowardice. Fine. You can return to your comfortable cell, and your betters will take care of retrieving Torval and finishing off the Savrakaths."

On cue, four Vigil officers entered the conference room. One placed a hand on Casmir's arm, and he wrenched it away. "You can't do this. Otto, Hannah? Ferdinand holds no real power here. Will no one defy him?"

Hannah studied her hands and kept silent, while Otto shook his head, possibly with a touch of sadness. "Machims do not show mercy to the enemy, Casmir. I'm sorry, but the Savrakaths have to be Eradicated, in the truest sense of the word. It's our duty."

Ferdinand nodded sharply in approval. "Guards, escort him to his room and see to it he does not leave it again."

This time, Casmir didn't fight when they grasped his arms. He'd lost...and he had no idea what to do now.

62

CONCORD HQ
CINT

Richard walked the halls of CINT, making it a point to stop and chat with everyone he passed. The very public arrest of Ferdinand's mole, Janice ela-Kyvern, risked kicking off a morale problem, but if he played things right, it also presented an opportunity.

He'd never considered himself a 'people person,' but he wasn't only his employees' boss, he was their leader. So he tried to project an aura of confidence and support, congratulating people on a job well done and reinforcing the importance of CINT's mission: to protect Concord's military, institutions and trillions of citizens.

He was fairly certain he was doing a dreadful job of it—

"Richard!"

He turned around to see Will striding toward him, urgency in his step and graveness on his features. Crap. "What is it?"

"You need to see something—but not here. Let's go to Cliff's room."

"Why not my office?"

"Because your office might be compromised."

He stopped short, dread creeping back into his bones. Was the mole only the beginning? "And yours?"

"I don't know. Cliff's room, please?"

He clearly wasn't going to get any answers standing around in the middle of the hall. They made their way across the atrium to CINT's other wing, where hardware and supplies were housed. All the way in the rear and through two layers of security sat the lab holding CINT's Artificial, Cliff.

As soon as they stepped inside, Will closed the door behind them, then entered a code on the panel to activate full surveillance shielding.

"Cliff, tell Richard what you found."

'We were running a sweep to clean up any sabotage, listeners or other malware that Janice ela-Kyvern could have left behind in CINT systems. We found one, but not from Janice.'

Richard groaned and dropped his head against the wall. "We have *another* leaker?"

'Possibly. We found a general-purpose listener routine embedded in the routing node. Its subtlety is quite ingenious, which is why we didn't detect it during our regular daily scans—'

"Focus, Cliff. Where did it originate?"

'The Consulate.'

His mind leapt to his contentious conversation with Senator Requelme regarding attacking the Savrakaths. "Mia?"

'Not precisely.'

Sometimes he longed for the old days, when Artificials lacked nuance. "It's been a long day, Cliff. Don't make me fish for it."

'Apologies, sir. The listener reports back to the network station in Marlee Marano's office.'

He exhaled in relief. "That I can actually believe. The girl's curious about everything we do here. It's likely harmless, but let's erase it. I'll talk to Mia about disciplining her. I mean, when she gets home." He'd seen Alex and Caleb pull off the impossible too many times not to believe they would successfully get themselves and Marlee off Namino and out of the Rasu's clutches.

'It's not so simple. A little over a week ago, the listener morphed into something more nefarious, and it was used to send a message using your access code to Taiv ela-Kyvern.'

"But...this doesn't make any sense. Marlee is trapped inside a quantum block five megaparsecs away. She couldn't have used it— shit."

Will drew closer, studying his countenance for clues. "What do you know?"

"Mia tried to convince me to pass along a tacit authorization, via Taiv, for Casmir to open up on the Savrakaths. Miriam rejected the idea. But now Machim warships are doing bombing runs across Savrak. Damn, would Mia really go behind my back and use CINT resources to co-opt my own informant? It's a major breach of security, not to mention a criminal offense."

'There is one more thing, Director. This morning, a message traveled in the opposite direction, from Taiv to you, but it was intercepted by the modified listener routine.'

"You're kidding me." He dragged a hand through his hair. "What did it say?"

'I do not know.'

RW

CONSULATE

Mia's fingertips caressed the scarf draped around her neck, and she let her mind wander to the night Malcolm had given it to her. It was woven of traditional tussar silk into a delicate jade and gold pattern he'd said complemented her eyes. Eyes she'd changed solely for him, in the first not-so-subtle clue that she cared about him.

Your listener routine has been scrubbed from the CINT system.

She jerked back to the present, her hands falling to her lap. *That's fine, Meno. It's done its job.*

Yes, but its erasure likely means CINT has discovered its origins.

She felt...was this relief? She didn't enjoy betraying the trust of her friends and colleagues. She didn't enjoy manipulating people to cause harm to others. But this was where the path of vengeance had led her, and there was no going back now. *So be it.*

One last thing to do—reach out to the one person who despised the Savrakaths as much as she did and might be in a position to strike the final blow. She sent them a message containing the information Taiv ela-Kyvern had intended to relay to Richard, then worked to busy herself with the mindless minutia of her job for a few last moments.

When Richard Navick walked in unannounced ten minutes later, she gave him a bland, professional smile. "What can I do for you?"

"We found and disabled your listener routine."

"I know."

She thought he looked a little sad. Or possibly it was pity. "You're not going to deny it was you?"

"What would be the point? You lead a spy organization, so I've no doubt you've uncovered the evidence you need. Besides, I find I don't have the energy for further subterfuge. I'm tired."

His gaze roamed around the office, possibly in search of another way forward—but this ended only one way. Still, she admired him for making the effort. "You realize you've committed a criminal offense. Not only will you lose your position in the Senate and at the Consulate, you could go to prison."

"I could. Are you planning to see to it that I do?"

"Mia, I don't understand. I mean, I *do* understand why you despise the Savrakaths. I truly do. You're grieving, and for that I am so sorry. But Concord is as much your brainchild as it is Miriam's or anyone else's. You've devoted the last fourteen years of your life to making this alliance work. Now you're just throwing it all away?"

"Just? No, not 'just.'" She stood and adjusted the scarf at her neck, letting her hand brush across the Caeles Prism resting below it. "But you've forgotten something about me. Before I was a businesswoman, I was a thief. Before I was a politician, I was a fugitive and a revolutionary. It turns out this is who I truly am, not the genteel public face I've worn for the world these last years." She laughed dryly, though doing so made her chest hurt. "It's funny. I spent so much time and effort convincing Malcolm that I wasn't a killer, merely a survivor. Now he's gone, and vengeance is my survival."

"What did the message from Taiv say? Tell me now, and I'll recommend leniency for you."

"It's too late for me. Goodbye, Richard." She let loose the building energy in her necklace, stepped through the open wormhole, and closed it behind her before he could follow.

63

E ren cringed as he opened his eyes...but no skull-splitting pain roared forth to greet him. Everything continued to hurt for certain, but in a normal bone-weary, existentially exhausted way.

He checked his arms to find multiple scrapes and two legitimate gashes scabbed over and healing. A headache throbbed rhythmically against his forehead but, again, an average and ordinary headache. His mind felt marginally clear.

He pushed up to a sitting position and peered around the cargo hold. The force field remained active, and Drae was nowhere to be seen.

He drew his knees to his chest, wrapped his arms around them, and buried his face in the cradle. Hot tears balanced precariously on his eyelashes, but he fought to keep them from escaping.

This ache, this all-consuming sorrow, hurt worse than the spiders or the brain swelling or the gouges he'd dug into his skin. He wasn't ready to deal with the grief. His brilliant plan had been to ensure he never need deal with it. Curse Drae for not letting him take the coward's way out on a one-way ticket to oblivion!

"Eren, are you all right?"

He hurriedly wiped his eyes dry while Drae climbed down the ladder. "'All right' is devastatingly relative, but I am feeling better. I guess this is where I'm supposed to thank you for saving me or some nonsense."

Drae crouched in front of him on the other side of the force field. "I hope one day you will, but I get that it's not today." He motioned over to the left, beside Eren, where a paper-wrapped package sat next to a fresh thermos of water. "I left you some food. You should eat."

"Sorry, I didn't see it." He scooted back to the wall and unwrapped the package to find a fresh roast beef sandwich inside. He turned up the thermos of cool water first, then set it aside to bite into the sandwich with surprising gusto. His stomach growled, though whether in thanks or protest, he didn't dare guess. How long had it been since he'd eaten anything?

While he chewed, he studied Drae. The man seemed rather sleep-deprived and stressed himself. Eren didn't remember much about the last...however long he'd been here, but he imagined he'd been a most troublesome patient. "When are you going to let me out of here?"

"When you agree to reconnect to the Concord regenesis server."

"That's what I thought you were going to say." He set the sandwich down on his thigh, his appetite gone. His heart yearned for escape from the sorrow welling up to drown him, for a permanent peace. Could he somehow bear to walk in a world that had been stripped of its light? Why even try? Once upon a time he'd proclaimed to Caleb and Alex that immortality was worth the fortune of galaxies, but now the notion of eternity stretching out in an endless string of forever days loomed before him like a dark and forbidding abyss.

"Eren, I know you think you're alone in this, but you don't realize the friends you have who care about you. Caleb and Felzeor went searching for you after you didn't come to the funeral. They hunted everywhere. Thelkt commed every former anarch he knows to ask whether they'd seen you. Director Navick has been searching, too, and he's the one who sent a frantic Mesme to me. There's a lot of bad shit going down out in the world right now, and it would be so easy for all of us to simply let you go in favor of attending to our crisis of choice. But we're not doing to do it."

The funeral...*arae anathema*. Part of him hated himself for not being there to honor her; the other part doubted his weak and battered soul could have withstood the trauma. "The funeral was nice?"

"I was locked in a regenesis lab, but Director Navick said it was beautiful."

Eren's jaw clenched for control. "Good. I'm glad."

"So what do you say? Are you ready to rejoin us in the land of the living?"

Could he do it? Could he face those endless days alone? Might the pain get better in time, easing away to reveal some light? Gods, Cosime would hate him for being such a histrionic, fatalistic sap. She would tell him there was still good he needed to do in the world, people who still needed his help, and he had damn well better get up off his whiny ass and help them.

But he still wanted to curl up in a ball on the floor and die, and she wasn't here to shame him into standing up and moving on.

His chin dropped to his chest. "Leave me alone."

"Dammit, Eren—"

"I don't know, okay? I'll think about it, but I can't do that when you're standing there judging me."

"I'm not judging you."

He squeezed his eyes shut, sapped of the strength to engage any further. After a few seconds, he was rewarded with the sound of Drae ascending the ladder to grant him his solitude.

RW

The insistent alert of a priority message jolted Eren from a deep, mercifully dreamless sleep. He clawed back for the darkness, desperate to remain in its silent, shrouded embrace...

...but no such luck. With a groan he stretched out on the floor and rubbed at his face. He'd finished the roast beef sandwich before succumbing to oblivion once more, and his headache had now lessened considerably. The scabs on his arms itched ferociously. Not because spiders skittered beneath them, thankfully, but they'd benefit from some medicated wraps to keep his fingernails off of them.

The alert flashed again. Right, the message. In his few hours of lucidity, he'd scrupulously ignored the deluge of messages waiting on him, for he didn't have the fortitude to bear the outpouring of well-meaning but empty and pointless condolences.

But someone believed *this* message was worth his immediate attention. He checked the sender...Mia Requelme? A nice and crafty lady, but not exactly one of his main chums. Interest piqued, he opened the message.

RW

A loud *thud* echoed from below. Before Drae could properly launch himself out of the cockpit chair, a second one followed it.

He leapt across the three meters to the ladder and slid down into the cargo hold, arriving in time to see Eren's fist hit the wall, leaving behind four streaks of blood from busted knuckles. "What's wrong?"

Eren grabbed for his hair as if to tear at it, only to come up empty. "Jhountar's planning to turn Torval over to the Anaden leadership in exchange for a temporary cease-fire. Zeus be fucking *damned!*"

"How the hells do you know that?"

"A little birdie whispered it in my ear. What does it matter how I know? The intel's solid. It's happening."

"Machim warships have been wiping the floor with the Savrakaths for the last week. I'm not surprised if Jhountar's searching for a way to make it stop."

"And I hope the Machims finish the job on Savrak, but Torval needs to suffer every last minute until they do." He stormed around the small, confined area, narrowly skirting the force field. "Fuck, fuck, fuck!"

Drae spoke carefully. On the one hand, it was a relief to see Eren spewing spitfire again. On the other hand, this level of rage couldn't be much healthier than wallowing in despair. "I'm sure it's been a most unpleasant stay on Savrak for Torval. The Savrakaths are not gentle with their prisoners."

"Damn straight it's been unpleasant. But it's not enough..." he sagged against the wall behind him and covered his face with his hands "...it's not enough of a price. Not for what he did."

"Maybe it has to be."

Eren peered at him from behind balled fists. "Fine. I'll reconnect to the regenesis server, on one condition."

"Name it."

"You help me crash the prisoner exchange. Help me blow up Torval, Jhountar and what I bet will be a good chunk of the Savrakath military leadership."

Leave it to Eren to go straight from suicide to explosions. "What makes you think Jhountar will personally show up for the exchange?"

"Because he'll want the promise of the cease-fire to be delivered directly to his snarling face. Because even in defeat, he's a proud, arrogant son of a bitch."

Drae conceded the point. "Granted. And how do you plan to blow them up?"

"The supplies I gathered before I liberated Torval from Detention included a couple of 'just in case' items. Go check the supply cabinet upstairs."

"I will, but why don't you simply tell me first? What manner of Hades did you bring on board this ship?"

"A small stash of antimatter belts I kept stored away from our old anarch days. The Savrakaths want to play around with antimatter? They can die by it."

64

CINT VESSEL 23A-X
SAVRAK STELLAR SYSTEM

I am deeply sorry, Eren, but I cannot.

You can't spare ninety seconds for one I-promise-is-the-last favor?

There is no need for it to be one last favor. But at present, I am actively involved in assisting the Asterions in retaking their planet of Namino from the Rasu. I am most pleased to learn you continue to draw breath among us, but no, I cannot spare ninety seconds.

Eren dragged a hand down his face. Fine. He'd relied on Mesme's ability to instantly put him wherever he wanted to be too much, anyway. He'd do it the hard way.

I understand. Good luck with the Rasu.

He studied Drae, who was cleaning up the mess Eren had made of the med kit while trying to bandage his wounds. His friend had only freed him from his force-field prison once he'd relented and officially reconnected to Concord's regenesis server. Even given the venomous rage he felt toward Torval, the decision had not been an easy one. He also strongly suspected that on Eren's reconnection, Director Navick had implemented a regular, remote cache backup of the data the connection transmitted, in order to prevent him from deleting his backup a second time.

If he severed the link again, they'd simply wake up a slightly stale version of him. He was supposed to be in charge of his own existence…but his friends weren't going to let him die.

"I imagine the Savradin defenses have taken a beating from the Machim attacks?"

"I expect so."

"How close to the meeting site do you think we'll be able to sneak unnoticed?"

Drae closed up the med kit and stored it in the cabinet. "With full stealth? Maybe inside half a kilometer. But Jhountar will be bringing a brigade of soldiers to ensure the Machims don't try any shenanigans."

"It's okay. I don't intend to approach from the ground. We're going to bomb the meeting from the sky—and I'm the bomb."

Drae sighed. "I appreciate your flair for the dramatic, and I'm glad to learn it's survived your hypnol poisoning. But there's no need for you to go through the hassle of regenesis this time. We can drop the antimatter belts from half a kilometer above the meeting and have time to escape the blast."

Eren forced a confident smile, pulling the correct muscles into a barely remembered pattern and holding them there. "This is where you're wrong—there is absolutely a need for me to go through the hassle of regenesis." He reached up and ran a palm over the stubble covering his scalp. "If I am going to continue living in this world, I have *got* to get my hair back."

Drae stared at him incredulously, then burst out laughing. "You know, that may be the first true thing you've said to me since this ordeal began. All right, fair enough. But if we're seriously planning to do this, why don't we go all-in? Let me crash the ship into the platform."

"Nah. You said it yourself. You just went through regenesis a few weeks ago, and you don't want to hop on that particular treadmill, trust me. No, as soon as I've cleared the airlock, you high-tail it out of there so you don't get disintegrated."

The effort of interacting as if the world were somehow normal was exhausting, but Eren drew on an empty well to add a touch of gratitude and sincerity to his voice. "Thank you for your help. Let's see this done, then I'll meet you at HQ in a few days, sumptuous tresses rightfully restored."

RW

SAVRAK

Eren peered out the open airlock. Ahead of them, a long, low building came into view. Apparently the Machim warships had leveled every military base on the planet, forcing the Savrakaths to conscript a random facility to effect the prisoner handoff.

A Machim frigate sat on the wide concrete strip that surrounded the facility, and a series of tiny, dark dots moved around between the two. No one there was worth saving, and it was a damn shame that some, including the worst of them, would wake up in a regenesis lab none the worse for wear. But not all of them. Jhountar was a scourge he was happy to eliminate from the face of the universe, and many of the Savrakath's lieutenants were even more unhinged than the man at the top. He believed eliminating them would save lives. Some kind of lives, somewhere.

Drae glanced back at him from the cockpit chair. "Get ready to jump in ten seconds."

Eren zoomed his vision in until he could make out a man in restraints being shoved toward the transport. *Torval.* Target acquired, he grabbed the end of the antimatter belt with two fingers and yanked. The antimatter slabs fell away from the belt to dangle from a thin ribbon, and the clock started running. When the buffer material dissolved, the antimatter would come into contact with matter—him—and obliterate everything for almost a kilometer in all directions.

"Five seconds. Last chance to give up on this stupid plan."

"I never have done the smart thing." Eren grasped the ribbon of deadly material tightly in both hands and took a deep breath.

"Now."

He extended a leg and stepped out of the airlock. The wind whipped him into a vicious spin as he tumbled away from the ship.

He surrendered to it, because it didn't much matter how he landed, or even where he landed so long as it was within a few hundred meters of those gathered.

As the concrete rushed up toward him, his pulse raced in longing for the brief but sweet oblivion awaiting him. The last of the buffer material on the slabs crumbled away.

He could almost see the whites of Torval elasson-Machim's tortured eyes when the explosion devoured them both.

65

SAVRAK

The walls of Malcolm's cell shook with such vehemence that jagged cracks opened up to spread across the floor and ceiling. A fine mist of debris rained down on him, and the force field sputtered and died.

He'd bet good money that the structure the Savrakaths had chained him up in, wherever it was and whatever other purposes it served, was being bombed from above. So the war had taken a real and bloody turn.

He hadn't seen a guard in several hours, and Torval had been gone for many hours longer. Maybe the Anaden finally goaded his torturers into killing him, thus freeing him from this captivity.

Malcolm, on the other hand, was going to have to free himself. A little ahead of schedule, as his shoulder was healing more slowly than he'd have liked—but by the sound and fury of it, now was the time. The force field remained dead, and the wide opening at the far end of his cell beckoned him to his freedom.

He peered at the wall above him to see jagged cracks splintering out in a cobweb shape from where his wrist restraint was attached to a large metal brace. As lucky breaks went, it would have to do. He sucked in air, steeled himself and tugged hard.

Fresh dust wafted down to coat his skin as the cracks widened. He tugged again. More dust fell, but the brace held.

He twisted around as far as he was able and locked his left foot at the wall. Then he shoved against the wall using his leg while he yanked his arm down and away.

Just when he was convinced his wrist was fracturing in the unforgiving grasp of the manacle, the brace tumbled out of the wall to land on the floor beside him. His shoulders sagged in relief, but there was no time for rest. Guards would realize the prison was breached and descend upon it in force any minute now.

He crawled along the wall to where his leg restraint was attached. The damage to this stretch of the wall wasn't as severe, but hairline cracks ran out from the restraint brace, so structural weakness had been introduced. He grabbed the chain with his good hand, braced both feet on the wall and pulled.

No movement; not so much as a fraction of give. He needed something to—

The walls, ceiling and floor shuddered again from a renewed strike, or possibly renewed collapse above, and he quickly breathed in and pulled again. This time the brace broke loose and went skidding across the floor.

He was free. But this was only step one.

He pushed himself up to his feet, then swayed unsteadily and grabbed for the wall behind him for support. He hadn't walked under his own power since being captured weeks earlier. Now, though, he must do more than walk.

He let his equilibrium settle and tested out his weight on each leg while he hunted around for anything he could fashion into a weapon, and belatedly realized one was attached to his wrist.

He gathered the chain up in his hands and swung the brace around a few times, getting a feel for its heft. It would substitute for a flail in a pinch.

Unfortunately, he'd also be dragging his leg manacle along behind him like some kind of ghost of Christmas past, at least until he located some way to unlock or smash it. He wouldn't be able to move quietly or swiftly, when he really needed to do both. He settled for winding the chain around his ankle several times before securing the latch inside it. There. That got it off the floor.

Now for a proper escape. Based on the reverberations, the explosions had all impacted high above this level, and he didn't dare count on being fortunate enough for his cell to be on the first floor of a tall building. Most likely he was located deep underground.

As soon as he stepped out of the cell, a high-pitched hissing sound began permeating the hallway. A pipe running along the wall had cracked, venting steam into the air. Hyper-heated water. In the dim light he couldn't make out many details, but it resembled the drainage system in place at the Okshakin...which meant two things: he was definitely underground, and this level was going to flood any second now.

He had no map and no helpful scans or schematics to point him toward an exit or merely a path toward higher ground. The guards had always appeared from the left, though, so he turned left and began walking as fast as his chain-bound leg permitted.

The staccato triple-thud of heavy Savrakath footsteps echoed from an intersection ahead. Malcolm pressed against the wall and readied the chain.

A guard had barely cleared the intersection when the sharp corner of the metal brace met him full in the face, knocking him to the ground and sending blood gushing from his nose. Malcolm leapt on top of him and drove the brace corner into the guard's throat with more strength than he'd believed he still possessed, then dragged it sideways. Blood bubbled out in a thin line behind it. The Savrakath jerked beneath him, long snout opening and closing in a weak attempt to find air.

The ceiling shook again—no time to dally. Malcolm stood and left the injured, but not quite dead, guard behind. The guard had come from somewhere...the right turn at the intersection. He retraced the guard's steps and hurried forward.

He passed what looked to be additional cells. Though the hallways weren't quite so labyrinthine as those comprising the Okshakin, this was without a doubt a prison.

Scalding water poured out of a ruptured pipe running the length of the hallway, and he skirted around the steam. What could have caused the water to boil? What kind of attack was this? If chemical or nuclear weapons were in play, he might find himself screwed upon reaching the surface. But Concord didn't utilize such toxic weaponry in ground combat.

The increasing volume of hissing steam made it harder for him to hear movement, and he ran smack into another guard at the next intersection. Before the guard was able to react, however, Malcolm had grabbed him by the shirt and shoved him beneath an escaping stream of boiling water. The Savrakath howled in agony, and Malcolm slammed him into the wall then took off running. His out-of-practice muscles screamed in protest and the chain around his ankle banged and jostled, but all complied with his demands.

Abruptly he reached a dead end, with branches to the left and the right. He didn't have time to hesitate, so he took the left hallway.

Fifty meters later he ran into a more distressing dead end: a solid wall of rubble. Hulking chunks of cement had fallen from above to form a landslide, blocking his progress. Dammit!

He peered up, struggling to make out details in the dark until he remembered the enhanced night vision routine they'd used on the Okshakin mission. Malnutrition and lethargy were making him stupid; with a curse directed at himself he switched to the routine. The debris and remaining walls took on an eerie, almost sickly fluorescent glow, but they also gained definition.

The rubble originated from higher up, possibly several floors above. It had torn through the ceiling, and where it sloped, he caught a glimpse of open space above. Not sky, but perhaps a path to reach it.

He secured the chain closer around his wrist so the brace wouldn't snag, and started climbing.

ASTERION DOMINION

66

MIRAI
OMOIKANE INITIATIVE

Dashiel watched Nika pace in a furious circle, hands at her mouth, her gaze focused three kiloparsecs away. She had been metaphorically distant since the initial attack, but now, with her consciousness split between here and Namino, the gap had become much more literal. The room buzzed with frenetic commotion as everyone rushed to prepare for the imminent gambit on Namino, but she moved in and through the activity like an apparition—a ghostly specter half-existing across multiple locations and dimensions.

He received a notification of twenty additional fighters leaving the assembly line, and he forwarded the update to Palmer on the off chance the commander could locate twenty more pilots in the next few hours. The adiaK-clad ships (his chosen moniker for the new metal fusion) might well turn out to be the greatest and most significant invention of his long career, but that judgment likely would not be rendered today. This fight was arriving too soon for the new ships to be properly measured and found fit or wanting. He'd grouse about it, but the universe rarely waited for perfection to be achieved before having its way.

In his peripheral vision, Nika absently wound her way through the middle of a group of three Administration officers cycling from one monitoring station to another. Unable to stand it any longer, he intercepted her course and placed a hand on her arm. "Is everything all right?"

She stopped and stared blankly at him, almost as if she didn't see him. Abruptly she blinked, and a flood of emotions broke across her expression. Her voice emerged in a cracked whisper. "If this doesn't work, I don't know what else to do. I fear we'll lose Namino forever."

He gave her the bravest, most confident smile he could conjure. "Then let's make sure it works."

"Right. Okay. The Concord fleet is standing by. The Kat fleet is standing by. Our tiny little DAF fleet is standing by. Even a few hundred Taiyok vessels are standing by, gods thank them for their overwrought sense of honor. Perrin and Katherine are standing by to receive a new influx of refugees. Every weapon in our arsenal is standing by." She leaned in to rest her forehead on his. "It's time."

NAMINO
CAMP BURROW

"It's time."

Nika lifted her shoulders into an unofficial command stance. "Joaquim, Ava, Selene, Dominic, grab as many large bags as you think you'll be able to carry when they're full. We're going to raid the DAF Command armory one last time. If we expect to make it across the city to the Rasu compound a second time, we need weapons. Lots and lots of weapons."

Ava returned from the supply room carrying a tall stack of empty bags and tossed them in the middle of the floor as Marlee hurried up to Nika. "You should take me with you. I've been to the armory before. I'm familiar with where the various weapons are stored."

"I appreciate the offer. But I need you and Grant to help all these people get packed up and ready to move out to the *Siyane*."

The muscles framing the girl's mouth twitched in displeasure; her lips parted, but she said nothing.

Nika tracked the variety of purposeful movements across the bunker, mentally checking items off overlapping lists. "What is it?"

"Grant and I..." Marlee's chin dropped to her chest "...well, we aren't exactly getting along so great right now. But it's not a problem. If you need me to work with him, I'll do it. I want to help everyone get to safety."

She started to brush the girl off, but stopped herself. "You know, Grant's a good man. A good man with a couple of deeply buried demons. If I could remember what they were, I might be able to help him, or at least tell you how you could try to do the same."

The girl's face screwed up in perplexity. "What?"

"Never mind. Make certain to take all the remaining food and water as well. I'm not confident the *Siyane* is stocked to support fifty people for very long."

RW

DAF COMMAND

The instant they crept off the lift into the DAF Command lobby, Nika sensed something was wrong—something beyond the generalized occupation of the planet by a terrible enemy. Shadows moved on the street outside of the blown-out entrance. The rumble of too-close machinery echoed threateningly off the damaged walls.

She leaned in close to Joaquim. "I thought you said they'd abandoned this location?"

"They had. I guess they've come back for another helping of secrets."

Joaquim had destroyed the primary server, but it didn't mean there weren't other secrets worthy of stealing in these halls. She listened to the insistent rumbling for several seconds, then made a decision. "Let's get to the armory."

"And if the building is crawling with Rasu?"

She handed him an archine grenade. "Then we'll shred them and run."

"Works for me." He pivoted and checked with Selene, who motioned them forward, and they headed into the interior of the complex.

Whatever nefarious deeds the Rasu machinery were up to, they were up to it on the top floors, and the group only had to dodge a single Rasu patrol on the way to the armory...the entrance to which was blocked by a solid wall of rubble. She muttered a curse through gritted teeth, but Joaquim grabbed her hand and guided her through a door just short of the rubble.

It led to a nondescript storage room. On the left wall, a jagged crack wound up almost to the ceiling, across and back down to the floor. She glanced at Joaquim. "Your handiwork?"

"Yep. The server room explosion blocked off the entrance, so when we came for the rocket launcher, I had to improvise." He walked up to the wall, placed both palms on the center of the cutout, and pushed, and a section of wall fell through to the adjoining armory. "And since we're vacating, we don't need to patch it up when we leave."

Nika strode through the opening, her eyes scanning the shelves upon shelves. "Everyone, stock up. Assault rifles, grenades, military Glasers, combat drones, power spikes. Whatever you think you can use to slow down Rasu attackers in the field or at the compound."

She went off in search of power spikes and electricity grenades. Her archine grenades were a preferable weapon in virtually any scenario, but her supply was already dwindling away. After emptying several cabinets her bag remained only half full, so she took a combat drone and two assault rifles to pass out to the others.

Five minutes later they all met at the jagged hole in the wall, bags stuffed and weighing down everyone's posture. "I know moving both fast and quiet is bound to be difficult while lugging thirty kilos of bulky gear, but let's do our best to get back to the lift unnoticed."

The trip back was nearly as uneventful as the journey to the armory, and she was almost about to relax a little. Then a deep, throbbing noise caused the walls, floor and ceiling to shake as they stepped into the lobby.

All her senses screamed in warning, and she locked eyes with Joaquim. "Run!"

They took off for the lift as a wide violet beam lit up the lobby for an instant before impacting two floors above them. The ceiling rained debris down on their heads and clogged the air, making it all but impossible to see where they were going. She felt more than saw a second strike impact the building, and the front half of the lobby began crumbling apart beneath the weight of the collapsing floors above it.

She motioned Ava onto the lift, then spun around just in time to see a huge chunk of ceiling slam into Dominic's back, knocking the man to the floor.

Joaquim was moving toward him before she could—another, larger section of ceiling collapsed, crushing Dominic fully beneath it when Joaquim was less than two meters away.

"No!"

Selene was acting as rearguard, and she grabbed Joaquim by the shirtsleeve as she ran past him. "Come on, you idiot. We have to get out of here!"

Still, he fought her for half a second before relenting and letting her drag him to the lift. Nika leapt onto the lift with them, and the lobby vanished beneath an avalanche of rubble as they descended.

CAMP BURROW

As soon as they returned to the bunker, Joaquim hurled his two full bags toward a vacant corner, then kicked them the rest of the way against the wall in an explosion of anger. Nika watched Selene watching him carefully for a moment, but the Justice Advisor didn't go over and try to calm him down. Instead, she dropped her bags in the center of the room, dragged his two bags beside hers and opened them all up.

Grant touched her arm, and she jerked in surprise.

"Sorry. What happened?"

"Dominic isn't coming back. And the Rasu finally blew up DAF Command, so we're going to need another exit route."

His expression flickered briefly. "The closest one is near Bunker #5. The exit will put us on the surface about three blocks from the Curio Market." He sighed. "It'll be slow going moving all these people through the tunnels."

"It's our only option. I'll get the updated coordinates to Alex." She scanned the bunker; it was much less crowded now that everything had been packed up, and most people were either double-checking the contents of their assigned bag or fidgeting quietly. "Is everyone ready to move?"

"I think so. Alex is helping Marlee bundle up the rest of the food from the refrigeration unit, and it's the last item on my list."

"Great, thank you. Let's plan to move out in five minutes."

Grant headed down the hallway to the kitchen, and Nika finally approached Joaquim. "We get home to Mirai, and Dominic will be back up and running in no time. But first we have to succeed today."

"About that. Nika, you know I try never to question you—"

"Are you kidding? You've basically done nothing but question me since the day I met you." She punched him lightly in the shoulder. "It's why you were an excellent second-in-command."

"True. In that case, I'll question you now. Are you sure you want to do this? I mean, what you're planning to do is...impossible."

"I've done the impossible before."

"With eight thousand copies of yourself, yes. Now there's only one of you here."

"Yes, but..." she stretched out an arm and studied the pale glow radiating off her skin "...it's a superpowered one of me. Also, this time I have you to watch my back."

He nodded soberly. "Yes, you do."

67

NAMINO

BENEATH NAMINO ONE

"It's only a little farther now, don't worry." Marlee patted the distressed woman on the back and gently nudged her to the left as the tunnel diverged in three directions.

She checked over her shoulder to confirm no one had fallen behind. Grant was taking up the rear of their subterranean convoy, though, so she needn't worry. He'd been friendly and kind to her all day, which only made her feel worse about yelling at him. And soon, if everything went according to plan, they'd be going their separate ways, perhaps forever.

But now was hardly the time for a heart-to-heart conversation to clear the air, so she let it go. If they didn't have an opportunity to talk before all this was over, she'd send him a note containing a proper apology in a few days. It might be the best she could do.

Bodies bumped into one another as they reached the exit and the front of the convoy came to a halt. Marlee nudged her way up toward the front until she reached Caleb. Beside the hidden door, Alex conferred in furtive murmurs and gestures with Nika and Joaquim.

After another round of murmurs, Nika nodded, and Joaquim broke off to say something to Ava. The woman scowled, and they argued in hushed tones for a moment before Joaquim squeezed Ava's shoulder then came up to her and Caleb.

Joaquim's chin dropped low, and his voice remained quiet. "Listen, if this goes the way I believe it will, I don't expect to walk back out of the Rasu compound."

Caleb frowned. "If you don't think this plan is going to work—"

"That's not what I said. It will work." Joaquim glanced up the tunnel toward Nika. "*She* will succeed in her mission, because I will spill my last drop of blood making certain she does. My point is, if I go down the way I expect to, when I see either of you again in the future, I won't remember you. So let me say this now: thank you. Thank you for helping us, and for sticking with a fight not your own. I'm not sure we'd be here doing this today if it weren't for the two of you."

Caleb offered Joaquim the most genuine smile Marlee had seen him display since bursting into the bunker more than a week ago. "You're most welcome. Thank *you* for helping to save Marlee's life. As far as I'm concerned, we're both still in your debt."

"Nah. Slate's clean." Joaquim shook each of their hands in turn, then headed to rejoin Nika. A few final murmurs followed, and the two of them headed off into the shadows of the right tunnel.

As Marlee understood the plan, they intended to stay in the tunnels for as long as possible, though the closest exit to the Rasu compound would leave them with several kilometers to traverse on the surface. The little scene between Joaquim and Ava made more sense now. He'd been breaking the news to her that she'd be staying with the main group instead of going to the compound. Hopefully they wouldn't need the woman's firepower, but Marlee found she was glad the people heading to the *Siyane* would have it in reserve.

She, Caleb and Alex were planning to create a distraction at the compound to help Nika's team slip in unnoticed, but not until they got everyone from the bunker on the ship and away from ground zero. She'd hadn't been briefed on the details of this distraction, but she was game for anything.

The device Alex had brought with her—she'd called it a 'walkie-talkie,' which was so silly a name that Devon Reynolds had to have made it up as a joke—emitted a static-filled squawking noise, and Alex held it up to her ear. "Understood. Two minutes, but no sooner. I don't want the *Siyane* sitting around like a giant, invisible target."

Apparently Alex had brought someone along with her to pilot the *Siyane* while she was groundside, since Valkyrie wouldn't have been able to penetrate the quantum block. Marlee hadn't thought to ask who it was.

Alex went up to Selene. "The ship's ready to land at the intersection above us. Are we ready?"

Selene's gaze passed across the huddled group of bedraggled refugees. "As ready as we can be." She raised her voice. "Everyone, it's time to move to the surface. We'll head up in groups of five, so no one has to stand around on the street exposed for longer than a few seconds. I'll stay at the top of the lift to help everyone out. The ship is stealthed, so once you're outside, wait for Caleb or Alex to guide you to the boarding ramp."

Marlee stared back down the tunnel in the direction from which they'd come. She most definitely wasn't sad to be leaving the claustrophobic, oppressive haven the tunnels and the bunker had provided, but she did feel a bit of wistfulness over it. The days she'd spent down here with these people would stay with her for a long time.

Caleb squeezed her hand. "Up we go."

NAMINO ONE

A hazy layer of dust hung in the air as they emerged from the storefront that hid a secret entrance to the tunnel network. The sidewalk was fractured into pieces every few meters, in several cases exposing the dirt below. The two streets meeting at the wide intersection had faired yet worse…the image that popped into her head was of a giant worm burrowing through the streets on its way to its next meal. A skeletal frame of a façade hung tattered and broken across the street, metal beams dangling off it like charms on a Khokteh headdress.

Alex came up beside her and Selene. "Hold here for one minute." Then she strode forward—and disappeared.

> *Marlee clutched her Mom's hand in a vice grip as they left the building lobby behind and walked toward an empty intersection.*
>
> *Caleb stood in the middle of the intersection; when he saw them, he turned and started walking away—then vanished!*
>
> *She gasped in surprise. Where did he go? Had the evil attackers opened up a giant hole and sucked him through? Had something—*
>
> *—he reappeared out of thin air wearing a grin. Behind him, a ship shimmered into existence.*
>
> *Marlee's eyes widened to giant bloodshot orbs as she let out a squeal of delight and ran to him. "Is this your ship, Uncle Caleb?"*
>
> *He crouched to her level. "Nope. It's my girlfriend's ship."*
>
> *That drew her enchanted gaze from the ship to him. "You have a girlfriend?"*
>
> *"I do."*
>
> *She considered him skeptically. "Is she pretty?"*
>
> *"She sure is—almost as pretty as you."*
>
> *Marlee giggled, covering her mouth with her uninjured hand in temporary embarrassment as she leaned against his shoulder.*
>
> *He tousled her dust-covered hair playfully. "Do you want to go for a ride in it?"*

Marlee chuckled to herself; Caleb really had been saving her ass ever since she'd been born. She reminded herself to continue being properly appreciative...and to repay him by helping him however she could once this was finished.

Alex reappeared a minute later, out of thin air, and motioned everyone forward. "The ramp's been extended. You'll be able to see it once you get inside the stealth bubble, so just watch your step."

Marlee had done this part before, so she stayed at the base of the ramp to help steward the groups of bunker refugees on board the ship. When only she, Selene and Ava remained, Caleb and Alex having gone ahead inside to organize what should now be a very full cabin, they headed up the ramp as well.

At the airlock, she took a last look outside to confirm the street was empty. "We've got everyone. You can close up the ramp now."

"Gotcha."

The familiar voice sent an electric shock racing through her, and she spun toward the cockpit. "Morgan?"

The woman sitting in Alex's chair glanced over her shoulder, and her brow furrowed. "Marlee, right? Caleb's niece? You've grown up."

"Uh-huh."

"You've got a cut on your cheek. You should get it patched up." Morgan spun the chair around and set to retracting the ramp and attending to pre-flight checks.

Marlee fumbled her way backward into the main cabin, sank against the cockpit half-wall, slid down to the floor and buried her face in her hands in abject shame. 'Uh-huh'? *Uh-huh*? For years she'd fantasized on an almost weekly basis about seeing Morgan again, and when it finally happened, all she could say was 'Uh-huh'? She might as well march right back outside and let the first Rasu she found kill her straightaway.

Also, why was she bleeding? She touched her cheek, and her fingertip came back dotted with a few specks of blood. She must have scraped it somewhere in the tunnels.

In her peripheral vision, Alex strode quickly through the crowded cabin toward the cockpit. She spotted Marlee as she passed and crouched beside her. "What's wrong? Are you all right?"

"Oh, sure. I'm fine. Just hanging out down here dying of mortification."

"What do you mean?"

She cast a mournful gaze around the corner of the half-wall toward the cockpit.

"Oh, crap! I'm sorry. I should have warned you Morgan was on the ship."

"That would have been *great*."

"Sorry." Alex patted her shoulder and stood to make her way into the cockpit. She leaned in to whisper something to Morgan, then promptly reversed course and wound her way back through the passengers and downstairs.

Marlee needed to stand up and get back to work. Neither Grant nor Selene were familiar with the ship, and their charges would be anxious and unsettled. She had a responsibility—

—a low rumble rippled through the cabin floor beneath Marlee. She bolted to her feet and lunged into the cockpit in time to see Caleb and Alex speeding off to the northwest on Caleb's bike.

She slammed both palms against the viewport. "You assholes!"

Morgan held out her walkie-talkie device toward Marlee, and Caleb's voice came through over the pervasive static. "Sorry, muffin. Next time, I promise. Look after everyone for us."

Morgan tucked the walkie-talkie away. "*Muffin?*"

Marlee groaned and propped against the dash. "Do not even get me started. I mean, it was cute when I was five years old, but...."

"But Caleb hasn't noticed how you're not five years old any longer?"

Had *Morgan* noticed? Her pulse spiked. "He's trying...except not today, apparently. Ugh, I hate them so much."

Morgan laughed dryly. "I doubt it, but I know how you feel. Maybe there wasn't room on the bike for you?"

"There was totally room on the bike for me."

"Yeah, there was." The woman checked a reading on the virtual HUD, then toed her chair around toward Marlee. "Alex left me alone on the ship in the middle of a field for *three days*. Well, not three literal days, but without a doubt some interminable span of time.

"But you know what? In less than an hour, we are going to get to unleash a storm of hellacious fireworks on this Rasu compound and blow their quantum block to smithereens. Join me up here in the cockpit, and you and I will have the best seats in the house for it."

Marlee smiled and casually eased herself into the second chair. "Now that's a show I want to see."

68

NAMINO
NAMINO ONE

A warm, dry, soot-soaked wind tore at them as they sped toward the outskirts of the city, where plains fought to reclaim the land from civilization. Nika had dialed up the range on Caleb's kamero filter to maximum for him, so hopefully it extended to envelop the bike in its cloaking field. If not, the Rasu were going to see them coming a kilometer away and respond accordingly.

Caleb worked to draw comfort from Alex's arms wrapped snugly around his waist, from the solidity of her chin resting on his shoulder and her chest pressed into his back. They'd been here many times before, racing across a planet headlong into danger, or at times racing away from it. He recalled the desperate drive across Cavare so long ago, when they were being hunted by assassins and he'd believed he'd lost her in more ways than one. He'd greatly underestimated her that night, but not since.

It's supposed to be you and me against the universe, come what may.

And so it would be today.

Akeso screamed in his mind for him to turn around, get on the *Siyane* and come home. To not execute this violence upon an enemy that Akeso struggled to comprehend. He filtered the cacophony out as best as he could, but the wall he'd rebuilt after those singular, extraordinary moments sharing one existence with Alex was proving to be weaker than before. He was exhausted from fighting this battle. From fighting against Akeso's nature, and against his own. It would be over soon, but he couldn't say what waited on the other side for him.

What if he couldn't come back from this?

Alex adjusted her hold on him and let her lips brush feather-light across his neck. As if she'd heard his question and given her reply. *No matter how far you fall, I'll bring you back.*

He made the only choice he could—the choice to believe it. But first—

—in the heart of the city, a thunderous crash roiled across the land to shake the ground beneath the bike. He skidded to a stop, and they both turned around in time to see Namino Tower collapse in upon itself. Clouds of hot debris rushed out in every direction to bury downtown in a sea of soot and shattered glass.

"My god."

He swallowed past the daggers lining his throat. "Our mission's all the more important now. We need to focus on it."

He floored the bike as a small Rasu vessel flew overhead without noticing them. It banked around to land inside the compound, and he breathed a sigh of relief that their plans weren't blown before they'd begun.

The walkie-talkie squawked static intermixed with Nika's voice. *"We're in position at the northwest entrance. On your mark."*

The transmission was too muffled to say for certain, but he thought he detected an undercurrent of rage in the woman's voice. "Fifteen seconds."

He brought the bike to a stop a hundred meters from one of the entrances cut into the outer barrier and tried to force levity into his voice. "One rocket launcher, please."

Alex unlatched the device from where they'd strapped it over the rear wheel, then hefted it up and passed it to him. "I don't get to shoot it?"

"I want the pleasure." He rested the tube on his shoulder and sighted down on the outer ring. He had no way to interface with the Asterion-designed targeting system, but accuracy wasn't really a factor here. He merely needed to draw lots of attention to the southeast section of the compound.

His finger pressed the trigger, and the rocket flew out of the casing. With such a short distance to travel, the rocket almost made it to the outer barrier before the defense lasers destroyed it.

He tossed the empty casing to the ground and floored the bike, sending it fishtailing to the east as they vacated the spot where Rasu were soon to be converging. He sped halfway around the compound, then finally slowed to a stop near another one of the cutout entrances. Once Alex climbed off, he laid the bike on the ground, hoping it would still be here and in one piece when they returned. "Are you ready?"

"Always." Alex stepped close enough for him to see her; he grabbed her hand tight. "Stay close to me."

She removed the Rectifier from its makeshift holster with her other hand. No time to waste now. They sprinted toward the entrance.

RW

Storm clouds churned across the ruined Namino One skyline. Rain was a rarity in this region of Namino, but perhaps the city wanted to express its displeasure with its new overlords. The clouds concealed many of the hovering ships, but they didn't drop so low as to obscure the spire at the center of the Rasu compound. Their destination.

Once exiting the tunnel network, Nika and Joaquim worked their way across the final two kilometers to their target. With it being just the two of them plus the fact that they'd worked together on missions for years, they moved as a single unit, silent and swift.

Nika tuned out the relentless destruction and the too-frequent corpses they crossed during their journey, because she had no other option. If she succeeded today, it would bring an end to all of it.

She'd filtered out most of the k-band ever since arriving, for in a crowded space such as the bunker, the strings were so widespread she could hardly see anything else. But once she'd reached the surface, she'd experimented with removing the filter, only to have her heart break at the realization of how few of the strings undulated through the city. There *were* people alive here, hiding in the ruins or below ground…but not many.

If she succeeded today, the dead would be avenged.

Joaquim held up a hand, and they halted at the last cover they were likely to find, the tattered remains of what had been a sports park. Beyond it waited the walled barricade of the Rasu compound.

"Are you set?"

She nodded firmly. "I am. Remember, this is an infiltration mission. I need to get to the room beneath that energy vortex. Unnoticed, if at all possible. Alex and Caleb are going to draw lots of attention away from us, but from here on out we have to value stealth over speed."

"You are not talking to a rookie here. I'll get you up that spire."

"And then we'll both get back out alive."

"Sure." He shot her a rare smile and checked his weapons—

—a Rasu beam from high above painted the sky violet, and a deafening roar exploded behind them. She spun around, only to gasp in horror as the apex of Namino Tower *melted* beneath the Rasu's unrelenting weapon. Structural beams were shorn away, and floor after floor crashed through those beneath them until nothing remained of the tower but a great advancing storm of debris.

A primal anger rose up in her chest, and her skin flushed hot. "DAF Command, now Namino Tower? They must believe they've stolen everything useful from us."

Joaquim shook his head in disgust. "What do you think they'll do now?"

She thought back to the Kat-created simex of the Rasu invading a primitive world. "Flatten every structure that still stands and kill everyone who remains."

"Then we need to hurry. Let's do this."

She followed him around the perimeter of the sports park toward the northwest side of the compound. Rasu transports and bipedals beat a busy path to and from the location, stealing away treasures and trash from the residents of Namino One. They gave the units a wide berth, but otherwise they had to count on the kamero filters to keep them hidden.

Still, it took time to pick their way across a span of open plains and reach the outer barrier. She cupped her hand over the walkie-talkie and whispered into it. "We're in position at the northwest entrance. On your mark."

Caleb's response came quickly. *"Fifteen seconds."*

She pocketed the walkie-talkie. The barrier wall was too high to see over, but the commotion, when it came, should be evident.

She counted down the seconds in her head—six laser beams erupted to converge on a point past the opposite side of the compound. A booming explosion roared beyond their sight, and all the nearby Rasu went scrambling toward the source of the blast. Perfect.

The way now clear, she and Joaquim slipped through the cut-out entrance in the barrier and inside. The spire towered above the center of the compound, but a hundred meters and three active rings still stood between them and their goal.

She stayed close enough to Joaquim to see his faint outline, though they each wore trackers that showed up on the walkie-talkie screen, just in case they got separated.

He pointed toward a gap in the first ring, and they crept along the Rasu metal comprising it until the opening lay directly ahead.

RW

RASU COMPOUND

When they were steps from the compound, Alex fired the Rectifier at a point thirty meters to the left, near where the rocket had almost impacted. A ten-meter section of the barrier dissolved. It was an impressive weapon.

Rasu flocked to the gaping hole that had just appeared, and Caleb and Alex slipped inside the entrance.

464 | G.S. JENNSEN

A full-scale industrial processing facility greeted them. He needed a target...a tall stack of shorn metal sat off to their right. It was Asterion metal, not Rasu, so he fired on it with his Daemon, cutting long slices through it until the metal tumbled into a jagged pile on the ground.

"Move." They jogged twenty meters to the left and flattened against a long storage module. Bipedal Rasu now scurried in every direction while drone models buzzed overhead, all hunting for the source of the attacks. On the other side of the compound, something tore the roof off a wide section of the middle interior ring.

He pressed the walkie-talkie button and whispered into it. "Status?"

"Halfway to the tower. Keep the hits coming."

He zeroed in on a conveyor moving large crates of items from the outer ring to the middle one. He reached out beside him and found Alex's arm, lifted it, and pointed the Rectifier at the track. "There."

"Nice choice." She fired, and a section of the conveyor track—and the outer ring—vaporized. When they got home, he was going to insist on the production of some oversized versions of that gun. And a personal one for himself.

"Move again."

They hugged the outer ring to try to avoid the stampede of Rasu heading for the damaged track, and ran smack into three Rasu racing in from outside.

He dropped the Daemon and drew both archine blades, adjusting his grip on them even as he lunged in front of Alex and sliced in opposite directions. A Rasu arm flew through the air as a torso slid to the ground. A metal fist connected with his shoulder; every bone in his body shuddered and threatened to crack, but he spun into the blow and severed the arm from its body. His pulse pounded in his ears until all he could hear was the rush of blood through his veins.

A second Rasu towered over him, one arm melting and morphing into a sledgehammer. He crouched and ducked beneath its legs, then brought both blades up at the center and wrenched them upward. He stood between the two halves as they fell away, then pivoted as the third Rasu barreled toward him. He feinted to the left and sliced up diagonally through the construct's torso. The intact arm swung around on him, and he lunged forward to take out both legs.

The sound of new movement behind him overrode the discordant symphony of his pulse, and he spun around, both blades raised—and jerked his arms to a stop with the blades less than ten centimeters from each side of Alex's neck.

Her eyes were wide and bright, her chest heaving from exertion...and he'd almost killed her.

RW

Another explosion rocked the far side of the compound, and Nika and Joaquim took advantage of the commotion to dash forward then creep through the gap to the other side of the ring.

Between here and the base of the spire, equipment, storage containers and disassembly rigs were packed into every available space. Nika couldn't help but wonder what they were doing with all these raw materials...but there was nothing and no one for her to rescue here. The people who'd been taken alive were transported to one or more of the ships in orbit, then probably to a new research lab. Beyond her reach, for now.

Transforming Rasu—growing weaponized limbs and small engines to speed their pace—rushed past them toward the increasingly raucous noises originating from across the compound, and she spared a thought to worry about Alex and Caleb's safety. They weren't Asterions, but they were risking their lives to save Asterion ones.

But she'd of necessity learned to trust in the abilities of her people while leading NOIR, and this was no different.

The newest commotion created a temporary lull in activity around them, and they darted through the center ring into the heart of the compound. The innermost ring stretched tall and imposing in front of them. It served as the wide base for the spire, so once they entered it, they would be trapped inside a living Rasu structure until the end.

The Rasu's bounty from pillaging Namino One now crowded around them so tightly they had to search for small gaps and weave agonizingly slowly toward the inner ring, then skate along it until they found an entrance. Then they had to wait for half a dozen Rasu drones to speed out of the entrance on their way to take out the mysterious attackers who were disrupting operations. As soon as the drones departed, she and Joaquim darted inside—straight into a bipedal Rasu meaning to leave.

Joaquim had sliced it into four pieces in the time it took her to blink, then shot each of the pieces with a concentrated fire of electricity from his Glaser, which should overload whatever counted for circuitry and prevent them from reforming for a minute or so. Now time was a factor, and every second counted.

She activated the walkie-talkie. "We're headed up the spire. Two more minutes."

"Acknowledged."

The base of the spire was surprisingly devoid of materials and equipment; it appeared to serve no purpose other than to provide access to the critical machinery higher up. In the center of the room stood two parallel vertical poles. She and Joaquim went up to them, nodded to each other, and grasped hold of them.

The poles instantly moved upward, carrying her and Joaquim with them. They must be used to ferry items of heavier weight up into the spire. She watched Joaquim as they rode upward, and he watched her. They needed to stay silent, but they didn't need words. He'd been her friend since finding her lost and broken in a rain-soaked alley almost six years ago. Since then, they'd performed these kinds of miracles together hundreds of times. He'd grown and changed, and so had she. But this, here? This they knew.

Clanging sounds began to echo down from above them. Machinery put to purposeful use—and possibly transforming into weapons designed to kill them? She peered up, and a brief scan identified three concentrations of Rasu signatures. Two on the left, one on the right. Joaquim pointed to her, then to the right.

A moment later they cleared the floor. Perhaps expecting Rasu visitors rather than intruders, the units in what seemed to be a control room were slow to respond. Slow enough that she had time to extend the dual blades built into her forearms—for this unique body, *archine* blades. She drove herself into the unit on the right, blades leading, ripped apart its torso and kicked the lower half of its body toward the corner.

In less than a second it had started reforming. She grabbed an archine grenade from her belt and lobbed it into the center of the roiling mass of metal.

"Take cover!" She hit the floor and covered her head with both hands.

Knife-edged shards of Rasu pelted her defensive shielding, and she winced from a sharp sting in her calf as a piece penetrated the shield and her skin. Most of the shards, however, shot over her head and hopefully not into Joaquim.

She lifted her head in time to see him repeatedly fire a Glaser into the chest of an advancing Rasu, until the sheer force of the blasts forced it to stumble backward and fall through the opening to the bottom floor far below. The last Rasu lay in overloaded pieces on the floor beside Joaquim.

She grabbed Dashiel's arm, interrupting his intense conversation with Adlai and Katherine mid-sentence. "Tell everyone to get ready. The quantum block will fall any minute now."

Nika leapt to her feet, ignoring the scream of protest in her calf; she had to hurry. She inventoried the components of the space. It was definitely a control room, because she'd seen these types of Rasu modules before, on the platform at their stronghold. But with no obvious and quick way to determine what module controlled which functions, her only option was to open one up and dive in.

While Joaquim kept watch for reinforcements arriving from below, she sliced open the cover of one of the modules and gripped one of the photal fibers. A working knowledge of the Rasu programming language was now deeply embedded in her own systems—

> *I dash among my fighting and falling sisters as they clear the path for me. The floor vanishes again, but I leap over the chasm and reach the bank of equipment. I look left, then right. It stretches for a hundred meters in each direction.*
>
> *How to locate the correct module? There can be no hesitation and will be no second chances. I stand flush against the equipment, where the Rasu cannot afford to dissolve the floor, and study the flashing lights, reading their output using the ceraffin's algorithms.*
>
> *Internal power flow. Engine stabilization. Radiation shielding and conversion—a module dances out a pattern of light, and the melody tells me its purpose is the one I seek.*
>
> *A shock erupts from beneath me. I fall.*

—and she soon identified the nature of the instructions passing through the fibers. She followed the relevant ones to the hub that controlled the defense grid.

"We've got company on the way. Faster would be better."

"Trying," she muttered through gritted teeth. Dammit, she couldn't corrupt the hub from this access point. She tried to visualize how the programming web must correspond to the physical equipment, then rushed to another module across the room as weapons fire shot up through the opening in the floor and Joaquim returned fire. She tore into the cover of the module, tossed it away and thrust both hands inside.

"I'm out of grenades, and we are not out of company."

She removed one hand to fumble through her pack and retrieve a grenade, which she tossed over her shoulder to him. "My last one. Make it count."

He nodded slowly, an odd wistfulness lifting his features. "I will. See you on the other side."

"What?" She gasped as he activated the grenade and leapt down through the opening.

The explosion shook the control room so violently she barely stayed on her feet, and enough chunks of blood and flesh flew up through the opening for her to recognize full well what had happened. Godsdammit!

Focus. This will all be for naught if you don't get the defense grid down. She choked off a cry and redoubled her efforts, letting the alien code flow around her. There—the central brain of the defense grid.

She opened up her internal pathways and let the virutox course out of her hands and into the photal fibers. Encased in a wrapper of Rasu programming, it shouldn't be flagged as a foreign invader until it was too late.

Her mind lingered as she watched the virutox begin to wreak its destructive havoc. Throughout the control room, alarms began to peal, and a module behind her shorted out in a flurry of sparks.

Still she watched, all the way until the signals necessary to operate the defense grid stopped reaching their intended destination. Then she withdrew her hands and tried to look around, but code and kyoseil had imprinted themselves on her vision like halos after a blinding solar flare.

Her fingers fumbled over the walkie-talkie until she was able to activate it with a thumb. "Virutox implanted. Alex, Caleb, get out of here. *Siyane*, you're up."

RW

"Let's move!" The conductivity lash at Alex's wrist whipped out through the air to strike what remained of the last nearby Rasu, stunning it in place. Then she grabbed Caleb's trembling hand, blade and all, and dragged him away from the temporary carnage.

They ducked inside a storage container, and his hands fell limply to his sides. No air reached his lungs. "Alex...."

"It was my fault. I shouldn't have gotten so close. You were doing what you needed to do to protect us."

"But I—"

"Focus, *priyazn*. We'll talk about it later."

How could she call him that when seconds earlier he'd nearly severed her head from her body?

Nika's hushed voice on the walkie-talkie jolted him out of the immediate shock. *"We're headed up the spire. Two more minutes."*

"Acknowledged." He tried and failed to meet Alex's gaze. "Let's see this through."

"You bet." She gave him a brave smile, shattering his overtaxed heart, and they headed out of the storage container and back into the fray.

Instantly she vaporized a large piece of passing machinery. He retrieved his Daemon from the ground and fired on a small vessel rising into the air, doing little damage but perhaps drawing some attention away from the spire.

Out of nowhere two motorized Rasu sped past them, and he shoved Alex into the outer ring. She exhaled harshly, aimed the Rectifier high above them, and took out a vessel accelerating in the direction of the spire. He tossed two archine grenades into an open door in the middle ring—then they were running again as explosions resounded behind them.

"Virutox implanted. Alex, Caleb, get out of here. Siyane, you're up."

Abruptly every Rasu unit in sight began racing toward the spire. One mind, one consciousness, and they now knew they had been corrupted.

Caleb fired one last shot at a distant section of the middle ring, then took Alex's hand in his and sprinted for the closest exit.

69

NAMINO
SIYANE

"Marlee, can you come here for a second?"

Marlee sighed and cast a sideways glance at Morgan as she stood and headed into the cabin. She and Morgan had been talking for the last twenty minutes. Nothing monumental, just mission stuff, but it was so nice. It had also taken her mind off the fact that twenty minutes had passed since Caleb and Alex took off for the Rasu compound—a reality that now came slamming back into the forefront of her mind. How long was it going to take them? The longer they were inside the compound, the worse things were bound to go for them.

She almost bumped into Ava, who was brushing up against everyone in her way as she wove a stormy path through the cabin and back again while stroking her (for now) dormant gun arm. Obviously not happy at having been left behind. Marlee maneuvered past the woman, then past Parc, who was busily playing with the data center controls—Alex would have a conniption fit if she found out—to finally reach Selene, who crouched beside a woman sitting on the couch with her head dropped low between her knees.

"What's wrong?"

Selene winced up at Marlee. "She isn't feeling well. I think it's merely stress from the evacuation today, but would it be all right if we got her some water and let her lay down in the bed downstairs?"

She was hardly the arbiter of Caleb and Alex's bed...except for the time being she kind of was. "I'm sure they won't mind. I can't promise her privacy, though. We don't have enough room up here to kick everyone out of the lower cabin."

"Understood." She patted the woman on the shoulder. "Come on, let's get you downstairs, nice and easy."

Marlee cleared a path to the staircase for them, even as her gaze kept returning to the viewport at the front of the ship. Once Caleb and Alex had departed on the bike, Morgan had vacated downtown for a quiet, non-Rasu-infested stretch of plains a few kilometers west of the compound. Clouds swept angrily across the sky, and she swore they grew more agitated as they approached the inky, ominous spire in the distance.

Abruptly several cruiser-sized Rasu broke off from their overhead patrols and accelerated toward the compound. Marlee bumped and elbowed her way to the cockpit, arriving as Morgan was straightening up in her chair and opening multiple HUD screens. "What's happening?"

"If I had to guess, one or both of our teams just kicked a hornet's nest in the compound." Morgan's voice rose above the din in the cabin. "Everyone should sit or grab onto something that's bolted down. Things ought to get interesting in the next few minutes."

Above the compound, a swarm of tiny Rasu dots made it impossible to discern any details about what might be transpiring inside. From the east, the first of the cruisers drew near the spire.

The walkie-talkie sitting in a makeshift cradle on the dash squawked to life. *"Virutox implanted. Alex, Caleb, get out of here. Siyane, you're up."*

Morgan cracked her knuckles. "Finally, I get to shoot something."

Concern gripped Marlee's heart in an icy fist. "What if the defense grid isn't down yet? We don't actually know how long it will take for the virutox to do its work. We shouldn't burn all our negative energy missiles until we're certain."

"True." Morgan rolled her eyes. "We'll test-fire the main weapon and see what it draws out."

The *Siyane* rose into the air and crept closer to the compound. A silvery beam shot out from beneath the ship and impacted the outer barrier of the compound without provoking any automated resistance. "Excellent! Bombs away."

Morgan tapped the center of the screen directly in front of her, and four aerodynamic missiles burst forth from the belly of the *Siyane*. The instant they were away, Morgan began strafing to port and rising higher in the air.

RW

RASU COMPOUND

Beneath Nika, renewed *thrums* signaled the arrival of yet more Rasu, and she no longer had her protector to fend them off. She wasn't getting out by going down, so she peered up. The power vortex writhed and contorted above her like a malevolent sun. Maybe the virutox was affecting it, too.

She'd given Joaquim her last archine grenade, so she couldn't blow a hole in the exterior wall and escape that way. She could always simply allow herself to die here, and her copy on Mirai—her original, in truth—would live on. But she didn't want to die. She was fucking *tired* of dying in sacrifice to the Rasu.

She thrust her hands back into the wiring. She'd seen something while she was rooting around, and it took her only a second to find it again. The power controls. The virutox had wiped away the failsafes and security protocols, and she was able to send an overload command directly into the main power line.

By the time she'd removed her hands, the vortex above her was thrashing about like a star going supernova. She crouched in the farthest corner, trying to make herself as tiny a target as possible, and readied her wingsuit to deploy.

The poles at the center of the room started sliding upward, ferrying Rasu to come kill her.

The vortex exploded in a cacophony of searing electricity, blowing out all the walls. She scrambled to her feet as the floor disintegrated beneath her, clambered past the remains of a cracked module, and leapt out of the spire.

SIYANE

All four missiles slammed into the apex of the spire. The explosion was like nothing Marlee had ever seen. A ball of obsidian flame erupted at the point of impact. It seemed to fall in on itself for an instant—then a shockwave of nothing but void rushed out in all directions, vaporizing everything in its path, including one of the approaching Rasu cruisers.

The other two cruisers, however, pivoted and accelerated in the general direction from which the missiles had come.

As the *Siyane* pitched up and to port again and their angle of ascent increased to at least thirty degrees, Marlee found her attention drifting away from the incredible rupture in the fabric of space-time ahead of them and toward Morgan's profile. All traces of projected boredom or ennui had vanished from her features. Her fingers flew over the virtual HUD panels with a grace and speed customarily reserved for virtuoso musicians. While her eyes swept across every screen and datapoint, she bit into the left side of her lower lip and poked the right side out, which…Marlee blinked. Was it hot in here? Of course it was hot in here; the ship was filled to capacity with terrified people.

In the span of a heartbeat they'd traveled to the opposite side of where the compound *used* to stand—it was now a dusty but serene crater—and cruised surreptitiously along the lower edge of the cloud cover. Meanwhile, ten kilometers away the two cruisers continued to scour the region for the source of the attack.

"Nice flying."

"Eh…" Morgan rubbed at her neck "…I'm embarrassingly out of practice."

"Then I'd love to see what it must be like when you're *in* practice."

Morgan stared at her, one eyebrow toying with arching. "Noted."

Marlee swallowed. *Definitely* too hot in here. She grasped for anything else to focus on, and belatedly remembered the whole 'her family and friends being in mortal peril' thing. She leaned forward to peer out the viewport in concern. "Do you think Caleb and Alex made it out of the blast zone safely? And Nika and Joaquim, too?"

Morgan gestured toward the walkie-talkie. "We'll know when they comm us."

RW

RASU COMPOUND

Nika's wingsuit deployed to halt her plummet to the ground, where hundreds of Rasu gathered to storm the spire. Too late.

She soared, once again invisible, above a compound in utter chaos. From this vantage, the Rasu seemed almost *vulnerable*. She only hoped one day soon the impression would become a reality.

As she cleared the outer barrier wall, four missiles soared past her to crash into the crumbling remains of the spire, and she smiled—

—a shockwave slammed into her and sent her tumbling through the air. Her momentum carried her forward while a powerful elemental force fought to drag her backward, into the hungry grasp of the void.

She forced her limbs straight and made her body into an arrow, both to arrest the tumble and to increase her aerodynamic momentum away from the miniature black hole writhing behind her.

The ground spun in dizzying circles beneath her, rapidly at first then gradually more slowly, until it finally settled into place when she'd sunk to a mere fifteen meters above it. Her brain continued to spin inside its skull casing, but she managed to tuck her legs into a ball against her chest, and her left shoulder took the brunt of the blow as she crashed into the ground. She rolled twice and came to a stop flat on her back.

She tried to gasp in air, but her diaphragm refused to respond. Her body convulsed until an emergency signal from her OS jolted the diaphragm back into operation. She rolled over and coughed up dirt and soot until her chest ached so much she was certain she'd cracked several ribs.

Everything hurt, and she was bleeding from multiple locations, but she pushed herself up to her hands and knees and wobbled around to look in the direction from which she'd come.

The spire was gone, along with the rest of the compound and all the Rasu. In their place, a deep crater had been carved into the soil.

A sweet, sweet deluge of messages began pouring into her OS.

A round of high-fives among most of the Advisors preceded a renewed flurry of activity as everyone swept into action. Dashiel wrapped her up in his arms and spun her around in the air. So dizzy.

On her hip, the walkie-talkie crackled out static. *"We've got your tracker location. On our way."*

Oh, good—a ride. She grimaced and forced herself to her feet, then tested out each of her limbs in turn.

Time to take this planet back.

SIYANE

Marlee snatched up the walkie-talkie and activated it. "Caleb, do you read? Alex, come in, please. Nika? Somebody answer me!"

She could feel Morgan's curious gaze boring into her, but she didn't back down. "I repeat, anyone on this channel, come in. The spire, the quantum block and its power source have been destroyed—the entire compound has been destroyed—but there is an increasing number of Rasu in the vicinity. Please respond with your location."

Her foot tapped impatiently. If any of them ruined the big day of triumph by dying, she was going to be righteously pissed.

A familiar voice filled the cabin. 'Morgan, please inform me if you require my assistance in any way regarding the operation of the Siyane. Alex says that as soon as it's safe for you to do so, land about three kilometers to the southeast of the compound. They will pick up the others and come to you.'

"Roger that, Valkyrie. Welcome back." Marlee flopped into the cockpit chair with a massive sigh of relief. "It's always like this with them, isn't it?"

Morgan shrugged. "It's been a while since I've kicked around in their orbit, but near as I recall, yeah." She kept one eye on the Rasu cruisers in the distance as she descended toward the plains below and eased the *Siyane* to the ground, her mouth drawn into a frown. "I hope they get here pronto. We are still way too close to ground zero for my comfort."

"Right. I'll go below and try to hurry things along." She maneuvered through a cabin full of shell-shocked passengers, hopefully free of bruises or broken limbs, and headed down the staircase. Once downstairs, she nudged a couple of people out of the way to open the hatch to the engineering well and descended the ladder.

The ramp had already been extended, and she peered out across a featureless landscape as the clouds finally loosed their contents and heavy raindrops splattered onto the ground.

When it was less than ten meters away, the bike suddenly materialized with Caleb, Alex and Nika on board.

Marlee grumbled under her breath, "I *knew* there was room on the bike," and waved them up the ramp.

She crossed her arms dramatically over her chest and readied to give Caleb an earful about tricking her and leaving her behind. But when Alex collapsed her helmet and climbed off the bike behind him, she shot Marlee a warning look and shook her head minutely.

She took the hint and eased off on her stance, watching Caleb closely as he collapsed his own helmet. Strain seemed to have burned itself permanently into the creases around his mouth and the rigid set of his jaw, and his eyes had darkened to a turbulent indigo. What had happened to him in the compound?

As soon as everyone had disembarked, Caleb secured the bike to the side of the well. "Morgan, we're all on board. Close the ramp and retreat to a safe distance."

Wait...Marlee gazed around in confusion. "What about Joaquim?"

Nika dropped her chin to her chest. "He didn't make it."

Marlee's chest panged with a confusing, tempered sorrow that always accompanied the 'death' of an immortal. "I'm sorry."

Caleb touched Nika's arm as he passed her on the way to the ladder. "If it matters, I think he knew going in that he wasn't walking out of the compound."

"Godsdamn asshole of a hero." Nika's face was covered in dirt and bloody scratches, and her left arm hung limply by her side, but she pushed past Caleb to scramble one-handed up the ladder ahead of him. "Come on. We need to meet Mesme."

70

CAF AURORA
CONCORD HQ STELLAR SYSTEM

Miriam stood at the overlook of her lovely new flagship. They idled in front of a Caeles Prism wormhole a full kilometer in diameter, waiting for the word to advance. When Nika Kirumase had relayed a three-hour estimate, she'd moved the fleets into position. Then the report had been 'within the hour' and now, literally any minute. And Alex was at Nika's side, risking life and limb to invade the heart of the Rasu's presence on Namino.

When she'd told her daughter to 'go to Namino and get the quantum block down,' she hadn't meant it *quite* so literally. But in retrospect, she should have expected no less.

Her eyes surveyed the bridge, where talented officers conducted final checks and ensured the new vessel maintained a state of hyper-readiness in anticipation of battle. Almost forty percent of her original crew had returned, coming out of regenesis ready to fight another day, perhaps with a touch of vengeance in their hearts. Another forty-nine percent had requested a medical leave of absence after being reawakened, for which she absolutely could not blame them. If she were anyone else, she would've welcomed taking one herself. But she was Miriam Draner Solovy, and she did not break. As for the rest of the former crew...they'd included 'no regenesis' clauses in their wills. Which meant she'd gotten them killed in the first Battle of Namino.

Getting people serving under her killed in pursuit of a higher purpose had been a fact of her life for more than half a century now. One day in the not-too-distant future it might stop being so, once regenesis became more widely accepted, then embraced. In her scant idle moments, she wondered how this was apt to transform the psychology of war. There must be a different path, a better path, than the one the Anadens had taken, but it would be up to humanity to blaze it.

But that was for later, and right now she needed to focus on the upcoming engagement. Having learned her lesson in too tragic a manner, she was not bringing a knife to this gunfight. She had six hundred thousand AEGIS vessels staged at multiple wormholes, not counting fighters or Eidolons, all ready to move on her order and bring thousands of tactical nukes and millions of negative energy weapons to bear on the Rasu. Four hundred Kat superdreadnoughts and their hordes of swarmers—in addition to the hundreds of superdreadnoughts already guarding Dominion worlds—were sworn to show up to *this* battle.

She'd forbade any Khokteh or Novoloume formations from participating in the mission. They'd suffered too many losses in the first encounter and needed time to rebuild and heal. In something of a surprise, the Machim *elassons* who had not defected to Ferdinand's rebellion insisted on sending the ships under their control. She didn't plan to count on their arrival, but they were certainly welcome to join the party. Commander Palmer was also emphatic about sending every new DAF ship the Asterions had built since the last battle. Seeing as this was his home they intended to reclaim, it was not her place to refuse him.

She was considering a bit of silent fretting over the passing seconds when a direct message arrived from Advisor Kirumase.

The quantum block is down.

Nothing about the state of the Rasu on the ground; nothing about Alex, Caleb, Marlee or the rest of the infiltration team. But battlefield discipline required that she set any concerns aside. It was time to go to war, properly this time.

There was no need for grand motivational speeches today. This battle had become personal, and every soldier knew full well the stakes.

Commandant Solovy (CAF *Aurora*)(*Namino Command Channel*): "*All ships, proceed to your assigned initial rendezvous points in the Namino stellar system. Once there, execute on TP-Epsilon 4.*"

In the hours when he wasn't tending to her every emotional and psychological need, David had spearheaded the development of a new tactical combat plan designed to take advantage of their strengths and the Rasu's weaknesses, such as they were. Though untested, it looked brilliant and devious in the simulations. She wished he were here to see it play out, but he correctly asserted the bridge belonged to her alone during hostile engagements. Also, she assumed he was camped out in her office—half to ward against any new surprises from Ferdinand, half to be able to watch the live command feeds as they streamed in.

She'd never fielded a fleet half as large as the one vaulting across five megaparsecs of space now. Of necessity with such a large force, most of the battlefield decisions devolved to the admirals and brigadiers in charge of the battle groups and often to the individual ship captains. This had been AEGIS' *modus operandi* since its founding, and the flexibility it provided should work to their advantage today.

'Executing Caeles Prism traversal.'

"Thank you, Thomas."

The golden light consumed them for an instant—then they were back in the Namino stellar system, twenty megameters from the planet. Many thousands of Rasu stood between them and their goal, and she had no doubt many more would promptly be en route.

The glut of menacing alien vessels in orbit around the planet was enough to trigger traumatic flashbacks if she possessed any true memory of the prior battle and her death during it. It was probably for the best that she only had Thomas' recordings of the disaster. Even so, she had to work to suppress a visceral shudder at the sight.

As one—like the hive-type mind they were—every Rasu currently orbiting this hemisphere of the planet turned outward and raced to engage her armada, exactly as she wanted them to.

"Thomas, take us in."

RW

NAMINO STELLAR SYSTEM
DAF FLIGHT #3

Lieutenant Kiernan Phillips fidgeted in the tiny cockpit of his new fighter. The ship's main body was half again smaller than his previous one; allegedly, this had something to do with adiamene rendering most of the hull reinforcements and defensive modules unnecessary. But he didn't care for the way it felt as though the void loomed *right outside*, like he could lower a window (if he had one), extend his arm and watch it freeze solid and break off at the elbow to float away into the black.

But the engine was faster and more agile and the weapons were more powerful, courtesy of some ceraff or other. Oh, and the hull changed shape on command. So all in all, an improvement on prior models.

*Commander Palmer (*ADV Dauntless II*): "All DAF forces, move in, make a nuisance of yourselves, and draw every Rasu target you can away from the planet."*

Kiernan adjusted his harness and accelerated toward the writhing cloud of Rasu. Honestly, he'd never expected to sit in the cockpit of a fighter again. This was all his fault, after all, and Commander Palmer should have demoted him, then dishonorably discharged him, then ordered him to report to a clinic for a comprehensive up-gen. Instead, the man had given him a coveted pilot's spot in one of only two hundred ten new fighters. A chance for redemption, maybe? He didn't know about that, but he *did* know he wanted to shoot a fuckton of Rasu today.

A mini-swarm of smaller Rasu solidified on his radar, and he marked them for the other members of his flight. Two additional fighters appeared on each of his port and starboard, and they spun up in a sixty-degree arc above the Rasu vessels, pivoted and dove in from above, weapons firing in unison on the first target.

The frigate-sized Rasu ruptured near center-mass, sending its constituent pieces shooting off in every direction. They immediately re-targeted the individual pieces, blasting them repeatedly into ever smaller pieces floating ever farther apart. It wasn't a death blow, but it should keep *these* Rasu out of the game for a while. Possibly for long enough until it didn't matter.

His tiny fighter shuddered from the broadside impact of weapons fire from another Rasu. Yet no alarms rang to pierce his ears or flash annoyingly across his HUD. The hull remained in ship-shop shape. *I'll be damned.*

He was grinning as he pivoted 180 degrees, in unison with his flight mates, and fired with renewed vigor on the next target.

RW

NAMINO

Plains transitioned to grasslands as the *Siyane* sped northwest across the continent, giving the cities and their Rasu occupiers a wide berth. They needed to be as far away as possible from the combat engagements for this next phase.

In the cabin, Selene, Grant and Marlee were patching up various bumps and bruises the passengers had suffered when the *Siyane* evaded Rasu pursuers in the aftermath of the compound's destruction. Alex had kicked Morgan out of the pilot's chair promptly upon her arrival, and now Morgan rested against the cockpit half-wall sipping on a beer. Caleb was…Nika hadn't actually seen him in several minutes.

Her head swam from a dizzying overload of information flowing into the Initiative back on Mirai, and the scene out the viewport blurred away as she focused on *the rapidly updating scoreboard at the front of the Initiative. On Dashiel's anxious but optimistic oversight of planetary defenses. On Perrin's happy relaying of the growing number of refugees arriving on Mirai soil through Prevo wormholes. On Lance's—*

"We're approaching the coordinates you gave Mesme."

Nika jerked back to this reality and pushed her other consciousness to the periphery. "Excellent. How's the radar look?"

Alex flicked at a screen on her left. "All clear."

"Go ahead and set down. Mesme says it'll be here in—"

"—two minutes." Alex shrugged. "It's talking to me, too."

"Of course it is."

The *Siyane* settled to the ground, and Alex opened the airlock and extended the ramp. "Morgan, keep the chair warm for me."

"And here I thought I was off the clock." The woman traded places with Alex and dropped her beer in the cup holder.

Nika beat Alex down the ramp and jogged into the knee-high grass. No artificial structure stood for two hundred kilometers in any direction. If the device wasn't safe here, it wouldn't be safe anywhere.

She peered up at the sky, shielding her eyes against the blazing sun with a hand, for the storm soaking Namino One had evaporated once they left the city behind.

Mesme, where is it?

A moment. I am adjusting the landing location so the Rift Bubble device is not deposited on top of the Siyane. *Alex would be displeased.*

That's the truth.

Abruptly, as if materializing wholly out of thin air two hundred meters above her, a sphere plummeted out of the sky. Just when she began to worry it was going to crash, it slowed and settled gently to the ground. The metal casing fell away and the obsidian lattice ignited in pale gold light. The air crackled with ionization, raising the fine hairs on her arms.

Mesme's undulating lights were faint in the bright sunlight. *The Rift Bubble is now active.*

"Show me."

On one of the panes along the front wall of the Initiative, the feed from one of the ships in their tiny reconstituted fleet displayed the snarl of Rasu vessels now engaged by the Concord fleet above Namino. The pilot searched around until it found a Rasu descending toward the surface of the planet. As the haze of the upper atmosphere began to engulf it, the vessel vanished from scans.

"You sent it into the heart of Namino's sun, yes?"

As is fitting.

No more Rasu would be ravaging Namino, today or any day, and the ones who remained on the surface would soon be eliminated. "I have no words to properly thank you, Mesme."

None are needed.

"Nevertheless."

Someone touched her arm, and she spun around to see Alex standing behind her. The woman still looked like she'd just emerged from a war zone, with stray streaks of blood and dirt decorating her face and clothes and her hair spilling wildly out of a low knot.

Nika smiled. "The Rift Bubble is working."

"Oh, I know. Want to do something cool?"

She chuckled. "I think I've earned something cool. Sure."

"Come with me." Alex strode off through the high grass toward the lattice. Nika followed, the beginnings of a remarkable lightness filling her chest.

Dashiel leaned in close and stole a quick celebratory kiss.

Mesme swirled ahead of them in some agitation. *Alex, I must ask that you—*

"Shut it, Mesme. You've done well today, but now you're going to let us have our fun."

Mesme didn't argue further, which Nika took for consent.

When they reached the lattice, Alex lifted her left arm and let her fingertips dance along the fringes of the power rippling out from the structure. "Here's your chance to get a crash course in Kat programming and engineering. Never know when you might need it."

"How?"

"We stick our hands inside this beautiful ball of energy."

"We do what?"

"I won't say it's safe, exactly, but I've done it before. In fact…" Alex smiled a little wistfully "…one could posit that nearly everything humanity has accomplished in the last fifteen years has happened because on Portal Prime, I decided to do the reckless, arguably stupid thing and stick my hand in a lattice exactly like this one. Given the long conflict that awaits us on the other side of today's battle, it strikes me as a good idea to do it again now, with you."

"Hells, yes, it does." Nika flexed her right hand and thrust it into the fire.

71

NAMINO STELLAR SYSTEM
CAF AURORA

*H*i, Mom. The Rift Bubble is operational, so why don't you send a couple of ships down here to get rid of the vermin on the surface? Oh, and we're all fine.

If anyone on the bridge happened to be glancing her way when the pulse arrived, Miriam would not have been able to disguise the rush of relief that briefly brightened her expression and softened her stance.

Good to know on all counts. Well done.

Commandant Solovy (CAF Aurora)(*Namino Command Channel*): "Fleet Admiral Bastian, you are authorized to begin Phase 2 operations on the Namino surface."

Fleet Admiral Bastian (AFS Leonidas)(*Namino Command Channel*): "Acknowledged. Battle Group #2, with me."

On the tactical map, twenty thousand ships broke off from the battle and adopted a trajectory that would quickly take them into Namino's atmosphere. They each broadcast a special signal to enable them to pass through the Rift Bubble barrier and reach the planet's surface. Any Rasu who chased after them were going to experience a very different fate.

On the opposite side of the planet, Kat superdreadnoughts had arrived as promised to engage the Rasu forces, and for now Miriam left them to do so however they best saw fit.

Splashes of light flared outside the viewport as three Rasu leviathans fired mercilessly upon the *Aurora*. She was accustomed to her vessel withstanding blistering fire without damage, but with the Imperium double-shielding active, the fire never even reached the hull to create so much as a minor, fleeting vibration.

She'd consciously readopted her ship's prior role as a 'damage sponge that shoots back,' almost as if to dare her still-shaky psyche to crack under the pressure. Trial by fire.

Her pulse beat a trifle too rapidly, and a few beads of sweat tickled the skin beneath her uniform collar, but so far she was weathering the storm.

'Commandant, the *AFS Trinidad* and the *MF Epsilon-16Bravo* are being targeted for potential intrusion by Rasu vessels.'

A shiver ran unbidden up her spine. "They know what to do...but let me see the feeds."

Two new screens manifested to her left on the overlook. They showed an AEGIS cruiser and a Machim battlecruiser fleeing at top speeds from pursuing Rasu leviathans—and from the vicinity of the planet below.

Even with late-breaking power allocation and programming enhancements that increased its propulsion by 12%, the AEGIS cruiser could not outrun the leviathan, while the Machim warship managed to match the leviathans' speed but not outpace it.

Which was fine.

When the ships crossed a pre-determined threshold distance, they each unloaded eight heavy negative energy missiles into their pursuers. Then, before the missiles impacted their too-close targets, the ships used their superluminal drives to jump a safe distance away. The leviathans were vaporized, the Rasu that comprised them reduced to a scattering of subatomic fundamental particles.

She breathed out carefully through her nose. "Express my commendations to the captains, would you, Thomas?"

'Of course, Commandant.'

"Then take us in closer to the planet. It's time for us to act as bait."

RW

DAF FLIGHT #3

Small, annoyingly agile Rasu vessels swarmed around Kiernan's fighter. Their strikes had taken out one of his two laser weapons by shooting straight through the open nozzle, and at this point his hull was basically bathing in Rasu weapons fire. Visual scans were useless, though at least wide-band scans assured him the battle continued to go well outside of his little party.

He frowned at the vicinity radar. Two of the dots making his life miserable had merged into one much larger dot.

He altered his course, falling into a spin for three seconds before yanking the ship hard to port and climbing toward the void.

The dot chased him. The others fell away, as did, thankfully, the relentless weapons fire. The blinding light on his visual scanner faded, revealing that the larger Rasu vessel had tracked him through his evasive maneuvers and was closing fast. At two hundred meters' distance, the vessel began splitting apart again—but not completely.

He'd heard about this. It was planning to surround him, then slither inside his tiny fighter and eat him for breakfast, or dinner, or whatever meal was next.

His heart pounded violently in his chest. Dammit, he hadn't spent weeks hiding from the Rasu on Livad, eating nothing but berries and twigs and catching fitful naps on hard dirt, only to get devoured by the monsters *now*.

The yawning mouth of the transformed vessel filled his viewport—and in his terror he'd almost forgotten his ship's new trick.

He transmitted the command to the defensive system for the adiamene to go into 'cocoon' mode, then set about trying his damnedest to flee, just in case.

The system told him the engine had to shut down to complete the cocoon transition. Because engine exhaust ports were weaknesses that allowed the Rasu inside.

He wasn't having much luck escaping anyway, so he brought the ship to a halt and killed the engine. Now he was naught but a floating minnow in space.

The stars, the planet and the sun all vanished as the Rasu swallowed his ship whole. *Oh shit, oh shit, oh shit....* He tried to focus on the defensive system readings. They claimed the cocoon was complete and all seams and holes closed tight.

No fluid Rasu slithered into the cockpit, so maybe it was telling the truth. Only one small problem: he was now trapped *inside* a fucking Rasu.

Lieutenant Phillips (DAF Flight #3): *"Hey, guys? Anyone want to come and shoot me out of this blasted thing?"*

Lieutenant Romescu (DAF Flight #3): *"Ha! On our way."*

RW

CAF AURORA

The outer wisps of the planetary atmosphere danced across the energy barrier of the double-shielding as the *Aurora* banked around, placing the planet behind it and the remaining Rasu armada in front of it.

"Confirm we are situated completely inside the Rift Bubble's perimeter."

'Confirmed.'

"Excellent. Weapons, pick a target and make them come to us."

Considering two leviathans and three Rasu cruisers had chased them all the way here, selecting a target was not difficult. They fired on the lead leviathan as it drew inexorably closer. Flashes of Thomas' recording haunted the fringes of Miriam's consciousness; she ignored them. "Increase fire. Make them want to take us out."

Four new streaks of laser fire joined the six already pouring into the hull of the leviathan. Though negative energy missiles were currently in prodigious use farther out from the planet, this close they didn't dare risk it. And they didn't *need* to.

The leviathan drew within four hundred meters, and she had to concentrate to keep her breathing normal. Three fifty....

The leviathan vanished. Caught in the Rift Bubble's trap, it was now disintegrating inside the corona of the system's star.

Her chin dropped to her chest for a mere half a second before rising high once again. "Excellent work. Let's see how many Rasu we can trick into falling into our trap before they start getting wise to it."

Commandant Solovy (CAF Aurora)(Namino Command Channel): "Vice-Admiral Ashonye, you have command of Battle Groups #1, #3 and #4. Begin Phase 3 operations."

What Rasu didn't fall into the Rift Bubble would now be mercilessly targeted by over five thousand Eidolons wielding a host of negative energy bombs, in addition to suffering the unremitting fire from the Concord fleet. There would be no escape for the Rasu. Not today.

Many hours remained before the battle could be declared 'won,' but in her own counsel she began to relax a little. This was not the end of this conflict, for the Rasu could reinforce any engagement with an effectively infinite number of ships. They could and likely would attack other planets, and before long those would include Concord planets. The Rift Bubbles alone did not bring victory, for they were at best a bandage designed to staunch the bleeding and buy them much needed time to engineer a proper offensive strategy.

No, this was not the end of the conflict. But perhaps it was the end of the beginning.

RW

NAMINO

Nika opened her eyes to see Caleb looming over them, his frame blocking out the sun, his brow drawn tight in consternation. "Do I even want to ask?"

Alex giggled beside her, which provoked a new round of laughter from Nika, and they lay there on the ground for another thirty seconds alternately laughing and trying to catch their breath.

Finally Alex stretched an arm into the air, and Caleb helped her to her feet. "Well, the lattice was right here and…."

"Ah. I see. Nika, you weren't responding to Grant's messages. Please do, so he'll stop hyperventilating to everyone on the ship."

"Oops!" She leapt up to her feet, then swayed as a bout of lightheadedness overtook her. The Kat code spun enticingly through her mind…but that was for another, less exciting day.

Sorry, Grant. I'm good. Everything is…good.

I'm glad.

A new message arrived then, and she grabbed Alex by the arm. "We need to head back to the city."

Alex grimaced. "What about getting all those people crowded into my ship to Mirai?"

"As soon as we do this one last thing."

RW

They landed well outside of downtown, on the opposite side of the city from the former Rasu compound. The cabin had grown quiet during the short trip; most everyone was too exhausted to stay afraid any longer.

Nika hurried down the ramp as two carriers of Asterion design broke through the clouds above her. One ship paused to hover fifty meters above the ground while the other landed. An airlock opened, and a man in DAF fatigues descended the ramp.

She met him halfway, and he snapped a formal salute. "Advisor Kirumase, I'm Major Benson. I bring you eleven hundred heavily armed and highly motivated special forces ground troops, courtesy of Commander Palmer and Advisor Ridani, to help clear this Rasu rabble out of the city. Tell me where you want them."

She gazed back at the broken downtown skyline. "Head in from the southeast corner and sweep every block until no trace of Rasu metal remains."

Overhead, a series of loud booms ruptured the sky, and they both peered up in surprise. Hundreds—no, thousands—of Concord warships had breached the Rift Bubble and were descending to engage the Rasu vessels above the city.

Alex appeared at her side once again. "Nothing like the cavalry arriving to brighten one's day, is there?"

A radiant grin broke across Nika's face. "No, there is not."

"Unfortunately, this means the air above Namino One is shortly going to get messy with space-time vacuums, so we should probably head out."

She nodded. "We should. I don't know about you, but I am ready to go home."

Dashiel touched her cheek while wearing a tender smile. "But my love, you are *home."*

CONCORD

72

CONCORD HQ
MEDICAL

F elzeor glided down the hallway toward the entrance to the regenesis lab, then forced himself to drift outside the door and wait for Drae. Walking took people *so* long!

"Excited to see Eren again, are you?"

"I am." He cooed as he landed on Drae's shoulder, but fell silent as a rush of worry overtook him. The action evoked memories of running around Concord HQ with Caleb, and that adventure had ended badly in so many ways.

In the days since, he'd remained at HQ, mostly hovering around the CINT offices when he wasn't catching a few hours' sleep in the small, Volucri-friendly lodging he'd procured. He needed to hear any news about his friends, about the wars, the instant it arrived. He needed to be where he might do some good, if given the opportunity.

Director Navick had assured him that Caleb was alive and slightly safe on the Asterions' Namino planet, but the last update had been too long ago. This morning he'd heard how a grand battle was now underway at Namino, and he feared for Caleb and Alex being caught up in it. The Rasu sounded like truly awful creatures.

Space battles were beyond someone such as him, however, so he could do nothing to help them. But he believed he *could* help cheer Eren up. He'd been so happy to see Drae yesterday, then shamefully annoyed when his teammate had spent most of the evening meeting with Director Navick.

But Eren was scheduled to be released from the regenesis lab shortly. He'd forgiven Eren for abandoning him on Akeso and for missing Cosime's funeral. If his dear friend promised not to vanish ever again, Felzeor might even forgive him for trying to kill himself. No matter how much someone's heart was broken, they ought to keep living, so it would be able to heal. After all, his heart still needed to heal, too.

"Eren's going to have his hair back, right?"

"He is." Drae stroked Felzeor's neck while he took his place at the end of a short line leading to the reception desk. "It'll even be clean and brushed."

Felzeor clucked in amusement at the thought. "Not for long, I bet!"

"I bet you're right." The line moved forward, and they stepped up to the desk.

The receptionist was an Anaden woman, but he couldn't decide if she was an Erevna or a Kyvern. Not all Anadens matched their Dynasty stereotype any longer. "How can I assist you?"

"CINT agents Drae Shonen ela-Machim and Felzeor to see Eren Savitas asi-Idoni. He should have woken up from regenesis this morning."

"Hmm." The woman scanned the screen in front of her. "Ah, there he is. I'm sorry, but the patient checked himself out an hour ago."

"What?"

"The medical system cleared him after a few tests, and he left promptly thereafter."

Felzeor's beak dropped to Drae's shoulder in dismay. Not again!

"Dammit. Can you tell me…never mind. Thank you for your time." Drae spun around to stride out of the lab, agitation roughing up his steps.

"Pardon me, sir? Did you say your name was Drae?"

His gait hitched, and he turned back to the receptionist. "I did."

"Mr. Savitas left a message for you, with instructions for it to be delivered to you when you came by."

Drae shot Felzeor a perturbed look and returned to the desk. "Why didn't he just send me the message the normal way?"

Felzeor chuckled a little, happy to find amusement among so much sadness. "Eren never misses an opportunity for showmanship."

"Truer words...." Drae motioned to the receptionist. "Give me the message."

She passed over a thin film, and Drae opened it.

> *Drae,*
> *Thank you for saving my life and not being* too *much of a prick about it. I'll see you again one day, my friend.*
> *—Eren*
> *P.S.: Felzeor, I love you. I hope you can find a way to forgive me for abandoning you.*

"Eren, you infuriating son of a bitch."

Felzeor shook a tear out of his eye. In his darkest moments these last several weeks, he'd selfishly wondered if Eren had forgotten all about him. He'd forgiven his friend anyway. "What are we going to do? We need to find him."

"Hang on for a second. I'm checking...he's still hooked into the regenesis server, thank Athena." Drae sighed and let himself sink against a nearby wall, and Felzeor adjusted his grip on his friend's shirt. "Maybe he simply wants to be alone for a while. And there's nothing else I can do for him, so maybe we should let him be."

"But we *can* do something for him. We can help him feel better."

"I know." Drae reached up and scratched the soft feathers under Felzeor's neck. "But not until he's ready to feel better, I think. Much as it pains me to say, we should be patient with him."

"I'm not very good at being patient."

"Me either. I tell you what. Why don't I buy you some baked apple tarts from the Consulate bakery, and we'll figure out what to do next while we eat?"

His eyes lit up. The bakery's tarts weren't as tasty as Thelkt's home-baked ones, but they were plenty delicious enough. "I accept your offer!"

RW

HIRLAS

NARAIDA/VOLUCRI HOMEWORLD
PEGASUS DWARF GALAXY

The dew-soaked leaves of the weald glistened luminously in the early dawn light. An olive-and-amber canopy welcomed Eren home as he ascended the winding steps built into the broad tree trunk.

When he reached the landing at the top, he nearly bolted back down the tree to flee in a panic. He couldn't do this. He wasn't ready. He was weak, and he needed to run away and hide for a while longer, to drown his grief in a sea of alcohol and hypnols until he found a way to forget.

But Cosime would be so disappointed in him if he followed his baser nature into the depths of Hades. She'd saved him from those depths once, and she hadn't done it just so he could relapse the instant she was gone.

Gone.

He took a deep and distressingly sober breath and stepped onto the wide platform encircling the tree. *Home. Their home.*

They'd spent little time here in recent years—so little, in fact, that a few months ago Cosime had suggested they sell it. He'd resisted, though. For one, he liked Hirlas, at least in small doses, before it had time to become too drearily peaceful. And while he'd never gotten her to admit it, Cosime always thrived here. Her skin glowed brighter; her step was lighter, her smile broader. So not only hadn't they sold it, he'd tried to make sure they swung by here more often, merely to refresh that exquisite glow of hers.

A woven thatch roof covered the necessary rooms—kitchen, bath, greeting area, bedroom—but no solid walls stood to block out nature. A curtain of gauze fabric hung around the bedroom for a modicum of extra privacy, but mostly they'd relied on the natural flow of the weald to create what privacy they'd desired.

He went in the bedroom and sat on the edge of the feather-soft bed situated low upon the floor. A mint-green shirt of hers lay crumpled in the middle of the covers, discarded and forgotten the last time they'd raced off on a new adventure. His touch was reverential as he picked the shirt up and clutched it against his chest.

Eren stretched his arms lazily above his head, eyes closed as he basked in the warming sunrise flowing through the gaps in the trees. "Another wonderful day in paradise."

"Mmm mfffm."

He shifted around on the porch and looked back into the bedroom. One of Cosime's legs jutted out from beneath the bedcovers, and her face was buried in her pillow. A shaft of golden light cut across the soft, creamy skin of her thigh, and he smiled. "What did you say, love?"

She rolled over and flung her arms wide atop the covers. "I'm bored."

He rested against the opening to the porch and gave her a pout. "With me?"

"No, not with you, silly." She grabbed a pillow and threw it haphazardly at him; it missed him by several centimeters and tumbled to the floor. "I'm bored with this perfectly peaceful day, and it hasn't even begun. Tomorrow will be yet another perfectly peaceful day, and another one will follow after that. I can hardly bear to consider it."

"Well, since the weather's so dreadfully perfect, do you want to go visit Shalemahr Peak?"

"We just went there a few weeks ago."

"We did." He returned to the bedroom and dropped to his knees on the bed beside her, then started playing with her exposed toes. A year had passed since the fall of the Directorate and the end of the anarch rebellion, and he felt the same wanderlust as she did. The

same yearning to fight and chase and scheme. But he was doing his damnedest to suppress it. The battle was over and they'd won the day; this was his reward, and he intended to enjoy it to the fullest.

In the months following The Displacement, they'd had plenty to do. First, Cosime and Felzeor both had to finish their rehab for the injuries they'd sustained during the Directorate's attack on Post Alpha. Next they'd helped Xanne and some of the other anarch leaders pack up the anarch posts and close up shop. They'd visited an unexpectedly reborn Caleb on Akeso and fixed up this quaint house in the trees on Hirlas. They'd visited every scenic vista on the planet, of which there were many, and made love under waterfalls and atop mountain peaks. Then they'd done it all again for good measure.

"That tickles!" She snatched her foot out of his grasp and sat up, feathery pearl hair falling across her features to obscure bleary emerald eyes. "Let's run wild somewhere. Let's find a defensible spot and stir up some trouble, maybe get into a fight—not with each other. Though if I grow bored enough, I'm not ruling it out."

"We could always go to Chalmun Station and sign up for the arena contests."

She flung her hair out of her face. "Ooh, can we?"

"No. Arae, Cosime. Those feral Barisan gladiators would rip our limbs off and use them as clubs on each other." He traced a winding pattern up her calf with his fingertip, his gaze dropping to hide the struggle he suspected was evident in his expression. She couldn't be caged, could she? Not even when the cage was an entire planet's worth of halcyonic beauty and the man she loved was her constant companion to enjoy it with. More relevantly, she shouldn't be caged. Not when she shone so fiercely when free. All right, then.

"So, I heard that Concord is instituting an intelligence agency—almost like it's planning to be a real government or something. Alex's friend, Richard Navick, is slated to head it up."

Excitement danced in Cosime's eyes. "Do you think he'll give us a job? We can do so much good as agents of chaos."

"Or stopping agents of chaos." He chuckled. "I think he already offered us one."

"What? When were you going to tell me?"

"I'm telling you now." He threw her back onto the bedcovers, pinned her arms above her head and leaned in close. "Are you sure this is what you want to do?"

"I am crazy sure."

"You are definitely crazy, and I love you madly for it." His lips brushed across hers. "Okay. If it's what you want, we'll do it."

For all that it had now cost him everything, he couldn't bring himself to regret the choice he'd made, or the thirteen years which had followed. They'd torn up this corner of the universe in service of their mission to stop—and occasionally cause—chaos, get into fights and generally keep the citizens of their new, better-than-the-Directorate empire safe.

He brought the shirt to his face and breathed in her lingering scent on the fabric before folding it and placing it atop the dresser along the far wall. Then he went out onto the porch, where their hammocks swung idly in the morning breeze.

He stood on the far rim of the porch, his toes curling over the edge. His muscles strained with the profound need to jump, to plummet to the forest floor below...but then everything would simply start over again.

During the trip here, he'd worked out how he'd be able to hack into the Concord regenesis server and delete the cache backup they were now keeping of his mind. Then he'd be free to disconnect his integral a final time and end it all, like he'd planned to do after delivering Torval to the Savrakaths.

A will to survive wasn't what stopped him from doing it. One day it might, but he hadn't found the strength of that will yet. No, duty stopped him. Drae had been right about one thing. A lot of people had worried over him, searched for him and helped him, though he didn't deserve any of it. It wouldn't be fair for him to let them down a second time.

So he would keep drawing air, for now, even as every breath cut his chest open in fresh welts of agony. For his friends, until he reached a place where he could do it for himself.

A songbird landed atop one of the tree limbs that teased the patio, sang a dulcet morning tune for him, then beat its wings and flew off.

Tears were streaming down his cheeks before he realized it. His chest heaved, all the air driven from his lungs, and he sank to the smooth teak floor. He couldn't hold the deluge at bay any longer—and this was why he'd come here, wasn't it? If he was going to mourn her, he needed to do it here in their home, where she'd infused everything she touched with rich, vibrant life.

Sobs wracked his body in punishing waves, and he at last surrendered himself to the grief.

73

SAVRAK

Malcolm struggled through a gap where two pieces of concrete had landed diagonally to one another and climbed out into the searing heat of the midday Savrak sun. He squinted, blinking away overpowering halos while his eyes adjusted to seeing real light for the first time in weeks.

When his vision finally cleared, he looked behind him to see...nothing. The entire landscape had been eradicated. He couldn't even tell what sort of building had once stood there, for no trace of it remained. There should have at least been clouds of soot and debris clogging the sky, but he inhaled only crisp if hot air.

To his left, a crater fifty meters deep and almost a kilometer wide had cleaved a cavernous bowl into the ground. The main force of the blast had missed the underground wing where he'd been held captive by less than a hundred meters; as much destruction as he'd just traversed, his prison had been spared the worst of it. Only nonconventional weaponry inflicted such damage. So who had inflicted it?

Two Savrakath ships approached rapidly from the southeast, and he broke into a loping run to get free of the destruction. His left leg ached from dragging the chain and brace up through four levels of jagged ruins and now mucky soil that wanted to pull him back down into its depths, but he forced himself to keep moving forward. No part of his bruised and weakened body was going to stop until he was off this planet, dammit.

He stumbled across multiple bodies thrown wide of the destruction. One or two of them might have still been alive...and he couldn't bring himself to stop and check. He'd deal with the guilt of not doing so later, once he was home and safe and wrapped up in Mia's arms.

Finally he reached a small copse of swamp trees a few dozen meters beyond the last of the debris. He dropped his hands on his thighs, winded and gasping for air. The instant he'd caught his breath, he straightened up and tried to remember how to comport himself like a soldier, then sent a message to AEGIS Operations at the Presidio.

"This is Fleet Admiral Malcolm Jenner, authorization ACZ-21Y18 Omega Zulu Mark 3.1. I need a priority Caeles Prism extraction at my location."

AEGIS Operations: "Sir? But you're—please repeat your authorization code."

He frowned but complied, one eye on the sky, where in the distance more Savrakath response units began arriving at the crater.

AEGIS Operations: "I see. Um...I need to check with my supervisor. Sir."

"Please do hurry. My position will be compromised at any moment."

No response was immediately forthcoming, and he crouched low beneath the trees' overhang to hopefully avoid being spotted by the approaching craft. He was so close to freedom, if the military bureaucracy failed him now....

It took three minutes before he got another reply.

AEGIS Operations: "Fleet Admiral, this is Brigadier Thompson. I apologize for the delay. I see that your location is the planet of Savrak in the Antlia Dwarf galaxy. Is this correct?"

"Affirmative. I was captured a month ago during a Godjan rescue mission."

"Yes, sir. We're...aware. A Caeles Prism will open at your coordinates shortly."

He exhaled in relief and tried to prepare himself. He'd be facing a tough few days of endless debriefs and medical treatments, but he would be home.

The air shimmered in front of him, then wrent apart to reveal...the Security Department on the Presidio, he believed. Three MPs, a man he assumed was Brigadier Thompson, and a medical team waited for him on the other side, which seemed like a bit of overkill.

He squared his shoulders and walked through the wormhole, chains and all.

RW

THE PRESIDIO
SECURITY WING

The MPs' hands went to their service weapons, and the brigadier took a half-step forward. "Sir, keep your hands at your sides. We need to confirm your identity."

Malcolm wanted to argue, but it was proper procedure. "Right, of course. As soon as that's done, if someone can grab a blowtorch and cut these shackles off of me, I'd greatly appreciate it."

One of the MPs held out a scanner and stared at it for a second. "Identity confirmed."

Thompson snapped a sharp salute. "Welcome back, Fleet Admiral. We, uh...the Savrakaths told us you were dead, sir."

Dead? The word shook him to his core. "Dead? No, I was a prisoner. They didn't—" His heart stopped as a realization hit him.

Mia, I'm alive and safely back on the Presidio.

Recipient is not accepting messages at this time.

What? What had happened while he was gone? Panic snaked through his chest to squeeze his poorly healed ribs, and his gaze snapped over to the brigadier. "Where is Mia Requelme?"

74

EPITHERO

Casmir's attention jerked toward the door to his luxurious cell when it opened to reveal his Machim guard. "Sir, you're wanted in the conference room."

Something had gone wrong with the 'mission' to trade for Torval. Whatever calamity had resulted, Ferdinand would now want him to patch up the wreckage and *fix it*. But he was tired of playing Ferdinand's errand boy whenever it suited the Kyvern, only to be locked up and denied a voice in decisions when it didn't.

He considered simply refusing to answer the summons. But then Ferdinand would barge his way in here, full of poisonous hot air and feckless declarations. Better to go to the conference room, embarrass Ferdinand in front of all the others and get himself hastily removed once more.

He stood, smoothed out his shirt and nodded to the guard. "Let's go."

RW

Ferdinand's head snapped up when Casmir entered. He had a frazzled, *glistening* air about him…regenesis?

Casmir snorted. "You went to the exchange yourself, didn't you? Got yourself killed?"

The Kyvern *elasson* rushed forward to get in his face. "Who did you tell?"

"Excuse me?"

"Who did you warn about the exchange?"

Casmir was careful not to scan the room in search of the Kyvern *ela* who'd passed him messages from Concord. "No one. Recall, you have me locked up and cut off from all communications."

"You found a way."

"I did not. What happened? Did the Savrakaths arrive armed and you insulted their honor?"

Ferdinand ran a hand through hair he'd already managed to tangle. "Someone *blew us up*. Everyone: myself, Otto, Torval, a dozen Machim officers and half the Savrakath military leadership."

"Then you should be pleased. You live again, while the Savrakath leadership has been decimated."

"Of course this is a welcome development, but I do not appreciate being blown up."

"No one ever does. Where is—"

The intercom burst to life. *"Sir, we've got an unauthorized ship landing on the lawn outside."*

"On the *lawn*? How did it get past the defense array?"

"I don't know, sir."

"Well, arrest whoever emerges, put them in shackles and take them to a secure room. I'll deal with them later."

No response arrived, and Ferdinand's perpetual sneer deepened. "Acknowledge my order."

"Um, sir...I'm afraid I can't comply."

"What?" Ferdinand and several others in the room gravitated to the tall windows at the other end of the conference room. After a second, Casmir followed behind them.

On the lawn far below, a dark-haired man in a charcoal suit and indigo turtleneck strode toward the building entrance, flanked by two of the Machim guards. No weapons or restraints were in sight.

"Has everyone lost their minds today?" Ferdinand pivoted toward the door, where two additional guards stood watch. "Go downstairs and intercept them. See that the intruder is properly restrained and isolated."

"Yes, sir." They turned on their heels and disappeared through the doors.

"Now, where were we? Ah, yes. Casmir, you were attempting to convince us you had no role in the explosion on Savrak."

"That's correct." Casmir shifted his focus to Otto, who sat at the conference table. The Machim *elasson* had endured many, many more regenesis cycles than Ferdinand, and he sat there acting calm and composed. "Otto, why don't you tell me what transpired?"

"We met the Savrakath contingent at a facility several hundred kilometers from the capital. They presented Torval, then—"

"Sir. You have a guest." The voice on the intercom sounded like it belonged to one of the guards who had just vacated the room.

Ferdinand ground his jaw in growing annoyance. "A 'guest'? What I had better have is a prisoner."

"But, sir, it's—"

"I don't give a flying fuck who it is. If they aren't in shackles, you soon will be."

Ferdinand paced anxiously along the length of the table while he waited on an update...that again never came.

The raucous sounds of a commotion echoed outside the doors, and Ferdinand started to order the guards to take up defensive positions, only to realize he'd dispatched all the guards to deal with the intrusion. He spun to Otto, and Hannah sitting beside him. "Be ready to shoot whoever comes through the door."

The *elassons* stood. Casmir's hand went to his hip but came up empty. No weapons for captives.

Five seconds later, the doors opened. The guards from before walked in first, weapons holstered at their sides.

"Well? What happened? Where's the intruder?"

None responded to the inquiry; they refused to meet Ferdinand's furious glare as they moved off to either side of the entrance.

A man walked deliberately through the door, unarmed but also unshackled.

Casmir sucked in a sharp breath, for the man wore a face every Anaden knew. It was also impossible that it appeared here before them now, for the face belonged to a dead man.

Corradeo Praesidis silently acknowledged every dropped jaw in the room, one by one, saving Ferdinand for last. "No prisoners will be taken today, *elasson.*"

Shock rendered Ferdinand speechless, his expression a caricature of terror, and Casmir started laughing. "Uh-oh. Daddy's home."

75

AKESO

At the sound of a ship emerging through the Caeles Prism and descending to the landing complex, Marlee took off running out the front door and across the mud-soaked meadow.

Caleb reached the porch in time to see Isabela exiting the airlock of her small ship and Marlee running into her arms. He smiled, leaning against the railing to drink in the scene. To let it warm his heart and reaffirm the rightness of all the painful choices he'd had to make.

After several more hugs, they walked arm-in-arm to the house. Isabela beamed at him as Marlee rushed up to take his hand. "If it's okay, I'm going to go stay with Mom for a few days." She leaned to whisper, "She's being all *needy*." Behind them, Isabela rolled her eyes.

"Of course it's okay. I got you home. Now your life is yours again."

"Right." She tapped her foot and studied him intently for a minute. "But I'm coming back to visit very soon."

"I look forward to it."

"Me, too." A grin broke across her features. "Let me grab my bag and say goodbye to Alex."

As soon as she disappeared inside, Isabela wrapped him up in a big hug, too. "Thank you. Thank you so, so much."

"How many times must I tell you? I will always rescue her—rescue both of you. Anytime, anywhere."

"I know you will." She drew back and wiped a tear off her cheek before gazing out at the wrecked meadow curiously. "What happened here?"

"Just a storm. It's passed now."

She turned to regard him with a questioning look not at all unlike the one Marlee had bestowed upon him. "Has it?"

Marlee returned to the porch in a flurry, her bag of souvenirs from Namino slung over one shoulder. She kissed him on the cheek, then grabbed her mother by the arm. "Come on—I need new clothes *so* badly. Maybe we can have lunch at *Fuori Barbeque?*"

He watched them stroll back to the landing complex, drawing every ounce of joy he could wring from the scene, then went inside.

Alex was drying her long hair with a towel in the kitchen. After her shower, she'd changed into a loose black tank top and flimsy gray shorts, which only served to remind him how utterly beautiful she truly was. "Did I miss Isabela?"

"Yeah. Marlee has a big day of shopping and feasting planned for them."

"Good. She deserves a little frivolity." She laughed faintly. "I talked to Mom a few minutes ago. Once the Rasu realized they were no longer going to be able to reach the planet, the armada in orbit cut their losses and fled. Our forces will be another day or two dispatching the remaining Rasu trapped on the surface, but we've got the upper hand on them."

"I'm glad to hear it."

"Me, too." She folded the towel on the countertop and came over to grasp him gently by the shoulders. One hand drifted up to his neck, the other along his arm. "So what do we do now?"

"Now...I need to go outside for a while."

"Caleb—"

"Listen. Something is broken inside of me, and I cannot continue on like this. It's not fair to you...or to me, or to Akeso."

Her brow furrowed in consternation. "But you can't sever your connection with Akeso, can you? I won't lose you, so if you're thinking of—"

"No, I can't sever it. And I don't want to. But we have to find another way."

She kissed him softly, tasting of mint, warm spice, and hope. "I'll be here. Yell, and I'll come running."

Her palm rested flat on his chest; though the connection was fading, he knew she could still sense him, still feel his heartbeat in her mind, for now. It made things easier, knowing he wasn't genuinely leaving her behind.

He squeezed her hand then stepped away. "I love you. I'll be back soon."

Outside, he picked his way through the strewn tree limbs and uprooted shrubs. The house had been spared all but the most minor of damage, but a lot of work lay ahead for Akeso to replenish what the two of them had destroyed.

The damage was even worse in his beloved forest, and his heart ached for the anguish and turmoil he had caused. But this was why it couldn't happen again—to either of them.

Finally he reached a stretch of grassy undergrowth that gleamed in the morning sun. He yearned to strip naked, lie down and drown himself in the rapturous melody of this living planet. But if he ever wanted to find balance, he needed to stand strong now.

So he let his fingertips drift along the hanging vines of a nearby tree, took a deep, cleansing breath and closed his eyes.

If you're ready to listen, I'm ready to talk.

Akeso's lilting voice manifested anxiously in his mind. *Things are going to change now, aren't they? Change causes All disquiet.*

The world has always been changing around us. We've shut it out all these years, and I fear it was a mistake for us to do so. We can't ignore it any longer. But you don't need to fear change so long as I am with you. We will find a new way forward, together.

The Story Continues In

ECHO RIFT

RIVEN WORLDS BOOK THREE

(AMARANTHE ♦ 16)

Coming This Winter

Author's Note

I published my first novel, *Starshine*, in 2014. In the back of the book I put a short note asking readers to consider leaving a review or talking about the book with their friends. Watching my readers do that and so much more has been the most rewarding and humbling experience in my life.

So if you loved **INVERSION**, tell someone. Leave a review, share your thoughts on social media, annoy your coworkers in the break room by talking about your favorite characters. Reviews are the backbone of a book's success, but there is no single act that will sell a book better than word-of-mouth.

My part of this deal is to write a book worth talking about—your part of the deal is to do the talking. If you keep doing your bit, I get to write a lot more books for you—which is a great opportunity to remind you that *RIVEN WORLDS* is not a trilogy, but a six book series. The story isn't close to over!

Of course, I can't write them overnight. While you're waiting for the next book, consider supporting other independent authors. Right now there are thousands of writers chasing the same dream you've enabled me to achieve. Take a small chance with a few dollars and a few hours of your time. In doing so, you may be changing an author's life.

Lastly, I want to hear from my readers. If you loved the book— or if you didn't—let me know. The beauty of independent publishing is its simplicity: there's the writer and the readers. Without any overhead, I can find out what I'm doing right and wrong directly from you, which is invaluable in making the next book better than this one. And the one after that. And the twenty after that.

Website: gsjennsen.com
Wiki: gsj.space/wiki

Email: gs@gsjennsen.com   Goodreads: G.S. Jennsen
Twitter: @GSJennsen   Pinterest: gsjennsen
Facebook: gsjennsen.author   Instagram: gsjennsen

Find my books at a variety of retailers: gsjennsen.com/retailers

APPENDIX

THE STORY SO FAR

View a more detailed summary of the events of the Amaranthe novels online at gsjennsen.com/synopsis.

AURORA RISING

The history of humanity is the history of conflict. This proved no less true in the 24th century than in ancient times.

By 2322, humanity inhabited over 100 worlds spread across a third of the galaxy. When a group of colonies rebelled two decades earlier, it set off the First Crux War. Once the dust cleared, three factions emerged: the Earth Alliance, consisting of the unified Earth government and most of the colonies; the Senecan Federation, which had won its independence in the war; and a handful of scattered non-aligned worlds, home to criminal cartels, corporate interests and people who made their living outside the system.

Alexis Solovy was a space explorer. Her father gave his life in the war against the Federation, leading her to reject the government and military. Estranged from her mother, an Alliance military leader, Alex instead sought the freedom of space and made a fortune chasing the hidden wonders of the stars.

A chance encounter between Alex and a Federation intelligence agent, Caleb Marano, led them to discover an armada of alien warships emerging from a mysterious portal in the Metis Nebula.

The Metigens had been watching humanity via the portal for millennia; in an effort to forestall their discovery, they used traitors among civilization's elite to divert people's focus. When their plans failed, they invaded in order to protect their secrets.

The wars that ensued were brutal—first an engineered war between the Alliance and the Federation, then once it was revealed to be built on false pretenses, devasting clashes against the Metigen invaders as they advanced across settled space, destroying every colony in their path and killing tens of millions.

Alex and Caleb breached the aliens' portal in an effort to find a way to stop the invaders. There they encountered the Metigen watcher of the Aurora universe, Mnemosyne. Though enigmatic and evasive, the alien revealed the invading ships were driven by AIs and hinted the answer to defeating them lay in the merger of individuals with the powerful but dangerous quantum computers known as Artificials.

Before leaving, Alex and Caleb discovered a colossal master gateway that generated 51 unique signals, each one leading to a new portal and a new universe. But with humanity facing extinction, they returned home armed with a daring plan to win the war.

Four Prevos (human-synthetic meldings) were created in a desperate gambit to vanquish the enemy invaders before they reached the heart of civilization; then they were given command of the combined might of the Alliance and Federation militaries. Alex and her Artificial, Valkyrie, led the other Prevos and the military forces against the alien AI warships in climactic battles above Seneca and Romane. The invaders were defeated and ordered to withdraw through their portal, cease their observation of Aurora and not return.

During the battle, hints of the consciousness of her deceased father manifested in the shared connection between Alex and Valkyrie. Alex reconciled with her mother during the final hours of the war, and following their victory Alex and Caleb married and attempted to resume a normal life.

But new mysteries waited through the Metis portal. Six months later, Caleb, Alex and Valkyrie traversed it once more, determined to learn the secrets of the portal network and the multiverses it held, leaving humanity behind to struggle with a new world of powerful quantum synthetics, posthumans, and an uneasy peace.

And in the realm beyond the portal, Mnemosyne watched.

AURORA RENEGADES

Following the victory over the Metigens, Alex, Caleb and Valkyrie set off to unlock the secrets of the Metigens' portal network. Discovering worlds of infinite wonder, they made both enemies and friends. A sentient planet, Akeso, that left a lasting mark on Alex and Caleb both. Silica-based beings attempting to grow organic life. A race of cat-like warriors locked in conflict with their brethren.

Behind them all, the whispered machinations of the Metigen puppet masters pervaded everything. In some universes, the Metigens tested weapons. In some, they set aliens against each other in new forms of combat. In yet more, they harvested food and materials to send through the massive portal at the heart of the maze.

But Alex and Caleb found yet another layer to the puzzle. In one universe, they discovered a gentle race of underground beings with a strange history. Their species was smuggled out of the universe beyond the master portal by the Metigens. They watched as their homeworld was destroyed by a powerful species known as Anadens; but for the Metigens, they would have perished as well.

Back home in Aurora, the peace proved difficult to maintain. The heroes of the war—the Prevos who melded their minds with AIs—found themselves targeted by politicians and a restless population desperate for a place to pin their fears. Under the direction of a new, power-hungry Earth Alliance PM, the government moved to cage and shackle them.

In desperation, the Prevos uploaded the AIs' consciousnesses into their own minds, fled from their governments' grasp and disappeared onto independent colonies. Devon published the details of the Prevo link to the exanet, unleashing its capabilities for anyone who wanted to follow in their footsteps.

Meanwhile, an anti-synthetic terrorist group emerged to oppose them, fueled by the rise of Olivia Montegreu as a Prevo. While the private face of Prevos was the heroes who defeated the Metigens, the public face became the image of Olivia killing a colonial governor and tossing him off of a building in front of the world.

Unaware of the struggles her fellow Prevos faced, Alex forged her own path forward. Rather than bringing the AI into herself, she pushed out and through Valkyrie, into the walls of the *Siyane*. Piloting her ship in a way she never dreamed, Alex was able to feel the photonic brilliance of space itself. Over time, however, that bond began to capture more of her spirit and mind.

On the surface of a destroyed planet, Mesme at last revealed all. The portal network, which the Metigens call the Mosaic, was above all else a refuge for those targeted for eradication by the Anadens. And the Anadens, rulers of the true universe through the master portal, were the genetic template upon which humanity was built. Aurora was nothing more than another experiment of the Metigens, created so they could study the development and nature of their enemy and the enemy of all life.

Alex and Caleb returned to Aurora to find a galaxy rocked by chaos. After the execution of Olivia Montegreu by Alliance and Prevo forces, Miriam had gone rogue. Under her careful planning, a resistance force, bolstered by help from inside the Senecan and Alliance militaries, moved to remove the despotic Alliance PM.

As Alex struggled with her growing addiction to an ethereal, elemental realm, she felt herself being pulled away from reality. Away from her husband, her mother, her friends. She watched as those she loved fought, but increasingly found herself losing her own battle.

When terrorists staged a massive riot on Romane, Dr. Canivon, the mother of the Prevos, was murdered in front of Devon and Alex. Overcome by her own and Valkyrie's grief, Alex unleashed the explosive power of the ethereal realm to destroy the terrorists' safehouse. Standing in the rubble of her destruction, Alex made a decision to sever the quantum connection between herself and the *Siyane*, choosing a tangible, human life. Choosing Caleb.

Miriam wrested control of the EA government away from the PM, bringing an end to the Prevo persecution. In the wake of victory, however, a shadowy Anaden hunter emerged from the darkness to attack Alex and Caleb. Caleb was gravely injured when the Anaden's power, known as *diati*, leapt into him, healing his wounds and helping him kill the alien.

Mesme revealed the ominous consequences of the attack. Soon, the Anaden leadership would discover Aurora. When they did, they would destroy it unless humanity could stand against them. Mesme told Miriam and the others to prepare, but knowing the end game was upon them, asked Alex and Caleb to come to Amaranthe. The master universe. The home and dominion of the Anadens.

AURORA RESONANT

In Aurora, Miriam led the formation of a multi-agency, multi-governmental (GCDA) and military (AEGIS) organization dedicated to meeting the imminent threat of the Anadens.

In Amaranthe, Alex and Caleb discovered an underground 'anarch' resistance movement against the Anaden Directorate. They made contact with an anarch agent, Eren asi-Idoni, and he helped them infiltrate the Anadens' Machim military command and steal secret information on the Machim fleets. Alex and Caleb were captured, but not before Valkyrie uploaded the information they sought. Eren 'nulled out' rather than being captured, for when Anadens died they underwent a regenesis procedure that returned their consciousness to a new body.

Valkyrie transmitted the data to AEGIS then returned to Amaranthe. When Eren reawakened, he joined Valkyrie and Mesme on the *Siyane*, and they rescued Alex and Caleb from the prison where they were being tortured for information.

The Directorate nonetheless learned the full truth about the Metigens/Katasketousya creation of Aurora and ordered a fleet to deliver a powerful weapon known as a Tartarus Trigger to Aurora and annihilate humanity. Forewarned, Miriam led a fleet of warships into Amaranthe to intercept them.

The battle commenced with the destruction of the one known gateway into the Mosaic, and Mesme sneaked onto the lead Machim warship and stole the Tartarus Trigger. Humanity used its Prevos, Rifts and other tricks to take the Anadens by surprise and prevail in the battle. Afterward, Alex, Caleb, Miriam and Mesme were summoned to a secret meeting with the leader of the anarchs, Danilo Nisi, and a tenuous alliance was formed.

AEGIS scored several early victories but also devastating losses. While the battles raged, Alex and the other Prevos developed a method for using sidespace to open physical wormholes, enabling AEGIS vessels to travel anywhere in known space without using the Anaden gateway system.

The AEGIS fleet attacked the Machim homeworld, destroying the Dyson rings encircling its sun and blowing up their orbital military command station. At the same time, Nisi broadcast an impassioned speech across the empire setting forth the Directorate's sins and the anarch's mission to free those oppressed.

In a flashback Caleb's *diati* showed him, it was revealed that Nisi was actually Corradeo Praesidis, the former leader of the powerful Anaden Praesidis dynasty. Many millennia ago, his son tried to kill him; thinking him dead, the son stole his name, face and power, and now served on the Directorate as the Praesidis Primor.

Valkyrie and her twin, Vii, had spent months rebuilding the consciousness of David Solovy that manifested during the final battle of the Metigen War. Using the Anadens' regenesis technology, they transferred his consciousness to a cloned body, and he and Miriam were reunited after twenty-five years.

The Directorate tracked an AEGIS vessel to the primary anarch base and launched a surprise attack, and a bloody battle followed in orbit and on the ground. To stop a Machim warship from bombing the base with antimatter missiles, Alex re-established her ethereal connection with the *Siyane* to bypass the warship's shielding and destroy it; in doing so, she found the connection no longer exerted the damaging hold on her it once did.

Alex soon discovered a way to use the supradimensional properties of the mysterious Reor mineral to access the contents of the Reor slabs used by the Directorate to store sensitive information. She uncovered the location of the Directorate's regenesis backups, and AEGIS and the anarchs devised a plan to take out the entire Directorate, permanently, in one massive strike.

For all but two of the Directorate members, the mission succeeded with minimal losses. However, the Machim Primor escaped his assassination attempt. Armed with the location of one of the Mosaic gateways, he acquired a new Tartarus Trigger and raced to wipe out the Aurora universe.

On Solum (Earth's twin), Caleb engaged the Praesidis Primor in a battle of staggeringly powerful *diati*, and the *diati* freed when the Primor died rampaged wild. Caleb couldn't wrestle it under control, and it killed millions before destroying the planet itself.

The anarchs learned that the Primors kept an additional regenesis backup stored on their secret space station, the Protos Agora, which orbited the Milky Way galactic core. The *Stalwart II* took the Tartarus Trigger Mesme stole at the start of the conflict and used it to destroy the station.

Just when they believed they had finally achieved victory, they discovered the Machim Primor's plans. The Primor had a head start, and the only way to try to prevent him from destroying Aurora was for the Kats to disconnect it from the Mosaic, rendering it unreachable forever. Caleb, however, instead used his now total control over *diati* to command the cosmic force to pull all the pocket universes in the Mosaic—including Aurora—into Amaranthe, then destroy the Mosaic.

He succeeded, but the energy the act required killed him. While Miriam and the others worked out what it meant for all of humanity to now exist in Amaranthe, Alex took Caleb to the living planet of Akeso and, via the deep connection they shared, Akeso brought him back to life.

ASTERION NOIR

On the planet of Mirai in the Gennisi galaxy, a woman woke up in a rain-soaked alley with no memory of who she was or how she'd gotten there. Two strangers found her and offered to take her in. When asked, she told them her name was Nika, though she didn't know why.

Fast forward to five years later. Nika, alongside her rescuers Perrin and Joaquim, led a group of rebels called NOIR against the despotic government of the Asterion Dominion. An insidious virutox was infecting people's programming, altering their personalities and causing them to commit inexplicable crimes. NOIR's investigation of the virutox brought them to Dashiel Ridani, who Nika learned was her lover in her prior life, before she lost her memory.

With her world thrown into disarray, Nika and Dashiel chased the threads of her lost identity while searching for the source of the virutox. Their search led them to the leaders of the Asterion Dominion, the Guides. Nika broke into the Guides' data vault, where she found they had ordered her psyche-wipe five years earlier after she pressed them on a series of disappearances.

Meanwhile, Gemina Kail, an Administration Advisor, traveled to an alien stronghold across the galaxy, where she delivered thousands of Asterions in stasis chambers to an alien species called the Rasu.

As the virutox spread, wreaking increasing havoc across the Dominion, Justice Advisor Adlai Weiss traced the source to the Guides' doorstep. They ordered him to drop the case and let the virutox propagate among the population. He disobeyed, developed a vaccine and contacted NOIR for help in distributing it.

Across the galaxy, Nika and Dashiel discovered the stronghold of the alien Rasu. A metal-based shapeshifting species of immense power, they'd constructed hundreds of thousands of warships and space stations. Armed with this terrifying information, Nika and Dashiel returned to Mirai.

One of the Guides, Delacrai, defied the others to help Nika. She shared how an Asterion scout ship encountered the Rasu eight years ago; the crew was captured and killed. The Rasu grew interested in the Asterions' unique bio-synthetic intelligence powered by kyoseil and quantum programming, and in return for not attacking Asterion Dominion worlds, they demanded a regular supply of Asterions to experiment on. The Guides agreed.

The other Advisors were told the terrible truth about the Rasu and the Guides' deal with the aliens. They scrambled to undo the damage eight years of the Rasu Protocol had inflicted while racing to find a way to respond to an impending Rasu deadline, when the aliens expected more Asterions to be delivered.

Nika's oldest friend from her former life, Maris Debray, revealed that both she and Nika were members of the "First Generation": Asterions who had never erased their psyches in the 700,000 years since they fled the Anaden Empire and created themselves as a new species by merging Anaden DNA, AI programming and the kyoseil mineral. Only a few dozen of the First Generation remained, and their history was kept secret from everyone else.

With time running out, Nika sought the help of the Sogain, an enigmatic species who once threatened the Asterions with extinction if they ever trespassed on Sogain territory. This time, the aliens disclosed the location of a single, stranded Rasu.

An Asterion team captured the Rasu and brought it to Mirai for interrogation. The creature revealed that the Rasu exhibited a collective intelligence when physically connected to other Rasu, but regained independent thought when they were separated. They intended to use kyoseil to control other Rasu over great distances, as kyoseil was supradimensional, deeply interconnected and one of the universe's oldest life forms.

Using this knowledge, the Asterions identified a way to link their consciousnesses together via kyoseil. They dubbed these connections 'ceraffin' and used them to develop a plan to face the Rasu.

They constructed volatile electricity bombs to be sneaked into the Rasu stronghold. The Rasu were expecting 8,000 Asterions in stasis chambers, so Nika used the ceraff structure to split her psyche into shards inhabiting 8,000 copies of herself.

The copies were delivered to the Rasu as expected, and they awoke inside the Rasu's lab on their primary space station. Chaos ensued as they fought to reach the power control center, even as they were cut down by the thousands. A mere dozen made it to the control center, and a single instance survived to override the power safeguards.

Dashiel detonated the electricity bombs, and a cascading power overload ripped through the stronghold. It destroyed the Rasu's Dyson lattice, which triggered an intense surge in solar flare activity, and all the Rasu stations and vessels were incinerated, save one vessel that escaped through a wormhole.

The Asterions recognized this was not the end of the conflict, but the beginning, and they needed to prepare for the Rasu's return. Nika was contacted by the Sogain, who informed her the Anaden Empire of old had fallen and suggested she might find allies among the new one which had risen to take its place.

Nika journeyed to the Asterions' ancestral home, the Milky Way. Before she arrived, however, a wormhole opened in the cabin of her ship, and Alex Solovy walked through it.

Acknowledgements

Many thanks to my beta readers, editors and artists, who made everything about this book better, and to my family, who continue to put up with an egregious level of obsessive focus on my part for months at a time.

I also want to add a personal note of thanks to everyone who has read my books, left a review at a retailer, Goodreads or other sites, sent me a personal email expressing how the books have impacted you, or posted on social media to share how much you enjoyed them. You make this all worthwhile, every day.

ABOUT THE AUTHOR

G. S. JENNSEN lives in Colorado with her husband and two dogs. She has become an internationally bestselling author since her first novel, *Starshine*, was published in 2014. She has chosen to continue writing under an independent publishing model to ensure the integrity of her stories and her ability to execute on the vision she has for their telling.

While she has been a lawyer, a software engineer and an editor, she's found the life of a full-time author preferable by several orders of magnitude. When she isn't writing, she's gaming or working out or getting lost in the Colorado mountains that loom large outside the windows in her home. Or she's dealing with a flooded basement, or standing in a line at Walmart reading the tabloid headlines and wondering who all of those people are. Or sitting on her back porch with a glass of wine, looking up at the stars, trying to figure out what could be up there.

CPSIA information can be obtained
at www.ICGtesting.com
Printed in the USA
FSHW010509280521
81918FS